KRISTA'S
JOURNEY

GEMMA
JACKSON

POOLBEG

Published 2020
by Poolbeg Press Ltd.
123 Grange Hill, Baldoyle,
Dublin 13, Ireland
Email: poolbeg@poolbeg.com

A catalogue record for this book is available from the British Library.

ISBN 978178199-350-7

www.poolbeg.com

Also by Gemma Jackson

Published by Poolbeg

Foreword

Dear Reader,

Thank you for coming on Krista's journey with me. This part of the series opens with Krista's sea journey.

I too left home at seventeen to take a sea journey to England and eventually to London by train. My journey was a great deal more downmarket than Krista's. I took what we then called the 'cattle boat' from Dun Laoghaire to Liverpool. The boat was used for moving cattle from Ireland to England. I don't think there was a great deal of hygiene practised on it in that day and time. The thing stank to high heaven, but I didn't care. I was off on my first foreign travel. I still remember the sheer thrill. I had no fear of the future or what might be ahead of me. Well, I was seventeen and we are immune to danger at that age, aren't we?

The passengers travelled in the bowels of the boat. There were long wooden benches bolted to the floor. The sea was stormy and an older woman (she was probably in her forties but to a seventeen-year-old she was ancient) clung to my arm, screaming in my ear that we were all going to die. The grip she had on my arm hurt. I remember patting her hands, trying to get her to release me while murmuring sympathetically (I thought), "It's all right, missus, we'll all die together."

London – what an eye-opener to a holy Catholic girl from Ireland! Thank heavens for my innocence. It protected me from so much. It is only in later years that I look back and think of the danger I was in, but my sheer ignorance of life kept me safe. The drugs, sex and rock-and-roll lifestyle those around me were living passed right over my head. I had no frame of reference. I only knew I didn't like it!

I didn't stay long in London. I had so many jobs in that short time. It was an era when, if you didn't like a job, you walked out and had a new job the same day. The one job that I think of often was with Lyons of Cadby Hall. It was the head office of the Lyons company that made tea and cakes and owned the Lyons tea rooms. It was a position for life with great prospects and I was picked for the top. In the name of God! At seventeen! I wanted to be a world traveller. I didn't want to climb the ladder of success. I sometimes sit and wonder how different my life would have been if I'd settled into the life of a well-paid executive. The path not taken.

I vividly remember what made me leave. I was an office worker on the top floor. There were factories on the ground floor. I thought it ridiculous that there was a huge social divide between the office staff and factory workers. I was taken on a tour of the factory so I would better understand the working of the company. What an experience! I was uncomfortable walking around the factory with my office manager who was lording it over the men and women working on the factory floor.

We stopped to watch a line of women, in overalls

with nets over their hair, sitting on either side of a moving conveyor belt. They were using their thumbs to put the dimple in doughnuts! I don't know why I thought that someday that could be me – but I was horrified. I tendered my resignation to a great deal of consternation and, looking back again, concern. I was giving up a bright future. I didn't care. I was off.

Merchant Ship *Swallow*
English Channel

Chapter 1

Krista Dumas stared out the porthole at the angry grey
sea foaming around the ship. She clenched her jaw,
trying desperately to stop her teeth from chattering.
What was she doing on a British merchant ship sailing
from Belgium to England? She was a citizen of France.
How would she support herself in a foreign country
where she knew no one?

"Christine, come join us. The steward has promised
a pot of tea and sausage sandwiches." The male voice
echoed around the room.

Krista, shocked at being called by a name not her
own, spun around. She'd been unconsciously waiting
to hear this voice. She stiffened her knees against the
shock of relief that ran through her body. How on

earth had he escaped the German soldiers that had detained him on the dock?

"Bertram, has your stomach settled?" Violet Andrews had stiffened her spine when he'd appeared and sat beside her. It wouldn't do to sink to the floor in relief.

"Quite." Gerhardt, Baron von Furstenberg, the man calling himself Bertram Standish, beckoned to Krista. "Come, my dear, join us."

He was still feeling delicate from his recent episode of emptying his stomach over the side of the ship. He refused to show any weakness to the females he had used to facilitate his escape from his home in Germany. He settled his body, encased in the 'fat' suit and ill-fitting tweed jacket, into the nearest chair, running his hand over his bald head. It had been difficult to sacrifice his fine head of hair and beard, but the disguise had worked to hide his identity to the casual observer. He would be glad to shed the uncomfortable 'fat' suit that turned his lean body into a rotund lump. He had never realised he was vain. He shook off his mental ramblings and turned his attention to the here and now.

"Good to see you looking hale and hearty, Bertram," Violet said as Krista took one of the seats bolted to the floor of the small lounge. She wanted to ask him how he had escaped the German soldiers – but now was not the time nor was it the place. One never knew who was listening.

"Miss –" Krista stopped abruptly when a male hand grasped her wrist.

"I think we should continue our charade," Gerhardt murmured. "It is safest for everyone concerned." He looked casually around the lounge as he spoke. They were the only passengers present.

2

"Christine, my dear, how are you feeling?" Violet had been Krista's English teacher and dare she say friend for many years. She was concerned for Krista who was leaving everything she knew. How would she cope on her own in a strange country? "The happenings on the dock were frightfully upsetting for all of us." She would offer every assistance she could to help the child settle into a new life. Krista spoke three languages fluently – surely they would find her a place that would suit?

"I am coping, Mama." Krista had no one to blame for the position she found herself in but herself. In order to escape an impossible situation, she had hidden in the backseat footrest of the car the man calling himself Bertram Standish – a man she had known all her life as Herr Baron von Furstenberg – had been driving. She was a stowaway. These people owed her no consideration.

"Good girl," Violet said.

Gerhardt listened, sighing internally. He stared at the young woman. She was a perfect mix of her parents. She had her mother's long slender figure and pretty face, but his elder brother had marked her with his white-blond hair and impossibly blue, blue eyes. Unknown to the girl, she was his brother's by-blow. Her care had fallen to him when his brother and his English mistress were killed in a motor accident. He'd had little to do with her after he'd placed her as an infant with a French family.

The steward entered before more could be said. He carried a tray with crockery that rattled as he walked slowly across the floor. He greeted them with a smile and with one hand unlocked a table that was latched to the wall. He pulled it down which released a leg.

3

When the table was secure, he began setting the thick white cup, saucers and side plates on it. "I'll have the food and a pot of good English tea out to you in a few moments." He placed a milk jug, sugar bowl and a heavy linen cloth, folded into an envelope shape around the cutlery, on the table. "They are forecasting rough seas so best get something into you while you can," he said cheerfully and, with the tray under his arm and another smile, he left the room.

Krista, who had grown up in her family's auberge, had watched the steward with fascinated eyes. He would not have been employed by the Dumas family with his casual attitude.

"*Ugh!*" Gerhardt held up one of the heavy white cups with a grimace of distaste.

"Don't be a snob!" Violet laughed at her companion's reaction. "We are on a merchant ship after all, not a passenger liner. One should be grateful for one's blessings." She, for one, was glad to be escaping the German bully boys they had seen on the docks. Her eyes had been opened to what was happening in the world around her. She had spent the last fifteen years living quietly in the village of Metz on the German-French border. She'd hidden her head in the sand in recent years, not wanting to acknowledge the frightening world around her. She had lived and served in one world war. She had refused to believe they could be once more marching towards war.

"Here we go!" The steward had returned. He put the tray and its contents on the end of the table and stood back with a wide smile. "Help yourselves." He turned and left the room.

"I'll be Mother." Violet laughed aloud at her companions' reaction to the lack of anything approaching servility from the crewman.

Krista watched her former teacher add milk to her tea and followed her example. The cups were very different to the wide-lipped coffee cups she used in the café/bar/tabac of the family auberge, whose shape allowed you to dunk your *pain au chocolat* or *croissant* as required.

"I haven't had an English sausage sandwich in years." Violet was salivating at the taste-memory the huge sandwiches aroused in her. She opened one of the sandwiches under the watching eyes of her companions and with glee shook some of the contents of a glass bottle onto the meat. "Brown sauce, how delightful!" She cut the sandwich into four pieces before picking up one piece and biting into it with relish.

The ship sailed towards England and an uncertain future while the three enjoyed their meal.

"When we reach England, we shall be in your part of the world, Ann," Gerhardt said to Violet, using her alias, when the remains of the meal had been removed and the table locked back into position. "We shall be relying on you for guidance."

"I have been giving some thought to the matter," Violet said. "Christine dear, let that table down again please and put my travelling bag on top if you would." She waited until her order had been carried out before saying, "My dear, there is no need for you to remain in here with us old fogies. You are young and I'm sure you would enjoy a brisk stroll around the deck."

"I will have you know I do not consider myself quite past it, old thing," Gerhardt objected.

Violet ignored him as she opened her small travel case and began to search for some items she needed. She wanted to speak to him without Krista present.

"Wrap up well, Christine," she said.

"I will enjoy a stroll," Krista said, pushing her arms into the trench coat she had borrowed from Gerhardt, which reached almost to her ankles. She wanted to be alone. She almost ran from the room. "I'll be back shortly," she threw over her shoulder as she went.

"Well, my dear," Gerhardt said as soon as Krista disappeared, "you have deftly got rid of our young companion. What do you wish to say to me?"

"Bertram, I am at my wit's end. I have been thinking about the people I could contact when we arrive in England," Violet practically snapped. "You gave me no time to prepare for this trip. You demanded I be ready at a moment's notice. There was no point in writing to my friends. I knew I would most likely arrive before the post."

She had been unwilling at first to join him. He had explained that Hitler wanted men of his social stature to be part of his entourage, but she still thought he was being alarmist in his frantic plans to escape the might of the German Reich. It was the thought of an all-expenses-paid trip to England that had tempted her to join him in his flight to freedom. She had been forced to change her opinion as they drove through France and into Belgium to the coastal town of Antwerp. The sight of German soldiers harassing fleeing refugees on the dock had sickened her. Were the people in power really going to allow the world to descend into the madness of war again? It beggared belief.

"I believe the best course of action for us when we arrive," Violet leaned back in her chair to say, "is to drive to Ipswich and book into a hotel. I have a friend living in the area. I shall call her from the hotel and make arrangements to meet with her. If anyone knows what is going on in the world it will be Abigail Winchester. We served together in the last lot."

"What are we to do with our young friend?"

"That poor girl!" Violet sighed. "You saw the letter that Philippe Dumas wrote to her." They had found the letter when Krista fell asleep on her hotel bed with it clutched to her chest. They had removed it from her hand while helping her under the covers.

"I could wish he had kept his suppositions to himself." Gerhardt had placed his brother's baby with the Dumas family on the understanding that they would raise her as one of their own. Krista had no idea of her true parentage nor apparently had her 'brother' Philippe, but he knew at least that she was not his blood sister and had told her so in that letter.

"Krista must be feeling lost and alone. We have taken her from everything she has ever known."

"We removed her from a dangerous situation." Gerhardt refused to feel guilty. The girl had stowed away in his car after all.

"What kind of people would allow a child they raised – no, no, let us be honest – they *assisted* in plans to allow Krista to be raped and beaten – then forced into marriage to a cruel bully." There were tears in Violet's eyes as she thought of what might have happened to

Krista, the child of her dear friend Constance Grace. Krista's mother had been an exceptional human being. Violet felt she had let her friend down by allowing her daughter to be raised as the daughter of innkeepers. She should have done something.

Krista, all unknowing, was thinking about the same subject. She walked the decks hunched up against the biting breeze that blew. She was heading into an unknown future while dealing with the shock of finding everything she had believed to be true was a lie. Who was she? Where did she come from? She had always known that physically she differed from the three men she thought were her brothers – but to discover that she was nothing to them! How was she supposed to deal with something so outrageous?

She found a small nook out of the wind and stared out at the sea stretching as far as the eye could see. What was to become of her? It was all very well for Herr Baron to say they would not desert her, but what did that mean? She could not tag along at their heels. She needed to plan a future for herself. She put a hand in front of her mouth, trying to force the sob that wanted to escape back down her throat. She looked around to be sure she was alone. She wanted no kind person asking what had upset her. How would she ever explain?

"I thought to consult Abigail about our young friend." Violet was still thinking about her friend Constance and how disappointed in her she would be. "She has girls a little older than Christine. She might have thoughts and ideas on the subject – about what Krista might do to improve her lot in life. And she may well have some clothing that she could allow her to have. The poor girl ran with only the clothes on her back."

"That is perhaps not a bad thing." Gerhardt could not believe that he was once more faced with the upkeep and protection of his brother's by-blow. He had enough problems of his own to be dealing with. He too was facing an unknown future. "The clothes she is wearing are suitable only for an under-housemaid, not a young woman seeking a new life in a new country."

"That was no fault of hers!" Violet felt desperately sorry for Krista.

"I shall give her some funds to see her on her way."

"It is not money she needs at this moment. She needs help finding a position that offers a roof over her head. She needs to know who she is. She must have so many questions about herself. We can give her answers to many of those questions. We must do that now because we cannot know what is to happen to us in the future." She was determined to tell Krista what she knew. The girl needed to know where she had come from.

"What can we tell her except that her parents are dead?" Gerhardt snapped.

"Even that much information will offer her some comfort. She will not be searching the faces of strangers to discover if she has anyone in the world that belongs to her! I cannot imagine being so alone in the world."

"You are beginning to sound like a bleeding heart."

"My heart is bleeding for the lost child we have in our company. I intend to do everything in my power to assist her."

Before more could be said the hatch opened and

9

Krista stepped into the room, bringing a blast of cold air with her and putting an end to the conversation.

"It is so cold out there. My nose and toes are frozen."

Chapter 2

The journey to England seemed to take forever and at the same time fly past. Krista spent the remainder of the journey curled up under a blanket, supplied by the obliging steward, semi-dozing in one of the chairs while her companions spoke of people she might never know and places she had only read about.

The steward escorted them off the ship and into a small dockside waiting room reserved for first-class passengers. Unlike the one in Antwerp, it had a public telephone for first-class passenger use. Miss Andrews was using the telephone, making a series of reverse-charge calls to friends and family. Krista had chosen to wait outside the room, uncomfortable listening to private conversations.

She stood, as she had on the docks in Antwerp, watching the strange world around her. The rush and hurry of the dock didn't upset her – this dock was smaller and less frantic than the Antwerp docks. But the shouting voices did. They were speaking English – she was sure of it – yet she understood less than one word in ten! What was she going to do? She had been so sure her English language skills were up to snuff, as Miss Andrews would say. How would she find employment if she could not understand the words spoken to her? She wasn't aware of time passing as she stood watching the ships being unloaded.

"*Christine, come along!*" Miss Andrews' voice carried over the noise of the dock.

Krista jerked in surprise. She had been so lost in her own thoughts she hadn't noticed the movements of her companions. She needed to be more alert. These two people could help her establish a new life in this country. She must remain vigilant and learn all she could from them.

They joined Gerhardt who was standing by the large British automobile that he had driven through France and Belgium. The car had been one of the first cargo items unloaded from the ship and now awaited its passengers.

They drove out of the dock area carefully. Krista almost bit her knuckles in fear. She had no papers to present to the port authorities.

When the luxury automobile was waved through the checkpoint without being stopped she dared to breathe again. It would appear port authorities were not so stringent when you obviously had money. They motored onwards – on the wrong side of the road! She wondered if her heart could take many more shocks!

Miss Andrews suggested they stop at the first village they passed through and purchase a road map.

The bright May evening made driving through the English countryside a delight. Krista wondered what crops were planted in the fields they passed. The world outside the window of the car was a sea of brown and green with patches of white where sheep grazed. They passed farmhouses with chickens pecking in the dirt and dogs barking. She looked for rows of grapevines but failed to see any.

The journey passed quickly with Miss Andrews, map in hand, issuing firm, crisp directions. They were soon in Ipswich town centre, driving towards the large hotel Miss Andrews suggested. The black-and-white Tudor buildings were strange to Krista's eyes. The people walking along smiling and passing the time of day were fascinating, she thought. Everything was so very different to the world she had spent her life in. She would enjoy walking the streets and exploring but didn't feel brave enough to suggest such a thing. She needed to stay close to her companions. She felt cast adrift – the two people who had carried her along with them were her only familiar landmarks.

"You two wait here," Miss Andrews said when the car pulled up in front of the building she'd indicated. After checking passing traffic, she opened the door and jumped out. She leaned in to say, "I'll see if they have rooms available. If not, I'll have them telephone around and find us somewhere suitable."

Krista watched her stride confidently into the hotel through the door held open for her by a uniformed doorman.

"That woman should be running this country." Gerhardt couldn't wait to remove the 'fat' suit he was wearing as part of his disguise. It had kept him safe and in some cases warm, but it was restricting and he wanted rid of it. He waited and watched the busy streets around them. Would Hitler send men after him? He thought he might. He could not be seen to have successfully escaped Hitler's clutches. Still, he sighed deeply, he was in England. Now he had to find someone willing to listen to his warnings and take action. England must be warned.

He almost jumped out of his skin at the sharp rap of knuckles on the car window.

"If you and the young lady would step out of the car, sir," a uniformed hotel attendant said as he opened the car door, "I shall have your luggage taken up to your rooms and the car parked in the hotel lot at the rear of the hotel." He left the driver's door open and opened the rear passenger door.

"Thank you." Gerhardt stepped out of the car and Krista joined him.

"I have booked three rooms for us," Violet informed them as soon as they had stepped into the hotel foyer. "They did not have an available suite." She would be glad of a space to think her own thoughts. Gerhardt would be paying for this stop and the man could afford the best.

"Excellent, my dear." Gerhardt looked around the foyer. It was not what he was accustomed to, but it was clean, polished and fresh-smelling. It would do for a first stop on their English journey.

"If you will follow me." A smartly uniformed porter stepped forward, pushing a trolley with their luggage. He led them towards the lift set to one side of the foyer, pushing open the iron lattice gate with an experienced hand.

Krista followed along silently, her eyes taking in the arrangements of fresh flowers and gleaming brass that decorated the large foyer. She stepped into the lift and held her breath. She'd have preferred to take the stairs. The lift seemed very shaky with the added weight of people and luggage.

Krista stared out of the window. The room she'd been given overlooked the main road. She stared down at the people hurrying about their business, wishing she had somewhere to go. She clutched the handkerchief-wrapped money in her skirt pocket and sighed. It was French francs. She would need to exchange it. She had no idea of its worth in British pounds sterling. One more thing for her to worry about. There was nothing she could do about it now. She needed a bath. She felt tired, thirsty and hungry. She had nothing to unpack. She had run away with only the clothes on her back. She spun away from the window at the sound of a sharp rap of knuckles on the door.

"Christine," Violet Andrews marched in without invitation, "I have arranged to meet a friend for dinner downstairs."

She examined her companion's appearance, supressing a groan. The girl looked like a waitress. She needed clothing. Her friend Abigail could not supply anything appropriate. Unfortunately, according to Abigail, her two girls resembled their mother – short and stout, not long and lean like Krista. Abigail had made the assumption that Krista was a servant of some sort and Violet was happy to leave it at that for the present. "I have ordered a tray to be delivered to your room. I'm afraid you simply cannot appear in the dining room dressed as you are." She didn't mean to hurt but Krista's clothing would be very similar to that of the people serving their food. "I suggest you take a bath and retire. We shall be up and about early in the morning, I shouldn't wonder."

She glanced around the room and, with a brief nod and without waiting for Krista to respond, turned and left, pulling the door closed at her back.

"My dear, it has been too long," Abigail, Lady Winchester, gushed over her friend. It had been so exciting to hear from her. She couldn't wait to hear the latest. Life had been tedious lately. "I love to receive your letters but that simply cannot equal meeting face to face. So much more satisfying."

"I have booked a table for us, Abigail."

Violet thought her old friend hadn't changed very much. She was older certainly and perhaps a little bit heavier but still the same smiling imp. Her grey-streaked brown hair and pale-blue eyes were complemented by her silver-silk evening dress and matching fur-trimmed wrap. The jewels bedecking her old friend were worth a fortune. It would be easy to discount Abigail as just another bored upper-crust lady of means but that would be a grave mistake. She had a first-class brain and used it wisely. Violet was counting on picking her old friend's brain for advice.

"Just the two of us? I thought you mentioned

travelling companions." Abigail looked around the foyer. It was decorated in ghastly shades of brown, the fresh flowers and gleaming brass the only dash of bright colour. It was the best Ipswich had to offer, she supposed. One didn't usually know which were the best hotels when one had a large house of one's own nearby.

"They have both chosen to dine in their rooms." Violet had been happy to hear Gerhardt preferred to take a tray in his room while he changed his appearance. "It will be just us two."

"Tell me all," Abigail said. "One is hearing such distressing news from the Continent."

The two women were sitting in the hotel dining room at a table hidden by greenery. They had made polite conversation while the waiters gushed over one of their local bright social lights. They had not discussed anything of import while dining and now, with delicate coffee cups in hand, prepared for the meat of the issue.

"Abigail, it is a nightmare." Violet closed her eyes briefly. It would be difficult to describe the changes taking place, but Abigail would surely have heard enough from friends of her husband to know there was cause for concern. "I need your advice and assistance. I have lost touch with British society and have no idea where to turn. I chose to stop in Ipswich, knowing you were nearby." She took a deep breath. "I cannot do what must be done, without you."

"Do you really believe we are once more heading towards war?" Abigail leaned forward to ask.

Both women were very aware of the staff dancing attendance on the diners.

Violet too leaned forward. "One of my travelling companions, a German aristocrat, certainly thinks so. He is fleeing in fear of his life!"

"*No!*" This was far more exciting than Abigail had supposed.

"Yes, indeed." Violet blotted her lips with her napkin. "I have seen the orders with my own eyes. He must present himself to Hitler or be shot down in the street like a dog."

"*No!*"

Violet looked around to insure they could not be overheard. "Because of his social status and his family concerns, he has seen and heard a great deal of very dangerous matters. He is desperate to speak to someone in our government. He wants to warn them of the coming storm – share his knowledge. I have no idea who to contact and thought of you as someone who would know better than I whom to consult."

"Are matters really that grave?"

"Abigail, they are pulling people from their homes – breaking the shop windows of anyone with any Jewish blood whatsoever – confiscating valuables. It is madness and must be stopped."

"You will need to speak with Winnie." Abigail signalled to a waiter and ordered more coffee and two brandies. This was far more than she had expected when her old friend telephoned and asked to meet with her.

"Winnie?"

"Yes, you must know him. Winston Churchill. He has been banging on about the danger Hitler represents for years. The only people listening to him at the moment are women, I believe. But then, they are the ones in danger of losing sons, brothers, fathers and lovers. If women ruled the world, we would have far less of war, let me tell you."

She paused while staff served the coffee and drinks.

"Of course," she continued then, "Winnie has made some very unpopular political decisions in recent years. He is very much out of favour." She took a sip of brandy, welcoming the warmth in her gullet. "Nonetheless, he is still someone who will know who to approach. *Yes!*" She slapped the tabletop with her dimpled, ring-adorned hand. "He is the man to talk to, I am sure of it."

"Would Bertie be willing to listen to the concerns of my travelling companion and make the necessary introduction, do you think?" Albert, Lord Winchester, Abigail's husband, was a man with many useful connections.

"There may be a problem." Abigail shrugged, sending her diamonds dancing. "He locks horns with Winnie regularly. But I do believe they respect each other. I can but ask."

"That would be of great assistance," Violet too sipped her brandy – for courage. "Abigail, the German aristocrat . . . it is Gerhardt, Herr Baron von Furstenberg."

"*No!* The one Constance –"

"No – his younger brother. Gerhardt inherited the title when Constance's paramour died in that dreadful car crash with her."

"Such a terrible tragedy – such a scandal." Abigail glanced at the platinum-and-diamond wristwatch she wore. She hated to be the one to cut this conversation short. It was simply too fascinating. "Violet, my dear, if I

19

am to consult with Bertie before he retires, my chauffeur must be sent for. My darling husband becomes a grouch if he does not receive a full night of sleep."

"Yes, Bertie needs to be put in the picture as soon as possible but we have not even touched on the second of my problems."

"There's more?"

"Oh yes, much more." Violet put her napkin on the table and pushed back her chair. "Are you free tomorrow morning, Abigail? We can continue our conversation then."

Abigail too arose, the waiter pulling back her chair to assist her. "I shall have my social secretary cancel any engagements I might have." She couldn't bear to be left out of exciting events. "I shall speak with Bertie and give you his opinion in the morning when we meet – if that is what you wish?"

"Please," Violet said as the two women began to walk from the dining room.

The doorman, upon seeing them, clicked his fingers at a nearby porter. He sent the boy running to the staff waiting room at the rear of the hotel to inform Her Ladyship's chauffeur that the lady appeared ready to depart.

"Do you want to meet here?" Abigail looked around the lobby and sniffed. "No, what am I saying? I shall send the car for you."

"There is no need. We have our own automobile and I have been to your estate enough times over the years to find my way." Violet touched her friend's arm gently with her fingertips. "I cannot thank you enough for your help, old friend."

"No need for thanks. I have done nothing yet." The

two women air-kissed. "Ten o'clock tomorrow morning! We shall discuss matters then in the comfort of my home. I shall have my staff arrange everything."

Violet stood watching as Abigail was escorted out by the doorman, before going to her room. She had a great deal to think about and plan, but the first small steps had been taken.

Chapter 3

"*Mon Dieu!*" Krista couldn't bite back the exclamation at the sight before her. The house was enormous to her eyes. A large white building sitting tall and long amongst sweeping green lawns.

"*Mein Gott!*" Gerhardt von Furstenberg echoed, slowing the car as they drove along the driveway towards the mansion.

"Indeed." Violet Andrews smiled in pleasure at the reaction of her companions. "The house is Jacobean. Kings and queens have slept in its rooms. The gardens were designed by the famous landscape gardener Capability Brown." She had stayed at the Winchester stately home many times. The impressive exterior was matched by the sumptuous interiors.

A group of servants appeared on the driveway. Gerhardt drove carefully, not wishing to splash mud or gravel onto the waiting group. Car doors were opened, and hands were offered to assist the visitors from their vehicle.

Krista had to consciously work at not standing with her mouth open staring at the building. She had never seen its like before in her life.

An older servant stepped forward to greet the visitors. "Miss Andrews, welcome back!"

"It's wonderful to be back, Dodd," Violet greeted the Winchester's long-time butler.

The butler's white-gloved hand waved a hovering maid forward.

"Wilson will take the young woman to the kitchen. If you would follow me, Miss Andrews – sir."

Krista followed the maid, trying not to stumble over her own feet as she tried to take in the many openings leading off the entryway into the house. Every wall was decorated in rich colours with paintings in tiers everywhere she looked. She would hate to be responsible for the cleaning of this place. It would take you years just to learn your way around, she was sure. The maid opened a doorway off the long hall.

"I was told to take you to the kitchen." Mary Wilson stepped onto the wooden landing on top of the stairs leading down into the kitchen. "Follow me, please."

Violet waited until the butler had announced them and closed the door at their backs before walking across the richly decorated room to greet their host. The red walls were a stunning background for the artwork and treasures placed around the large room. "Albert, how lovely to see you! Abigail, Albert, allow me to introduce you to Herr Baron von Furstenberg – Gerhardt."

She waited while the men shook hands.

"I knew your brother slightly, Herr Baron," Abigail said when Gerhardt clicked his heels and carried her hand to his lips. Such lovely manners these foreigners had, she thought. "I was dreadfully sorry to hear of his passing."

"Your Ladyship is most kind." Gerhardt smiled sadly.

"Oh, call me Abigail."

"And you must call me Gerhardt."

"Abigail," Violet said, "I have informed Gerhardt that I approached you for assistance with sorting out his concerns."

"I brought the matter to my husband's attention. I hope you do not feel we are discussing you without your permission, Gerhardt?"

"Not at all, Abigail. I need all of the help I can get at this time." Gerhardt looked at the tall thin man who was watching his every move with discerning brown eyes set under bristling black brows. "I do indeed wish to discuss matters of great importance with His Lordship, if he would care to listen?"

"Of course, Herr Baron," Albert replied.

"Well, then, Albert, best you speak in private in the library." Abigail had no wish to stand on ceremony. They could spend an age dancing around politely. She simply did not have the time to indulge in social niceties. There were matters to attend to. She knew her dear husband would be mentally rolling his eyes, but she did not care.

"Yes, indeed. Herr Baron . . ." Albert waved his

hand in the direction of the door, hiding his smile at his wife's attempt to get them out of the way of her and her friend. The best decision he ever made was to marry Abigail Smithers twenty years ago.

Violet laughed when the door closed behind the men. "That was very well done, Abigail!"

"Oh, they will want to rattle their sabres and beat their manly chests, I have no doubt. I have no time for all of that nonsense." Abigail led the way towards two hand-embroidered silk-covered chairs in front of the fire. "I've ordered tea for us. The men no doubt will have something stronger." She pulled an embroidered hanging cord to signal to the servants to bring the tea.

"You never change, Abigail." Violet sat back into the comfortable chair and waited for her friend to join her.

"*You* certainly have." Abigail had been surprised when her butler mentioned sending Violet's maidservant to the kitchen. "I never expected you to travel with a French maid! *Oh, la, la!*"

They were interrupted by a knock on the door.

The butler entered, followed by a footman and a maid, each carrying a tray.

"Put everything on that table," Abigail pointed to a nearby circular table. "We shall serve ourselves."

Violet hid a smile at the obvious displeasure on the butler's face at this instruction, but her friend made her own rules.

"My maid!" Violet sighed deeply when they had served themselves tea and retaken their seats before the fire. "That is something I need to discuss with you, Abigail. Again, I desperately need your assistance."

Abigail sipped her tea and waited for her friend to speak. Violet had never been one for shilly-shallying.

"The young woman is not my maid. She has been dragged along in our efforts to escape notice by the Germans seeking Gerhardt." Fighting tears, Violet looked across the fire. "She is the daughter of Constance Grace, Abigail."

"*I beg your pardon!*" Abigail dropped her cup into its saucer with a rattle. "Are you telling me I have sent the daughter of a baron, the granddaughter of a duke, into my kitchen with the servants?"

"I hadn't thought of it quite like that." Violet was forced to laugh.

"How would you think of it then?" Abigail stared at Violet as if she had run mad.

"She is a by-blow, Abigail – illegitimate."

"Stuff and nonsense! Half the dukedoms of England were set up for the by-blows of royalty!"

"Does your husband know what a radical he has married?"

"Of course. It is one of the reasons he married me – that and my fortune. Even his sour parents couldn't sniff at that – though they tried."

"I have missed you, Abigail. You were the first person I thought of before starting out on this journey home. Abigail, Krista – the young girl in your kitchen – has no idea who she is or where she comes from. She has been raised to believe herself the daughter of innkeepers. A most disagreeable family as I know only too well."

"That is disgraceful!"

"I agree with you. Gerhardt was left with a great

many responsibilities he had never expected when his brother died. He didn't know how to contact Constance's friends. He did the best he could with what was laid before him."

Violet then proceeded to tell Abigail all she knew of Krista's life up to and including the horrific situation she had fled at a moment's notice – ending up a stowaway in Gerhardt's car.

Abigail thought of her own two daughters and was horrified

"I am at my wit's end." Violet didn't know where to go from there. "Krista has only the clothes she stands up in. Your butler, at one brief glance, sent her to the kitchen. I had expected nothing less." She almost wailed. "What am I to do?"

"Is she presentable? Surely she cannot be slovenly – not Constance's daughter!"

"She is the very image of her mother except for her white-blonde hair and startlingly blue eyes. Those she got from her father. She speaks three languages and has worked in the family auberge since she could toddle as far as I've been able to ascertain."

"We shall send for her shortly so that I may meet her." Abigail was thinking frantically of the best way to go about matters. "You asked if I had clothing of my daughters'. Did you plan to dress her in the cast-offs of others? Violet, she is Constance's daughter. We must do our best by her."

"Easy for you to say, Abigail, with a fortune behind you. I do not have that luxury. The girl needs everything. I cannot finance such an outlay of cash." Violet would like nothing better than to dress Krista in a fashion that would elevate her, but she simply did not have the necessary funds.

In the kitchen Krista had been given a mug of tea and a thick slice of what the cook had called a fruit cake. She had never seen its like before. She was sitting at a table well out of the way of the staff who bustled around the busy kitchen.

Albert, Lord Winchester, was sitting behind a carved paper-covered desk in the library while Gerhardt sat in a chair across from him. Both men were drinking whiskey from crystal glasses.

Gerhardt had just finished giving Lord Winchester a full and frank account of all he had seen and heard on his travels around Germany and Austria. He felt drained after recounting the horrors that he had witnessed.

Glass in hand, Albert rose and walked over to a table bearing crystal decanters.

"I know it's early," he said, "but, after hearing what you have to say, I need another drink." He splashed a healthy dose of whiskey into his glass. "Will you join me?" He held up the decanter.

"Please."

"I have seen Hitler in the news reels at the cinema." Bertie served his guest before seating himself back at his desk. "Quite frankly he comes across as a most unpleasant fellow. How is he leading the German people into this madness?"

"That is difficult to answer. Hitler has been fiendishly clever. His offensive started almost as soon as the papers were signed at the Treaty of Versailles.

That document ended the First World War but I am afraid it also sowed the seeds for what is happening now." Gerhardt sipped the whiskey, enjoying the warm, smooth, smoky flavour for a moment. He closed his eyes and sighed. "We were all too busy enjoying peace after years of conflict, and trying to turn our lives back into something we could be proud of, to notice what he was doing. Your own Prince Edward is a frequent visitor to Hitler and his cronies."

"Yes, well," Bertie sipped his whiskey, "the Royals and indeed a great many of the English aristocracy have family connections in Germany." Queen Victoria's mother was German after all and so was her husband, Prince Albert, his own namesake. Then she had married most of her nine children to members of the German royalty. Those connections proved a problem in the last war and could well be again if what this German chap feared came to pass.

"The French Revolution gave the people the aristocrats to hate. Hitler is giving our people the Jews to hate." Gerhardt sipped whisky while the two men sat in silence for a while.

"I believe we need to speak to Winston Churchill with some urgency." Bertie looked at the telephone on his desk. "I shall not telephone to set up a rendezvous. Heaven knows the telephone operator listens in to any conversation she believes might be of interest – completely against the company rules of course – but that has never stopped them."

"My name must not be mentioned anywhere it might be overheard." Gerhardt too looked at the telephone. A marvellous instrument but it could be

29

misused. "There is a warrant out for my arrest. I have been travelling – with the owner's permission – using papers in the name of Bertram Standish."

"I know the Standish family – good people." Bertie put his elbows on his desk and dropped his head into his hands. He wanted to push the memories back. The trenches, the smell, the screams, the crippling fear. Dear Lord, was it all to happen again? "Is it wrong of me to be glad my sons are too young to serve? The thought of my boys in the trenches sickens me."

"*Nein!*" Gerhardt hit the top of the desk with an open hand, causing Bertie to jump. "It will not be that kind of war. We must never think of trenches. This will be a war of machines. It will be man against machine in the most terrible battle if we do nothing to stop this madness."

"My government speaks of peace." Bertie tried to fight off the very thought of such a battle.

"I would that I could believe it," Gerhardt sighed.

"I shall travel to London with you." Bertie pulled a piece of paper towards him and started to make notes. They would need to open the London house. His wife would deal with the staff, but he had estate matters to take care of. Spring was a busy time of year. "I shall introduce you to Winston Churchill. He has no official role in government at the moment, but the man has been shouting to all who will listen about the danger Hitler represents. He will know who to contact."

"I thank you." Gerhardt wanted to crawl into bed and hide his head under the covers. He did not want another war but what could one do? He had to make people listen to him. He had to try and avert the coming disaster in any way he could.

* * *

"We must travel to London." Abigail began to make mental lists of what needed to be done to move her household to the capital. "I shall have staff open the London house. You must stay with me, Violet. There is much to be done."

"I had thought to get in touch with some of our old comrades from the Wrens." Violet was being swept along in the whirlwind that was Abigail.

"We must." Abigail nodded in agreement. "They will have more knowledge of what is going on than we do."

"Abigail, my dear, you will always be in the thick of things," Violet said with a laugh.

"We need to have a meaningful conversation with your ward." Abigail nodded her head, sending her curls dancing. "Yes, that is how this little Krista I have not yet met must be known. Your ward. It will give the child a certain cachet. Now, my dear Violet, while we shop to outfit your ward – really, my dear, we must do something about your own wardrobe. You look quite the frump."

Chapter 4

"You are the French maid?"

Krista's head jerked at the flow of French. She stared at the woman addressing her. "I am French but I am no one's maid."

"Oh, not bashful, are you?" Emmanuelle Doumer stared at the young girl. "Stand up and let me see you." She waited, foot-tapping, until Krista obeyed. "You are tall certainly, and your figure is not unpleasant."

"Excuse me, who are you?" Krista stared at the thin elegant woman dressed all in black with her black hair pulled into a tight bun at the back of her head. She was tiny, barely coming up to Krista's chest.

"I am Emmanuelle Doumer, Lady Winchester's French maid."

"You are not French."

"No," Emmanuelle laughed softly. "I am from Belgium and proud of it, but in this country it is quite the thing to have a French maid." She shrugged. "So, I am French."

"*The visitors are staying for lunch, Mrs Bennett!*" a footman shouted, pushing open the door into the kitchen.

"Joe Major," Mrs Bennett the cook stood erect, her white cap wobbling, "you will give me a heart attack one of these days. Will you please come into my kitchen like a human and pass the message along in a correct manner! Honest to goodness, I don't know what the world is coming to when loudmouth young terrors like you get taken on to train. You'll never make a good house servant if you don't learn to behave." She belted the long-handled wooden spoon she was holding against the delft mixing bowl sitting on the well-worn kitchen table in front of her.

"I am having great difficulty understanding what people say," Krista whispered to Emmanuelle.

"Ah yes, the English language!" Emmanuelle laughed gently. "They swallow consonants and exaggerate vowels until it is difficult to understand a word. Then there are the regional accents. This too is a nightmare. But we have local accents too of course. You knew immediately I was not a citizen of France, did you not?"

"But I have studied English for years and have passed all of my exams with distinction!" Krista almost wailed.

"The schoolroom is nothing like real life. You must find something that will allow you to practise your

33

English speaking until you are confident." Emmanuelle didn't think working in a big house as a servant was suitable for the young woman in front of her. There was something about her – a touch of class – that would set her apart.

"Mad-a-moe-sell Emmanuelle!" Joe Major, after flirting outrageously with the kitchen maids, walked over to join the two women. The young one was a bit of all right is his opinion. He wouldn't mind getting to know that one. He wondered if she'd be employed here. He'd have a chance to have a go at her if she was – he'd seen her first after all. "Her Ladyship wants you to take the young woman upstairs."

"You took your time passing along that message!" Emmanuelle snapped. She would be the one in the wrong if Her Ladyship decided to take offense at being kept waiting.

"Had to find you first to pass on the message, didn't I?" Joe Major gave the fussy little Frenchwoman one of his best smiles. "This old house is a bloody maze."

"Come along, Krista, it does not do to keep one's employer waiting." Emmanuelle ignored Joe and grabbed Krista by the elbow, almost towing her around the young man standing in their way, and out of the kitchen.

"You can keep your eye off that one, Joe Major," said Mrs Bennett with a laugh.

"So, you are Krista." Abigail sat in her chair by the fire and examined the young girl standing so stiffly in front of her. She felt her heart lurch. She looked so much like her dear departed friend Constance. What were they to do with the poor waif?

34

Krista nodded.

"Krista, we have been discussing what we are to do with you." Miss Andrews had introduced Krista to her friend after the French lady's maid had been dismissed.

"She is tall, as you said, Violet." Abigail was examining the girl in great detail. "And so slim. Why, she could be one of the models my London modiste uses to show the clothing in her salon. She is delightful."

"Abigail, I have already told you. She will need somewhere to live when we reach London and a way of earning her living. I would not be happy to see her working as a clothing model. It is most probably a perfectly respectable way of earning one's living but I don't like it for Krista."

Krista looked at the two women, wondering what they expected her to say or do. The way they were both looking at her made her feel like she was an animal that was not quite ready for market.

"Sit down, my dear." Abigail waved towards a delicate chair pulled close to a round table. She didn't wait to see if her instruction was obeyed but turned to Violet with a beaming smile. "I have had a thought!" She clapped her little dimpled hands in delight. "Cordelia – that is the answer – Cordelia!"

"Cordelia?" Violet prompted. She had forgotten how Abigail was always mentally one step ahead of everyone else.

"Yes, indeed. Cordelia, my husband's youngest sister. She is married to a Naval Officer. Charles Caulfield is captain of a Royal Navy ship."

"And?" Violet had no idea what her friend was planning.

"Cordelia's husband is away so much, as you can imagine. She has two delightful boys – twins – I think they are about three years old. I believe she needs help, but she refuses to employ a nanny. Cordelia grew up watching the antics of the 'bright young things' of the twenties. She has some rather strange ideas." Abigail wondered why problems came along in groups. She had been floating along living her life calmly – now this. The need to move her household to London and discuss matters of state came far before the problem of a young girl – but still – she was Constance's daughter – they must help her.

"What do you have in mind?"

"I am sure Cordelia would be happy to employ Krista." Abigail wasn't quite sure what the position would entail but she would have a word with Cordelia. Surely between them they could think of some way of occupying the young woman's time until Abigail herself was free to take the girl in hand? The girl needed social polish before she could be sent out into the world. They owed that to her dear departed mother.

Krista sat and listened as the two women batted her life around without ever asking her opinion.

"What about clothing?" Violet was happy to think of Krista being in the employ of Abigail's relation. It would give the girl time to become accustomed to her new life. It would be a relief to know Krista was safe while she herself got in touch with friends from her past. She had much to do and could not take care of Krista at the same time. Yes, this would indeed be ideal.

"Ipswich has many fine shops." Abigail had thought to take the girl shopping herself, but she simply did not have the time. "It should be possible to purchase everything needed to get the girl set up."

"Do you sew?" Emmanuelle was driving the small car set aside for staff use.

"I was taught to darn and mend in school. That is all." Krista had been almost weak with relief when she was informed Miss Andrews and Her Ladyship were too busy to travel into Ipswich with her to shop. She had been sent off instead with Emmanuelle. A much better state of affairs, in Krista's opinion.

"Shame, one can do so much to improve the fit of clothing with a little skilled nip and tuck. Never mind, we will see what is available in the Ipswich shops. You need some of everything, is this not so?"

"Yes, thank you." Krista had been delighted to learn that Emmanuelle had been ordered to charge all of her purchases to the accounts Her Ladyship held at the local shops. "I do have a little money of my own, but it is French. I need to go to a bank and change it if that would be possible today?" Krista had never been shopping for her own clothing. Madame Dumas, the woman she had believed to be her mother, had ordered everything Krista might need.

"We will visit the bank of course – it is good to have money of one's own." Emmanuelle had never known Her Ladyship to be so generous. She wondered what it was about this young French girl that had caused Her Ladyship to pay so much attention to her. Still, it was none of her business. She had been given a chore and she would fulfil it to the best of her ability. It would be a joy to shop for someone so attractive.

The Winchester daughters were nice women but little dumplings like their mother. It was a challenge to make them look fashionable.

The following hours were the strangest Krista had ever spent. After her flight from France that was saying a great deal. Emmanuelle Doumer appeared to know every shop and salesperson in Ipswich. She swept Krista in and out of shops at speed. She demanded the best with orders to send all invoices to the Winchester home.

"That hair must go." Emmanuelle stopped in front of the town's most popular hairdresser's salon. "It makes you look like a schoolgirl. Do you have any objection?"

"None at all." At least she asked her opinion, Krista thought.

Krista was pulled into the hairdresser's and parked in a chair while Emmanuelle gave instruction to the stylist.

"I will leave you here while I pick up some things we need." Emmanuelle disappeared before Krista could respond.

"We have been given our orders." Beryl Stewart put a hand on Krista's shoulder, bending to meet her eyes in the mirror. "Are you happy to have me style your hair?"

"Please." Krista met the kind brown eyes smiling at her in the mirror. "It is only hair. It will grow back."

"A good attitude to have." Beryl ran her hands through the mass of white hair, thinking about the style the little Frenchwoman had demanded. It would suit the young woman's face certainly, but she would not cut if she was not confident it would suit the hair as well. "I will give you instructions on how to keep the style fresh. You will need to have a trim every six weeks if you want to keep the style."

Krista allowed the stylist to do with her what she would. Her hair was washed, her head massaged in a delightful way that had her almost groaning aloud. It felt wonderful. She moved where instructed and once more arrived in front of the mirror. She closed her eyes and sat back, listening to the snip of the scissors through her hair. She didn't care about the style. She was glad to be allowed to sit and rest. Today had been exhausting and it wasn't over yet.

"Miss," Beryl's voice was soft, "let me show you some styles you can have with this cut."

Krista snapped her eyes open, staring into the mirror at the wet strings of hair that had been cut to her jawbone.

"Do you have any idea how fortunate you are to have this white-blond hair without the use of bleach and chemicals?" Beryl leaned forward to say. "There are women I know who would kill to have hair like this." She laughed. "Honestly, I have my work cut out for me bleaching their hair until it is almost tow, but will they listen to my advice? Will they heck?" She continued to finger the wet hair. "Now, with just a few minutes of attention in the morning you can decide the style you need for the day. I am going to give you the most glamorous style today which you can easily attain yourself."

While fixing large rubber curlers Beryl began to give Krista a lesson in haircare that had her mouth dropping in shock. How was she supposed to find the time to do all of that – and first thing in the morning?

It was insane. Beryl walked Krista over to take a seat under a tall stand. A rubber hood was placed over her hair and hot air began to pour over her head.

Krista watched from under the dryer when Emmanuelle stepped into the salon. She spoke briefly with Beryl before disappearing again. Krista sat back to enjoy this novel experience.

"Right!"

The noise of the hot air-blower had disappeared and Krista could hear Beryl speak.

"You're cooked." Beryl laughed, removing the hood from over Krista's hair. "I've been ordered to do nothing more until Madame comes back." She led Krista over to her styling station. "Ah, here she is now. That was well timed."

"Thank you, Beryl." Emmanuelle made a space on the workstation for the little vanity case she had carried into the salon with her. "I want to make a few changes before you style her hair. I hope you do not mind? The lighting here is excellent for what I have in mind." She swung the styling chair and Krista around to face her.

"Not at all." Beryl got the impression it wouldn't matter whether she minded or not. Still, this woman was acknowledged as a bit of a miracle worker – look how she made the Winchester women look so attractive. She'd keep her mouth shut, watch and learn.

"Krista, you are young and do not need much in the way of cosmetics." Emmanuelle removed a tweezers from the case and began to pluck at one of Krista's eyebrows. "You must however do some maintenance. All women should." She glared down at Krista. "I will show you once then it is up to you." She tutted when Krista winced at the pain of having hair removed. "We must all suffer for beauty."

At last she stood back to examine her work and nodded in approval. She put the tweezers back in the space designed for it in the case.

"You must moisturise your skin."

With experienced hands – using a pot from the case – she applied cream to Krista's face.

Then Beryl watched in fascination as with a few skilled strokes Emmanuelle defined and darkened Krista's eyebrows and lashes. It was subtly done but made an enormous difference in the girl's appearance. A sweep of pink lipstick and the girl looked as if she had stepped from a magazine.

"Finished!"

Emmanuelle packed what she had used into the little case, closed it and stepped back.

Krista was swung around to face the mirror again. She stared at her own image in surprise. It didn't look like her.

When the curlers were removed and her hair swept back and to the side, with soft curls framing her face, the change was complete. Who was that woman? She felt more lost than ever but stiffened her spine and listened half-heartedly to the compliments Emmanuelle and Beryl were paying each other. She was just the model, it would appear.

Chapter 5

Krista held the door of her hotel room open for the porter. Emmanuelle had ordered all of their parcels to be delivered to the hotel. She stared at what appeared to her eyes to be a mini-mountain of wrapped packages, trying to remember what they had bought. Some packages she didn't recognise as Emmanuelle had purchased a variety of items while she was having her hair styled.

She had the porter put everything on the bed and, using some of her own precious English coins, tipped him. She hoped it had been enough – English money and its value was something she would need to study and understand.

She put the large brown-leather suitcase on the luggage stand at the foot of the bed and stood back to admire the article. Emmanuelle had bought it at a good price since it was slightly scratched. Krista didn't give a hoot about scratches – it was now hers – and it looked *rich*. She had never thought to own such a thing. She opened the straps and snapped open the locks and with a smothered laugh put her head inside the suitcase, taking a deep sniff of the rich aroma of new leather.

The small matching vanity case that Emmanuelle had used at the hair salon was on the bed. She opened it with a wide smile of delight, spending time examining all of the little pockets and wonderful articles stashed within. Imagine, the bottle-tops were silver! She had seen such cases used by guests staying at the auberge in Metz but to own such a thing – what luxury!

She danced over to the large hotel wardrobe and opened its doors for the first time. She'd had nothing to put in it before. Now she took covered hangers from its depths, enjoying the sandalwood scent. She began to open the packages, taking time to enjoy each item revealed. She hung blouses, cotton dresses, knit twinsets, skirts. She stashed shoes, silk stockings and all manner of small clothing in the room's tallboy of drawers.

Krista pulled back the net curtain. She had been hoping for something to take her mind off her own concerns, but everything was foreign to her. She turned to look back at the wardrobe and tallboy, thinking of the delightful items hidden now in their depths. She was still wearing the outfit she had travelled in. She wasn't ready to dress in the new clothes that had been purchased for her – not yet. It seemed to her that when she did wear the articles, so different from anything she had ever owned, then she would be leaving her old life behind forever and stepping out into an unknown world.

Her stomach rumbled, not from nerves but hunger. It had been a long time since lunch. Miss Andrews and Herr Baron had not returned to the hotel. She could not walk into the dining room in the hotel alone. She should have thought of buying something to eat and drink. She was alone now and responsible for her own wellbeing. She bit back a sob and pulled the note from Philippe from her skirt pocket. It was crumpled and hard to read now but she knew the words by heart.

He wrote that she was not a Dumas. Who then was she? Where had she come from? Did it matter? She was here, in England, alone in a hotel room with people who appeared to want to help her. Shouldn't she just accept that help without wondering and worrying about where she came from and who she was? She had never felt like a member of the Dumas family. She had always felt like the Ugly Duckling, being too tall and blond to fit into the short dark Dumas mould. It was time to sink or swim. She pushed to her feet and paced the small room. She needed to be doing something – but what!

She would take a bath, protecting her hair as the stylist had shown her. She walked over to the tallboy and pulled one of the drawers open. She had her own linen nightdress now and a heavy dressing gown to cover it. She would take a bath and get ready for bed – hunger wouldn't kill her.

"Christine, my dear, there you are." Violet Andrews, a waiter carrying a tray at her heels, walked down the hotel corridor. "You may drop your clothing into your room and come into mine." She examined the tall figure standing outside the bathroom door in her dressing gown, with her clothes in her arms. "I wish to speak with you."

Krista hurried to open her room door. She threw her clothing on a chair before standing inside the door, listening, waiting to hear the waiter leaving. She was decently covered but could not feel comfortable being observed in her night attire by an unknown male.

"The hot chocolate is for you." Violet drew a snifter to her lips. "I am in need of something a great deal stronger."

The two women sat at a circular table placed before the long windows overlooking the main street of the town. Violet's room was much larger than Krista's.

Krista tried not to fall upon the dainty sandwiches arranged so appealingly on a large platter. She poured chocolate from the silver jug into a thick glass goblet.

"Herr Baron is downstairs in the bar." Violet waved her hand at the tray, inviting Krista to partake of the food she had ordered for her. "The poor man has spent most of the day being interrogated by people who found it difficult to believe what he was telling them."

There was silence while Krista ate. Violet leaned back in her chair, sipping at the cognac in her glass, and trying to organise her thoughts. What she had learned today had shocked and terrified her. The information Gerhardt shared had changed her own plans drastically.

"You look upset, Miss Andrews." Krista wiped her lips with her napkin.

"I am more than upset, Krista." Violet closed her eyes for a moment, then opened them, sat forward and stared at Krista. "Do you know what is happening in Germany at the moment?"

"I have heard a great many rumours but know nothing for certain." There were a great many things happening in Germany at the moment. She had heard whispers but did not know what to believe.

"Today has been one shock after another. My dear friend Abigail never has let the grass grow under her feet." Violet pressed her fingers into her brow, trying to suppress the images that wanted to form. "Being so close to London is a blessing. She was on the telephone demanding the presence of a group of people she hopes will be able to assist Gerhardt in spreading the word about what is happening in Germany – what has been happening for some time, to hear him tell." She waved her hands about. "That is neither here nor there. Today Gerhardt tried to convince us that Germany has been stealing children away from their parents for years." She hit the table, rattling the dishes. "*Years* that man has been running unchecked." She fought tears at the very thought of those poor frightened children.

Krista stared at her, shocked. "My brothers, Jean-Luke and Henri Dumas, often threatened me with special homes for children like me when I was growing up."

"Children like you?" Violet was unsure of her meaning.

"Blond, blue-eyed children. They told me that Hitler's people would take me away. That they had homes where they were rearing such children." Krista had thought they were just trying to frighten her – she hadn't believed such places existed.

"Well, according to Gerhardt, they did."

Krista might well be feeling lost and adrift right now, but she was glad, so glad that she was no relation to men who had never shown her any affection or respect.

"And there was more," Violet said. "The White Slave Trade." She didn't want to think about it, but her eyes had been opened. She no longer had the luxury of hiding her head in the sand. "One hears of it, of course. We were warned of it as young women stepping out into the big bad world. But I never thought – have difficulty believing – that a man who is the head of a civilised country could sanction such a thing! It is past believing."

"I do not understand 'white slave trade'." Krista could see how upset Miss Andrews was becoming.

"It is the vile practise of stealing young women off the streets and forcing them into lewd acts." Violet gulped cognac, wishing she had asked for the bottle.

"*Ah, yes* – I have heard men in the village boasting of visiting such places." Krista had thought it was just that – idle boasting by men drinking in the company of men.

Violet wanted to weep at a young innocent like Krista hearing of such things.

"I did not quite understand what the men were talking about. They quickly silenced each other if they thought I was paying attention to what they were saying." She had heard many things while serving in the café/bar/tabac over the years.

"Shameful." Violet had not really believed Gerhardt when he had first told her of Hitler's plans. It had seemed fantastical but more and more she was being forced to believe. She had listened to Gerhardt tell of factories producing tanks, guns, bombs but it was the plight of women and children that most shocked her. How could the world have been so blind to what was happening?

"What Gerhardt shared with us today has changed my own plans." Violet finished the dregs in her glass. "I had not truly believed him when he spoke of the danger that faced us all. I had thought to use his dramatics to visit friends and family in this country before returning to my little cottage and quiet life." She leaned back in her chair. "Your presence in the car, was of course, the first shock." She smiled softly at Krista before continuing. "The gang of ruffian soldiers at the docks – they too were a shock to me."

She fell silent.

"What will you do?" Krista asked when the silence became uncomfortable.

Violet spoke after a long pause. "My mind is in a whirl. I have not packed up my life in France. There are items there it will sadden me to lose but returning is out of the question." She leaned forward, resting her elbows on her knees and burying her head in her hands. Her voice was muffled when she continued. "I have to remain here. I can be of help to Gerhardt. I have no clear knowledge of where I will go from here." She sat upright in the chair. "I am concerned for you, Krista."

"I thought my fate had been decided?"

"Yes, for the moment." Abigail had spent time on the telephone convincing her young relative to employ Krista as something of an assistant. Someone who would help watch over the children and also turn her hand to anything asked of her. It would protect Krista until something could be planned for her future. "You are a young woman alone in a strange country and the idea of working for Abigail's relation is a good one – but it is not long term. What is to become of you?"

"I do not know."

"Abigail has arranged for her driver to take you to London – Knightsbridge – in the morning. You will be safe there. I have the address." Violet leaned over to put her hand over Krista's resting on the table. "I want you to think of me as an aunt – an eccentric one perhaps – but I do care what happens to you." She sighed deeply. "I will write to you and I insist you keep me informed of your news. I do not want to lose contact with you."

"That is most kind." Krista would be happy to know that she had at least one person in England who was concerned for her.

"If I were truly kind, I would have removed you from the Dumas home years ago and taken you to England." Violet had kept her distance from Krista, happy to oversee her studies in English, but she had never put herself out to really worry about the girl. Constance would be ashamed of her. She was ashamed of herself.

"Why?" Krista could tell there was something Miss Andrews was keeping from her.

"I saw the note Philippe Dumas wrote to you." Violet stiffened her backbone. "You fell asleep with it clutched to your breast. I removed it from your hands at the hotel in Belgium. I read it. I am sorry."

"So, you know I am not a Dumas – it came as a shock to me. I do not know who I am or where I came from. I thought to begin a search for my own beginnings. Madame Dumas must know where I came from – don't you think?"

"You would be only opening yourself up to a world of hurt, child." But how could she leave Krista in the dark?

"I need to know who I am, can you not understand? I feel adrift. I wonder if I have family who would welcome me. I never felt as if I belonged to the Dumas family even before I learned the truth."

"Child," Violet sighed, "I knew both your mother and your father ..."

"You did?" Krista stared, unable to believe the words she was hearing. Did everyone in the world know who she was except her?

"I am sorry to tell you, but they are both deceased."

"No!" She sucked in a breath, feeling as if someone had punched her in the chest. How was it possible to learn of her true parents' existence only to be told in the next breath that they were both dead. How was she supposed to react? She clasped a hand to her mouth, fearing she was going to vomit.

"Yes, they died in a tragic accident when you were a babe-in-arms." Violet wished she had more experience at telling uncomfortable truths.

"But surely I have grandparents, uncles, aunts, cousins." Krista's head was spinning. "I must have family somewhere."

"Your parents were never married." Violet could feel her heart breaking. Krista did have family – a lot of family, if the truth be known, but they would not welcome her into their midst. "Well, your father was married, just not to your mother." She felt as if she had slapped the girl, but she needed to know the truth.

"I am illegitimate – a bastard child?" The word *bastard* was practically the same in English and French. She well understood its meaning.

"You were a much-loved and cherished baby. Had your parents lived, your life would have been very different." Violet was tired. She longed to close her eyes and sleep – escape the world that was shattering around her. She too felt as lost as Krista looked at this moment.

"Will you tell me about my parents?" Krista wasn't sure she really wanted to know.

"Not tonight." Violet stood up. "I am tired. I will tell you all I know of your parents at some time. I promise. But tonight I simply must sleep. There is so much to do. At this moment in time, Krista, the simplest plan is for you to travel to Knightsbridge. You must work on your English conversation. In time we can make more plans. But please, I beg of you, not tonight!"

Chapter 6

Krista jerked awake at the soft sound of a key being turned in her bedroom door. The chair she had put under the doorknob stopped whoever was outside from entering her room.

"*Who is there?*" she croaked.

"*Your wake-up call, miss!*" a soft female voice called.

Krista hadn't asked for someone to wake her. She pushed up onto her elbow, trying to see the hands on the small enamel clock she'd put on the bedside table. She'd purchased the clock the previous day from a pawnbroker. She hadn't slept very well. She had tried to sleep with curlers in her hair as her stylist suggested. She finally tore the torture instruments out of her hair sometime in the small hours of the morning.

"*One moment!*" She rolled out of bed, her feet searching for the slippers she'd left on the floor by the side of the bed. She almost fell over to the door. She pulled the chair away before putting her head in the opening, hiding her nightdress-clad body behind the door.

"I didn't ask for a wake-up call," she said.

"The gentleman asked that you be awakened this morning, miss." The fresh-faced young chambermaid smiled. "He ordered breakfast for three to be served in his room." She turned to leave then turned back to say. "He said not to dress for the day but come in your dressing gown and slippers, miss."

"Thank you." Krista closed the door and almost fell into the nearby chair. Well, at least she had a dressing gown and slippers to wear. It would feel strange, but she would be decently covered. Before anything else she needed the toilet. She put the chair back in its place before shoving her arms into the sleeves of her heavy woollen dressing gown.

"Christine, good morning." Miss Andrews, in her dressing gown, stepped out of the toilets and into the hotel corridor. "Have you too received orders to present yourself?"

"The chambermaid woke me."

"Well, hurry along. Bertram is not a man who likes to be kept waiting."

"I will not be long," Krista stepped around her and with relief entered the toilet.

"We need to discuss our plans for the future while we have this time alone." Gerhardt wiped his lips with a

53

napkin. He found a cooked English breakfast a delightful way to start the day.

The three travelling companions were seated around a round table, helping themselves to breakfast from the tiered wooden trolley pushed into the room by a waiter. The trolley was laden with silver-domed serving dishes. Tall carafes holding tea, coffee and hot chocolate sat tall on top.

"We are to part ways today." Gerhardt sipped from his cup, wincing at the dreadful coffee. "Young Krista, you will travel to London to take up your new position. Miss Andrews and I will be guests of the Winchesters for a time." He sat back in his chair, staring at his companions. They had been instrumental in helping him escape those who sought to detain him. "Krista, I wish you well in your future endeavours."

"Thank you." Krista pushed the coffee cup from her. The Baron was someone she had seen around her village all of her life. He was someone to bow your head before and watch from afar. What was she doing sitting in his company as if they were social equals?

"We are sending you out into the world alone, Krista." Violet Andrews sipped her tea with delight. It had been years since she'd been able to enjoy a pot of superior English tea. She hid her grin in her teacup. She had noticed her companions' disgust at the bitter coloured water served as coffee. Well, now they knew how she felt when she'd tried the truly dreadful tea served in France. "We need to work as one to explain your presence here in England." She had shamed Gerhardt into helping her establish Krista in England. The man had educated his brother's two legitimate daughters. He had seen them settled with husbands. She was determined to see he helped Krista get settled too, even if he never wanted to publicly acknowledge their connection.

"I have no papers," Krista fretted. "How can I seek employment without the proper paperwork?"

"In the normal scheme of things," Violet replaced her cup on its saucer, "you would have to present your papers to the nearest police station and be declared as a foreign national. Then you would have to undergo a medical examination and seek a work permit. You entered the country illegally, as all here know."

"I could write to the Mayor's office in Metz and request copies of my papers to be forwarded to me," Krista said. The words *police* and *illegal* rang in her head.

"I do not think it is a good idea to tell anyone of your whereabouts." Gerhardt continued to enjoy his cooked breakfast. "You are not yet of legal age. It is quite possible the Dumas family would send one of their sons to take you back or indeed approach the police here to have you returned to them. They would be within their rights."

"What shall I do?" Krista was horrified at the thought.

"Abigail and Gerhardt have connections in the Foreign and Home Office." Violet refilled her teacup. "I truly believe, dear girl, that it would be better for you to start over in this country with new papers. It makes no sense to apply for your old identity papers from France."

Krista felt the food she'd eaten congeal in her stomach.

"You may leave all of that in my hands." Violet

intended to do all she could to make Krista's way as easy as possible. After all, she was the innocent in all of this. She had connections of her own whom she would persuade to help her in establishing Krista as the daughter of an Englishwoman. If she had to, she would approach Constance's family. She would do what she could to embarrass them into helping the girl. But that would be a last resort. In her opinion, the matter of papers for Krista would be best managed discreetly.

"But I will need to present papers to my new employer."

"No, no – I will arrange all of your paperwork," Violet gave a brief pat to Krista's fist clenched tightly on the tabletop. "Today you will arrive at your place of work in a chauffeur-driven Rolls Royce. No one will dare to question you. I do not suggest you lie but allow people to form their own opinions. Abigail's dresser did purchase a dress outfit for you, did she not?"

"Yes, she was most insistent I would need such an outfit."

"Good. Now your story, my dear, is that your mother was English, your father French. They died when you were a babe-in-arms and you were raised by a family friend. It is simple and almost the truth. It is best to stick as closely as possible to the truth when you are on sticky ground. There will be no need to mention you were raised in an auberge and worked in a café/bar/tabac." Violet was determined to give Krista a good start in her new life.

"But ..."

"This is a new life for you, Krista, and you must start as you mean to go on," Gerhardt said. "The position being offered to you – as I understand it – is one of gentility. You will be a companion and help to a lady from a titled family."

"But I will not know –"

"You should give some thought to what you would like to do," Violet said, ignoring her protests. "It may well be possible for you to take evening lessons in shorthand and typing. You are fluent in three languages. That is a great achievement and will be much sought after. You need make no decisions now but, when you have your papers in hand, then you may decide what you want to do with your life."

"It is all very complicated," Krista sighed. "I had thought to seek a live-in position in a hotel."

"Krista," Violet leaned forward to emphasise what she was about to say, "this is your chance to change the course of your life. Grab it with both hands. I will be on hand to advise you. I will not desert you, my dear. I want to see you flourish in your new life. You will have a new life in a new country, with a new name if you so desire."

"I do not wish to be known by the name Dumas any longer." Krista wanted to forget everything about her past life.

"We need to decide on a family name for you. Your forenames of Krista Grace are, of course, quite acceptable." Violet knew Constance Grace chose these names for her child. It had gladdened her heart the first time she'd seen them written down in Krista's English exercise book. Gerhardt, in this at least, had seen to it that Constance's wishes were carried out. "We cannot put your father's name on your papers." She didn't look at Gerhardt when she said that – even if they could, the name was too German in these troubled times. "We must choose a name that sounds very French. Something not too difficult to pronounce for the English – something easy to remember."

"Lestrange," Krista said without thought. It would suit, as everything was very strange indeed to her at this moment in time.

"Krista Grace Lestrange." Violet gave a quick nod of her head. "I like it."

"Then we are decided." Gerhardt pushed his chair back and walked to the nearby desk. He made note of the name before putting the paper carefully into his wallet.

"We must get ready for the day ahead." Violet could not think of anything more they needed to discuss. "Krista, the chauffeur will be outside the hotel at ten o'clock. You must not keep him waiting. I will come to your room at nine thirty. We will wait together in the hotel lobby."

"I will say goodbye to you here." Gerhardt had matters he needed to take care of before leaving the hotel. "I wish you the best of luck, young Krista Grace Lestrange." He stood and clicked his heels. It didn't have quite the same effect while wearing slippers.

"Goodbye, Herr Baron." Krista stood and gave him a nod of her head.

"Gerhardt!" Violet snapped, giving a jerk of her head in Krista's direction.

"Ah, yes, of course." Gerhardt turned back to the desk. He picked up his wallet and removed two large white papers from it. "Take this," he pushed the money into Krista's hand. "You may have need of it."

"That is a ten pounds, Krista." Violet said. "It is a great deal of money to the everyday working man. It is good to have money of your own in case of need."

"Thank you." Krista could not afford to be proud and refuse.

"Krista, my dear, you look wonderful." Violet stood in Krista's room, examining her from head to toe. This is how she should always have looked. A young girl of good family. The royal-blue floral dress revealed by the open royal-blue coat she wore was in the best of taste. Her legs gleamed in silk stockings running down to T-strap leather shoes in the same royal blue. The Peter Pan style white hat that was so in fashion at the moment sat on her shortened hair.

"I am not overdressed?" Krista had found it difficult to believe her eyes when she had seen her own image in the mirror. "I have white kid gloves and a clutch handbag too."

"You look a treat and very much as you need to appear before your English employer for the first time." Violet clasped her hands to her breast, thrilled with this new image of her charge. "You are packed?" She looked around the room.

"I am." Krista was shaking. "Miss Andrews, I wish to thank you for all of your help. You have been very kind to me." She felt and looked like a different person from the one who had climbed out the laundry window and hidden herself in the back of Herr Baron's car.

"Your late mother was a very dear friend of mine, Krista." Violet smiled sadly, wishing her friend Constance Grace could be here to see her lovely daughter. "I will keep in touch with you. I want to know how you go on. I had not intended to make this journey a permanent move to England. I am afraid I do not have firm plans for my own future. But that is neither here nor there. We will keep in touch and see what the future brings." She turned towards the door. "Now, come along, it would not do to keep Abigail's driver waiting." She started out the door. "We will send the porter for the luggage." She laughed. "You will find, Krista, that protecting your silk stockings from runs is quite difficult. That luggage with its belts and buckles would shred them."

Krista locked the door behind them as they left the room, wondering how much she would have to tip the porter.

Violet felt very emotional as they stood watching the chauffeur load Krista's luggage into the boot of the Rolls Royce Silver Ghost car sitting, engine throbbing, in the street. "Remember, Krista Grace Lestrange, I will let you have my address as soon as I know it. Should you have need of me, your new employer will know who to contact. I am always at your service."

"Thank you. For everything." Krista couldn't take her eyes from the gleaming, beautiful motorcar. She had never seen anything like it before in her life. Was she really to travel in such a vehicle? She wanted to pinch herself. "I do not know what I would have done without your help." She refused to think of the horror she had left behind. She was entering a new stage of her life.

Chapter 7

Krista travelled in the back of the Rolls Royce, feeling like
royalty. The view outside the sparkling windows was
delightful and strange to her eyes. She longed to know
what the crops growing in the field were but the chauffeur
had not lowered the thick glass wall that separated him
from his passengers. Perhaps it wasn't the done thing to
speak to the chauffeur? She had to content herself with
sitting back and enjoying this unique experience.

The old men sitting outside their cottages in the
villages they passed through doffed their hats as the
car passed. Young people on bicycles pulled over to the
side of the road and waved. The chauffeur never
acknowledged these greetings but drove steadily on
towards London.

* * *

Krista's eyes were burning. She was afraid to blink in case she missed something – she was in London. It was beautiful. Tall white buildings, bright green hedges, flowers in pots everywhere. She couldn't wait to explore this new world. She recognised the Royal Albert Hall from the many photographs she had seen in magazines and newspapers. The open spaces of a park were green and thronged with people. The chauffeur turned into a street off the park then into a square of tall white buildings that surrounded a charming square of parkland. She had to snap her mouth shut when the car came to a stop in front of one of the houses.

The door was set back from the road with a walkway of black-and-white tiles. It opened and a smiling young maid stood there. Krista felt her stomach turn – she was here – what was she going to find behind that door?

The chauffeur opened the car door for Krista and offered a white gloved hand to assist her from the depths of the leather interior. She accepted the hand gratefully and took her first step onto London soil.

"We didn't know what time to expect you, Mr Johnson!" the young maid called cheerfully. "I've been keeping my eye out for you."

"Yes, thank you, Matthews." Johnson didn't approve of the familiarity of this generation.

"Mrs Acers said you would be welcome to step into her kitchen for a sup of tea and a bite of cake." Peggy, though she didn't know it, sounded exactly like her

Irish mother when she was addressing someone she didn't like. She didn't think the old sourpuss would accept the offer of tea and cake, but she'd been told to make the offer and she had.

"I must be on my way." Johnson carried the luggage he'd taken from the boot into the black-and-white tiled entrance hall, placing the items at the foot of the wide staircase. He turned to leave with a touch of his fingers to his peaked hat.

"Thank you for getting me here safely, Mr Johnson." Krista wasn't quite sure of the etiquette of the situation but manners cost nothing.

"You are welcome, miss." The chauffeur stepped smartly across the hall and out the front door, pulling the door closed after him.

"Hello, my name is Peggy – Peggy Matthews – how do you do?" Peggy examined the girl standing in front of her. Foreign, she was told. She wasn't half dressed lovely. "I thought we could take your things up to your room."

"My name is Krista Lestrange. It is nice to meet you, Peggy." Krista hoped she could make friends with this girl. "Is there a toilet nearby?" She desperately needed to use the facilities. If they were off the premises she would prefer to use them before going upstairs.

Peggy's peal of laughter echoed around the high ceiling of the hallway. "Yes, I can't imagine asking that auld sourpuss Johnson to stop for a pee-break." She continued to laugh as she pointed to a nearby door. "The necessary is through there. I'll wait here for you and take you up to your room." She continued to laugh while Krista hurried to attend to her needs.

* * *

"The Missus is off to one of her exercise classes." Peggy carried the suitcase up the stairs while Krista carried the vanity case, being mindful to keep it away from her legs and silk stockings. "She goes to the classes three times a week. If she had to run up all these blessed stairs as many times a day as I do, she'd have no need for exercise classes I can tell you."

"Where are the children?" Krista tried to take in everything as they continued to climb. The walls were painted white with paintings all along their length. To her surprise they were not paintings of relatives but colourful pictures of country life. She would take her time to examine them – when she was free to do so.

"Those two holy terrors are with their grandmother. The Missus will pick them up after her class." Peggy looked over her shoulder with a smile. "It's a blessing they weren't here this morning. They're lovely boys but they love that Rolls Royce and who can blame them? It's a thing of beauty to anyone's eyes but you can't stop young lads from touching, now can you?"

Krista couldn't comment and it seemed it wasn't necessary.

"You should have seen auld Johnson's face the last time the boys got their hands on that car. It was a picture no artist would paint." She stopped on the landing of the third floor – Krista had kept count. Peggy opened one of the three doors opening off the landing. "This is the lads' room right next door to your room." She gave Krista only a moment to peek at a room decorated in shades of blue with two single beds. "You can look at that later – we need to get on. This is the playroom."

The room revealed by the open door was a delight, with items Krista wanted to examine. There appeared to be a great many toys. She would enjoy playing with them herself, never mind the little boys.

Peggy closed the door and opened another. "This room is yours." She stepped back, waiting for Krista to enter.

"How lovely!" Krista didn't know what to say or do. The room was beautiful in shades of cream and coffee. The wide lace-draped window let in plenty of light. The big brass bed was covered by a cream lace bedspread. The wardrobe and tallboy gleamed. The wooden floors were covered with a beautiful carpet. The high ceilings delighted her.

"Here, give me your coat and I'll hang it up." Peggy put the suitcase on the floor and took a padded hanger from the wardrobe. "I don't want you to think I'm bossing you around or anything, but I suggest you change your clothes before you meet the boys."

"Shouldn't I meet my new employer in my best clothing?" Krista passed over her coat.

"Bless you, you can't stand around all day like a shopfront dummy." Peggy wanted to see what the girl had in her luggage. The outfit she was wearing had her salivating. She wished she had the money to own something like that.

"Thank you for your advice but I'll wait to change until I have met the mistress of the house." She felt wonderful in these clothes and was reluctant to remove them just yet. Besides, she wanted to make a good impression on her employer. "Perhaps you have a suggestion as to what I should wear when dealing with the boys?" Krista removed her hat and gloves, putting them on top of the tallboy. "I have no experience in being a member of an English household or indeed caring for young people," she dared to admit.

She needed help and this friendly young woman seemed willing to share her opinions.

"I'll help you all I can." Peggy couldn't insist she changed but those stockings she was wearing were silk if she were any judge – not the thing to wear while running after young boys. Still, it was none of her business. "You've fallen lucky to come to this house. It's nothing like what me auld ma told me about the house she worked in as a maid before she was married. I couldn't have worked somewhere you had to watch yourself every minute. Still, there are rules and regulations to follow." She took a wooden folding table out of the wardrobe and, opening it to reveal a canvas top, she set it at the bottom of the bed. "You can put your suitcase on here."

"Thank you." Krista heaved the heavy leather suitcase onto the foldaway.

"Before you get started putting your stuff away, why don't we go down and have a cup of tea and a bite of cake with Mrs Acers? She's waiting to meet you and the arse will be boiled out of the kettle if we don't go down soon." She turned towards the door. "One word of advice and I hope you don't take it wrong ..."

"I am happy to be guided by you, Peggy."

"Put anything you don't want little fingers tampering with in the wardrobe." She pointed. "It has a key you can turn and put away. It will save a lot of bother."

"Thank you. I will do that."

"Come along then. We have time before the family returns." She walked through the door they had left open.

Krista looked around the room and with a small sigh followed along.

"Mrs Acers, I've brought the foreign girl to meet you." Peggy pushed open the door of the basement kitchen. "Her name is Krista and she talks like one of them off the radio."

"I thought you'd lost your way, young Peggy, you were that long." A tall big-boned woman, dressed all in black with a large white smock apron wrapped around her body and tied at the waist, looked over her shoulder as she poured boiling water from a black kettle into a teapot sitting on the black range. She turned back around when she'd put the heavy kettle on the back of the range.

Krista stood on the red-tiled floor of the kitchen, trying to take everything in at once.

"I am Mrs Acers the cook. It's nice to meet you. I hope you will be happy here." She smiled at the shy youngster standing looking lost in her kitchen. "Sit yourself down and we'll have a pot of tea and get to know each other. I've a cake not long out of the oven that we can slice." She gestured towards the heavy wooden table pushed to one side of the kitchen.

"Thank you." Krista pulled a wooden chair away

from the table. "I am happy to meet you."

* * *

"Now," Mrs Acers said when they were all seated around the table, tea and cake in front of them. "The Missus said you are French but you speak English?"

"Yes." Krista swallowed the bite of cake she had just taken. "I am from a small village in France. I have studied English for many years but I need to practise speaking."

"Your parents must be sad to see you travel so far from home?"

"My parents are dead, Mrs Acers." Krista tried not to blush. It might well be the truth but she felt as if she was lying to this kind woman.

"Oh, I am sorry, dear."

Peggy drank her tea and ate her cake as if she hadn't eaten in weeks, but her ears were wagging. She didn't want to miss a word.

"They died when I was a baby. My mother was English. I have no close family. I was raised by friends of my French father." It was the first time she had told the story that Miss Andrews insisted she tell.

"Fancy that." Wilma Acers didn't know what to say. She didn't want to make the poor lass sad on her first day in the house, but she liked to know what was going on in what she thought of as her domain. "And you are here now to look after the little lads?"

"How come you arrived in that Rolls Royce?" Peggy had been burning with curiosity and couldn't keep her mouth shut any longer.

"I arrived in this country in the company of my guardian Miss Violet Andrews." Krista moistened her mouth with a sip of the cooling tea. "Miss Andrews is a close personal friend of Lady Abigail Winchester." She waited to see if they had questions. When both remained silent, seemingly hanging on her every word, she continued. "I had thought to seek employment in a hotel, but Lady Winchester insisted I needed to improve my knowledge of spoken English."

"Lady Abigail won't steer you far wrong, girl." Mrs Acers was a great admirer of that titled lady.

"I am grateful for her interest in my welfare," Krista said. "But I have no experience in taking care of the young. I am nervous."

"Well, you won't go far wrong if you watch and listen to young Peggy here." Mrs Acers was glad the girl wasn't claiming to be something she wasn't. She'd been nervous when she heard the latest member of the household was arriving in style in the back of Her Ladyship's Rolls Royce. "Peggy is the eldest of ten."

"*Ten!*"

"You sound shocked." Peggy laughed. "I was that glad to get away from all of them. My little room here in the basement is a palace to me. I love taking care of this house – keeping everything clean and sparkling."

"Peggy has already kindly offered to advise me how best to deal with the young boys in my charge." Krista was thrilled to know she had an expert to run to for information and guidance. "I will be happy for any help you might offer too, Mrs Acers."

"They are good little lads, aren't they, Mrs Acers?" Peggy waited for the cook to nod before saying, "But

69

you need to establish who is boss or they will run you ragged."

"I will do my very best by them." Krista tried to sound positive, but she was trembling at the thought of caring for young boys. The males she had thought of as her brothers had not been kind to her while they were growing up.

"Well, sitting here yakking won't get the baby a bonnet." Mrs Acers used her hands on the tabletop to push to her feet. "I have lunch to finish and I daresay you will want to get settled into your room, Krista."

"I'll take you up and get you started." Peggy began to remove the dishes from the table.

Krista picked up some soiled crockery and waited to see what she should do with it.

Mrs Acers watched the two youngsters, pleased to see Krista lend a hand. They had no use for anyone who wasn't willing to help out in this house. The girl wouldn't be expected to scrub floors but in a house this size there was always something needing doing.

"I'll wash these later, Mrs Acers." Peggy turned from the sink. She knew Mrs Acers couldn't abide untidiness in her kitchen and would wash the dishes before she could get to them.

"If we do them now, they will be out of the way," Krista said innocently. "I will wash if you will dry and put everything away. You know where things go but I will learn."

"That shook you, young Peggy!" Mrs Acers laughed, well aware of Peggy's habit of leaving dishes for her to clean away. "Here." She took an apron from the back of the kitchen door and passed it to Krista.

"You don't want to dirty your lovely dress."

Krista put the apron on and in no time at all the two young women had the dishes washed, put away and the table scrubbed. They left the kitchen laughing together, heading towards the stairs and what would become Krista's domain.

Chapter 8

"You must be Krista."

Krista almost dropped the children's books she'd been stacking. She turned on her heel to smile in the direction of the voice. The woman was wearing slacks! How shocking! She had seen women wear such things in magazines from Hollywood but could not imagine being daring enough to wear them.

What a handsome picture, Krista thought, as she stood up from where she'd been crouched restoring order to the bookcase. The woman standing in the doorway was tall and slim, very attractive with her russet hair and blue eyes. She was smiling, thank goodness. The two boys standing close to her side were like matching bookends. Twins and identical.

How on earth would she tell them apart?

"What are you doing with my books?" one boy demanded.

"Are you going to read to us?" asked the other.

"Boys, manners!" Cordelia – Lia to friends and family – Caulfield put a gentle hand on the shoulder of each of her boys and led them into the room she had set aside as their playroom. "Krista, meet your charges, Edward and David." She switched to fluent French to say, "They will try to deceive you about which is which. Edward has a widow's peak like myself. David does not." She pointed to her own forehead. The shining russet hair was thick and rich with a pronounced widow's peak. "The only thing either of my boys got from me. They are the very image of their father."

"Your husband must be a very handsome man," Krista replied in French. The two boys were enchanting with black hair and stunning green eyes.

"Mother, it is rude to speak when we can't understand." David crossed his arms and glared.

"Do you not speak English?" Edward looked with concerned eyes at Krista.

"I do speak English." Krista smiled down at the two boys.

"Krista, we will go down and share a pot of tea while getting to know each other." Lia Caulfield turned the boys towards the door. "The boys will have juice and a snack with Mrs Acers while we talk."

Krista followed after the little family, still in shock over the lady's apparel. The brown slacks were pleated and high-waisted. The coffee-coloured twinset and pearls gave the outfit a dashing appeal.

* * *

"Now we will have some peace while Mrs Acers and Peggy keep the boys entertained." Lia reached for the teapot which had been delivered by a smiling Peggy.

They were sitting in a comfortably furnished lounge. The room was at the back of the house and was obviously furnished to withstand the wear and tear of two young boys. The large chair Krista sat in almost swallowed her. She was having difficulty sitting erect. The coffee table holding the tray of tea seemed miles away.

"Tell me about yourself," Lia said.

"I am French ..." Krista repeated the story agreed upon with Miss Andrews.

"Violet Andrews is your guardian." Lia opened a box sitting on the coffee table. She took a long cigarette and a match out, using the side of the box to strike a light. When the cigarette was burning brightly, she blew a stream of smoke towards the ceiling. "I haven't seen her in years."

"She has been living close to my home in France," Krista said simply.

"Indeed." Lia tapped her ash against the rim of a nearby ebony ashtray. "Look here, Krista. I am in rather a quandary as to how to treat you. I have never wanted or needed someone to help me look after my sons."

"I have been imposed upon you by Lady Winchester." Krista felt her heart sinking.

"Oh, Abigail always has the best of intentions," Lia waved away smoke, "and I like the thought of having someone be there to oversee the boys. They will be going to school in September. That will of course change everything. It will force me into a schedule." She fixed her pale blue eyes on Krista. "I have not been looking forward to being constrained by time." She blew smoke rings at the ceiling. "It will help me enormously to have someone get the boys ready in the morning and be available to pick them up from school."

There was silence while they sipped their tea.

"I was raised with servants constantly underfoot." Lia sighed. "I imagine many would think that a wonderful situation, but I can't like it. Mrs Acers does not live in and Peggy is a rule unto herself. I enjoy her free spirit. I do not want someone who can't think for herself. We will have to take each day as it comes, I suppose. Abigail was insistent I take you on. But I simply do not know what to do with you."

Krista wondered what she was supposed to say to that. She was in a foreign country in a strange household and had no idea what she was supposed to do or think. If the mistress of the house was confused, she was floundering.

"Perhaps we could learn together," she suggested. "I have never been employed to watch over children before. We will both be starting off fresh. We can decide what is and isn't acceptable." She wanted to stay in this charming house with its rather avant-garde mistress. "I had not expected the boys to be going to school. Lady Abigail thought the boys were only three years old." What would she do when the boys were in school?

"Abigail does not like to notice the passing of the years." Lia laughed softly.

"Madame ..."

"No, no. You must call me Lia. If I understand what Abigail has in mind, you are not to be my servant. Perhaps this would work best if we think of you as my protégé?"

"Lia?"

"Yes, my nanny always referred to me as Cor-de-*lia*." She mimicked her nanny's voice. "I grew up thinking my name was Lia and answered to nothing else." She shrugged. "I prefer it."

"Thank you, Lia." Krista wondered if she would be able to comply.

"How old are you, Krista?"

"I will be eighteen this summer." Would she think that too young?

"You are just starting out in life." Lia stared at the uncertain young girl sitting across the coffee table from her. What was she supposed to do with her? She was alone in a strange country. How frightfully terrible would that be? "If we are to think of you as my protégé I will endeavour to guide you. However," she leaned forward to tap the ash from her cigarette, "I must warn you that I am not someone who follows slavishly the strict rules and regulations of society. You would perhaps be better in a household that is strict in its manner." Did she have what it took to guide this young person?

"Madame … L-lia," Krista stuttered. "I was sent here to learn to speak English fluently. Perhaps we could take this summer to see if the situation we find ourselves in works for both of us?" She'd like to learn to stand on her own two feet. The summer would give her time to become familiar with an English household.

"We can do that." Lia mashed her cigarette into the ashtray. "The boys won't remain in the kitchen for very much longer. They are bundles of energy, always seeking new adventures." She waved a hand at Krista. "Your clothing, while charming, will not withstand the pressure of running after my two whirlwinds." Before Krista could react to this comment on her dress and silk stockings, she continued. "I noticed your reaction to my slacks. It is not common attire for a woman but I run after two boys all day long. I need to be dressed in a manner that allows me to join them in their endeavours.

"I have never worn slacks." Krista wondered if she would be brave enough to appear in such a thing.

"They are incredibly comfortable and much more sensible for running around after two children." The sound of running feet could be heard. "We will see how we go on. As you suggest, we will learn what is best together."

The door to the room flew back against the wall as the two boys ran into the room.

"*Mother!*" two voices cried in unison.

"Boys, is that any way to enter a room?" Lia braced herself for the charge as the two boys threw themselves into her arms.

"Peggy told us that this lady is going to look after us!"

Krista thought it was David who spoke.

"Why do we need someone to look after us? We are big boys of five." He held up one hand, fingers splayed. "We don't need looking after."

"Now, David, you are being quite rude –"

"Mother, she is dressed like a girl," Edward

interrupted with all the disgust of a young boy appalled at the thought of being around girls. "How can she play football with us? She'll be afraid of getting dirty. She won't be any good at playing trains."

"That is quite enough!" Lia tried to keep her face straight. If she laughed her two little mischief-makers would win. "Krista and I are discussing her duties. She is not here to look after you two. She is here to assist me."

Edward leaned in and put his two hands on his mother's face while staring intently into her eyes. "But we are your two best assistants," he said solemnly.

David added his voice to his twin's. "We always help you."

Krista watched the scene with a lump in her throat.

"You two will be going to school soon." Lia had been avoiding thinking about the changes the school year would bring to her own life. She had rejected all suggestions of sending her sons to boarding school. She wanted them with her. Trust her sister-in-law to force her into facing facts. She needed a new purpose in life. She had devoted the last five years of her life to her sons and enjoyed every second. She had no regrets. But what would she do with herself when they were in school and making new friends?

"Mother, if you have someone else to help you," David narrowed his green eyes and smiled innocently at his mother, "may we have a puppy?"

"Mother, you've always said you couldn't look after more than two naughty boys but you will have help now. May we have a puppy, Mother?" Edward shared a delighted grin with his twin.

Krista clenched her teeth. Something else she had no experience of – a pet!

"You see what you will have to deal with?" Lia laughed at her sons' cunning. "Krista, while I have these two in hand perhaps you would like to change your clothing?"

"I am afraid I have no slacks."

"But you perhaps have something that will withstand rough treatment?" Lia said. "Running around after these two will shred your stockings." She tickled the boys who were snuggled so close to her, enjoying the sweet sound of their laughter. "Peggy wears thick black stockings. If you do not have wool stockings, we can purchase them. Perhaps you could go barelegged just for today?"

"I have thick stockings." Krista almost groaned. She would be back in the dread thick black stockings. Well, she wanted to protect her silk ones. They were expensive and she was counting her English money carefully.

"Then run and change," Lia said. "We will wait for you. We will take these two tearaways across the road to the park. They can run off excess energy while you and I chat some more." She wanted to ask the girl about affairs in Europe. Would someone so young be aware of the changes taking place in the world?

Lia, wearing a long jacket that matched her slacks, kicked the football back towards the twins. They were running and shouting around the grassy area of the park while the two women strolled along the gravel path.

"Krista, you have recently travelled from France?"

"Yes." Krista was once again wearing the thick black stockings and laced shoes she'd worn as part of her uniform. The dark gaberdine skirt she wore with a pale-green knit twinset was new. She tried to count the days since she had run away from the auberge in Metz. It seemed so long ago but was only a matter of days.

"How are matters in France? We are hearing so much disturbing news."

"Miss Andrews believes we are heading towards war." Krista wouldn't hide how serious matters were becoming.

"No!" Lia grabbed onto Krista's arm, pulling her to a stop. She stared into Krista's brilliant blue eyes, her own paler eyes silently begging. "Please don't tell me that. My husband is a sea captain. He would be in the thick of things if we cannot keep the peace."

"I'm sorry." Krista couldn't deny what she had seen and heard. "I lived in a village on the French-German border. In the last two years the world I lived in changed beyond all recognition. Hitler has been making plans for years. He will not accept peace."

"Dear Lord!" Lia was trembling.

"*Mother, the ball!*"

Krista ran and kicked the football towards the twins. She walked back towards a pale-faced Lia.

"I need to sit down." Lia almost collapsed onto a park bench. She dropped her head into her hands, fear for her husband almost crippling her. She knew of course that he didn't simply sail calm seas and look out at the ocean. He sailed into danger. He had never hidden that from her. But no one was dropping bombs on him!

Krista ran onto the grass to keep the twins occupied. Lia needed time to gather her composure. She had been given a rude shock, but Krista couldn't lie and pretend everything was alright in the world. Her eyes had been opened to what was happening in her country. Britain needed to prepare for what was coming. There would be no stopping Hitler.

"Why is Mother sitting down?" David demanded.

"Your mother has some thinking to do. She thought I could kick the ball around with you two for a while." Krista wasn't very experienced at kicking a football, but she could do it. How hard could it be?

"Perhaps we should go sit with her?" Edward stared at his mother, his eyes glistening. She looked so sad there all on her own.

"I think your mother would prefer to see you two running around." Krista wanted to give the woman time to think about the horror that might well be heading her way. It would not be easy to hide her fear from these two. "She will call us if she needs us."

David too was staring at his mother.

"Why don't you two teach me how to play football?" Krista was determined to win at this first chore. She needed to keep the boys occupied.

"Don't you know how?" David looked at Krista in horror.

"I knew it would be a problem to have a girl try to play ball with us," Edward said in disgust.

Chapter 9

"Peggy, what are you doing up at this hour of the morning?" Krista was fixing the waistband of her navy slacks when she pushed open the kitchen door. She loved the freedom the slacks gave her but was still nervous of wearing them in public. She was surprised to see the light shining brightly in the kitchen, the kettle steaming on the hob.

"I thought I'd give you a hand getting ready," Peggy said, admiring Krista's slacks – she had been tempted to buy a pair herself but hadn't dared. She was enjoying having this girl in the house. In the six weeks she'd been living with them Krista had proved a blessing.

"I thought to make a flask of hot chocolate. I made snacks last evening. They are in the cool box in the pantry. I'll carry them in my haversack." Krista had learned never to leave the house without drinks and nibbles for the two boys.

"I'll make a pot of tea while you get your bag ready." Peggy hadn't bothered to dress. She was going back to bed as soon as this lot left the house.

"What would I do without you, Peggy?" Krista went to the pantry and pulled out everything she'd left to hand last night. She began to pack her haversack.

"Listen to you!" Peggy poured tea into two china cups. "I'll make the flask of chocolate while you wake the lads. Although what you are thinking of getting them out of bed at this hour of the morning I don't know. Drink that tea first."

"Edward!" Krista shook the little shoulder. "Edward, you need to wake up." He was the easiest of the two boys to wake in the morning.

"Is it today?" Edward rolled out of bed. He hurried across the carpet separating his bed from his twin's. "David!" he added his voice to Krista's, urging his twin up. "It's today."

"Come on, boys, into the bathroom – teeth, face, hands and hair must be clean." Krista had the clothes they would wear ready and waiting.

"It's very dark," David grumbled.

"It is very early." Krista hurried the boys through washing and dressing.

"Have Mother and Father left already?" Edward asked from under the jumper he was struggling to pull over his head.

"I don't know but we have to get there early so we

find a good place to watch."

The twins insisted on exploring the world whenever she took them out and about. There was no point in hurrying them along. She just had to leave the house early in order to allow them time to move at their own pace.

"Now, remember what I have told you." Krista followed the two boys down the stairs.

"We can't shout or wave at Mother and Father," Edward said with a longsuffering sigh.

"We can't frighten the horses," David added.

Captain Caulfield had arrived home for an extended stay. His ship was in dry dock for refitting. He and his wife rode out each morning with the King's Horse Guard at the nearby Hyde Park. They were civilian members who assisted in exercising the horses under the Guards' command. The boys had been demanding a chance to see their parents ride with the famous horsemen.

"Look at the two of you!" Peggy stood ready to open the front door. "You look like midshipmen in your duffle coats and trousers."

"Have you both got your flashlights?" Krista examined both boys.

"*Yes!*" The boys danced impatiently. They had insisted on wearing their new leather schoolbags on their backs in imitation of Krista's haversack.

"Come along then." Krista grabbed each by the hand and smiled her thanks at Peggy as they passed out into the gas-lamp lit street.

The clip-clop of hooves could be heard as they

walked slowly along towards the nearby Hyde Park. Automobiles, their lights like enormous bug-eyes broke through the darkness. The two boys took great delight in pointing their flashlights in all directions. It wasn't necessary but they were enjoying themselves and didn't object to Krista towing them swiftly in the direction they needed to go.

"*Look at that rabbit!*" David shouted.

"Keep your voice down," Krista reminded him. "It is very early. Take your light off the poor rabbit. He is frozen in terror."

"Sorry, rabbit." David removed his light instantly, allowing the rabbit to hop away.

"Look at the way the trees dance." Edward was pointing his light towards the sky.

"Yes, indeed, now come along." Krista continued to tow her charges in spite of their stop-start actions.

"Sorry, miss." A deep voice stopped them in their tracks. "You need to find another route to where you're going."

The two boys swung their flashlights, almost blinding the Horse Guard standing in their path.

"We have come to see Mother and Father ride out." David trust his chin out.

"We will be very good!" Edward smiled. "We are early so we can get the very best seats."

"Captain and Mrs Caulfield are riding out with the Guards this morning. These are their sons." Krista held up the hands she clutched tightly. "They will be on their very best behaviour."

"These two likely lads might be carrying contraband." The Guard Sergeant had been advised of the planned appearance of these lads by Captain Caulfield. He swung David around, examining the leather bag on his back carefully.

"Krista," Edward whispered, "do we have any con – con – what he said?"

"I'll be the one to answer that, my lad!"

Finished with David's schoolbag, the guard swung a delighted Edward around so he could examine his.

Krista swung her back to the man, offering up her haversack for inspection. She waited while he gave a cursory examination of the supplies she had packed so carefully.

"Now, lads!" the guard barked. "You use those lights to guide this lady around the cordoned-off area. There is a bench just off the path over there." He pointed in the general direction. "Find it, sit down and remain silent. Those are your orders. Do you understand?"

"*Yes, sir!*" Edward saluted.

"Come along, Krista." David puffed out his chest. "We have our orders."

"Thank you." Krista tried not to laugh. She could see the Guard was delighted with the little boys.

The boys took their orders very seriously and led Krista by the hand towards a bench off the gravel pathway. The cordoned-off area was a sand riding-space for the horses.

"Krista," Edward whispered, "we won't be able to see if adults stand in front of us."

"We can stand on the bench," David whispered.

"Boys, I don't think there will be many people out and about at this hour of the morning."

The crowds that would gather later to watch the

men in full uniform ride out to take part in the Changing of the Guard would be too rough for such young boys. This morning was a chance for them to see something not everyone could enjoy. She began to unpack her haversack.

"We will be able to see the horses coming out of the gates and crossing the road to the park," she said. "Now, each of you take your tin cup out of your bags. We will have a drink of chocolate while we wait."

The three settled down, Krista trying to keep the boys entertained. The park became alive with the sound of birdsong as the sky began to lighten. The boys jumped onto the bench, frantically trying to see the birds in the trees.

The gates across the street from the park began to open. Krista had to poke each boy in the back to attract their attention. It was a breathtaking sight. The dark horses, their bridles jingling, came out one by one. The boys froze like little statues as they watched.

"Where is ..."

"*Shhh* ... watch." Krista put a finger to her lips.

Finally, the civilian riders appeared. They looked attractive in their hacking jackets, jodhpurs, knee-high boots, a riding hat pulled onto each head making it difficult to tell them apart.

One of the riders approached the bench, his horse dancing impatiently under him.

"Have to give the horse its head for a while, boys! We will be back." Captain Caulfield turned his horse and followed the other riders along the bridle path.

The two boys danced on the bench, waving their arms wildly, but they remained silent.

It was an exciting morning for the two boys. They watched everything in wide-eyed wonder. Krista knew she'd be hearing all about this morning for hours on end. She didn't mind. It was wonderful to her to share their joy in the world around them.

Chapter 10

"Excuse me, miss."

Krista looked up at the waitress standing over her table.

"Could this gentleman join you?" The waitress was dressed in the black-and-white uniform of the Lyon's tearoom. She gestured towards a tall handsome young man leaning on crutches by her side. "This table is out of the way and allows him to stretch out his injured leg. Would you mind? I can guarantee his good behaviour. He is a regular."

"Please do." Krista waved her hand at the chairs across the table from her.

Today was her eighteenth birthday. Time to be brave. She had chosen this table because it was tucked away out of the busy traffic of the Lyon's Corner House tearoom. The boys were with their parents visiting the zoo. It would soon be time for the captain to return to his ship. They were spending these last days as a family, freeing her to explore London and her future.

"Thank you, Betty." The handsome young man allowed the nippy, as the Lyon's waitresses were called, to assist him into a chair.

"I'll be back to take your order in a moment." Betty hurried away.

"Thank you for allowing me to join you." He put his hand out. "My name is Perry Carter." They shook hands. "I've seen you in here before, but you have been accompanied by two little people." He smiled charmingly, flashing twin dimples.

"Krista Lestrange," Krista felt a fluttering in her stomach. He really was very attractive with his thick brown hair, light-brown almost amber eyes and charming smile.

"What will you have?" Betty, notepad in hand, stood over their table.

"Will you join me for afternoon tea – my treat?" Perry offered. He'd been watching this young beauty for weeks, hoping for a chance to meet her. It seemed his gammy leg was good for something.

"Thank you." Krista bowed her head slightly. Why not? She couldn't afford to treat herself and he had offered.

"Afternoon tea for two, Betty, please."

Betty snapped her notepad closed and took to her heels.

Perry laughed softly, turning to Krista. "You can see

why they are called nippies. It's the speed they move around the place." He settled more comfortably in his wooden seat and leaned on the table. "Am I interrupting something?" He jerked his head towards the newspaper open on the table in front of her.

"I am trying to decide my fate." She closed the newspaper offered free to clients of the tearoom.

"That sounds frightfully dramatic." Perry was surprised. He had expected her to say something frivolous about fashion or some such.

"Doesn't it?" Krista laughed.

"The two young lads I've seen you with cannot be yours. Are you their nanny?"

"I am French and as such I am employed as a companion and general assistant to their mother. I have come to England to improve my spoken English."

"With your family?" he dared to ask.

"No, no – alone."

Perry was saved having to say anything by the arrival of their waitress with a tray laden with tea, tiny sandwiches and delicious cakes. He was even more fascinated by this young woman now. How brave of her to come to a strange country alone! The riding accident that had crushed his lower left leg had changed his view of life. His friends had been sympathetic but quickly dropped him from their social rounds when he'd been unable to join in their frivolity.

"I should have ordered coffee," Perry said. "You being French."

"I have joined the English in their love of tea." Krista laughed and leaned forward to whisper. "I must. The coffee served is not what I am used to."

91

"No," Perry was forced to agree. He had drunk coffee in Europe and it was far superior to anything served in England outside high-class hotels.

"So," Krista held the brown teapot aloft, "tea it is. How do you take yours?"

They became busy with the business of preparing their tea and making a selection from the tiny sandwiches.

"Were you serious when you said you were deciding your fate?" Perry asked when they had both enjoyed a first taste of tea.

"I was." Krista didn't know why she was being so open with this young man as they were passing strangers. But perhaps that was why she felt at liberty to discuss her life with him. "I speak three languages fluently and thought to take classes to improve my choice of employment, but I have no great idea of what I wish to study."

"That is a dilemma." Perry bit into a salmon sandwich and was thoughtful for a moment before asking, "Could your parents not advise you?" He couldn't imagine being alone in a strange country, responsible for his own future.

"I am an orphan," Krista offered simply.

"Tough luck." Perry was embarrassed, hoping he hadn't caused her pain. "You are all alone in the world?"

"I have a very caring guardian." She did not want him to think she had no one looking out for her welfare. One heard such stories about women disappearing. He seemed a nice chap but one never knew.

"Could he not advise you?"

"She," Krista said with a smile. "And she is allowing me to decide my own future."

"How very liberated!" Perry felt like a fool but what could he say? He had never encountered a situation like this before. He had been protected all of his life. It was only since his accident that his eyes had been opened to the world around him. He was twenty years old and felt like a schoolboy before this self-possessed young woman.

"Perhaps, but at the moment it feels rather daunting."

"It would appear that we are in the same position." Perry pointed towards his injured leg stretched out past the table. "This has changed all of my own plans."

"So, we are two strangers wondering about our place in the world." Krista wondered what had happened to his leg but didn't like to ask – they had only just met. "Is your injury really life-changing?" Was that question too forward?

"The doctors have told me that the leg will heal but I may have a limp." He tried to smile. "I am very fortunate, I know." He shrugged away the nights of sleeplessness as he worried and wondered what was to become of him. He'd had plans to be an officer in the King's Household Guard. Now he was floundering. He was a younger son – he needed to plan a future for himself. He had always been so physically active. What would become of him with a gammy leg?

"We will be crying into our tea soon!" Krista tried to lighten the subject. Surely two young people with their lives in front of them could come up with a plan of action?

Chapter 11

"Hello, Jacob! Are you getting a cap too?"

David's voice snapped Krista out of her daydream about Perry and the fun they'd been having together, exploring London and the surrounding countryside. She was supposed to be keeping an eye on the twins while Lia shopped for the last items the boys needed for their school uniforms.

"Cordelia Caulfield, I must talk to you!" A short stout matron dressed all in black with a porkpie hat pulled low over her brow sailed through the Oxford Street children's haberdashery, forcing people to jump out of her way.

She was followed by a maid Krista knew from the park in front of the Knightsbridge house. She often met up with Sarah when she took the twins out to run wild in the little park. Jacob, a shy boy the same age as the twins, loved to join in their fun. She gave Sarah a discreet nod of greeting.

"Ruth Abrams, how nice to see you," Lia said through clenched teeth. The lady didn't approve of Lia and let no opportunity go to state her opinions at great length. "It does not seem possible that the children are ready for school. Where do the years go?"

"Yes, yes, I have no time for all of that now. You know Jacob is my youngest. Five boys!" She threw her hands dramatically in the air. "Why could I not have been blessed with a girl? Someone to share my burden."

"Krista, would you help the boys chose their caps, please?" Lia stifled a sigh.

Krista nodded and left.

"It is your German maid I want to speak about." Ruth Abrams had the wonderful habit of only listening to her own voice.

"Krista is not German nor is she a maid," Lia said. "She is French and my assistant."

"Yes, yes, that is all very fine." Ruth took firm hold of Sarah's shoulder, ignoring the girl's wince of pain. "Sarah, tell them. Tell them what you had the Rabbi tell me. Go on." She pushed the girl towards Lia with such force that Lia had to steady her before she fell.

"Mrs Caulfield ..." Sarah's voice was almost a whisper.

"*Speak up!*" A poke in the back from Mrs Abrams stiffened Sarah's spine.

"Mrs Caulfield, I spoke with the Rabbi about Krista and her kindness towards Jacob and me. I know she speaks German. There is such a need for people who know the German language, Mrs Caulfield."

"So, what do you say, Cordelia? The Rabbi wants to speak with your German maid." Ruth Abrams had shopping to do and had no time to stand about chatting like some people.

"Ruth Abrams ..." Lia sucked air through her nose and out of her mouth as she had been taught in class. She counted backwards from ten and when she felt capable of speaking civilly, said, "We live five doors down from each other. Could you not have simply sent a message to my house?" She didn't allow the other woman to answer. "I have no time now for chitchat." She pointed to her two boys who had returned to her side and were now hanging on every word spoken. "I have matters to attend to – as you must." She took the twins by the hands, refusing to allow this woman to run her from the shop. "I have last-minute shopping to do. It is a beautiful day. I will speak with Sarah this afternoon in the park in front of our houses." She couldn't imagine what the Rabbi needed with Krista, but she'd far rather hear it from Sarah without her officious employer listening and commenting.

Krista returned. "I believe I have everything we need." She pointed to the items sitting on the waist-high wooden counter. While the two women had been speaking, she had been busy selecting items with the help of a sales assistant. She had ticked the items off the list the school had sent to all parents of new pupils.

"Very well." Lia could have kissed her – Ruth Abrams simply rubbed her up the wrong way and it had nothing to do with her religion. She was an obnoxious woman whatever her faith. "I will settle up and arrange to have everything delivered." She opened her handbag and, while searching for her purse, said again, "The park this afternoon, Sarah. We can speak then." She glared at Ruth Abrams when the woman opened her mouth to object. "Or I can go to the synagogue and speak with the Rabbi."

"That will not be necessary." Ruth Abrams bristled. If she had been a cat, all of her hair would have been standing up.

"Do you know what that was all about, Krista?" Lia asked.

"Yes, I do."

"*Mother, slow down!*" David who Lia had by the hand shouted. "*I have little legs!*"

"I am so sorry." Lia stopped on the busy street, smiling down at her son.

"We know what it is about, Mother," Edward, holding Krista's hand, said. "It is very sad."

"Come," Lia's eyes latched onto a nearby Lyons' tearoom. "You boys can have ice cream while Krista explains to me." It was impossible to keep secrets from the boys. They heard everything you didn't want them to, it seemed.

"Now, Krista," Lia demanded when they were all seated around a white linen-topped table. The boys were enjoying colourful ice cream served in glass bowls while Lia and Krista had tea with the addition of a cigarette in Lia's case. "Explain."

"Very well. Synagogues around the world are

receiving hundreds if not thousands of letters from Jews begging for help in getting their children out of Germany and Austria, to name but two of the countries Sarah mentioned to me. There is a plan in place here in England to remove as many children as possible to safety. People are opening their homes to these children but they will not speak English and will be so frightened. I offered to help in any way I could."

"Why have I not heard of this?" Lia held up the hand holding her cigarette. "I have been so involved in my own little world." It had been wonderful to have Charles home for an extended period of time. She had wanted to enjoy every single moment. She had spent the summer months filling every moment with her sons before they entered school and became independent of her. She had been selfish. "I must know more." She stared across the table at Krista. "I will get details of the local Rabbi from Sarah this afternoon. I will telephone the man and arrange to meet with him. This is not a matter for only Jews to deal with – every mother in England would want to help, I am sure."

"Sarah has told me that a lot of people have offered to open their homes to the children. They want to remove as many children as humanly possible. I want to help in any way I can. I have been welcomed with great kindness into this country. This is a way I can pay back the kindness offered to me."

"We must speak with the Rabbi, Krista." Lia mashed her cigarette into the ashtray on the table.

"We want to help too, Mother," Edward, an ice-cream moustache on his upper lip, said.

"We can give the children toys," David said.

"Krista and Peggy can sort our clothes and give some of them too."

"That is a wonderful idea, boys." Lia fought back tears. Her boys had been more aware of what was going on in the world than she had – shame on her. "We can certainly do that." She turned to Krista. "I will write to my husband. We can offer a home to some of the children. It will be vital to try and keep brothers and sisters together." She signalled for the cheque. "Yes, indeed, there is much we can do to help." She leaned forward. "I can speak to the ladies in my exercise class. Those who cannot open their homes can give money." She watched Krista clean the children's faces with one of the cloths she always seemed to have to hand. "I shall speak with Peggy and Mrs Acers. They too will want to help, I'm sure."

Chapter 12

When Lia Caulfield got the bit between her teeth there was no holding her back. Krista felt as if she had been picked up by a whirlwind. The house in Knightsbridge became a hive of activity. Krista worried that Lia would start pulling strangers in off the street and demanding their assistance. Perry, walking with one crutch now, was pulled in to help. Krista thought it was doing him a world of good to focus on the problems of others. The two boys were delighted to turn their hand to any chore. They listened, wide-eyed, to the talk of children like them being removed from their parents and families. Krista believed having the two constantly underfoot made the volunteers Lia was gathering more aware of what was at stake.

* * *

The day Lia had been dreading arrived. The boys' first day at school.

"I am being ridiculous, I know, Wilma." Lia sat in the kitchen, a cup of tea and cigarette to hand. "They are going to school, not leaving the country. I am determined not to weep when I see them disappear into that school building." She searched for a handkerchief in her slacks pocket. "Dear God, if I feel such pain at this moment how on earth are the people getting ready to send their young ones so far away coping? They must be devasted."

Peggy had started on her tasks around the house and Krista was upstairs getting the boys ready.

Wilma Acers, who was standing boiling eggs and making toast for the boys, was feeling emotional too at the thought of the two little boys she'd seen grow up being ready for school. "I know what everyone has been saying about the need to get the Jewish children to safety, but I'll tell you the God's honest truth. I find it hard to believe such horrible things that we've heard about could really be going on in the world."

"My eyes have been opened, Wilma. If that man Hitler is not stopped and soon, we will be at war." Lia heard the sound she'd been waiting for – the thunder of her boys on the stairs and Krista's soft voice reminding them to go carefully. She stood to butter the warm toast and cut it into finger-lengths – soldiers – to dip in their soft-boiled eggs.

"Mother," David arrived first, "we are going to school."

"You will miss us," Edward said.

"Let us get you two seated." Krista smiled around the room. "Good morning."

Two leather cushions were kept on kitchen chairs to help the boys reach the table. She helped each boy up under Lia's tearful eyes. "I want no egg yolk on your school shirts." With a flick of her wrist she shook out the two large linen napkins she took from the tabletop and put one in each boy's shirt collar.

"They were so brave." Lia, walking along the street with Krista at her side, wiped her pink eyes.

"I think we embarrassed them." Krista too had been tearful watching David and Edward settle into their schoolroom without a backwards glance.

"We were not the only women crying."

Then Lia gasped as they turned into her square.

The large luxury car parked in front of her house could mean only one thing. Lady Abigail had come to call.

"My dear Lia, your fundraising efforts have been quite spectacular." Abigail, Lady Winchester, sat in the formal lounge of the Knightsbridge house and beamed at her sister-in-law. "I am not the only one who has been impressed."

"The work you have done is splendid." Violet Andrews, who had arrived with Lady Winchester, smiled.

"Shall I order tea to be served?" Lia wished she could have escaped into the kitchen with Krista.

"I wish to speak with my ward while you two chat." Violet Andrews stood. "With your permission, Lia, I will tell your cook to send refreshments."

102

"Thank you." Lia wasn't surprised that she was losing control in her own home. Abigail had always been a force to be reckoned with.

"What is going on, Abigail?" Lia asked after Violet left the room.

"There is so much more going on than you are aware of." Abigail, in company with the Baron and Violet, had been in talks with the leaders of the country. "I have been very impressed with all you have achieved in assisting in the plans to get children out of Germany but, my dear, matters are so much more grave than we are being told about." She closed her eyes, trying not to think of the horrors she had been exposed to in the last months.

"Our leaders speak of peace." Lia was trying desperately not to believe a war was coming. Charles would be in the thick of it. The sea was a demanding enough mistress without people chucking bombs.

"Our leaders are fools," Abigail snapped. "I have spent months trying to beat sense into the heads of some of the leaders of our country. They refuse to see what is in front of them. They refuse to listen to people who know what is really going on in Germany. War is coming, Lia, and we must be ready for it."

In the kitchen Krista greeted Miss Andrews with pleasure. They had kept in touch with letters but it was wonderful to see her.

"Slacks, Krista?" Violet Andrews was delighted to see Krista looking so well. It had been a good idea to send her here.

"They are wonderful for running around after young children." Krista smiled when Mrs Acers tutted.

"I am enjoying wearing them although I was shocked to see Lia wearing them when I arrived."

"Your English has improved immensely since you have been here." Violet was impressed.

"She still sounds like someone off the radio to my ears." Wilma Acers was preparing a tray to be carried upstairs. The kitchen was her domain and she felt free to offer her opinion.

"She fits right in here, Miss Andrews." Peggy was waiting to carry up the tray. "You don't have to worry about her. We are keeping an eye on her."

Violet Andrews felt comfortable sitting in the kitchen with these lively women. Abigail's home was so terribly formal at all times. Sometimes she felt stifled.

Before anyone could comment, the kitchen door was pushed open.

"I have decided it will do Abigail a world of good to sit and have a cup of tea in the kitchen, Wilma." Lia led the way. "She has probably never even seen a kitchen before in her life. Times are changing, Abigail, and we shall have to change with them." Lia was frightened and trying to hide it.

"Greetings, everyone," Abigail said cheerfully and took a seat at the kitchen table, ignoring her sister-in-law's comment on her lifestyle. She put her elbows on the table and beamed around at the stunned company. "Has Violet told you we wish you to travel to Germany, Krista?"

To Be Continued

Printed in Great Britain
by Amazon

Vancouver
& Canadian
Rockies

Matthew Gardner

Credits

Footprint credits
Editor: Alan Murphy
Editorial assistants: Elysia Alim,
Danielle Bricker
Layout and production: Angus Dawson
Maps: Kevin Feeney

Managing Director: Andy Riddle
Commercial Director: Patrick Dawson
Publisher: Alan Murphy
Publishing Managers: Felicity Laughton,
Nicola Gibbs
Digital Editors: Jo Williams, Tom Mellors
Marketing and PR: Liz Harper
Sales: Diane McEntee
Advertising: Renu Sibal
Finance and administration:
Elizabeth Taylor

Photography credits
Front cover: Steven Castro/Shutterstock
Back cover: Karamysh/Shutterstock

Every effort has been made to ensure that
the facts in this guidebook are accurate.
However, travellers should still obtain
advice from consulates, airlines etc about
travel and visa requirements before travelling.
The authors and publishers cannot accept
responsibility for any loss, injury or
inconvenience however caused.

Publishing information
Footprint *Focus Vancouver & Canadian Rockies*
1st edition
© Footprint Handbooks Ltd
August 2011

ISBN: 978 1 908206 22 0
CIP DATA: A catalogue record for this book
is available from the British Library

® Footprint Handbooks and the Footprint
mark are a registered trademark of Footprint
Handbooks Ltd

Published by Footprint
6 Riverside Court
Lower Bristol Road
Bath BA2 3DZ, UK
T +44 (0)1225 469141
F +44 (0)1225 469461
footprinttravelguides.com

Distributed in the USA by Globe Pequot Press,
Guilford, Connecticut

The contents of this book have been taken
directly from Footprint's *Western Canada
Handbook*.

Contents

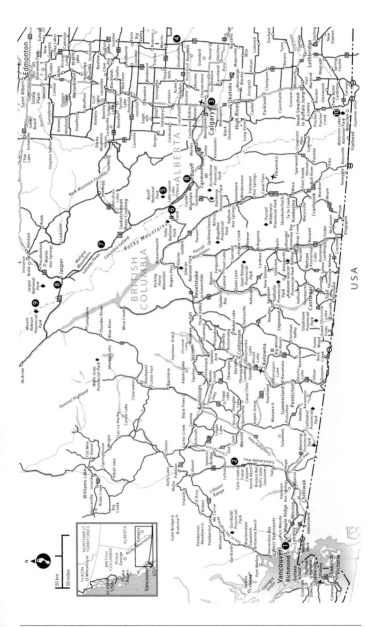

All the elements that have allowed Vancouver to top the list of the world's most liveable cities also make Western Canada's gateway a great place to visit. The beautiful Coast Mountains tower over the city, providing a breathtaking backdrop, as well as skiing, hiking and mountain biking of the highest calibre. The ocean is equally pervasive, offering a lively beach scene, a 28-km sea wall promenade, and easy access to world-class kayaking, canoeing, sailing, scuba-diving and whale watching.

British Columbia's southern interior is criss-crossed with towering mountain ranges, broad river valleys and long skinny lakes. In two days you can drive through snowy peaks and glaciers in the Coast Mountains; arid, semi-desert hills covered with orchards and vineyards in the Okanagan; the forested slopes, pristine lakes and glaciers of the Columbia Mountains in the West Kootenays; moonscapes of muted colours in the Thompson Valley; and the sheer cliff walls of the Fraser Canyon.

The Canadian Rockies are like the Egyptian Pyramids: it's hard to imagine why anyone would visit the country without seeing them. If you go feeling that the reality will never live up to the hype, you'll be proved wrong, as the Rockies deserve their reputation as Canada's premier attraction and one of the natural wonders of the world. Hiking is the obvious activity in the parks and the best way to commune with the exceptional scenery and wildlife, but every other major outdoor activity is pursued here: canoeing, whitewater rafting, mountain biking, climbing, fishing, caving, skiing, skating, golf and soaking in hot springs.

Calgary is the most convenient entry point for visiting the parks. Most people concentrate on Banff, which contains the lion's share of scenery and hikes; Jasper is further away, less busy, much bigger and wilder; between the two is the astonishing Columbia Icefield; Yoho, a compact jewel, combines with Kootenay to make a nice loop back to Banff.

Planning your trip

When to go

Western Canada's weather is fickle, unpredictable and highly localized. The West Coast receives copious amounts of rain year-round, but is blessed with Canada's mildest winters and earliest springs. Weather in the mountains can change from blazing sunshine to blizzards in a single day, even in July.

With so much water to play in and around, an uninterrupted string of great festivals, outdoor pursuits galore, and (usually) as much sun as you could want, summer is the obvious time to visit. Most hikes in the Rockies and other mountain regions are only snow-free between July and September, which is also the most reliable time to see those snowy peaks free of cloud. Many attractions, campgrounds and visitor centres only open from Victoria Day (third Monday in May) to Labour Day (first Monday in September). When we say 'summer' or 'May-Sep', this is what we mean. In the Yukon, the summer days are extremely long, with the sun barely setting at all around the summer solstice.

Many places (the Rockies in particular) are overrun with tourists during the summer. Accommodation rates are higher and coastal ferries tend to get booked up, so reservations for both are highly recommended. The best overall time is perhaps mid-August to September: the crowds are thinning, the trails are still open and the autumn colours are spectacular in the mountains. Spring is a good time for visitors concentrating on the coast, as the blossoms are out in Vancouver.

Winter in Canada is a different matter entirely. Tourism is still very much alive, but attracting a different group of people: those who come to ski or snowboard. Canada offers some of the best, most affordable skiing in the world, as well as many other snow-related activities. Most sights are closed in winter, however, and transportation can be slow. Late February to March is the best time for skiing: the days are getting longer and warmer but the snow is still at its best.

Getting there

Arriving by air

For visitors other than those from the United States, who have the option of driving or taking a train and bus from Seattle, the only feasible way of getting to Canada is by air. The best-served city in the west is Vancouver, though Calgary is a much more obvious starting point for those focusing on the Rockies. One-way and return flights are available to both destinations. Since return flights these days are essentially booked as two singles, it is no more expensive, and could be very advantageous, to fly into one and out of the other.

It is advisable to start looking for your ticket early, as some of the cheapest have to be bought months in advance and the most popular flights sell out quickly. On the other hand, those with the flexibility to leave at a moment's notice can sometimes snap up last-minute bargains. It's a gamble and a game. You can tip the odds in your favour using sites like www.cheapflights.co.uk, www.justtheflight.co.uk or www.travel supermarket.com/c/cheap-flights/, but the cheapest flights often limit your stay to two weeks. The prices below are approximate for return fares in the high season, including all taxes, fees and charges.

Don't miss

1 **UBC Museum of Anthropology**, page 31.

2 **River rafting out of Fraser Valley or Golden**, page 87.

3 **Calgary's Glenbow Museum**, page 76.

4 **Drumheller's Badlands and Dinosaur Museum**, page 92.

5 **Hiking in Banff National Park**, page 109.

6 **Lake Louise**, page 111.

7 **Driving the Icefields Parkway**, page 114.

8 **Ice canyon tours in winter**, page 124.

9 **Mount Robson's Berg Lake trail**, page 136.

10 **The Crypt Lake trail in Waterton National Park**, page 157.

Numbers relate to numbers on map on page 4.

Typically, this means July and August only; the rest of the year – even June and September – is roughly 65% of this price, with a further drop in November and January.

Getting around

Regional flights

The easiest way to cover Western Canada's vast distances is with internal flights, mostly operated by **Air Canada**, www.aircanada.com, its subsidiary **Jazz**, www.flyjazz.ca, and **West Jet**, www.westjet.ca. Their prices are usually identical these days. Many mid-sized towns such as Kelowna, Kamloops, Cranbrook, Castlegar, Prince George and Prince Rupert have an airport, and some communities in the north are only linked to the outside world by air. To give an idea of prices from Vancouver, one-way to Kelowna costs $80-90; one way to Calgary costs $120. Returns are double and advance booking secures a better deal. ▸▸ *For further details, see Ins and outs sections throughout the guide.*

Bicycle

Canada can be a wonderful country to explore by bicycle, but remember how vast the distances are, and try to stick to lesser-used roads. For information, ask at bike shops or visit www.cycling.bc.ca.

Bus

Due to long distances and regular stops, travel by bus can be very slow and seriously limits your flexibility. The network operated by **Greyhound**, T1800-661 8747, www.greyhound.ca, concentrates on towns close to the TransCanada and Yellowhead highways. Getting from Greyhound depots to sights and accommodation can also be very difficult, and may mean shelling out for a taxi. If relying on public transport, it's best to keep your schedule simple and concentrate on one area, such as the Rockies or Vancouver.

An excellent and very economic way to get around BC and the Rockies is with **Moose Travel Network**, T604-297 0255, www.moosenetwork.com. They run 15 different well-planned routes – from two days for $80 to 15 days for $1059 – usually starting and ending in Vancouver, covering most possible itineraries and all the best sights. For example, their most popular tour, Hoodapus ($560), runs from Vancouver to Banff on the TransCanada, to Jasper and back, then back to Vancouver via Kelowna. Travel is in mini-coaches seating up to 24 people, with most routes covered three or four times a week. You can get on and off where and when you want, with no time limits, allowing for maximum freedom and flexibility. They also schedule stops for sights such as hot springs, include numerous sporting activities like hiking and kayaking, and have negotiated a number of discounts for their customers.

Car

The best way to explore Western Canada properly is by car, since many sights cannot be reached by public transport. If hiring a vehicle seems expensive, consider offsetting this cost against accommodation by camping; in summer, a car and a tent are all you need. Older travellers tend to favour **Recreational Vehicles** (RVs), but these can be prohibitively expensive. Before hiring a vehicle, be sure to check if there is a mileage limit, and whether the insurance covers forestry roads. All-wheel, 4WD or front-wheel drive vehicles are useful if you are planning to go off the beaten track. **Hitchhiking** is a way of life in some rural areas, but even in Canada this carries a certain risk, especially for lone women.

Rules and regulations You must have a current driving licence to drive in Canada. Foreign licences are valid up to six months for visitors. If crossing the border in a vehicle, be sure to have your registration or ownership documents, and adequate insurance. Throughout Canada you drive on the right, and seat belts are compulsory. Speed limits are 90-110 kph on the open road, usually 50 kph in built-up areas. The police advise people to drive with lights on even during the day. Compared to most countries, driving is easy and relaxed, with wildlife representing the main hazard. In many towns, traffic lights are replaced by four-way stops: vehicles proceed according to the order in which they arrived. Turning right at traffic lights is legal if the way is clear.

Fuel costs Fuel (called 'gas' here) is easy to come by anywhere but the far north. It's expensive (around 115 cents a litre), unless compared with British prices.

Maps We recommend investing in Rand McNally's good-value *BC and Alberta Road Atlas*, which includes the whole region covered in this book, even the Yukon, and also has larger scale maps of key areas such as the southern interior and Rockies, and most towns and cities, with additional city centre maps for the biggest. Those who really want to get off the beaten track could invest in a *Backcountry Mapbook* (2010), Mussio Ventures, $26, which shows all the secondary and forestry roads, with full details on free and forestry campsites, hot springs, and other useful features. For transport information throughout Canada, visit www.tc.gc.ca.

Vehicle hire Details of rental agencies are given in the transport sections of Vancouver, Calgary and Whitehorse. Some companies have a one-way service, meaning you can rent a car in one place and drop it off elsewhere. Prices start at about $25 per day, $170 per week, $650 per month plus tax and insurance. Another option would be to rent something you could sleep in. A mini-van works out at about $350 per week all-inclusive. RVs are the expensive but luxurious choice. **Cruise Canada**, www.cruisecanada.com, and CanaDream, www.canadream.com, are the biggest companies. Prices start at about $1250 per week for a small unit, $1180 for a 22-footer, and $1250 for a 30-footer plus tax and insurance. All hire vehicles are registered with the **Canadian Automobile Association** (CAA); in case of breakdown, simply call their T1800 number and give directions to where you are, and a towing operator will take you to the nearest CAA mechanic.

Buying a car For long-term travellers, it would work out cheaper to buy a vehicle and sell it at the end of your trip. Bargains can be found in Vancouver. The classified section of the *Vancouver Sun* is a good place to start looking.

Sleeping

Until you stray far from the beaten track, accommodation in Western Canada is plentiful and easily found across the price ranges. Mid-range, usually characterless, **hotels** and **motels** dominate the scene, especially in smaller towns. Rooms are typically clean but uninspiring, with generic decor, a TV, tub, small fridge and coffee maker. Facilities such as saunas, hot tubs, fitness rooms and indoor pools are often small and disappointing. Many of the most impressive hotels, operated by the **Fairmont** chain, were constructed by the Canadian Pacific Railway (CPR) at the turn of the last century, and resemble French chateaux. Motel rooms are usually side by side, with an exterior door and often a parking spot right outside.

For the same price as a mid-range motel, you can usually find an attractively furnished room in a small **B&B** or **guesthouse**, with a hearty breakfast included, representing much better value. Generally operated by friendly, helpful and knowledgeable hosts, these offer an excellent opportunity to meet Canadians on their own ground, but might deter those who value their privacy or can't shake off that feeling of staying with their auntie.

In a similar vein, many travellers have had wonderful experiences when staying in **lodges**. Often found in remote spots, sometimes associated with outdoor activities, these usually consist of a large central building containing facilities and rooms, with cabins scattered around the extensive grounds. Some of the gorgeous log constructions, for which the West Coast is famous, are exceptional and well worth a splurge. For something more exotic, consider staying on a working **ranch** or **farm**, which abound in Alberta and the Cariboo. For more details contact the BC Guest Ranchers' Association, www.guestranches.com. **Resorts**, primarily found on the coast, tend to have cabins, huts or chalets of varying standards, along with their own restaurants, beaches and other facilities. There has not always been room to mention these, so seek them out in the excellent *BC Approved Accommodation Guide*, www.hellobc.com.

Almost all Canadian towns have a **hostel**, many affiliated to **Hostelling International** (HI), with a reduced fee for members. For information and reservations contact www.hihostels.ca. There is no age limit. A typical hostel has dormitories with four or more beds, usually single sex, and a few private rooms for couples and families. Facilities include shared washrooms with showers, a common room with TV and sometimes games, and a library, a kitchen/dining room, and lockers. Many organize activities or tours. Almost all are clean, friendly, a bit noisy and great for gleaning information and meeting fellow travellers. In the Rockies, a string of rustic HI hostels enjoy locations second only to the campgrounds, making them a great budget option. **SameSun**, www.samesun.ca, also have a string of excellent, well-equipped hostels in some key locations, like Vancouver, Kelowna and Banff. For the latest other non HI-affiliated hostels, and they have started proliferating of late, check www.backpackers.ca. A number of other low-cost options can be found at www.budgetbeds.com.

Camping is the cheapest option, and the best way to immerse yourself in Western Canada's magnificent countryside. Where the scenery is wildest, camping is often the only choice. The best campgrounds are those within provincial parks, which are not driven by profit margins and tend to have more spacious sites, with plenty of trees and privacy. The busier ones often have shower facilities and hot running water. Campsites in big towns tend to be far from the centre, expensive and ugly, making a hostel a better option. Those that cater to RVs, with pull-through sites and hook-ups, often resemble car parks, with few trees and no privacy.

Seekers of calm will gravitate towards the small campgrounds that have no facilities beyond an outhouse and a water pump. Even cheaper are forestry campgrounds, which are almost always situated in remote spots on logging roads (ask at local visitor centres). 'Guerilla camping' means finding out-of-the-way spots where you can pitch your tent for free, or sleep in the back of your van, without being bothered. Much of Western Canada (but not the Rockies) is remote enough to make this possible. Logging roads are always a good place to look (and you may stumble on a forestry site). Anyone interested in this approach might want to buy Kathy and Craig Copeland's *Camp Free in BC* (Voice in the Wilderness Press). Volume one covers the south, volume two the north.

Eating and drinking

Food

Western Canada, unlike the country as a whole, has developed a strong culinary identity, focused on the gastronomic playground of Vancouver. **West Coast cuisine** combines Asian, Californian and European techniques with a strong emphasis on the use of very fresh, locally produced ingredients, a genuinely innovative, creative, eclectic philosophy, and the extensive use of seafood. Elements are also taken from traditional Native American cooking, such as the grilling of salmon on cedar or alder, and the use of wild game like caribou and buffalo. Many different ethnic cuisines are fused with the West Coast sensibility, and are usually healthier for it.

Not surprisingly, **vegetarians** are well catered for in Vancouver, and in bohemian areas like the Gulf Islands and West Kootenays. The more you move into the redneck communities further north and east, however, the harder it gets to avoid the meat-and-potatoes mentality. However, if you are a meat-eater, Alberta AAA beef is as good as it gets, so if you like steak this is the place to indulge.

In Canadian cities you can find any kind of food you want, until late at night. Most towns will have an expensive 'fine-dining' establishment, which usually means old-style European, predominantly French, with the emphasis on steak and seafood. In smaller communities, however, you're often stuck with unimaginative 'family' restaurants, Chinese restaurants of dubious authenticity, pizza, and early closing. Certain ubiquitous chains like **Earl's** and **Milestone's** cover most of the comfort-food bases, and really are fine, especially if you're travelling with kids. Equally ubiquitous are the family chains like **Denny's** and **Smitty's**, which are alright for big breakfasts, but the coffee leaves a lot to be desired. All the American fast-food outlets are here too; **Subway** is always a good bet for sandwiches.

Drink

While Vancouver has its share of sophisticated cafés, bistros and tapas bars, as well as the inevitable Irish pubs and phoney English boozers, the typical small-town Canadian pub has a pool table, a TV set screening sporting events, soft-rock or country music, a burger-dominated menu and a handful of locals propping up the bar playing keno (a lottery game). Chances are, though, they'll be a friendly bunch.

Sleeping and eating price codes

$$$$ over Can$260 **$$$** Can$140-260 **$$** Can$70-140
$ under $70

Accommodation price grades in this guide are based on the cost per night for two people sharing a double room in the high season, with breakfast, not including tax (see page 13). Many places offer discounts during low season or for long stays. Prices are in Canadian dollars. Almost all the campsites listed in this guide are in the **$** price category.

Eating price codes

ψψψ over $40 **ψψ** $20-40 **ψ** under $20

Prices refer to the cost of a main meal (often called an entrée) and an appetizer or dessert. Prices are in Canadian dollars.

Sadly, most of the **beer** sold here is tasteless, weak, watery lager, such as Molson, Kokanee and Canadian. Yet Western Canada has pioneered the concept of **microbreweries**, which produce small-batch, carefully crafted beers using natural ingredients. All styles of beer are available, served carbonated and chilled. Very small but excellent breweries include Raven (Vancouver), Crannog (Shuswap), Driftwood (Victoria), and Salt Spring (southern Gulf Islands). Unibroue, based in Québec, brew Canada's best beers.

While here, you should also make a point of trying some BC **wines**, the best of which are made in the Okanagan Valley. This region specializes in German-style whites, sparkling wines, pinot noir, and the sweet and sophisticated ice-wine. It's hard to recommend specific wineries, but Tinhorn Creek and Red Rooster never disappoint.

Canadians take their **coffee** pretty seriously. Locally brewed examples to look out for include Kicking Horse (Invermere, East Kootenays), Oso Negro (West Kootenays), and Salt Spring (southern Gulf Islands).

Essentials A-Z

Accident and emergency

Contact the emergency services on T911 and your embassy or consulate (see below). Remember to get police/medical records for insurance claims.

Electricity

Canada uses 110 V, 60 cycles, with a US-style plug, usually 2 flat pins, sometimes with a 3rd earth pin which is round. UK appliances will not work in Canada without a heavy-duty inverter to up the voltage to 220 volts.

Embassies and consulates

For a full list of Canadian embassies abroad, or foreign embassies in Vancouver, see www.embassy.goabroad.com.

Health

Western Canada must be one of the safest places on earth: it has good medical facilities, and there are no prevalent diseases, so no vaccinations are required before entry. Tap **water** is safe to drink, but drinking water from dubious sources, especially slow-moving streams, can lead to giardia, commonly known here as 'beaver fever'. The result is vomiting, diarrhoea and weakness.

The health service in Canada is maintained by provincial governments. Travellers should make sure their insurance covers all medical costs and visitors suffering from a condition that may need immediate care, such as those with serious allergies or diabetes, are advised to carry what they need in case of an emergency. Medical services are listed in each town's directory.

Pharmacies are plentiful and stock all the usual provisions. They are often large retail outlets that stay open late, even 24 hrs in big cities. As elsewhere, many drugs are only available with a doctor's prescription.

Money → *US$1 = $0.97, €1 = $1.38, £1 = $1.54 (Jul 2011).*

Prices throughout this book are in Canadian dollars. The Canadian currency is the dollar ($), divided into 100 cents (¢). Coins come in denominations of 1¢ (penny), 5¢ (nickel), 10¢ (dime), 25¢ (quarter), $1 (called a 'loonie' because it carries a picture of a loon, a common Canadian bird), and $2 (called a 'toonie'). Banknotes come in denominations of $5, $10, $20, $50 and $100. The loonie has been very strong lately, making Canada a more expensive place to travel, especially for those coming from the US, whose own currency has plummeted.

What to take

As in most countries today, the easiest and safest way to travel in Canada is with a credit or debit card using ATMs, which are found in all but the smallest, remotest communities. The major credit cards are also accepted just about everywhere. Traveller's cheques (TCs) remain a safe way to carry money, but mean more hassle. **American Express (Amex)**, Visa and **Thomas Cook** cheques are the most widely accepted. You're never far from one of Canada's big banks: **Royal Bank**, **Bank of Montreal**, **CIBC**, **Scotiabank** and **TD Bank**. They all give reasonable rates for TCs and cash. Minimum opening hours are Mon-Fri 1000-1500, but they're usually open until 1630. Bureaux de change, found in most city centres, airports and major train stations have longer hours but worse rates. Avoid changing money or TCs in hotels, the rates are usually poor. The quickest way to have money sent in an emergency is to have it wired to the nearest bank via **Western Union**, T1800-235 0000, www.westernunion.com, or **Moneygram**, www.moneygram.com.

Cost of travelling

The cost of living is considerably lower in Canada than in the UK. Things that will cost £1 in England will often cost $1 in Canada. Notable exceptions are luxuries like beer and cigarettes which are roughly on a par with the UK and therefore more expensive than they are in the US. Petrol (gas) is cheaper than in the UK but more expensive than the US.

Canada is not a budget destination, and is less affordable for those coming from Britain than it was a few years ago. Apart from accommodation, the single biggest expense is travel, due to the vast distances that need to be covered. Petrol gets considerably more expensive the further north you go. Accommodation and restaurant prices tend to be higher in popular destinations such as Whistler and Banff, and during the summer months (or winter at ski resorts).

Budget

The minimum daily budget required per person for those staying in hostels or camping, travelling by bus and hitching, and cooking their own meals, will be roughly $50-80 per day. If you stay in cheaper motels or B&Bs and eat out occasionally that will rise to $80-100 per day. Those staying in slightly more upmarket places, eating out daily and visiting attractions can expect to pay at least $120-150. The best way to budget is to move around less and camp a lot. In destinations like the Rockies, this is also about the best way to experience the country. Single travellers will have to pay more than half the cost of a double room in most places, and should budget on spending around 60% of what a couple would spend.

Opening hours

Shops tend to stay open 0900-1730. Bank hours vary, but typically they are open Mon-Fri or Tue-Sat 1000-1600. Visitor centres are typically open 0900-1700, longer in summer. Some are only operational May-Sep. All shops and businesses keep longer hours in cities, with everything shutting down earlier in smaller and more remote communities.

Public holidays

Most services, attractions, and many shops close on public holidays, or greatly reduce their opening hours. Accommodation and transport tends to be more heavily reserved, especially ferries between Vancouver and Vancouver Island.

National holidays

New Year's Day, 1 Jan; **Good Friday**; **Easter Monday**; **Victoria Day**, 3rd Mon in May; **Canada Day**, 1 Jul; **Labour Day**, 1st Mon in Sep; **Thanksgiving**, 2nd Mon in Oct; **Remembrance Day**, 11 Nov; **Christmas Day**; **Boxing Day**.

Provincial holidays

Alberta Family Day, 3rd Mon in Feb; Alberta Heritage Day, 1st Mon in Aug.
BC British Columbia Day, 1st Mon in Aug.
Yukon Discovery Day, 3rd Mon in Aug.

Safety

Few countries are as safe as Canada. Even here though, common sense should prevail in cities. Avoid walking alone in remote, unlit streets or parks after dark. Elsewhere the biggest danger is from wildlife, though there are no poisonous animals. Never approach wild animals, even the ones deemed safe. More people are injured annually by elk than by bears, see page .

Telephone

For international calls to Canada, dial your country's IDD access code (00 from the UK) **+1**, then the local code, then the number. Local codes are: **250** for all of BC, except Vancouver, the Sunshine Coast and Sea to Sky Highway, which are **604**; most of Alberta is **403**, except the Edmonton region (including Jasper), which is **780**; the Yukon is **867**. These codes have been included throughout the guide.

Time
BC and the Yukon are 8 hrs behind GMT in summer, 7 hrs behind GMT in winter. BC and the Yukon operate on Pacific Time. Alberta is on Mountain Time, which is 1 hr ahead.

Tipping
Western Canadians take tipping very seriously and in restaurants the customary tip is 15%. Bars and pubs usually have waiter/waitress service, and these too are tipped 10-15%. Even if you buy your drink at the bar you are expected to leave a tip, usually change up to around 10%. Taxi drivers and hairdressers should also be tipped 10-15%. Naturally, this all depends on service.

Tourist information
Visitor information centres can be found in almost every Canadian town and are listed in the relevant sections of this book. Many are only open mid-May to mid-Sep and tend to be well stocked with leaflets. In **British Columbia**, T1800-534 5622, www.hellobc.com, literature includes a *Vacation Planner*; the indispensable *Approved Accommodation Guide*, which also includes addresses and toll-free phone numbers for visitor centres; vacation guides for each region; the extremely informative *Outdoor Adventure Guide*; and other guides covering topics such as fishing and golf. **Alberta**, T1800-252 3782, www.travel alberta.com, produces an *Accommodation Guide* and a separate *Campground Guide*, a very useful *Vacation Guide* full of attractions, and some regional brochures. The **Yukon**, T1800-661 0494, www.touryukon.com, produces a helpful *Vacation Planner*.

Most visitor centres will provide information on local transport and attractions, and sell relevant books and souvenirs. Many also produce self-guiding walking-tour maps of their towns, and have illustrated directories of local B&Bs. **Parks Canada**, www.pc.gc.ca, operates its own offices, usually in conjunction with the local tourist board. These tend to be excellent facilities, especially in the Rockies. Their website has lots of information, but finding it can be frustrating.

Visas and immigration
Visa regulations are subject to change, so it is essential to check with your local Canadian embassy or consulate (see page 12) before leaving home, or at www.cic.gc.ca. Citizens of the EU, Scandinavia and most Commonwealth countries do not need an entry visa, just a full valid passport. Residents of South Africa, the Czech Republic and Turkey do need a visa. US citizens require a US birth certificate or passport, or a green card, and are also advised to carry proof of residence such as a driver's licence. All visitors have to fill out a waiver form, which you will be given on the plane or at the border. If you don't know where you'll be staying just write 'touring', though immigration officers may then ask for an idea of your schedule. They will decide the length of stay permitted, usually the maximum of 6 months. You may have to show proof of sufficient funds, such as a credit card or $300 per week of your proposed stay. If you wish to extend your stay beyond the allotted time, send a written application to the nearest Canada immigration centre well before the end of your authorized time limit.

Weights and measures
The metric system is universally used, though many Canadians still talk about feet rather than metres. Hectares and acres are both used.

Contents

Vancouver & around

Metro Vancouver

Vancouver's compact Downtown peninsula contains most of the city's sights, but none compares with the pleasure of discovering its many neighbourhoods and incredibly diverse architecture. Surrounded by water on all sides, and largely undeveloped, Stanley Park is a green oasis, containing some giant trees and possibly the peninsula's best sight, the Aquarium. South of False Creek, Granville Island is another must, combining a Covent Garden-style market with BC's finest collection of arts and craft studios and galleries in an attractive marina setting. A short stroll away are museums in Vanier Park, and trendy Kitsilano, which boasts one of the city's finest beaches. Further west is the remarkable Museum of Anthropology in Point Grey. South and East Vancouver have some fascinating neighbourhoods, such as Commercial Drive and Main Street, and some beautiful parks and gardens, but if nature calls, the semi-wilderness parks that head up into the giant mountains on the North Shore are hardest to resist.

Ins and outs

Getting there

All international flights land at **Vancouver International Airport** (YVR) ① *T604-207 7077, www.yvr.ca*, 13 km south of Downtown. There is a **Visitor Information** desk on the arrivals floor (Level 2) and an airport information desk (which operates a lost-and-found service) in the departure lounge, along with most of the shops. There are also plenty of phones and ATMs, a children's play area and a nursery. Specially built for the 2010 Winter Olympics, the new SkyTrain branch – the Canada Line – connects YVR with Downtown in 26 minutes. Follow signs from the Arrivals lounge. A $5 levy is added to single ticket fares, but not to day passes, which thus work out cheaper. Taxis operate around the clock, charging $28-32 for the 25-minute trip downtown; a limousine from **Aerocar Service** ① *T1-888-821-0021, www@aerocar.ca*, costs from $39 plus tax for up to eight passengers. All the major car rental agencies are located on the ground floor of the indoor parkade (multi-storey car park). **Pacific Coach** ① *T1800-661-1725, www.pacificcoach.com*, run direct buses to Squamish and Whistler (SkyLynx, seven daily, three hours, $55 one way); and Victoria (seven daily, four hours, $49). Tickets can be bought at their counter in the Arrivals lounge, or on the bus. Look for the bus stop to the left when leaving the terminal.

All long-distance buses and trains arrive at **Pacific Central Station** ① *1150 Station St*, a short **SkyTrain** ride from Downtown. **BC Ferries** arrive from Victoria and the southern Gulf Islands at Tsawwassen, about 30 km south of Vancouver. City buses connect with the SkyTrain to get you downtown from the ferry terminal ($5). Ferries from Nanaimo in central Vancouver Island arrive at Horseshoe Bay, 15 km northwest on Highway 99, with two direct buses downtown ($3.75). ▶▶ *See Transport, page 56.*

Getting around

Many of Vancouver's attractions are concentrated within the Downtown peninsula, which is best explored on foot. The public transport system operated by **TransLink** consists of buses, an elevated rail system called the **SkyTrain**, and a passenger ferry called the **SeaBus**. The same tickets are valid for all three. The SkyTrain is the quickest, most efficient way to get around, but its routes are of limited use to visitors. Buses run everywhere but can be slow, and information on routes is rarely displayed. If time is limited, think about taking taxis. A couple of private mini-ferries also ply the waters of False Creek. ▶▶ *See Transport, page 56.*

Orientation

Unlike most North American cities, Vancouver's downtown streets have names rather than numbers, making orientation more tricky. If in doubt, remember that the mountains are always north. Block numbering is divided into east and west by Ontario Street, which runs in a north–south direction just east of the Downtown core. So, the address 39 W Broadway is in the block immediately west of Ontario, whereas 297 W Fourth Avenue would be in the third block west.

Unlike most cities built on a grid, the numbers of avenues in Vancouver do not correspond directly to block numbers. To work out the block number from a numbered avenue, add 16. So numbers between 18th and 19th Avenue will start at 3400.

Best time to visit

As with most of Western Canada, there is little doubt that summer is the best time to visit Vancouver, unless you're looking for winter sports. Temperatures are high but not uncomfortably so (average 21.7°C), Vancouver's lively residents take to the beaches, parks and mountains, and a string of great festivals keep the party spirit flowing.

Climate

Vancouver is a rainy city, with an average of 170 days of precipitation per year. Since the local topography involves a jump from sea level to mountains within a few kilometres, plus close proximity to the Pacific Ocean, the Georgia Strait and the mountains of Vancouver Island and Washington's Olympia Range, it's not surprising that the weather here is unpredictable. Forecasts are definitely not to be trusted. Having said that, a warm Pacific Ocean current combined with a strong airflow originating near Hawaii help make Vancouver's climate the mildest in Canada. Spring flowers start blooming in early March, and winter snowfalls are rare enough to throw the city's motorists into confusion. For these reasons Vancouver has been called the Canadian city with the best climate and the worst weather.

Tourist information

At Vancouver's main **visitor centre** ① *Plaza Level, Waterfront Centre, 200 Burrard St, T604-683 2000, www.tourismvancouver.com, daily 0830-1800*, staff are friendly and extremely efficient, and the range of facilities is excellent. A broad range of literature is available on the city and province, as well as illustrated details of hotels and B&Bs, travel information, a reservation service, currency exchange and branches of **Ticketmaster** and **Tickets Tonight** (see page 47). For up-to-date listings and information, there are three magazines: *Official Visitors' Guide*, *Where Vancouver* and *Visitors' Choice Vancouver*. For nightlife and entertainment listings with a more streetwise angle, pick up a free copy of the *Georgia Straight*.

Downtown → *For listings, see pages 37-58.*

In keeping with its status as the heart of one of the world's youngest cities, Vancouver's Downtown presents the visitor with a fine example of postmodern aesthetics; a constantly evolving hotchpotch of architecture, where sleek glass-and-chrome skyscrapers rub shoulders with Gothic churches, Victorian warehouses and a handful of curiosities. The best way to appreciate this jamboree bag is on foot, so the peninsula is presented here as a walk, starting at the **visitor centre**, following an anticlockwise circle around Downtown, Yaletown, Chinatown, East Side and Gastown, then shooting north through the West End to Stanley Park.

Canada Place and around

Built to resemble an ocean liner, with five giant white masts rising from its 'deck', **Canada Place** is the main terminus for Vancouver's thriving cruise-ship business, and begs comparisons with Sydney's famous opera house., It's an important and attractive landmark, but there's little reason to go inside.

Opposite the **visitor centre** on Burrard is the magnificent **Marine Building**, the British Empire's tallest building for more than a decade after its completion in 1930, and described by Sir John Betjeman as "the best art-deco office building in the world". In keeping with the architects' vision of "some great crag rising from the sea", the relief frieze around its base and the brass surroundings of its double revolving doors are dotted with marine flora and fauna. The art deco façade is decorated with panels illustrating the history of transport. Over the main entrance, Captain Vancouver's ship *Discovery* is seen on the horizon, with Canada geese flying across the stylized sunrays. The lobby is designed to resemble a Mayan temple.

Up the road is the old **Canadian Pacific Railway (CPR) Station** ① *601 West Cordova St*. Built in 1914, this neoclassical beaux-arts-style building with its arches and white columned façade is now a terminus for the **SeaBus** and the **SkyTrain**. The 1978 restoration retained many features of the original interior such as the high ceilings, woodworking and tile floor. Almost opposite, on the flying-saucer-shaped 29th floor of the Harbour Centre is **Vancouver Lookout** ① *555 West Hastings St, T604-6890421, www.vancouverlookout.com, mid-Oct to Apr daily 0900-2100, May-Sep daily 0830-2230, $15, youth $10, child $7, infants free, hourly guided tours included*. Glass-walled elevators on the outside of the building whisk you up 130 m to the observation deck in a mere 40 seconds. No longer the tallest building in BC, it still boasts the best close-up 360° views of the city, particularly striking at sunset on a clear day. In, From up there it is much easier to get a feeling for the layout and architecture of the city. The ticket is expensive, but allows as many visits on the same day as you wish.

Vancouver Art Gallery and around

① *750 Hornby St, T604-662 4719, www.vanartgallery.bc.ca, daily 1000-1700, Tue until 2100, $22.50, under 12 $7.50, under 4s free, family $54, suggested donation of $5 on Tue after 1700.* The Art Gallery occupies an imposing neoclassical marble building designed by Francis Rattenbury in 1910 as Vancouver's original courthouse, and renovated in 1983 by Arthur Erickson. The four spacious floors are typically dedicated to five or six temporary exhibitions, at least one borrowed from another institution, the others mostly drawn from the gallery's own 10,000-work collection. Though the focus is frequently on contemporary artists, exhibitions are deliberately varied enough that everyone should find something that appeals, and there are usually some top names on offer. Only the Emily Carr Gallery is a permanent fixture, and this justifies a visit in itself. The world's largest collection of works by this prominent Victoria artist (see page) are accompanied by a video about her life. The gallery also has an offsite exhibition space at the base of the Shangri-la Hotel at Georgia and Thurlow, and hosts various tours, talks, events, and family programs, plus concerts and performances on select Friday afternoons and evenings. The Gallery Store is one of the city's best places to buy original crafts, and the café offers decent food and a gorgeous outdoor patio.

Hotel Vancouver across the road is one of the city's most distinctive landmarks. A typical example of the grand hotels erected across Canada by the Canadian Pacific Railway, this hulking Gothic castle sports a striking green copper roof, gargoyles, some fine relief sculpture and an admirably opulent interior. Dwarfed by the surrounding modern giants, **Christ Church Cathedral** (finished in 1889) is Vancouver's oldest surviving church. Built in Gothic Revival style, this buttressed sandstone building features a steep gabled roof, impressive pointed-arch, stained-glass windows and some splendid interior timber framework. **Cathedral Place**, next door, has a neo-Gothic lobby full of art deco features that leads to a lovely grassy courtyard. Next door is the **Bill Reid Gallery**

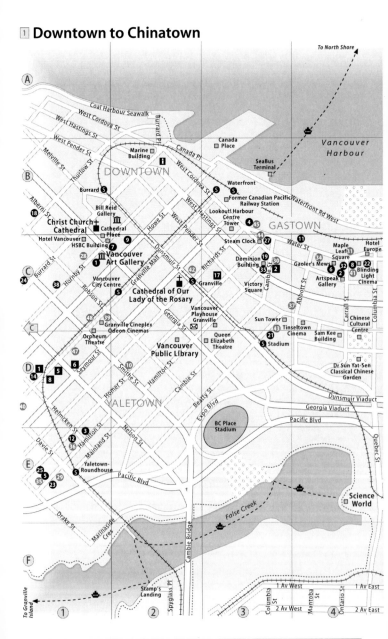

200 metres
200 yards

Sleeping 🛏
Cambie Hostel Gastown
  & Cambie Pub **2** *C3*
Comfort Inn
  Downtown **5** *D1*
HI Vancouver Central **1** *D1*
Moda **6** *D1*
Patricia **13** *C6*
SameSun Backpacker
  Lodge **8** *D1*
Victorian **17** *C3*

Eating 🍴
Bambo Café **19** *C3*
Blake's **2** *C4*
Blue Water Café
  + Raw Bar **3** *E1*
Café Ami **7** *C2*
Café Medina
  & Chambar **21** *D3*
Caffe Dolcino **8** *C4*
Coast **5** *E1*
Cobre **22** *C4*
Diva at the Met **9** *C2*
Gallery Café **1** *C1*
Ganache Patisserie **25** *E1*
Guu with Otokomae **4** *B3*
Hon's Wun-Tun
  House **15** *D5*
Joe Forte's Seafood &
  Chop House **18** *B1*
Judas Goat Taberna
  & Salt **6** *C4*
L'Abbatoir **32** *C4*

La Luna Café **11** *C4*
Le Crocodile **24** *C1*
Nuba **35** *C3*
Plan B **12** *E1*
Rodney's Oyster
  House **23** *E1*
Salt **6** *C4*
Templeton **14** *D1*
Water Street Café **27** *C3*
Wicked Café **38** *C1*

Bars & clubs 🍸
Alibi Room **26** *C5*
Bacchus **28** *C1*
Bar None **29** *E1*
Barcelona Ultra
  Lounge **40** *D1*
Cambie **30** *C3*
Chambar **43** *C3*
Chill Winston **31** *C4*
Fabric **34** *C4*
George Ultra Lounge
  Wine Bar **36** *E1*
Honey Lounge **37** *C4*
Irish Heather **41** *C4*
Lennox Pub **39** *C1*
Post Modern
  Dance Bar **31** *C4*
Railway Club **42** *C2*
Republic Nightclub **47** *D1*
Shine **44** *B3*
Steamworks **45** *B3*
Subeez Café **10** *D2*
VENUE Nightclub **48** *C1*

ⓘ 639 Hornby St, T604-682 3455, www.billreidgallery.ca, Wed-Sun 1100-1700, $10, under 17s $5, under 5s free. This important new gallery, opened in 2008, features many works by the master Haida artist himself, including his monumental bronze frieze, *Mythic Messengers*, and the *Restoring Enchantment* collection of over 40 gold and silver masterworks. Another highlight is the *Celebration of Bill Reid Pole* carved for the gallery by Jim Hart. There is also a temporary exhibition intended to promote understanding of and appreciation for Aboriginal art of the Pacific Northwest. Opposite, the **HSBC Building** *ⓘ Mon-Thu 0800-1630, Fri 0800-1700*, has a towering atrium lobby containing the world's largest pendulum, and one of Vancouver's best unofficial art galleries and cafés.

Robson Street is Vancouver's undisputed shopping focus, and Granville is the heart of the justly named **Entertainment District**. The junction of these two busy streets is the unofficial pivot of this bustling city, and makes for great people-watching.

Yaletown and the Public Library

A small triangle of land to the south, hemmed in by False Creek, and Homer and Nelson streets, and concentrated on Hamilton and Mainland, **Yaletown** was once Vancouver's rowdy warehouse district, with more saloons per kilometre than anywhere else in the world. Today, most of the massive old brick buildings have been converted into spacious apartments, offices, trendy bars and upmarket restaurants which line the narrow streets whose atmosphere owes much to the raised brick walkways of former loading docks. Finally mellowing into a genuine sense of style, this is a fascinating and unique area to explore, especially at night.

The curving walls and tiered arches of nearby **Vancouver Public Library** bear a resemblance to the Roman colosseum, whatever architect Moshe Safdie might say, and this postmodern masterpiece, classical and futuristic in equal measure, contains a pleasant shop-filled atrium spanned by elegant bridges. Nearby is the Gothic Revival **Cathedral of our Lady of the Rosary**, built in the late 1880s with asymmetrical towers, a vaulted ceiling and some decent stained-glass windows.

BC Place and Science World

ⓘ 1455 Québec St; SkyTrain; bus No 3 or 8 on Granville or Hastings, or No 19 on Pender.
Just east of Yaletown is the vast air-supported dome of **BC Place Stadium**, and the **BC Sports Hall of Fame and Museum** *ⓘ T604-687 5520, www.bcsportshalloffame.com, closed at time of writing, but due to reopen in 2011*. From behind here a ferry runs across, and the sea wall promenade runs around, False Creek to another of Vancouver's unusual structures, a giant silver golf ball that makes a suitably futuristic venue for **Science World** *ⓘ T604-443 7443, www.scienceworld.ca, daily 1000-1800, $21, youth $17.25, child $14.25, with Omnimax $26.50, youth $22.75, child $19.75*. Educational, fascinating and entertaining in equal measures, this place is a delight for adults but particularly kids. You can investigate the wonders of your own body and mind in the **BodyWorks Gallery**, explore the mysteries of water, light, sound and motion in the **Eureka! Gallery**, explore the natural world in the **Sara Stern Search Gallery**, and learn about energy and sustainability in the **Our World Gallery**. There are always exciting temporary galleries, and a Kidspace Gallery to keep the younger children happy. There are lots of lessons to be learned, but the emphasis throughout is squarely on hands-on interaction and fun. There are live demonstrations on the Centre Stage, free high definition films in the science

theatre and an **Alcan Omnimax** theatre whose 27-m-diameter dome screen and 10,000-watt wrap-around speakers have the edge even over the giant IMAX.

Chinatown

Main Street heads north to Vancouver's bustling Chinatown, which, in keeping with the city's east-meets-west persona, is the third biggest in North America after New York and San Francisco. The restaurants here are as authentic as you'll ever find outside China and the streets are lined with noisy shops selling the kind of weird and wonderful ingredients only the Chinese know how to cook (look out for the geoducks). An experience not to be missed is the open-air **Night Market** ① *Keefer and Main St, www.vcma.shawbiz.ca, mid-May to early Sep Fri-Sun 1830-2300, T604-682 8998*, featuring 100 stalls plus cultural performances. Ninety-minute tours of the district are offered by the **Chinese Cultural Centre** ① *50 E Pender, T604-658 8883, www.cccvan.com, Jun-Sep, $8, child $7, $11/10 with museum tour, $13/10 with a slide show*, and inevitably include the disappointing **Sam Kee Building**, aka 'Slender on Pender'. The story goes that when the city appropriated most of Chang Toy's 30-ft lot for street widening, his neighbour expected to get the remaining 6 ft at a bargain price, but to frustrate him Toy built the world's skinniest building.

Infinitely more worthwhile is the **Dr Sun Yat-Sen Classical Chinese Garden** ① *578 Carrall St, T604-662 3207, www.vancouverchinesegarden.com, May to mid-Jun 1000-1800, mid-Jun to Aug 0930-1900, Sep 1000-1800, Oct-Apr 1000-1630, $14, child $10, under 5s free, family $28, bus No 19 or 22 east on Pender*, the first authentic Ming classical garden built since 1492, and the first ever outside China. Created by 52 experts from Suzhou, this is a carefully planned realm of symmetry, simplicity and symbolism, where buildings, rocks, water and plants recreate a microcosm of the world. There are walls within walls, courtyards within courtyards, pavilions, bridges and galleries. Hourly guided tours, included with admission, are recommended for an understanding of the Taoist principles at work. Music events and art exhibitions are hosted in summer.

East Side

Just a block north of Chinatown is Vancouver's seediest quarter, the East Side. Over a century ago, when the city's first trams connected Gastown to a newly emerging business district along Granville, Hastings Street entered a decline that has led to its current rating as Canada's lowest-income postal district. The corner with Main in particular has become notorious as a meeting place for Vancouver's homeless and drug addicts. Some of the last remaining examples of neon have survived here from an era when Vancouver had 18,000 such signs. There are also some interesting buildings. In 1910, the distinctive French classical-style **Dominion Building** ① *207 West Hastings*, was the British Empire's tallest and most modern structure. Two years later, its record height was topped by the nearby **Sun Tower** ① *100 West Pender*. Opposite the Dominion Building is **Victory Square**, now run-down and nicknamed 'Pigeon Park'. Just east of Main, on Cordova, is the **Firehall Arts Centre** and **St James Anglican Church**, which combines touches of the Romanesque, Gothic, Byzantine and modern.

Gastown

Keep walking north and you arrive in **Gastown**, site of Vancouver's first industry and, maybe more importantly, the saloon of 'Gassy' Jack Deighton, after whom the district was

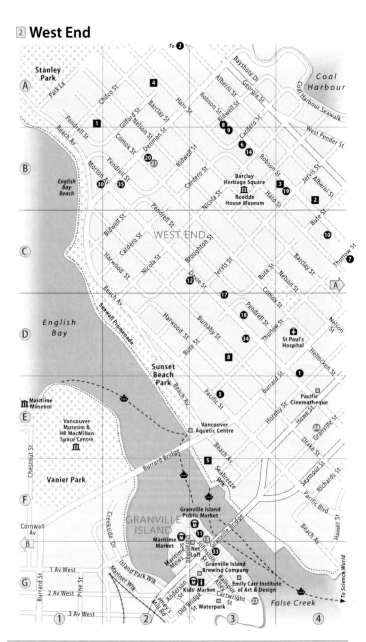

Stanley Park

Park La

Coal Harbour

Coal Harbour Seawalk

Bayshore Dr

Georgia St

Alberni St

Robson St

Bidwell St

Cardero St

West Pender St

Chilco St

Pendrell St

Gilford St

Barclay St

Nelson St

Comox St

Denman St

Haro St

Bidwell St

4

1

8 9

6

14

Robson St

Alberni St

Jervis St

Bute St

3

19

2

English Bay Beach

Morton Av

Pendrell St

30

35

20

21

Cardero St

Pendrell St

Nicola St

Haro St

Barclay Heritage Square

Roedde House Museum

10

WEST END

Bidwell St

Harwood St

Cardero St

Nicola St

Broughton St

Jervis St

Bute St

Nelson St

Barclay St

Thurlow St

7

12

Davie St

17

Comox St

Ⓐ

English Bay

Beach Av

Seawall Promenade

Harwood St

Burnaby St

Bute St

Pendrell St

Thurlow St

18

34

8

St Paul's Hospital

Nelson St

Helmcken St

Sunset Beach Park

Beach Av

Pacific St

5

Burrard St

1

Pacific Cinematheque

Hornby St

Howe St

Granville St

24

Drake St

Maritime Museum

Vancouver Museum & HR MacMillan Space Centre

Vancouver Aquatic Centre

Seymour St

Richards St

Chestnut St

Vanier Park

Burrard Bridge

Beach Av

Seabreeze Wlk

Pacific Blvd

Beach Av

Homer St

5

Cornwall Av

Ⓑ

Creekside Dr

Island Park Wlk

GRANVILLE ISLAND

Granville Island Public Market

Maritime Market

Net Loft

11

15

Granville Bridge

33

Granville Island Brewing Company

Burrard St

Pine St

1 Av West

2 Av West

3 Av West

Mariner Wlk

Lameys Mill Rd

Anderson St

Duranleau St

Johnston St

Cartwright St

Old Bridge St

Kids' Market

23

Emily Carr Institute of Art & Design

Waterpark

Railspur Alley

False Creek

To Science World

English Bay Beach

Vancouver maps
1 Downtown to Chinatown, page 20
2 West End, page 24
3 Kitsilano, page 30

N

200 metres
200 yards

Sleeping

910 Beach Ave **5** *F3*
Blue Horizon **2** *B4*
Buchan **4** *A2*
English Bay Inn **1** *A1*
HI Vancouver
  Downtown **8** *D3*
The Listel Hotel **3** *B4*

Eating

Bin 941 Tapas Parlour **1** *D4*
Café Luxy **17** *C3*
Chilli House Thai Bistro **5** *E3*
CinCin Ristorante
  & Bar **10** *C4*
Delilah's Martini Bar
  & Restaurant **20** *B2*
E-Hwa **6** *B3*
Granville Island Coffee
  House **33** *G3*
Guu **7** *C4*
Guu with Garlic **8** *A3*
Gyoza King **14** *B3*
India Bistro **18** *D3*
JJ Bean **11** *F3*
Lift Bar Grill View **2** *A3*
Lolita's South of the
  Border Cantina **12** *C3*
O'Doul's **19** *B4*
Raincity Grill **30** *B1*
Sand Bar **33** *G3*
Sushi Mart **9** *B3*
Stepho's Souvlaki Greek
  Taverna **34** *D3*
Tanpopo **35** *B2*
Teahouse **2** *A3*

Bars & clubs

Backstage Lounge **15** *F3*
Comox Long Bar
  & Grill **21** *B2*
Dockside Brewing Co **23** *G3*
Morrissey Pub **24** *E4*

named. One of Vancouver's favourite historic characters, he is remembered for rowing across the Burrard Inlet and offering a bunch of thirsty workers at Stamp's Mill all the whisky they could drink if they helped him build a bar. Within 24 hours the **Globe Saloon** was finished. A statue of the legendary Yorkshireman standing on a whisky barrel graces the quaint **Maple Leaf Square**. Behind him is the site of his second saloon, along with **Gaoler's Mews**, an attractive little courtyard. Opposite is the thin curved end of the wedge-shaped **Hotel Europe** (1909), the first reinforced-concrete building in Vancouver and certainly one of its most charming constructions.

Just west of here is Gastown's main drag, Water Street, site of the much-touted **Steam Clock**, which entertains tourists every 15 minutes by tooting and erupting in a cloud of steam. Still overrun with souvenir shops, the street is finally becoming less tacky and is positively gorgeous when illuminated at night. Many handsome old red-brick buildings and cobbled streets redeem Gastown, which also holds some of the city's best antique shops, commercial art galleries, bars and clubs.

West End to Stanley Park
→ *For listings, see pages 37-58.*

West End
The most interesting way to get to Stanley Park is via **Robson Street**, which is lined with fashionable boutiques and restaurants, and perpetually thronged with trendsetters, posers and Japanese students. It marks the northeast boundary of the **West End**, Western Canada's most densely populated area, whose proximity keeps the Downtown core perpetually buzzing through the night. The rectangle is completed by Denman and Davie streets,

both packed with restaurants and cafés, creating a neighbourhood vibe that gains much of its character from the district's large gay community.

Most of the area's traditional buildings were replaced with high-rises during the 1960s. The best surviving block is **Barclay Heritage Square**, where a park-like setting contains nine historic houses built 1890-1908. One 1893 Queen Anne Revival-style home, furnished in Edwardian style and attributed to architect Francis Rattenbury, has been converted into the **Roedde House Museum** ① *1415 Barclay St, T604-684 7040, www.roeddehouse.org, guided tours only, mid-May to mid-Sep Tue-Sat 1000-1700, $5, tea and tour Sun 1400-1600, $6, bus No 5 to Broughton*, which provides an opportunity to see inside one of these buildings.

Stanley Park

① *T604-257 8400, www.vancouverparks.ca, Stanley Park never closes but isolated trails should be avoided after dark, bus No 19 from Pender, keep your ticket for a $2 discount at the Aquarium, in summer, extra shuttle buses run from Pender & Cambie, parking $2.50 per hr or $10 per day Apr-Sep, $2 for 2 hrs, $5 per day Oct-Mar; Vancouver Trolley Company, T604-801 5515, www.vancouvertrolley.com, runs a 15-stop, hop-on hop-off tour around the park, mid-Jun to mid-Oct, $10, under 11 $5, under 4 free.*

Looking at a map, the head and beak of the duck-shaped downtown peninsula are green, entirely devoted as they are to the 400-ha Stanley Park. Miraculously, the lion's share of this evergreen oasis, predominantly filled with second-growth but still giant cedar, hemlock and fir, has been allowed to remain undeveloped. Almost all of the park's many attractions, which merit a whole day of exploration, are concentrated in the beak, the narrow spit that juts out north of sheltered Coal Harbour.

At the park's main entrance on Georgia St. is the extensive **Lost Lagoon**, a haven for swans, ducks, geese and the occasional blue heron. The Ecology Society based in the newly renovated **Nature House** ① *T604-257 6908, www.stanleyparkecology.ca, mid-May to mid-Sep Tue-Sun 1000-1900, mid-Sep to mid-May Fri 1200-1600, Sat-Sun 0930-1630*, offers ecological information and useful maps, and organizes two-hour Sunday **Discovery Walks** ① *T604-257 8544 1300, $10, under 18 $5, 2-hr birdwatching tours at 0900 on the last Sun of every month (free), and various children's activities*. A short walk east along the seawall from here, past Vancouver Rowing Club, a granite-fronted Information Booth makes a handy second stop, at least to pick up a free map. Next to here is a kiosk selling tickets for one-hour **horse-drawn tours** ① *T604-681 5115, www.stanleyparktours.com, Mar and Oct 0940-1600, Apr-Jun and Sep 0940-1700, Jul-Aug 0930-1730, every 20-30 mins, $29, under 13 $16*. North of here and the rowing club are a beautiful **Rose Garden**, the **Malkin Bowl**, which is home to **Theatre Under the Stars** ① *T604-687 0174, www.tuts.ca, Jul-Aug alternating nights 2000, $29-42, under 16s $27-40*, and Painters' Corner, a kind of informal outdoor gallery.

Further north are a number of kid-friendly attractions, including the park's biggest draw, the **Vancouver Aquarium Marine Science Centre** ① *T604-659 3474, www.vanaqua.org, mid-May to mid-Sep daily 0930-1900, mid-Sep to mid-May 0930-1700, $30, under 18s $23.50, under 13s $19, bus No 19 from Pender*. One of Vancouver's prime rainy-day activities, this is even better when the sun shines since the most exciting animals – seals, dolphins and otters – live outside. Even these are utterly upstaged by a pair of giant and graceful white beluga whales that can be watched from an underwater viewing room downstairs, where a wealth of background information includes a video of the female giving birth. It's best to

The sea wall promenade

The 9-km sea wall around Stanley Park has long been celebrated as one of Vancouver's highlights. An unbroken sea wall promenade now runs from the end of Burrard Place near Canada Place, along Coal Harbour, round Stanley Park, through Sunset Beach Park, round False Creek, past Science World, around Granville Island, through Vanier Park and Kits Beach, and all the way to Spanish Banks Beach in Point Gray, 28 km in all. This waterfront environment represents an integral facet of Vancouver's complex personality, as important as any of the city's neighbourhoods, and we strongly recommend getting at least a taste of it. Cycling is the ultimate way to explore; for details, see Activities and tours, page 54.

save the belugas until last though, as the other 60,000 creatures from the world's many seas tend to pale by comparison. Indoor highlights include the Treasures of the BC Coast gallery, with a giant Pacific octopus, coral, anemones and some eerily beautiful jellyfish; a large collection of handsome frogs; and the Tropic Zone and Amazon Rainforest galleries. There are several talks and shows daily where everyone's favourite animals can be seen up-close or performing. Outside, look out for Bill Reid's magnificent bronze sculpture of a killer whale, *The Chief of the Undersea World (1984)*.

Opened in 2010, and hopefully set to become a permanent attraction, **Klahowya Village** ① *www.aboriginalbc.com/KlahowyaVillage, Jul-early Sep, free*, offers the chance to experience First Nations culture. The highlights are a 13-minute ride into the forest – and Aboriginal history – aboard the **Spirit Catcher Train**, and a **Children's Farmyard** with over 100 animals ① *T604-257 8531, Feb-May 1100-1600 weekends, Jun and school holidays 1100-1600 daily, Jul-Aug 1000-1800 daily, railway or farmyard $7, under 18s $5, under 13s $3.50, railway and farmyard $11/7/7*. There are three dance performances per day at 1200, 1400 and 1600, cultural tours every hour from 1100-1700, artisans carving wood and weaving, an Elder's Area, where the Elders speak about their life experiences, a Story Telling Circle, and kiosks selling arts, crafts, and authentic Aboriginal cuisine. To the west, by the sea wall, is a great **Water Park** ① *Jun-Aug 1000-1800, free*.

Particularly in summer, a great way to experience the park is to walk, jog, rollerblade, or cycle around the 8.8-km sea wall, which follows the park's perimeter between a number of viewpoints, and most of the park's other attractions. A further 13-odd km of sea wall continues round False Creek, past Kitsilano and almost to UBC. Equipment can be hired from shops at the north end of Denman Street. All cyclists and roller-bladers must do the circuit in a counter-clockwise direction. Following Coal Harbour past the Info-booth and the Royal Vancouver Yacht Club, you soon arrive at **Brockton Point**, which has a picturesque old lighthouse, a decent stand of Kwakiutl and Haida totem poles, and, fronted by three beautiful carved cedar gateways, the newly expanded Brockton Visitor Centre. At the southern point is the **9 O'clock Gun**, a cannon that has been fired at that hour every evening since a century ago, when it signalled the end of the day's legal fishing.

At the park's northwestern tip is **Prospect Point**, offering fine views of the North Shore. A couple of decent beaches hug the western shore, including **Second Beach**, where facilities include a heated ocean-side **swimming pool** ① *T604-257 8371, $5.70, youth $4, child $2.80*. Nearby, skirting the pitch and putt, the **Rhododendron Garden** shelters a collection of ornamental trees, including azaleas, camellias and magnolia, which are at their best in May. The bulk of the park's interior is devoted to shady walking paths, which were once skid roads used by early loggers to drag mighty trees down to the water. Look for the stump of one such, now endangered, giant known as the **Hollow Tree**. Between here and Third Beach is a living cedar believed to be one of the largest trees and oldest cedars in the world, it's almost 5 m across and roughly 1000 years old.

Granville Island to Point Grey → *For listings, see pages 37-58.*

Granville Island
ⓘ *Although Granville Island is always open, many attractions are closed on Mon, and parking can be a nightmare, so avoid driving and take the ferry ($2.50, and the best way to arrive) from the Aquatic Centre next to Burrard Bridge, or bus No 50 from Granville St and then walk.*

When Vancouver was first settled, the waterfront area of False Creek was five times the size it is today. Land has been reclaimed all around the inlet, much of it for Expo '86. Nowhere has this process been more successful than at Granville Island. Originally no more than a sandbar, the area was built up into an industrial zone, then transformed into an attractive yachting, shopping and arts district, with an atmosphere similar to London's Covent Garden, a magnet for tourists and locals alike.

Though not strictly pedestrianized, the island is well geared to aimless strolling. Meander at will, but be sure not to miss the **Public Market** ⓘ *daily 0900-1900, T604-666 5784.* As well as a mouth-watering collection of international fast food stalls, the place is packed with tempting produce from gourmet breads to seafood and sausages. The building itself is a fine lesson in the renovation of industrial structures, making great use of the natural lighting, large windows and doors, heavy timber and steel. The courtyard outside and adjacent bars are good places to watch the aquatic world float by. The island houses arguably the most concentrated collection of arts and crafts galleries, stores and studios in Western Canada, many of them concentrated in the **Net Loft** ⓘ *opposite the Public Market, daily 1000-1900*, and Railspur Alley. Also worth a visit is Canada's first microbrewery, **Granville Island Brewing Company** ⓘ *1441 Cartwright St, T604-687 2739, www.gib.ca, tours run daily 1200, 1400 and 1600, $9.75, 40 mins, and include 4 tasters and a souvenir glass.*

Close to the road entrance on Cartwright Street is a **Visitor Information Centre** ⓘ *T604-666 5784, www.granvilleisland.com, daily 0900-1800*, which provides a *Visitors' Guide* with discount vouchers and a very useful map. Almost next door at 1496 is the **Kids' Market** ⓘ *T604-689 8447, www.kidsmarket.ca, daily 1000-1800*, with 28 shops and services for kids and a multi-level indoor play area called **Adventure Zone** ⓘ *T604-608 6699, www.theadventurezone.ca, daily 1000-1800*. At the back is **Waterpark**, an aquatic play area with multiple slides and a playground.

Vanier Park
ⓘ *Bus No 2 or 22 from Burrard to Cornwall & Cypress, then walk up Chestnut St, or take the ferry from the Aquatic Centre. Contains 3 fairly important sights, which can all be seen with an Explore Pass, $30, under 18s $24.*

A pleasant walk north along the seawall promenade leads from Granville Island to Vanier Park, a small but pretty and popular summer hang-out. Housed in a building whose interesting shape was inspired by the hats of Haida natives, the **Vancouver Museum** ① T604-736 4431, www.museumofvancouver.ca, daily 1000-1700, to 2100 Thu, $12, under 18s $8, under 5s free, with Space Centre $17, under 18s $11, has four permanent exhibitions – Boom, Bust and War; You Say You Want a Revolution; Gateway to the Pacific; and The 50s Gallery – which together tell the story of the city's past. There's also one temporary exhibit, often a little more interesting and quirky.

Sharing the same building is the more upbeat **HR MacMillan Space Centre** ① T604-738 7827, www.spacecentre.ca, daily 1000-1700, $15, under 18s $10.75, under 5s free, observatory open Sat 2000-2330, free. A host of interactive exhibits in the Cosmic Courtyard talk you through the Earth's geological composition, the nature of life in space and the logistics of space travel. Tickets include entrance to **Ground Station Canada Theatre**, whose hourly demonstrations use video and live experiments to get kids excited about science, and hourly shows in the domed **Planetarium Star Theatre** ① also hosts Sat evening astronomy shows, 1900, $10.75, and laser and light shows on Fri and Sat evenings, set to the music of bands like Radiohead and Pink Floyd $10.75. Tickets include a 15-minute ride in the Virtual Voyages Simulator.

The front section of the nearby **Maritime Museum** ① 1905 Ogden Av, T604-257 8300, www.vancouvermaritimemuseum.com, mid-May to mid-Sep daily 1000-1700, mid-Sep to mid-May Tue-Sat 1000-1700, Sun 1200-1700, $12.30, under 18s $10.50, under 5s free, has a distinctive, steep triangular shape because it was built around the RCMP vessel, St Roch, which has been lovingly restored to its original 1944 condition. Before exploring this hardy little ship, watch the video about all the firsts it achieved: first to travel the treacherous and long-sought Northwest Passage, a 27-month journey from Vancouver to Halifax; first to make the same trip back via the faster, more northerly route; and first to circumnavigate North America. This is the museum's highlight but there's much more to see, with lots of artefacts and stories, a fun exhibit on pirates, a hands-on area for children and some bigger pieces on the lawn outside. There is usually also an interesting guest exhibition or two.

Kitsilano
① Bus No 2 or 22 south on Burrard to Cornwall then walk.

Continuing westwards on the well-used sea wall, Vanier Park melds seamlessly into **Kitsilano** (or **Kits**) **Beach**, the most popular stretch of sand in the city, with great views of English Bay, Downtown and the Coast Mountains, and a saltwater **Outdoor Pool** ① T604-731 0011, mid-Jun to early Sep Mon-Fri 1200-2045, Sat-Sun 1000-2045, $5.70, youth $4, child $2.80, which is Canada's longest. In the 1960s, Kitsilano was the main focus of Vancouver's subculture. By the 1980s, many of the local hippies had got high-paying jobs, bought and restored their houses, and helped turn Kits into a Yuppie's dream. Many of the old wooden town houses have been replaced by condos, but plenty of character remains in the area's two main drags, **West Fourth between Burrard and Vine** ① bus No 4 or 7, and the less interesting **West Broadway between MacDonald and Waterloo** ① bus No 10 or 16, offer some of the city's best browsing strips, with plenty of interesting speciality shops, trendy hair studios, snowboard outlets and good restaurants. Weekend brunch here is a Vancouver institution, but parking can be a nightmare (try Fifth).

Point Grey

From Kitsilano, Fourth Avenue and the more scenic Point Grey Road lead west to the jutting nose of Point Grey, home to some of the city's best beaches, the University of British Columbia (UBC), some botanical gardens and Vancouver's best sight, the Museum of Anthropology (see below). On the way is Vancouver's oldest building, **Hastings Mill Store** ① *1575 Alma St, T604-734 1212, mid-Jun to mid-Sep Tue-Sun 1100-1600, mid-Sep to mid-Jun Sat-Sun 1300-1600, entry by donation, bus No 9 Broadway or No 4, 7 or 44 to Alma and walk.* Transported from its original Gastown site in 1930, today it houses a small museum with displays of First Nations and pioneer artefacts.

From here, a clutch of beaches and parks run almost uninterrupted around the edge of Point Grey. First of these is **Jericho Beach**, set in a large, very scenic park with a fine youth

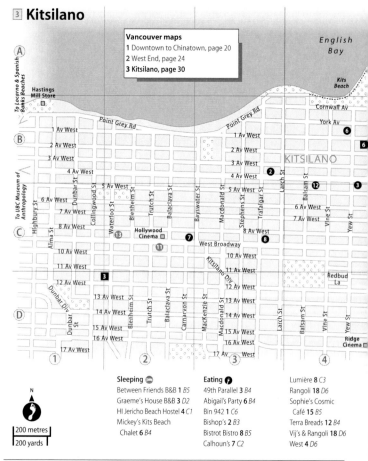

③ **Kitsilano**

Vancouver maps
1 Downtown to Chinatown, page 20
2 West End, page 24
3 Kitsilano, page 30

Sleeping	Eating
Between Friends B&B **1** *B5*	49th Parallel **3** *B4*
Graeme's House B&B **3** *D2*	Abigail's Party **6** *B4*
HI Jericho Beach Hostel **4** *C1*	Bin 942 **1** *C6*
Mickey's Kits Beach	Bishop's **2** *B3*
Chalet **6** *B4*	Bistrot Bistro **8** *B5*
	Calhoun's **7** *C2*

Lumière **8** *C3*
Rangoli **18** *D6*
Sophie's Cosmic
Café **15** *B5*
Terra Breads **12** *B4*
Vij's & Rangoli **18** *D6*
West **4** *D6*

hostel, a sailing school and a bird sanctuary. Three unbroken kilometres lead to **Locarno Beach**, a quiet area popular with families, and **Spanish Banks**, which has a beach café and warm, shallow water that's ideal for paddling. From UBC, roughly where Marine Drive meets University Boulevard, about 100 steps lead down through the forest to the 6-km strip of **Wreck Beach**. On a hot day as many as 10,000 sun-worshippers take advantage of its clothing-optional status, while wandering peddlers supply them with cold beers, food and the ubiquitous BC Bud.

Museum of Anthropology at UBC

ⓘ *6393 NW Marine Dr, T604-822 5087, www.moa.ubc.ca, daily 1000-1700, Tue 1000-2100, closed Mon mid-Oct to late-Jan, $14, under 18s $12, under 6s free, Tue 1700-2100, $7. Bus No 4 or 10 south on Granville then walk, or change to No 42 at Alma.*

Founded in 1949, and situated on native Musqueam land, the extraordinary, newly renovated Museum of Anthropology is the only attraction in Vancouver that absolutely must be seen. Designed by Arthur Erickson to echo the post-and-beam structures of Northwest Coast First Nations, it contains the world's finest collection of carvings by master craftsmen from many of these Nations, most notably the Haida of Haida Gwaii (Queen Charlotte Islands) and the Gitxsan and Nisga'a from the Skeena River region of Northern BC. Be sure to pick up a *Gallery Guide* at the admissions desk ($1.50). As well as providing a commentary on the exhibits, it gives a brief but excellent introduction to First Nations cultures, the stylistic differences between them and an overview of their classic art forms.

Take your time at the beginning, down the ramp and in the Great Hall, as many of the finest sculptures are here, grouped by cultural area, and informatively labelled. Most date from the early to mid-19th century, but an encouraging number are recent including several exceptional works by the late master Bill Reid, such as *Bear* (1963), *Sea Wolf with Killer Whales* (1962), and a 7.5-m inshore cedar canoe (1985). Outside, and visible from the Hall, is a Haida House complex, fronted by a collection of memorial and mortuary poles. The Museum's highlight is Bill Reid's

Bars & clubs 🎵
Fringe Café **11** *C2*
Lou's Grill & Bistro **13** *C2*

exquisite masterpiece, *The Raven and the First Men* (1980) housed in a natural light-filled rotunda. The Multiversity Galleries make some 15,000 objects from around the world accessible to the public: overwhelming as it is, this is still less than half of the museum's permanent collection. Then there are three or four temporary exhibits, and the extensive Koerner Ceramics Gallery. It's hard to do all this justice in one visit, especially as a bit of energy should be reserved for the small gift shop in the lobby, which is packed with splendid books, carvings, jewellery and prints.

Nitobe and UBC Botanical Gardens

A short stroll from the museum is the **Nitobe Memorial Garden** ① *T604-822 9666, www.nitobe.org, Apr-Oct daily 0900-1700, shorter hours Oct-Apr, $6/4.50/3, $12/10/6 with UBC gardens, by donation in winter*. An authentic Japanese tea garden, this is a subtle experience, with every rock, tree and pool playing its part in the delicate harmony to create an ambience that encourages reflection and meditation. There are cherry blossoms in spring, Japanese irises in summer and Japanese maples in autumn. Moving anticlockwise, the garden represents the stages of a person's life.

A further 3 km south on Marine Drive are the much more extensive but equally delightful **UBC Botanical Gardens** ① *6804 SW Marine Dr, T604-822 3928, www.ubcbotanical garden.org, mid-May to mid-Sep daily 0900-1630, mid-Sep to mid-May 1000-1630, $8, under 18s $6, under 12s $4, family $20 for botanical gardens alone; $12/10/6/30 with Nitobe; $20/15/10/44 with Nitobe and Walkway; $24, under 18s $20.50, family $60 with Nitobe and the Museum of Anthropology, free tours Wed and Sat 1300, bus No 4 or 10 south on Granville*. Spread over 30 ha are a number of expertly maintained themed gardens, such as the Physick Garden, devoted to traditional medicinal plants from 16th-century Europe. The experience is as educational as it is aesthetic, with well-labelled exhibits and regular lectures. New to the gardens is the 308-m Greenheart Canopy Walkway which takes visitors up to a height of over 17.5 m, offering a bird's eye view of the forest canopy.

South and east Vancouver → *For listings, see pages 37-58.*

Neighbourhoods

The broad swathe of Vancouver south of Burrard Inlet is dotted with small, interesting neighbourhoods each with its own particular atmosphere. The most worthwhile is **Commercial Drive** ① *bus No 20*. Once known as Little Italy, the area still has a number of Italian coffee shops, but has taken on a much more cosmopolitan, alternative and bohemian character, that makes it popular with artists, numerous minority groups, and the counterculture community. There are no 'sights' as such, but it's a fascinating place to wander, eat, drink and people-watch. A similar, but younger, vibe is found on Main Street from Seventh to 16th Avenues. Known as 'Uptown', it's dominated by trendily gritty cafés and restaurants, boutiques and galleries. **South Main** or 'SoMa,' stretching roughly from 16th to 30th Avenues, has lots of antique and second-hand shops, and more boutiques. Further south on Main between 49th and 51st Avenues is Vancouver's Indiatown, the **Punjabi Market**. If in the area, pay a visit to the splendid **Sikh Temple** ① *8000 Ross St*, another Arthur Erickson special. **South Granville**, from the bridge to 16th Avenue abounds with antiques shops, private art galleries, boutiques and cafés.

Queen Elizabeth Park and VanDusen Botanical Garden
ⓘ *For information on both parks, visit www.vancouver.ca/parks.*

Conveniently close together near Granville, Cambie and 33rd Avenues, South Vancouver's two main pieces of green are both worth a visit. It's easy to see why the 53-ha **Queen Elizabeth Park** ⓘ *33rd Av/Cambie, bus No 15 on Burrard or Robson*, is Vancouver's second most popular green space. The ornamental Quarry Gardens, built on the site of an old basalt quarry, are beautiful indeed, as is the extensive rose garden, and there's an arboretum said to contain a specimen of almost every tree found in Canada. Paths lead to Vancouver's highest point (150 m), the peak of an extinct volcano, with good if rather obstructed views of the city below and the wonderfully romantic **Seasons in the Park** restaurant (see Eating, page 43). Nearby is the wonderful **Bloedel Floral Conservatory** ⓘ *T604-257 8584, May-Sep Mon-Fri 0900-2000, Sat-Sun 1000-2100, Oct-Apr daily 1000-1700, $5.30, youth $3.73, child $2.72*, a giant triodetic dome that contains 500 varieties of exotic plants from tropical rainforest, subtropical and desert ecosystems, as well as floral displays that change with the seasons, koi carp, and about 100 species of free-flying tropical birds.

The 22-ha **VanDusen Botanical Garden** ⓘ *5251 Oak St and 37th Av, T604-257 8335, www.vandusengarden.org, daily from 1000 to 2100 Jun-Aug, 2000 May, 1800 Apr, 1900 Sep, 1700 Oct and Mar, 1600 Nov-Feb; prices vary by season, in summer $9.75, under 18s $7.25, under 12s $5.25, under 6s free; bus No 17 on Seymour or Howe*, contains over 7500 different plants from around the world, including some rare species. Set around lakes, ponds and waterfalls, and dotted with sculptures, the 40-odd themed gardens are considerably more romantic and contemplative than those at UBC, and they feel bigger. A favourite with children is the Elizabethan hedge maze. In December the gardens host the **Festival of Lights** (see Festivals, page 51).

North Shore → *For listings, see pages 37-58.*

The mountainous landscapes, tracts of semi-wilderness and potential for outdoor pursuits offered by Vancouver's North Shore represent for many people the city's finest feature, though it's not the place to stay or eat. The obvious way to get there is on the SeaBus, a lovely inexpensive chance to get out on the water. It leaves from behind the Waterfront SkyTrain in the old CPR building and docks at **Lonsdale Quay Market**, the North Shore's only real focal point. Local buses continue from here. The glazed and galleried interior of the market, a throwback to 19th-century industrial architecture, is well worth a look.

East from Lion's Gate Bridge
The other main route to the North Shore is from Stanley Park across the **Lion's Gate Bridge**, the British Empire's longest suspension bridge when it was built in 1938, inspired by San Francisco's Golden Gate. Roughly 8 km east from here, Lynn Valley Road leads to **Lynn Canyon Park** ⓘ *www.lynncanyon.ca, daily from 0700 to 2100 in summer, to 1900 in spring and autumn, to dusk in winter; exit 19 from Highway 1, bus No 229 from Lonsdale Quay*, 250 ha of relatively unspoilt forest, consisting of 80- to 100-year-old second-growth trees. The **Lynn Canyon Ecology Centre** ⓘ *3663 Park Rd, T604-9903755, www.dnv.org/ecology, daily 1000-1700, Oct-May 1200-1600 Sat-Sun, guided walks Jul-Aug daily 1400*, has displays, films and information about the park, as well as a free map. The 68-m suspension bridge that hovers 50 m above the rushing waters of Lynn Creek is free to walk across.

Many hiking trails of varying length begin on the other side, including a 15-minute stroll to a wooden footbridge that crosses the creek at Twin Falls.

At the eastern end of the North Shore, Mount Seymour Road climbs steeply up 1000 vertical metres to **Mount Seymour Provincial Park**, passing two stunning viewpoints, both worth a stop. Other than the commercial ski hill, Mount Seymour, the park's semi-wilderness old-growth forest and sub-alpine wild flower meadows make for some excellent hiking. **Flower Lake Loop**, a pleasant 1.5-km stroll through bog and ponds, is a good place for spotting birds. **Mount Seymour** ① *T604-986 2261, www.mountseymour.com, Mon-Fri 0930-2200, Sat-Sun 0830-2200, day pass $44.50, under 18s $39, under 13s $23, under 5s free, family pass $129, night skiing 1600-2200, $33.50, under 18s $33, under 12s $19, snowshoeing, $26.50, concessions $20; prices include rentals and snowphone, T604-986 2261,* is the most affordable ski hill in Vancouver, and good for beginners. The 80 ha of terrain features 39 trails (40% novice, 40% intermediate, 20% advanced) serviced by five lifts. There are also four snowboard terrain parks, including one that's geared toward beginners, plus 10 km of maintained snowshoe trails, and eight toboggan runs. Ski and snowboard rentals are available, as are lesson, ticket and rental packages. A **shuttle bus** (T604-986 2261, December-March), runs every hour in the afternoon during the week and from the early morning at weekends from Parkgate Mall ($6 one-way) and Lonsdale Quay ($8).

At the North Shore's eastern extremity is **Deep Cove** ① *www.deepcovebc.com*, a picturesque spot that has retained the unspoilt feel of a seaside village and enjoys great views across the bay to snowy hills beyond. As well as prime kayaking and biking, there's a nice green park by the water, a few good restaurants and the best neighbourhood pub in Vancouver. To get there, take the SeaBus, then bus No 229 to Phibbs Exchange, then bus No 211 or 212. ▸▸ *See Activities and tours, page 53.*

Capilano Valley and Grouse Mountain

Almost due north from the Lion's Gate Bridge, Capilano Road runs parallel to the eponymous river, valley and regional park all the way to the dammed Capilano Lake and beyond to Grouse Mountain. **Capilano Suspension Bridge** ① *3735 Capilano Rd, T604-985 7474, www.capbridge.com, daily 0830 or 0900, closing hours vary, $29.95, under 16s $18.75, under 12s $10, under 6s free, parking $3, bus No 246 from Georgia or No 236 from Lonsdale Quay, free shuttle from Canada Place or various downtown hotels, see website for schedule,* is Vancouver's oldest and most vaunted attraction. The current bridge is the fourth to span the 137 m across Capilano River 70 m below, making it the longest and highest suspended footbridge in the world, and very exciting to cross. On the other side, the new **Treetops Adventure** consists of a series of smaller suspension bridges strung between Douglas firs up to 30 m high, offering a unique perspective from which to appreciate the astounding beauty of the surrounding rainforest. Opening in 2011, new vistas will be offered by **Cliffhanger**, a series of cantilevered and suspended walkways, some with floors of glass, that jut out from the granite cliff face above Capilano River. There's also a small collection of totem poles, and a small First Nations Cultural Centre, with live demonstrations of traditional weaving and beadwork.

For a free and more genuine taste of the valley's natural beauty, head up the road to the 160-ha **Capilano River Regional Park**, which protects the Capilano River as it heads south to Burrard Inlet, a journey followed by the 7.5-km one-way **Capilano Pacific Trail**, the longest of 10 trails through unmanicured forest. Trail maps are available at the car park or from information centres, and they outline a number of pools and other features. The park also contains the **Capilano Salmon Hatchery** ① *T604-666 1790, free,* one of the best places to see the salmon run and learn the extraordinary story of their journey.

Grouse Mountain ① *T604-980 9311, www.grousemountain.com, SeaBus then bus No 236 from Lonsdale Quay,* is the most popular and easily reached ski hill on the North Shore, its lights seeming to hang from Vancouver's night-time skyline like Christmas tree decorations. It has easy access, tremendous views, and the best facilities. Any visit begins with a ride on the **Skyride Gondola** ① *daily 0900-2200, every 15 mins, $40, under 18s $24, under 12s $14, under 5s free,* which whisks visitors up some 1100 m in about eight minutes. At the top are year-round panoramic views, 5-m chainsaw sculptures, and all kinds of facilities, including a couple of fine restaurants. The Gondola ticket includes access to 30-minute multimedia action films in the **Theatre in the Sky**, a round-trip up to the peak on a quad chairlift, and a refuge for endangered wildlife such as grizzly bears and wolves; plus a Lumberjack Show, a Birds of Prey demonstration, eco-walks, mountain biking, and hiking, including the famous Grouse Grind, in summer; or, in winter, an 750-sq-m Ice Skating Pond, four snowshoeing trails, and sleigh rides.

Daily ski passes cost an additional $55, under 18s $45, under 12s $25, night skiing 1600-2200, $45, under 18s $40, under 12s $22; five-day passes are $225, under 18s $200, under 12s $110. The 26 runs are predominantly intermediate, with a vertical drop of 384 m. There are also two terrain parks. A new feature is the **Eye of the Wind tour** ① *$25, under 12s free,* which leads you to glass observation deck at the top of a giant wind turbine, within metres of the massive rotating blades. For hard-core adrenalin junkies, there's also **mountain ziplines** ① *daily, 1000-1800 every 20-30 mins, $65,* a set of five lines that lead around Blue Grouse Lake, then across mountain peaks at speeds of 80 kph. If that's not enough, there's **tandem paragliding** every hour in summer ($210), and **helijet** tours.

West from Lion's Gate Bridge

Some 7 km west the access road to **Cypress Provincial Park** can be seen ascending the mountainous terrain in wide, drunken zigzags. This has been a popular recreation site since the 1920s, and offers the same range of summer and winter activities as Grouse Mountain, though with less extensive facilities or attractions, and thinner crowds. Some of the North Shore's best hikes are here (see Activities and tours, page 54), leading to panoramic views that take in the city, Howe Sound, Mount Baker to the southeast, and the Gulf Islands, Georgia Strait and Vancouver Island to the west. There's also a lift-assisted mountain bike park. **Cypress Mountain Ski Area** ① *T604-926 5612, snowphone T604-419 7669, www.cypressmountain.com, ski pass $50, child $26, daily 0900-2200, night skiing $17, child $10, T604-922 0825,* has benefited greatly from improvements made for the 2010 Winter Olympics, including the brand new Cypress Creek Lodge. The hill is geared towards more serious and advanced skiers, with a vertical drop of 610 m, some 10 m of snow per year, and 240 ha of terrain that divides up as 13% beginner, 35% intermediate, 37% advanced, 8% expert, and 8% freestyle. Nine chair lifts lead to 53 runs on two mountains, with night skiing on all main runs. It also has a snowboard park with half-pipe, 19 km of groomed Nordic trails ($17, under 18s $12, under 12s $11, under 5s $5), 7 km of which are lit up at night and 10 km of snowshoeing trails $26 including rental, under 12s $20. The tubing park ($17 for two hours, including rental) is great fun for kids and adults alike. A winter-only **shuttle bus** ① *T604-419 7669, www.cypresscoachlines.com, $20/15 return*, runs to the hill five times daily from Lonsdale Quay, twice daily from Kitsilano at Fourth and Burrard, and West End at Davie and Thurlow.

Further west still, is the comparatively tiny **Lighthouse Park** ① *free, bus No 250 from Downtown*, one of the most accessible parks and the best for strolling. It contains some of Vancouver's most rugged forest, including one of the last remaining stands of old-growth Douglas firs. A number of short trails lead to arbutus trees, cliffs and the (out of bounds) Point Atkinson Lighthouse, which has been staffed continuously since 1875.

Highway 1/99, which experienced an extensive and expensive overhaul for the 2010 Winter Olympics, swings north towards Squamish, passing Horseshoe Bay, terminal for ferries to Nanaimo, the Sunshine Coast and **Bowen Island**. A mere 20 minutes away, the latter offers visitors a quick and easy taste of the Gulf Islands' laid-back atmosphere, its population of 3500 characteristically including a large number of writers and artists. Ferries leave more or less hourly from 0605 until 2135, with a break for lunch. Just off the ferry landing is the island's main hub, **Snug Cove** where there's an **information kiosk** ① *432 Cardena Rd, T604-947 9024, www.bowenisland.org, May-Sep daily 1000-1700*, where you can pick up a free copy of the *Bowen Island Guide* with maps, restaurant and accommodation listings, activities and everything else you may need. Many people come for the fine boating and kayaking in the sheltered bays that surround this 50-sq-km island. **Mount Gardner** is an excellent 16-km return day-hike that is possible almost year round.

Hiking around Vancouver (east to west)

Mount Seymour ① *9 km round trip, 440-m elevation gain. Trailhead: Mt Seymour Provincial Park National Park car park.* Providing one of the easiest routes to astonishing summit panoramas, this trail is understandably very popular. But it is certainly no pushover. The route can be confusing, and is dangerously exposed to bad weather. Views from the top are some of the most extensive around. The route is rarely snow-free before August.

Brothers and Lawson Creeks *10 km loop, 437-m elevation gain. Trailhead: From Highway 1 or Marine Dr take Taylor Way north. Turn left onto Highland Dr and continue until you can turn left onto Eyremount Dr. Park where this road intersects Millstream Rd.* Walk west on gated road and look for signs for Brothers Creek Forest Heritage Walk. This short, undemanding hike takes in a gorge and some cascades, but is best recommended for the ease with which you can see some really big cedars in their natural environment.

Mount Strachan ① *10 km round trip, 534-m elevation gain. Trailhead: by the ski area map next to the car park in Cypress Provincial Park.* A first-rate hike, this route follows the Howe Sound Crest Trail for a while before heading through Strachan Meadows then steeply up the edge of a gorge, alongside precipitous cliffs and through a beautiful stretch of old-growth forest. The north summit offers the best views. This trail is rarely free of snow before mid-July.

Hollyburn Mountain ① *8 km round trip, 405-m elevation gain. Trailhead: by the ski area map next to the car park in Cypress Provincial Park.* This is one of the finest and easiest trails on the North Shore with panoramic views from the top. You also walk through what is probably the finest stand of ancient giant cedar, fir and hemlock within reach of the city. Snow-free from mid-June to mid-November.

Mount Gardner ① *16 km round trip, 750-m elevation gain. Trailhead: take the ferry from Horseshoe bay to Bowen Island.* Directions are complicated so ask at the information centre or consult *Don't Waste Your Time in the BC Coast Mountains.* This is a fairly demanding but highly rewarding hike that is possible almost year round. Catch an early ferry to allow plenty of time. Panoramic views from the top are spectacular.

The Lions ① *15 km round trip, 1525-m elevation gain. Trailhead: at Lions Bay on Highway 99, turn east onto Oceanview Rd then left onto Cross Creek Rd, right onto Centre Rd, left onto Bayview Rd, left onto Mountain Dr, left onto Sunset Dr and park at the gate.* This is a steep hike, but the views are great from the base of the Lions, especially if you can scramble down to the gap between them.

Metro Vancouver listings

For Sleeping and Eating price codes and other relevant information, see pages 9-11.

● Sleeping

Downtown *p18, map p20*

$$$ Comfort Inn Downtown, 654 Nelson St, T604-605 4333, www.comfortinndowntown.com. A smart and fairly stylish hotel, conveniently located in the heart of Downtown, with a variety of rooms. Continental breakfast and fitness pass included.

$$$ Moda Hotel, 900 Seymour, T604-683 4251, www.modahotel.ca. A genuinely stylish and modern hotel, sleekly furnished in black and red, and just removed from the heart of the Entertainment district. Comfortable, attractive rooms, and friendly, helpful staff. There are decent bars and restaurants on site.

$$ Patricia Hotel, 403 E Hastings, T604-255 4301, www.budgetpathotel.bc.ca. Housed in a nicely renovated 1914 building enlivened with many plants, the **Patricia** is surprisingly classy given the seedy area, and certainly the best non-hostel budget option in town. Rooms are simple, clean and comfy, with en suite bathrooms. Some have fine views. There's a brewpub downstairs. Off-season weekly rates available. Staff on duty 24 hrs.

$$ Victorian Hotel, 514 Homer St, T604-681 6369, www.victorianhotel.ca. A renovated 1898 house, with small but comfortable rooms tastefully decorated in pastel shades with hardwood floors. Can be noisy. Continental breakfast.

$ Cambie Hostel Gastown, 300 Cambie St, T604-684 6466, www.cambiehostels.com. Well run and handily situated, the vibe of this busy backpacker hostel is somewhat influenced by the popular down-to-earth pub downstairs. Dorms and a few private rooms, all with lockers and shared bathroom. The common room (with TV) is a good place to meet travellers and pick up information. There's a small kitchen, laundry facilities, internet, luggage storage, and free coffee and muffin from the excellent bakery next door. Their smaller, sister hostel is nearby at 515 Seymour St, T604-684 7757.

$ HI Vancouver Central, 1025 Granville St, T604-685 5335. Situated in the heart of Downtown, this modern and efficient hostel offers 2- and 4-bed dorms and private rooms, as well as a common room, express kitchen (microwaves, no cooker) and lockers. They also organize daily activities.

$ SameSun Backpacker Lodge, 1018 Granville St, T604-682 8226, www.vancouverhostel.com. This centrally located, colourful hostel has everything you need. There are lots of dorms, double rooms with en suite bathroom, a huge kitchen, 2 large common rooms, a pool table, a TV room, a cheap bar-restaurant with nightly music, an outdoor patio, internet access, laundry, lockers and a travel information desk. Also organizes activities around town.

West End to Stanley Park *p25, map p24*

$$$ 910 Beach Ave, 910 Beach Av, T604-609 5100, www.910beach.com. This apartment hotel has a very wide range of attractive, open-plan, fully equipped suites, some with patio/balcony. All have floor-to-ceiling windows that take full advantage of the hotel's prime location on False Creek, with views of the water and Granville Market or the city. Continental breakfast included.

$$$ Blue Horizon Hotel, 1225 Robson St, T604-688 1411, www.bluehorizonhotel.com. The biggest and best of a cluster of mid-range hotels nicely situated on Robson. Rooms are large and plain but well appointed, with balconies and good views. Those with 2 beds ($10-20 more) sleep 4 and are much bigger. There's a small pool, hot tub, sauna, gym, bistro and café.

$$$ English Bay Inn B&B, 1968 Comox St, T604-683 8002, www.englishbayinn.com. Hidden away close to Stanley Park, this friendly B&B in a pretty Tudor-style house offers 4 attractive and comfortable en suite rooms and 2 suites. Huge gourmet breakfast.

$$$ The Listel, 1300 Robson St, T604-684 8461, www.thelistelhotel.com. Smaller than most high-end hotels, **The Listel** is beautiful and stylish throughout, with highly attentive staff. 'Museum suites' are decorated with First Nations art and exquisite hand-carved wood furnishings, while each 'Gallery suite' is dedicated to displaying original works by a different established artist. All are immaculately equipped, with big windows. Facilities include a fitness centre and hot tub, and there is live jazz in the restaurant.

$$ Buchan Hotel, 1906 Haro St, T604-685 5354, www.buchanhotel.com. Small and affordable, plain but pleasant, with a great location on a residential street close to Stanley Park.

$ HI Vancouver Downtown, 1114 Burnaby St, T604-684 4565, www.hihostels.ca. This clean and professional hostel on a central but quiet street has 4-bed dorms and simple private rooms with shared bath. Top-notch facilities include a large kitchen, TV room, library, games room with pool table, laundry, lockers and dining room. Many cheap activities can be arranged, free shuttle from bus/train station and a buffet breakfast.

Kitsilano *p29, map p30*

Kitsilano is taken as stretching east to Granville and south to 15th.

$$$ Mickey's Kits Beach Chalet, 2142 W 1st Av, T604-739 3342, www.mickeys bandb.com. 3 bright and pleasant rooms in a quiet spot close to **Kits Beach**, with a friendly and helpful host and a garden. Breakfast included.

$$ Between Friends B&B, 1916 Arbutus St, T604-734 5082, www.betweenfriends-vancouver.com. 3 small but very nice and distinctive rooms, a small suite and an apartment (**$$$**) in a classic Kitsilano home close to 4th Av. Guests share a pleasant sitting room and the friendly hostess serves up a big breakfast.

$$ Graeme's House B&B, 2735 Waterloo St, T604-732 1488, www.graemewebster.com. 3 rooms in a pretty heritage house with lots of interesting features, and a deck and flower garden. Close to the most interesting section of Broadway.

$ HI Jericho Beach Hostel, 1515 Discovery St, T604-224 3208, www.hihostels.ca. Built in the 1930s as barracks for Jericho Air Station, this vast and interesting building is the largest hostel in Canada. It has 288 dorm beds and 10 private rooms, all with shared bath. All the usual facilities are here: a massive kitchen and dining room, TV room, games room, library, laundry, lockers and bike rental. Free or cheap tours, hikes and activities. The main factor here is the location, it is in a beautiful and quiet spot right on the beach, but a very long way from Downtown.

South and east Vancouver p32

$$$ Delta Vancouver Airport, 3500 Cessna Dr, T604-278 1241, www.deltavancouver airport.com. The nicest place to stay close to the airport, thanks to a riverside location by a marina, a pub housed in a small pagoda and lovely gardens. There's also an outdoor pool, exercise room, restaurant and access to riverside trails.

$$$ Douglas Guest House, 456 W 13th Av, T604-872 3060, www.dougwin.com. 5 fairly large rooms/suites in a restored Edwardian manor, with elegant decor, and en suite bath in all but 2. Breakfast served in a sunroom with patio. They also have a sister guesthouse, the 11-room **Windsor Guest House**.

$$ Best Western Uptown, 205 Kingsway, T604- 267 2000, www.bestwestern vancouver.ca. Situated near the happening intersection of Main and Broadway, this standard but comfortable hotel consistently offers good value, especially off-season. Breakfast, fitness solarium and parking included.

$$ City Centre Motor Hotel, 2111 Main St, T604-876 7166, www.citycentermotor hotel.com. Handy for transport connections and the interesting section of Main, this brightly coloured hotel has simple but clean rooms with TV and bath, and plenty of parking. A bargain.

Camping

Capilano RV Park, 295 Tomahawk Av, near Lion's Gate Bridge, T604-987 4722, www.capilanorvpark.com. Very much an RV park, but centrally located with great facilities including full hook-ups, tent sites, free showers, a swimming pool, jacuzzi, play-ground, laundromat and lounge area with TV and games.

🅿 Eating

Eating out is one of the highlights of a trip to Vancouver, whose culinary scene is now as dynamic as anywhere in North America. Since the turnover of restaurants is except-

ionally high, these listings concentrate largely on reliable, established favourites. Details of the latest exciting newcomers can be found in *Eat Magazine*, www.eatmagazine.ca, or at www.urbanspoon.com or www.urbandiner. ca. Gastown has increasingly established itself as the most exciting area for culinary window-shopping.

Vancouver's chefs have pioneered a style of cooking known as West Coast cuisine (see page 11), emphasizing fresh, local produce and embracing an innovative, pan-global fusion mentality. Given the cosmopolitan population, it's no surprise that you can find whatever international cuisine you crave. We have favoured venues that offer a unique Vancouver experience.

Downtown p18, map p20

ⓎⓎⓎ Diva at the Met, 645 Howe St, T604-602 7788. A contender for the best restaurant in town, the food here is classic nouveau French, prepared with flair, creativity and a West Coast sensibility. Decor is bright and elegant, sophisticated but far from stuffy. An extensive wine list includes many offered by the glass.

ⓎⓎⓎ Joe Forte's Seafood and Chop House, 777 Thurlow St, T604-669 1940. Dominated by a large horseshoe-shaped bar, this exceptionally opulent room makes for a special dining experience, though you're paying for the setting rather than the food or service. Seafood is the speciality, with a broad choice of oysters. The selection of wines and beers is great and there's a roof garden and live piano music nightly.

ⓎⓎⓎ Le Crocodile, 909 Burrard St, T604-669 4298. Classic French cuisine, whose sophistication lies in its simplicity. The ambience is upscale bistro and the prices reasonable for food of this calibre.

Ⓨ Café Medina, 556 Beatty, T604-879 3114. Very popular for breakfast, brunch and lunch, serving food that is simple but creative, wholesome but sophisticated. Try the fricassée.

The Templeton, 1087 Granville St, T604- 685 4612. An authentic 1930s diner with jukeboxes and booths, offering typical diner comfort food with a healthy, original twist. Try the *ahi* tuna.

Cafés

Café Ami, 885 W Georgia St, in the HSBC building, T604-688 0103. A very relaxed and attractive spot for a coffee.

Gallery Café, in the Art Gallery, 750 Hornby St, T604-688 2233. A hidden gem. The patio is a fantastic place for a coffee or glass of wine on a sunny day, the atmosphere is relaxed and the light food menu is impeccable.

Wicked Café, 861 Hornby, T604-569 5480. Great coffee, great location.

Yaletown *p22, map p20*

Blue Water Café & Raw Bar, 1095 Hamilton St, T604-688 8078, www.bluewatercafe.net. Oozing genuine, unpretentious chic and upmarket class, this spacious venue is consistently celebrated for serving some of the best, freshest seafood in town, both raw and cooked. The drinks menu and service are also excellent

Coast Restaurant, 1257 Hamilton St, T604-685 5010. Dominated by pale wood furnishings, high ceilings, a waterfall and a large 'community' table, this is a tranquil and elegant location to enjoy all manner of West Coast-style seafood creations, including multi-course tasting menus.

Rodney's Oyster House, 1228 Hamilton St, T604-609 0080. Classic converted warehouse space with brick walls and huge wooden beams. Downstairs is casual with stools at the bar, upstairs is a little smarter. Clientele is slightly older but the ambience is lively and crowded. Focusing on oysters, mussels and chowder; the food is excellent.

Cafés

Ganache Patisserie, 1262 Homer St, T604-899 1098. If you like cakes, this is the place. A bit pricey but worth it.

Chinatown *p23, map p20*

For a snack try one of the numerous local bakeries for a curry beef, BBQ pork or honey bun; they quickly become addictive.

Hon's Wun-Tun House, 268 Keefer St, T604-688 0871; also at 1339 Robson, T604-685 0871. There are countless options in Chinatown and it's hard to go wrong, but this is the obvious choice, having for some time scooped up most awards for best Chinese and best restaurant under $10. The decor is cafeteria-style, the menu huge.

Gastown *p23, map p20*

Cobre, 52 Powell St, T604-669 2396. Sophisticated and delicious pan-Latin American cuisine in an interesting space, creatively wrought from brick, dark wood and installation art.

Guu with Otokomae, 375 Water St, T604-685 8682. Perhaps the all-round best of the **Guu** restaurants. Try the oyster gratin, deep-fried brie, and a cocktail or 3.

Judas Goat Taberna, 27 Blood Alley, T604-681 5090. Like it's older sister, **Salt** (see below), this Spanish-inspired tasting bar is all about eating while you drink wine. The small plates, offering tastes like pork belly, foie gras and ceviche, are delicious but tiny, so if you're hungry it can get expensive.

L'Abattoir, 217 Carrall St, T604-568 1701. A new local favourite that delivers on every front. The natural wood and exposed brick decor is modern but classic, with a delightful atrium. The French-influenced West Coast cuisine is imaginative and beautifully executed. The drinks menu and service are equally impressive.

Nuba, 207 W Hastings, T604-688 1655. A romantic room in the basement of the Dominion Building, serving exceptionally tasty, very reasonably priced Lebanese dishes, with plenty of options for vegetarians and vegans.

Salt, 45 Blood Alley, T604-633 1912. In a scary dark alley, in a minimalist, rather loud, urban-warehouse space, this 'tasting room' is quite an experience. Artisan dried meats and cheeses are sampled with bread and condiments and can be washed down by 1 of the 40 wines available by the glass.

†† Water Street Café, 300 Water St, T604-689 2832. The menu seems unimaginative, mainly pasta, with some steak and seafood, but it's always fresh and very reasonably priced. The interior is classically elegant and the massive windows and outdoor seating make the most of an excellent location.

† Bambo Café, 301 W Cordova St, T604-681 4323. A cosy, casual little café that's great for breakfast or lunch, with superior focaccia sandwiches, home-made soups and unusually tasty omelettes. Outdoor seating on summy days, and warm service.

Cafés

Blake's, 221 Carrall St, T604-899 3354. Exceptional, downbeat, tasteful coffee house in a prime location, with good music, brick walls, beer on tap, a modest menu and internet access.

Caffe Dolcino, 12 Powell St, T604-801 5118. Perfectly situated on picturesque Maple Leaf Sq, with a couple of tables outside to take in the scene.

La Luna Café, 131 Water St, T604-687 5862. Well-situated and comfy. They roast their own beans, so the coffee is great.

West End to Stanley Park *p25, map p24*
The West End's large and lively population breathes constant life into the city's most competitive culinary district, with Robson, Denman and Davie representing the finest streets for restaurant window-shopping.

††† CinCin Ristorante + Bar, upstairs at 1154 Robson St, T604-688 7338. Often rated as the best Italian food in town, it has lots of awards, many for its wine list. The Mediterranean decor is warm, romantic, sophisticated and comfortable, with balcony seating for summer evenings.

††† Lift Bar Grill View, 333 Menchion's Mews, off Bayshore Dr, T604-689 5438. On the water, with floor-to-ceiling windows offering views of Coal Harbour and Stanley Park. A modern, sophisticated interior and an upbeat West Coast menu that concentrates on seafood. Try their signature 'whet' plates.

††† O'Doul's, 1300 Robson St in the **Listel Hotel**, T604-661 1400. This long-standing survivor offers warmth, sophistication, class and impeccable service. Emphasizing fresh- ness, the eclectic West Coast menu is reliable from breakfast to dinner. With a fine wine list and live jazz every night, it's also a great place for a drink.

††† Raincity Grill, 1193 Denman St, T604-685 7337. One of the original exponents of West Coast cuisine. Ingredients are fresh, locally produced, organic when possible, and used with subtlety and panache. The decor is simple and elegant. The award- winning wine list focuses on BC's finest and many are available by the glass.

††† Teahouse, 7501 Stanley Park Dr, Ferguson Point, T604-669 3281. The nicer of the park's 2 restaurants, set in a bright and breezy summerhouse with lots of plants and big windows that offer fabulous views of English Bay. The menu has eclectic West Coast inclinations.

†† Bin 941 Tapas Parlour, 941 Davie St, T604-683 1246. This small and intimate bistro combines quirky decor, a lively atmosphere, inspirational tapas, and a well-stocked bar.

†† Chilli House Thai Bistro, 1018 Beach Av, T604-685 8989. Perfectly situated right on the water, spacious yet intimate, with a summer patio, and evocative decor. It's almost a bonus that the Thai food here is so good.

†† Delilah's Martini Bar and Restaurant, 1789 Comox St, T604-687 3424. With its delightfully louche, camp atmosphere, hand-painted ceiling, velvet drapes and nightly entertainment, this place provides an all-round enjoyable experience. Justly famous for its martinis, but the set menus are also fine and very reasonable.

¶¶ **E-Hwa**, 1578 Robson St, T604-688 1322. The full Izakaya experience, Korean-style.

¶¶ **Guu**, 838 Thurlow St, T604-685 8817. Izakaya joints, serving small tapas-sized Japanese dishes washed down with beer, sake or a martini, are all the rage in Vancouver these days. They tend to be dark, atmospheric, loud, social, lots of fun and open late. They are an all-round unique experience. The 3 **Guu** restaurants are among the best, with staff shouting back and forth, and food that is fresh, tasty and very authentic.

¶¶ **Guu with Garlic**, 1698 Robson St, T604-685 8678. The least hectic **Guu** restaurant. Daily specials are worth exploring.

¶¶ **Gyoza King**, 1508 Robson St, T604-669 8278. This is an atmospheric and very popular spot for Japanese-style tapas and sake. It's calmer than the **Guu** restaurants and the food is possibly even better.

¶¶ **Lolita's South of the Border Cantina**, 1326 Davie St, T604-696 9996. Highly inventive and original take on Mexican food, with a tapas sensibility and an emphasis on cocktails. Small, packed and noisy, the party continues until 0200.

¶¶ **Tanpopo**, 1122 Denman St, T604-681 7777. A long-standing favourite for the all-you-can-eat sushi. Resting on its laurels a bit, and not as cheap as it used to be, but still a good experience

¶ **Café Luxy**, 1235 Davie St, T604-669 5899. Exceptionally well-priced and tasty Italian food, but often disappointingly empty.

¶ **India Bistro**, 1157 Davie St, T604-684 6342. Dimly lit and very busy, a fine spot for everyone's favourite Indian classics. Lunch buffet for just $9.

¶ **Stepho's Souvlaki Greek Taverna**, 1124 Davie St, T604-683 2555. Why are there always such long queues snaking around the generic exterior at Stepho's? Because the portions are epic, the prices very low, and the food tasty and comforting. Besides, it's a neighbourhood institution.

¶ **Sushi Mart**, 1668 Robson St, T604-687 2422. This tiny, unassuming place serves the best and freshest sushi in an area teeming with competition, and at very reasonable prices. The service is also quick and friendly.

Granville Island to Point Grey
p28, map p24

¶¶ **The Sand Bar**, 1535 Johnston St, Granville Island, T604-669 9030. A beautifully renovated warehouse with high ceilings, industrial metal trimmings, vast windows overlooking False Creek, and a heated roof patio. The West Coast menu includes tapas, wood-grilled burgers, and pizza, but the seafood is your best bet. It's a loud and fun spot, with a fine selection of ales and wines, but the service can be poor.

¶ **Granville Island Public Market**. Countless excellent, cheap fast-food stalls selling all kinds of international cuisine, with seating outside by the water.

Cafés
Granville Island Coffee House, 1551 Johnston St, on the boardwalk behind the **Sand Bar**, T604-682 7865. Cosy little spot away from the hustle and bustle.

JJ Bean, 1689 Johnston St, T604-685 0613. Great coffee.

Kitsilano *p29, map p30*
Kitsilano contains many of the city's most celebrated restaurants and also the best selection for vegetarians.

¶¶¶ **Bishop's**, 2183 W 4th Av, T604-738 2025. The quintessential West Coast eatery. Owner John Bishop is famous for his impeccable hospitality and for changing his menu frequently to highlight the best locally grown organic ingredients available. The extensive wine list favours BC's best.

¶¶¶ **Lumière**, 2551 W Broadway, T604-739 8185. Though its famous 'Iron Chef' owner Rob Feenie has gone, word is that this remains one of the city's (if not country's)

finest restaurants. There's no à la carte, just French-inspired tasting menus from $85-180 without wine, apparently worth every penny. The modern interior is stylish to the point of being intimidating.

₤₤₤ Vij's, 1480 11th Av, T604-736 6664. The only Indian restaurant that is regularly cited as one of the city's finest overall eateries. Skilful, innovative variations on old favourites. Reservations not accepted, so queues are common. Dinner only.

₤₤₤ West, 2881 Granville St, T604-738 8938. Large and idiosyncratic, dominated by a library of wine bottles. Another superlative purveyor of imaginative, fresh and tasty West Coast cuisine, regularly cited as one of the city's best.

₤₤ Abigail's Party, 1685 Yew St, T604-739 4677. A neighbourhood favourite close to Kits Beach, serving West Coast cuisine made from fresh, local produce. Equally fine for brunch or dinner, with prime people-watching from the small summer patio.

₤₤ Bin 942, 1521 W Broadway, T604-734 9421. A thin room stuffed with weird and wonderful pieces of art, trendy and lively with modern but mellow dance music. Reasonable beer selection and an incredible menu of involved, delicious tapas.

₤₤ Bistrot Bistro, 1961 W 4th Av, T604-732 0004. The decor here is crisply modern, refreshingly unpretentious, and for once authentic French cuisine is served in satisfying portions at reasonable prices. The *prix fixe* menu is particularly good value.

₤₤ Rangoli, 1488, 11th Av, next door to **Vij's**, T604-736 5711. A more casual and inexpensive version of **Vij's**, only open for lunch.

₤ Sophie's Cosmic Café, 2095 4th Av, T604-732 6810. An eccentric, diner-style Kitsilano institution that is legendary for its weekend brunches (hence the queues) and large portions. Almost too popular for its own good but a great spot to observe Vancouverites in their natural habitat.

Cafés
49th Parallel, 2152 W 4th Av, T604-420 4900. Roasted on site, the coffee here is just about perfect. The pastries are a revelation.

Calhoun's, 3035 W Broadway, T604-737 7062, open 24 hrs. A huge and lively coffee shop with a slightly rustic feel, serving coffee, juices, breakfasts and cakes.

Terra Breads, 2380 W 4th Av, T604-736 1838. The baking here is to die for. Breads, croissants, muffins, cakes and sandwiches to eat in or take away. Good coffee too.

South and east Vancouver *p32*
₤₤₤ Seasons in the Park, Queen Elizabeth Park, T604-874 8008. One of the most romantic, high-class choices in town, with a sumptuous interior and exquisite views. Fresh seafood and steak, good appetizers and brunch.

₤₤₤ Tojo's, 777 W Broadway, T604-872 8050. A favourite with visiting celebrities, the undisputed best (and most expensive) Japanese restaurant in Western Canada, with the freshest fish, best sake and most beautiful presentation. Recent renovations have made the interior even more impressive.

₤₤ Addis Café, 2017 Commercial Dr, T604-254 1929. There are many ethnic restaurants on the Drive, but most ultimately disappoint. This small, authentic Ethiopian-Eritrean eatery does not. Tasty food, good prices, and friendly service.

₤₤ Cascade Room, 2616 Main St, T604-709 8650. Very popular in the neighbourhood, especially with the 20- or 30-something crowd. The food is reliable – calamari, burgers, pizza – reasonably priced, in decent portions, and the drinks are very good.

₤₤ Havana, 1212 Commercial St, T604-253 9119. The food is nothing special and the service poor, but the busy patio is still the best place for soaking up the Drive's unique atmosphere.

₤₤ Les Faux Bourgeois, E. 15th Av near Fraser/Kingsway, T604-873 9733. A little out of the way, but totally worth it. All of your bistro faves like steak-frites, escargots, or duck confit, perfectly executed and reasoanbly priced. A cool, somewhat retro 1970s space, that's always packed, so book ahead.

♔♔ **Seb's Market Café**, 592 E Broadway, T604-298 4403. A casual, inviting bistro with an ever-changing menu of eclectic but consistently tasty dishes. Brunch is especially popular, and there's live jazz at weekends.

♔♔ **WaaZuBee Café**, 1622 Commercial Dr, T604-253 5299. Now somewhat dated, but still a comfortable, atmospheric space, dimly lit, with loud upbeat music. The food is fairly predictable, and nothing special, but the portions are large, there's a decent selection of drinks, and the overall experience is consistently positive.

♔ **Café Deux Soleils**, 2096 Commercial St, T604-254 1195. Spacious, downbeat and friendly, with a little play area. Frequently packed with young couples and families. Large portions of reasonably priced vegetarian food, best for breakfast.

♔ **Nice**, 154 E 8th Av, T604-874 4024. A quaint neighbourhood greasy spoon, cheap, cheerful, fast, friendly, and very popular.

Cafés

Continental Coffee, 1806 Commercial Dr Large, busy and dimly lit. Good prices for speciality coffees, beans roasted on site.

JJ Bean, Main/14th Av, and 2206 Commercial Dr. The nicest and busiest café on Main these days. Elegant but cosy inside, with armchairs by the wood fire. Roasted on site, the coffee is fresh and very tasty.

La Casa Gelato, 1033 Venables St, near Commercial Dr. Tucked away in this unlikely spot is Vancouver's finest ice cream emporium, with 218 wonderful (and often weird) flavours to choose from and servers who are pleased to let you taste before you buy.

The Prophouse Café, 1636 Venables, off Commercial Dr. A unique spot with a wonderful, friendly and laid-back ambience.

Put on a record if you like. There's some well-priced, tasty food items, but it's mostly about the coffee.

Turk's Coffee Lounge, 1276 Commercial Dr. A long-running contender for the best coffee in town. A small but elegant interior, and the outdoor seating area is great for people-watching.

North Shore *p33*

♔♔ **Burgoo**, 3 Lonsdale Av, T604-904 0933. Also at 3096 Main St, T604-873 1441; and 4434 W 10th Av, T604-221 7839. A quaint little place, handily close to the Quay, offering tasty soups, stews, sandwiches, and comfort food.

♔♔ **Raglan's Bistro**, 15 Lonsdale Av, T604-988 8203. Also close to the Quay and market, this place looks like a Hawaiian surfer-bar, and offers up some of Vancouver's tastiest burgers, as well as pulled-pork, and some fabulous brunch options. It's also a great place for a drink, including cocktails and Sapporo on tap.

♔ **The Raven**, 1052 Deep Cove Rd, T604-929 4335. Superb neighbourhood pub, with enormous portions of superior pub-style food, and an unfeasibly large selection of beers on tap.

🎧 Bars and clubs

Like most big cities, Vancouver offers something for everyone and has developed a reputation for excellent microbrewed beers and a panoply of funky, atmospheric little bistros and tapas bars (see Eating).

For the short-term visitor, there are more than enough nightclubs to check out. Those listed here tend to host DJs spinning different music every night. Most charge $5-10 for entry (cover), and drinks can be on the pricey side. These days Granville from Drake to Smithe is the place to be, its many clubs packed, with long queues at the weekends. Gastown is more genuinely trendy and Yaletown more sophisticated.

Look out for the quarterly magazine *Nitelife*. For more specific night-to-night details consult the indispensable *Georgia Straight* or the useful www.clubvibes.com. Details of gay bars are listed on page 47.

Downtown *p18, map p20*

Alibi Room, 157 Alexander St, Gastown, T604-623 3383. This 2-level, long-standing favourite is as hip and visually enticing as ever, minimalist, laid-back, and charming. The food, mostly small plates, is very good, as is brunch, but the real draw is the beer menu, which offers 19 draft and 3 cask beers, always changing.

Bacchus, 845 Hornby St, the **Wedgewood Hotel**, T604-608 5319. This plush restaurant is a wonderfully romantic place to splash out, and is excellent for brunch or afternoon tea. For most of us, though, it's best recommended as a fantastic venue for cocktails.

Barcelona Ultra Lounge, 1180 Granville St, T604-249 5151, www.barcelonanights.ca Based on boutique style clubs of Las Vegas and Miami, with a state-of-the-art sound system, and DJs spinning dance and hip hop.

Bar None, 1222 Hamilton St, Yaletown, T604-689 7000. Housed in a minimalist industrial warehouse space, all brick and wood, this uber-chic, New York-style club is a favourite with Yaletown's hip and wealthy urban elite, who come to dance and sip cocktails.

The Cambie, 300 Cambie St, Gastown, T604-684 6466. Gritty, down-to-earth and friendly, this huge, English-style boozer is understandably popular for its wide selection of cheap beer and food, pool tables and crowded summer patio.

Chambar, 562 Beatty St, T604-879 7119. For what it is, this celebrated restaurant strikes us as a bit overpriced, but it's still great for drinks, with a fine wine menu, and an unparalleled selection of craft bottled beers.

Chill Winston, 3 Alexander St, Gastown, T604-288 9575. In a prime location and effectively illuminated at night, the red-brick building is gorgeous. Spacious, dimly lit and packed to the gills, this is the place to be in Gastown. The island kitchen puts out good food and there are plenty of well- priced wines and beers on tap.

Fabric, 66 Water St, Gastown, T604-683 6695. A fantastic, recently renovated basement space with brick walls, wood floors and different areas for music, dancing and lounging. DJs play a variety of music ranging from house to hip-hop to reggae. One of the biggest and best clubs in town.

George Ultra Lounge & Wine Bar, 1137 Hamilton St, Yaletown, T604-628 5555. Sophisticated and chilled, specializing in cocktails and wines by the glass. Music runs from jazz and Motown to more modern beats.

Honey Lounge, 455 Abbott St, Gastown, T604-685 7777. This hip bar sucks you in with impossibly comfortable couches smothered in huge velvet cushions, and a good drinks menu. Dark, capacious and open plan with loud, conversation-killing music that creates a club-like atmosphere without the dancing.

The Irish Heather, 208 Carrall St, Gastown, T604-688 9779. Not quite the same since it changed location, but still full of character and charm, and very popular. Equally great for food or drinks. Their café next door is wonderful for breakfast, and boasts a 12-m communal table.

Lennox Pub, 800 Granville St, at Robson, T604-408 0881. Standard pub with some outstanding but overpriced beers. Located on Downtown's busiest corner, the small patio is an ideal spot for watching the city rush by.

Post Modern Dance Bar, 7 Alexander St, Gastown, T604-684 3044. A new club in a heritage building, fitted out with state-of-the-art sound and light systems, with top DJs spinning modern dance music. Great location next to **Chill Winston**, and comparatively reasonable drink prices.

The Railway Club, 579 Dunsmuir St, T604-681 1625. This upstairs bar is cosy and atmospheric, with lots of wood, knick-knacks and intimate corners. There's varied live music every night, sometimes with a cover charge.

Republic Nightclub, 958 Granville, T604-669 3266. A 2-level club featuring a dance floor with live music or DJs and a long bar, and a comfortable lounge upstairs with table service and a glassed-in patio.

Shine, 364 Water St, Gastown, T604-408 4321. Smart, colourful and intimate, with club and lounge areas, and varied DJ-led music, attracting a 20-30s crowd that's a bit more well-heeled than usual. One to dress up for.

Steamworks, 375 Water St, Gastown, T604-689 2739. Different bar and restaurant spaces cater to different tastes, but the real draw here is the range of fine beers brewed on site.

Subeez, 891 Homer St, T604-687 6107. An expansive venue, whose industrial-style decor features enough quirky details to intrigue, delight or repel.

VENUE Nightclub, 881 Granville St, T604-646 0064. Varied live music shows Mon-Thu, then DJs playing rock, pop and retro on Fri and Sat nights. The space is huge, with glam rock-inspired decor, plush velvet booths, a top-notch sound and light system, and huge dance floor.

West End to Stanley Park *p25, map p24*

Comox Long Bar and Grill, 1763 Comox St, T604-688 7711. Not much to look at, but a firm favourite with locals, and so a great place to experience Vancouverites in their natural habitat. Lots of food and drink specials, pool tables, and friendly service.

Morrissey Pub, 1227 Granville St, T604-682 0909. Big and stylish with a river-stone fireplace and lots of dark wood and leather. Choice of beers on tap, decent cheap food, DJs and nightly drink specials.

Granville Island to Point Grey
p28, map p24

Backstage Lounge, 1585 Johnston St, T604-687 1354, in the **Arts Club**. Great, airy spot with a lively patio, decent food and live music most nights.

Dockside Brewing Co, 1253 Johnston St in the **Granville Island Hotel**, T604-685 7070. Tucked away from the hordes, with comfy leather armchairs and fine in-house beers. The menu is mid-range with wood-oven pizza and seafood.

Kitsilano *p29, map p30*

The Fringe Café, 3124 W Broadway, T604-738 6977. Tiny, downbeat bar with a bohemian attitude.

Lou's Grill and Bistro, 3357 W Broadway, T604-736 9872. Large, trendy bar and restaurant with terracotta walls, interesting art and a patio. Dim lighting, jazzy music and a great selection of beer on tap.

South and East Vancouver *p32*

Eight ½, 151 E 8th Av, T604-568 2703. A cute neighbourhood pub in a heritage building, with a great beer selection, and superior food.

Habit, 2610 Main St, T604-877 8582. A South Main institution with a trendy 1970s retro look, imaginative variations on comfort food favourites, and a fine drinks menu featuring lots of beers, whiskeys, and DIY cocktails.

The Whip, 209 E 6th Av, T604-874 4687. Combining the look of a local art gallery with the sensibility of an English pub, this is a warm and welcoming space, whose food (especially brunch) is as good as its selection of local microbrewed beer on tap.

North Shore *p33*

The Raven, 1052 Deep Cove Rd, T604-929 3834. English-style pub with the best selection of draught beers in town, including 19 microbrews and 6 imports. Lots of malt whiskies and the food comes in mammoth portions. Live music once or twice a week. Understandably popular.

The Rusty Gull, 175 E 1st St, T604-988 5585. Lively neighbourhood pub with good ales on tap, food and frequent live music. Magical views of the city from the patio, with shipyards and derelict warehouses in the foreground.

Metro Vancouver *p16,*
maps p20, p24 and p30
The first place to look for weekly listings is the *Georgia Straight*, available free on most major streets. The visitor centre has a branch of **Ticketmaster**, T604-280 4444, www.ticket master.ca, through which tickets to most events are available, inlcuding sports; and **Tickets Tonight**, T604-280 4444, www.tickets tonight.ca, which has half-price same-day tickets for many events.

Art galleries

Apart from the major galleries already mentioned, Vancouver has a wealth of smaller spaces, usually highlighting the work of contemporary local artists. Details of commercial galleries, which are usually just as interesting, are included under Shopping (see page 51).

There are a few worthwhile artist-run galleries in Gastown, such as **Artspeak Gallery**, 233 Carrall St; and **Vancouver Access Artist Run Centre**, 206 Carrall St. Granville is good for commercial galleries and there is an active art scene on the North Shore. Elsewhere, the **Grunt Gallery**, 116-350 E 2nd Av, and **Or Gallery**, 208 Smithe St, usually have interesting displays. **Charles H Scott Gallery**, in the **Emily Carr Institute**, entrance by donation. Always has interesting, sometimes controversial, displays. **Contemporary Art Gallery**, 555 Nelson St, T604-681 2700, www.contemporaryart gallery.ca. Usually has 3 temporary exhibits. **Presentation House Gallery**, 333 Chesterfield Av. One of Vancouver's oldest and has a good reputation for its photography and media arts exhibitions. **Western Front**, 303 E 8th Av. Tends to exhibit video and performance art.

Cinemas

Cinemark Tinseltown, 88 W Pender St, 3rd Floor, T604-806 0799, www.cinemark. com. One of the best screens in town for 1st-run movies, and reasonably priced too. **Fifth Avenue Cinemas**, 2110 Burrard St, T604-734 7469, www.festivalcinemas.ca. Gets most of the mainstream international films, as well as the usual 1st-run items. **Granville 7 Cinemas**, 855 Granville St, T604-684 4000, www.empiretheatres.com. The most convenient downtown location, but small screens. **Hollywood**, 3123 W Broadway, T604-738 3211, www.hollywoodtheatre.ca. A great repertory theatre, screening double-bills of well-chosen films just off the 1st-run circuit at very reasonable prices. **Pacific Cinematheque**, 1131 Howe St, T604-688 3456, www.cinematheque.bc.ca. The main venue for repertory, independent, art-house, foreign, documentary, or just plain off-the-wall films. **Ridge Theatre**, 3131 Arbutus St/16th Av, T604-738 6311, www.ridgetheatre.com. Housed in a delightful 1950s building, this is another fabulous repertory cinema offering carefully selected double-bills at a bargain price. **VanCity Theatre**, 1181 Seymour St, T604-683 3456, www.vifc.org. State-of-the-art cinemascreening high-calibre international films.

Comedy

The Improv Centre, 1502 Duranleau St, Granville Island, T1888-222 6608 for tickets, www.vtsl.com. The new home of **Vancouver TheatreSports League**, world champions of comedy improvisation, has shows running Wed to Sat, and a bar lounge overlooking the marina. Half price on Thu.

Gay and lesbian

The **West End**, and **Davie St** in particular, is the most gay-friendly part of a very gay-friendly city and host of the summer **Gay Pride Celebration**. To find out what's going on pick up a copy of *XtraWest*, or check out www.gayvancouver.net. **Little Sister's Book and Art Emporium**, 1238 Davie St, is a gay and lesbian bookshop where you can get a free copy of the *Gay and Lesbian Business Association Directory*, www.glba.org.

1181, 1181 Davie St, T604-687 3991, www.tightlounge.com. An extremely hip and stylish lounge, that's unpretentious and casual. A great bar in its own right, which just happens to be gay-friendly.

Celebrities, 1022 Davie St, T604-681 6180, www.celebritiesnightclub.com. A very busy and exciting gay-friendly club, with state-of-the-art light and sound systems, a big dance floor, top DJs, theme nights, and speciality performers.

The Fountainhead Pub, 1025 Davie St, T604-687 2222, www.thefountainheadpub.com. Gay-friendly neighbourhood pub, with a heated and covered patio, and traditional pub food, including a popular weekend brunch.

Lick Club, 455 Abbott St, T604-710 7457. A nightclub/lounge that's the city's main lesbian venue, usually open Thu-Sat.

Numbers, 1042 Davie St, T604-685 4077, www.numbers.ca. Vancouver's longest-running gay bar. Karaoke and a heaving dance floor entertain a very cruisy, older denim/leather-type crowd.

Oasis Ultra Lounge, 1240 Thurlow St, T604-685 1724, www.oasisondavie.com. A cool, gay-friendly lounge for tapas, martinis and cocktails. The heated garden patio is a civilized place to unwind.

PumpJack Pub, 1167 Davie St, T604-685 3417, www.pumpjackpub.com. A friendly and casual pub that always has a large gay clientele. Sun afternoons are popular enough top generate line-ups.

Live music

For information on jazz performances, see www.vancouverjazz.com.

Backstage Lounge, Arts Club Theatre, 1585 Johnston, Granville Island, T604-687 1354. A small but atmospheric venue for local and/or progressive acts.

Cellar Jazz Club, 3611 W Broadway, T604-738 1959, www.cellarjazz.com. The principal jazz venue in town, with local or visiting musicians every night.

The Chan Centre for the Performing Arts, 6265 Crescent Rd, T604-822 2697, www.chancentre.com. Mostly dedicated to classical performances, this UBC venue has 3 stages in 1 complex; the main hall is among the city's finest.

Commodore Ballroom, 868 Granville St, T604-739 4550. A wonderful old venue with a 1000-seat capacity and a massive dance floor built on rubber tyres. One of the best and most popular venues for international touring acts.

Media Club, 695 Cambie, T604-608 2871, www.themediaclub.ca. A small, understated venue with plain black walls and a great sound. Hosts music, including occasional big names, almost every night.

O'Doul's, 1300 Robson St, T604-661 1400, www.odoulsrestaurant.com. An upmarket restaurant and bar in the **Listel Hotel**, hosting live jazz every night.

Orpheum Theatre, 884 Granville St, T604-665 3050. Probably the best venue in town for highbrow acts of all types (no dancing allowed). When it was built as a part of the vaudeville circuit in 1927, this 2800-seat venue was the largest theatre in Canada. The elegant Spanish baroque-style interior with its arches, tiered columns and marble mouldings was almost converted into a cinematic multiplex before the city intervened. Home to the **Vancouver Symphony Orchestra**, it hosts most major classical events.

Queen Elizabeth Theatre, Hamilton and Georgia streets, T604-299 9000. This 1960s modernist building with almost 3000 seats is one of the main venues for classical music but also hosts ballet, musicals and major rock and pop acts.

The Yale Hotel, 1300 Granville St, T604-681 9253, www.theyale.ca. A rough-looking bar that's the city's premier blues and R&B venue.

Spectator sports

General Motors Place, 800 Griffith Way. Home to the Canucks ice hockey team (www.canucks.com), a Vancouver obsession.

Nat Bailey Stadium, Queen Elizabeth Park, T604-872 5232. Home to the Canadians baseball team Jun-Sep (www.canadiansbaseball.com).

Pacific Coliseum, 100 Renfrew N/Hastings St E, at the **PNE**, T604-444 2687. Home to the Vancouver Giants junior hockey team (www.vancouvergiants.com).

Hastings Park Raceway, Renfrew N/ Hastings St E, at the **PNE**, T604-254 8823, www.hastingsparkcom. Has been hosting thoroughbred horse racing since 1889.

Theatre and performing arts

The main season for concerts, opera and ballet is Oct-Apr, but a number of festivals run continual shows throughout the summer (see opposite). As well as a lively theatre scene, Vancouver has achieved recognition for its dance scene. The 2 main areas for theatre are Granville Island (see page 28) and the Entertainment District of Downtown (see page 22).

Arts Club Granville Island Stage, 1585 Johnston St, T604-687 1644, www.artsclub.com. Small venue for casual theatre such as musical comedies.

The Centre in Vancouver for the Performing Arts, 777 Homer St, T604-602 0616, www.centreinvancouver.com. Opposite the main library, and designed by the same architect, this state-of-the-art theatre is Vancouver's main Broadway-type venue for large-scale and popular theatre, dance and musicals.

Firehall Arts Centre, 280 E Cordova St, T604-689 0926, www.firehallartscentre.ca. An operating fire hall from 1906-1975, the building now provides a small, intimate setting for quality dance and theatre.

Stanley Theatre, 2750 Granville St/12th Av, T604-687 5315. An elegantly restored 1931 cinema, now an Arts Club Theatre venue for drama, comedy or musicals.

Vancouver East Cultural Centre, 1895 Venables St, near Commercial Dr, T604-251 1363. This converted Methodist church is one of the best performance spaces in the city, thanks to great acoustics, sightlines and an intimate 350-seat capacity. It hosts a range of events including theatre, music and dance, with an emphasis on the modern and sometimes controversial.

Vancouver Playhouse, Hamilton St/ Dunsmuir St, T604-873 3311, www.vancouverplayhouse.com. Fairly intimate venue for mostly serious theatre, including many modern Canadian works.

❂ Festivals and events

Metro Vancouver *p16,*
maps p20, p24 and p30

Jan Polar Bear Swim, T604-665 3424. Every year on 1 Jan, since 1819, lunatic locals have proven themselves by starting the New Year with an icy dip at English Bay Beach. **PuSh International Performing Arts Festival**, T604-605 8284, www.pushfestival.ca. Takes place at numerous venues around town for 2 weeks at the end of Jan.

Feb Chinese New Year Festival, T604-632 3808, www.vancouver-chinatown.com. Held mid-month, this includes a massive parade in Chinatown, and numerous activities such as fortune telling, t'ai chi, music, crafts and demonstrations at the Dr Sun Yat-Sen Chinese Garden. **Winterruption at Granville Island**, T604-666 3619, www.winterruption.com. A 9-day creative celebration, featuring music, theatre, dance, film, food and the visual arts.

Mar CelticFest Vancouver, T604-683 8331, www.celticfestvancouver.com. A parade and 60 events, including food, crafts and lots of music, some of it free, for 5 days around

St Patrick's Day. **Vancouver Playhouse International Wine Festival**, T604-873 3311, www.playhousewinefest.com. Includes 60 events involving 1600 wines from 16 countries, for a week at the month's end.

Apr **Vancouver International Boat Show**, T604-678 8820, www.vancouverboatshow.ca. An excuse to see lots of boats.

May **International Children's Festival**, T604-708 5655, www.childrensfestival.ca. Runs for a week in mid-May and involves a host of shows, events and activities to delight the youngsters in Vanier Park.

Cloverdale Rodeo, T604-576 9461, www.cloverdalerodeo.com. The 2nd biggest festival of its kind in the west after the Calgary Stampede (see page), attracting cowboys from all over the continent.

Jun **Eat! Vancouver Food and Cooking Festival**, T604-689 8654, www.eat-vancouver.com. Brings 3 days of culinary obsession to the new Covention Centre at Canada Place. **Vancouver Storytelling Festival**, www.vancouverstorytelling.org. Check website for dates and venue of this popular 3-day event. **Rio Tinto Alcan Dragon Boat Festival**, T604-688 2382, www.dragonboatbc.ca. 3 days of racing and cultural activities on False Creek.

International Jazz Festival, T604-872 5200, www.coastaljazz.ca. A major festival involving 400 concerts on 40 stages around town over 10 days. Also includes free shows.

Jun-Aug **Pride Season**, T604-687 0955, www.vancouverpride.ca. Culminates in the Gay Pride Parade in late July, a massive party that moves down Denman to Beach Av and on to the main party zone, Sunset Beach on English Bay.

Jun-Sep **Bard on the Beach Skakespeare Festival**, T604-739 0559, www.bardonthebeach.org. 4 months of the master's plays under tents in Vanier Park.

Jul **Dancing on the Edge Festival**, Firehall Arts Centre, T604-689 0926, www.dancingontheedge.org. Canada's largest showcase of independent choreographers runs for 10 days at the beginning of the month.

Vancouver Folk Music Festival, T604-602 9798, www.thefestival.bc.ca. Has been going for over 30 years and involves 3 days of music and storytelling at Jericho Beach and other venues. **Theatre Under the Stars**, T604-687 0714, www.tuts.ca. A month of classic musicals in Stanley Park's Malkin Bowl.

Aug **Celebration of Light**, T604-738 4304, www.celebration-of-light.com. An international fireworks competition held on 3 non-consecutive nights at the beginning of the month. The most popular places to watch it from are the West End beaches and Vanier Park. **MusicFest Vancouver**, T604-688 1152, www.musicfestvancouver.ca. 10 days of concerts at various venues around town, featuring hundreds of classical, jazz and world musicians. **Vancouver Chinatown Festival**, T604-632 3808, www.vancouver-chinatown.com. A free 2-day block-party featuring all manner of entertainment, with lots for kids. **Powell Street Festival**, T604-739 9388, www.powellstreetfestival.com. 2011 will mark the 35th anniversary of this 2-day event, which celebrates the city's Japanese community. **Abbotsford International Air Show**, T604-852 8511, www.abbotsfordairshow.com. Held on the 2nd weekend in Aug, this is the 2nd-largest air show in North America. Aircraft from around the world compete and perform.

Vancouver Queer Film Festival, T604-844 1615, www.queerfilmfestival.ca. For 2 weeks starting mid-month, 200 films are screened mainly at Tinseltown and Empire Granville.

PNE Fair at the Pacific National Exhibition, T604-253 2311, www.pne.ca. Includes live entertainment, exhibits, livestock and the Playland Amusement Park.

Sep **Vancouver International Fringe Festival**, T604-257 0350, www.vancouverfringe.com. Performances by an eclectic mix of over 80 international theatre companies in indoor and outdoor venues over 11 days. Voted the city's best arts festival 5 years in a row.

Oct Vancouver International Film Festival, T604-685 0260, www.viff.org. For 16 days at the start of the month, the city's many screens host over 300 films from 50 countries, celebrating cultural diversity and the art of cinematography. **Vancouver ComedyFest**, T604-683 0881, www.vancouvercomedyfest. com. 11 days of stand-up, improv shows and free street entertainment on Granville Island.

Dec Festival of Lights, T604-736 6754, www.vandusengarden.org. For most of Dec the VanDusen Gardens are illuminated with 20,000 lights and seasonal displays.

O Shopping

Metro Vancouver *p16, maps p20, p24 and p30*

Antiques
Many antique, junk and consignment shops are clustered on stretches of South Main and South Granville. There are also many on Richards between Hastings and Pender.

Arts and crafts
Gastown has some interesting galleries but the best place for art-seeking is Granville Island. Cartwright St contains some of the key galleries and Net Loft, opposite the public market, also houses many fine shops. Railspur Alley is a nucleus for small and unique artists' studios. South Granville is the best place to pick up works by established artists.

Art Emporium, 2928 Granville St, T604-738 3510. Open since 1897, selling big-name domestic and international artists from the famous Group of Seven to Picasso.

Buschlen-Mowatt Fine Arts, 1445 W Georgia St, T604-682 1234. Knowledgeable staff and an extensive collection.

Crafthouse Gallery, No 1386 Cartwright St, T604-687 7270. Collection of quality work including pottery, textiles and jewellery.

Equinox, No 2321 Granville St, T604-736 2405. Contemporary Canadian and international art, as equally revered as **Art Emporium**.

Federation Gallery, 1241 Cartwright St, T604-681 8534. Operated by members of the Federation of Canadian Artists.

Industrial Artifacts, 132 Powell St, T604-874 7797. A stunning collection of furniture and art, ingeniously fashioned from reclaimed pieces of old industrial machinery.

Monte Clark Gallery, 2339 Granville St, T604-730 5000. Specializes in avant-garde paintings, prints and photography.

Potters' Guild of BC, 1359 Cartwright St, T604-669 3606, www.bcpotters.com. Large selection of top-notch pottery that changes monthly.

Books
The best selection of new books can be found at **Chapters**, 2505 Granville St, T604-731 7822, and the more likeable **Duthie Books**, 2239 W 4th Av, T604-732 5344. For second-hand books try **Macleod's Books**, 455 W Pender St, T604-681 7654, and **Pulp Fiction Books**, 2422 Main St, T604-876 4311. **The Travel Bug**, 3065 W Broadway, T604-737 1122 or **Wanderlust**, 1929 W 4th Av, T604-739 2182 stock travel books and accessories, and **Does Your Mother Know?**, 2139 W 4th Av, T604-730 1110, is the place for magazines and newspapers, they carry a wide range including some internationals. **Granville Book Co**, 850 Granville St, T604-687 2213. A wide selection of interesting books and magazines, great for browsing and open till midnight.

Little Sister's Book and Art Emporium, 1238 Davie St. A gay and lesbian bookshop where you can get a free copy of the **Gay and Lesbian Business Association Directory**. **Tanglewood Books**, 2932 W Broadway, T604-731 8870. A second-hand bookshop specializing in non-fiction.

Clothes and accessories

Most big name fashion and shoe boutiques are situated on Robson St between Burrard and Jervis, or nearby in the gigantic **Pacific Centre Mall** at Georgia St and Howe St. Granville St is good for off-the-wall new and used clothing and footwear shops. More exclusive designer labels are found in gorgeous heritage buildings on and around W Hastings St between Burrard St and Richards St. South Main is the area for more original boutiques, many showcasing local designers, such as **Eugene Choo**, No 3683, T604-873 8874; **Pleasant Girl/Motherland**, No 2539, T604-876 3426; and **Smoking Lily**, No 3634, T604-873 5459. There's also 4th Av west of Burrard in Kitsilano. For those interested in retro clothing, head to Gastown and the shops around W Cordova St including **Deluxe Junk Co** at No 310, T604-685 4871.

The Bay, 674 Robson St, T604-681 6211. Forever having sales, bargains can often be found.

LuluLemon Athletica, 1148 Robson St, T604-681 3118. Sells unique items designed for sports and yoga, but is phenomenally popular for fashion.

Pharsyde, 860 Granville, T604-683 5620. Stocks hip, casual clothing, and shoes for men and women.

First Nations arts and crafts

The best place to start looking for native art is on Water St in Gastown.

Hill's Native Art, 165 Water St, T604-685 4249, www.hillsnativeart.com. Contains 3 floors of Northwest Coast arts and crafts, including some spectacular pieces.

Inuit Gallery, 206 Cambie St, T604-688 7323, www.inuit.com. North America's leading Inuit art gallery, with very beautiful modern and traditional sculpture and prints.

Spirit Wrestler Gallery, 47 Water St, T604-669 8813, www.spiritwrestler.com. Works by major artists of various First Nations, with some very high-class pieces of sculpture.

Gifts

For touristy souvenirs head to Water St in Gastown. For more unusual ideas check out the speciality shops on 4th Av in Kitsilano.

Obsessions, 595 Howe St, T604-684 0748; 1124 Denman, T604-605 8890. A wide range of gift ideas.

The Postcard Place Net Loft, Granville Island, T604-684 6909. Has the city's best selection of postcards.

Salmagundi West, 321 W Cordova, T604-681 4648. For something more off the wall. This is a really fun shop, packed with eccentric oddities, toys and tit-bits.

Vancouver Art Gallery Shop, 750 Hornby St, T604-662 4706. Has lots of inspiringly beautiful items.

Kids

Kidsbooks, 3038 W Broadway, T604-738 5335; **The Games People**, 123 Carrie Cates Ct, North Vancouver, T604-986 5110; **It's all Fun and Games**, 1832 Commercial St, T604-253 6727; and **The Toybox**, 3002 W Broadway, T604-738 4322, are all shops dedicated to children.

Kid's Market, 1496 Cartwright St, Granville Island, T604-689 8447. Contains 25 shops just for children. Many of the toys and clothes here are one-offs, educational and handmade locally.

Markets

The best place for food shopping is the **Granville Island Public Market**, T604-666 6477, a mouth-watering high-end food hall and produce market open daily 0900-1900.

Lonsdale Quay Market, T604-985 6261, www.lonsdalequay.com, where the SeaBus arrives at the North Shore, is a good second choice and is open daily 0900-1830.

Vancouver Flea Market, 703 Terminal Av, off Main St, T604-685 0666. For bargain-hunting.

Vancouver Chinatown Night Market, Keefer and Main, T604-682 8998, www.vcma.shawbiz.ca, May-Sep Fri-Sun 1830-2300. In our opinion, the only unmissable shopping experience in town, featuring hundreds of booths offering just about everything, including food.

Music
A&B Sound, 556 Seymour St, T604-687 5837. Best deals on new music. Large selection and listen before you buy.
Zulu, 1972 W 4th Av, T604-738 3232. Good selection of new and used music of all kinds, with an emphasis on modern or alternative sounds.

Photography
Dunne & Rundle, 305-595 Burrard, T604-681 9254, and **Lens & Shutter**, 549 Howe St, T604-669 4696; 2912 W Broadway, T604-736 3461, carry new and used equipment.

Sports equipment
The biggest sports equipment shops are grouped together around W Broadway and Cambie and this is also the area for ski and snowboard shops, such as **Pacific Boarder**, 1793 W 4th Av, T604-734 0212. For a great selection of used equipment head for **Sports Junkies**, 102 W Broadway, T604-879 6000, or **Cheapskates**, 3644 W 16th, T604-222 1125; and 3208, 3228 and 3496 Dunbar.
Coast Mountain Sports, 2201 W 4th, T604-731 6181. The other biggest and best all-round supplier.
Mountain Equipment Co-op, 130 W Broadway, T604-872 7858. Has the widest and best selection. Often has great deals but you'll have to buy a $5 membership first though.
Sigge's Sport Villa, 2077 W 4th Av, T604-731 8818. Has the biggest selection of cross-country equipment and offers lessons and rentals.
Sport Mart, 735 Thurlow St, T604-683 2433. For general supplies.

▲▲ Activities and tours

Metro Vancouver *p16, maps p20, p24 and p30*
Adventure tours
For general information visit www.bca dventure.com For impartial, enthusiasts' information on just about any outdoor pursuit in BC, visit www.trailpeak.com.
Lotus Land Tours, T604-684 4922, www.lotuslandtours.com. Offers a broad range of activity-based tours including eagle watching, snowshoeing, whale watching, rafting, sea kayaking and hikes.
Moose Travel Network, T604-777 9905, www.moosenetwork.com. Runs a wide selection of 2- to 25-day tours around BC departing from hostels, aimed at young, independent travellers. The Whistler 'Sea to Sky Pass' costs $62, while trips around BC and the Rockies cost from $259 for 4 days to $729 for 13-14 days, including tax.

Birdwatching
George C Reifel Migratory Bird Sanctuary, Westham Island, Richmond, T604-946 6980, www.ducks.ca/reifel. Daily 0900-1600, $5, child $3. A 360-ha sanctuary in the Fraser River for thousands of birds on their way from Mexico to Alaska. There's a good viewing tower close to the car park. Shore birds start arriving in mid-Aug, followed by mallard and pintail ducks. Numbers rise during Sep-Oct, and peak in early Nov, when about 20,000 snow geese noisily arrive. Many birds remain all winter. Nesting occurs Apr-May.

Boating/fishing
Granville Island has plenty of operators. Check the **Charter Information Centre** by the Maritime Market for information and **Granville Island Boat Rentals**, behind Bridges Restaurant, T604-682 6287.
Bites-on Salmon Charters, 200-1128 Hornby St, T604-688 2483, www.bites-on.com. 10-hr guided fishing tours.

Coal Harbour Boat Rentals, 1525 Coal Harbour Quay, T604-682 6257, www.boatrent.ca. Speed-boat rentals.

Boat tours

Accent Cruises, 100-1676 Duranleau St, T604-688 6625, www.champagnecruises.com. Sunset dinner cruise, 1745-2015, $60.

False Creek Ferries 1804 Boatlift Lane, T604-684 7781, www.granvilleislandferries.bc.ca. Runs tours every 15 mins, $10, child $6 for 40 mins, or $7/4 for 20 mins. Tours can be joined at any stop en route.

Harbour Cruises, north tip of Denman St, T604-688 7246, www.boatcruises.com. Tours include the sunset dinner cruise, 2½ hrs, $75; Indian Arm luncheon cruise, 4 hrs, $65; and Vancouver harbour tour, 1 hr, $30.

Bus tours

Grayline, T604-879 3363, www.grayline.com. Bus tours anywhere. Tour Vancouver in a double-decker bus.

Vancouver Trolley, 875 Terminal Av, T604-801 5515, www.vancouvertrolley.com, daily 0900-1430, $38, under 18s $35, under 12s $20. 2-hr trolleybus tours with 23 stops and on-off privileges. Starts in Gastown.

Climbing

Cliffhanger Indoor Rock Climbing

Centre, 670 Industrial Av, T604-874 2400, www.cliffhangerclimbing.com. Over 4500 sq m of climbing terrain with views of the North Shore Mountains. Programs and courses for ages 6 and up. For the best climbing nearby, head to Squamish.

Cycling

Possibly the best way to discover Vancouver is by riding the 28-km sea wall trail (see page 27).

There are a lot of 1st-class, hard-core mountain bike trails around Vancouver, not for the inexperienced. The 3 main areas are Cypress, Seymour and Fromme Mountains. Seymour is probably the least difficult trail

but Burnaby Mountain and Fisherman Trail are more appropriate rides for intermediates and beginners. Trail maps of these areas, along with some much-needed advice, are available at bike shops. See also *Mountain Biking BC* by Steve Dunn. For professional information or tours contact **Bush Pilot Biking**, www.bushpilotbiking.com. Note that by law you must wear a helmet.

There are a number of rental shops, such as **Simon's Bike Shop**, 608 Robson St, T604-602 1181, **Bicycle Sports Pacific**, 1380 Burrard St, T604-682 5437, and **On Top Bike Shop**, 3051 Lonsdale Av, T604-990 9550.

Bayshore Bicycle Rentals, 745 Denman St, T604-688 2453. For rollerblades and pushchairs.

Spokes Bicycle Rentals, 1798 W Georgia St, T604-688 5141. Road bikes, tandems, child trailers and baby joggers.

Golf

There are some excellent golf courses in and around Vancouver, the best are situated outside the city and a handful are listed below. Those closer to town are **Fraserview**, 7800 Vivian Dr, T604-280 1818; **McCleery**, 7188 MacDonald St, T604-257 8191; and **University Golf Club** at UBC, 5185 University Blvd, T604-224 7799.

Meadow Gardens, Pitt Meadows to the east, T604-465 5474. Constructed by Les Furber and aimed at experienced players.

Morgan Creek, T604-531 4653. The par-73 home to BC's CPGA. Course designed by Arnold Palmer which includes a 14-ha wildlife refuge. Set in naturally attractive landscape.

Westwood Plateau, in Coquitlam, T604-694 1223. Famed for its spectacular natural features and mountain setting.

Hiking

For a short walk, it's hard to beat sections of the sea wall promenade, especially around Stanley Park, or west from Vanier Park. For something longer, hiking in the Coast

Mountains on the North Shore is prime (see page 55), but even better trails are found further north around Squamish, Whistler and Garibaldi.

Natural Trekking, T604-836 2321, www.naturaltrekking.com. Offers hikes and snowshoeing around Vancouver.

Kayaking

The best local kayaking is up Indian Arm, reached from Deep Cove. This 30-km fjord reaches deep into the Coast Mountains, passing old-growth forest and waterfalls, with ample chance to view wildlife.

The second-best local starting point is Bowen Island, from where the 8 Paisley Islands can be visited as a day trip. English Bay and False Creek offer mellow paddling in the heart of the city. For rapids, head for the Capilano and Seymour rivers. The following companies offer rentals and 3-hr lessons or tours for around $65.

Bowen Island Sea Kayaking, T604-947 9266, www.bowenisland kayaking.com.

Deep Cove Canoe and Kayak, 2156 Banbury Rd, North Vancouver, T604-929 2268, www.deepcovekayak.com.

Ecomarine Ocean Kayak Centre, 1668 Duranleau St, Granville Island; 1700 Beach Av, English Bay; 1500 Discovery, Jericho Beach; T604-689 7575, www.ecomarine.com.

Takaya Tours, 3093 Ghum-Lye Dr, North Vancouver, T604-904 7410, www.takaya tours.com. Runs trips up Indian Arm from Deep Cove with First Nations guides.

Sailing

The Yellow Pages is full of luxury yacht cruises. For something more authentic, **Cooper's Boating Centre**, 1620 Duranleau St, T604-687 4110, www.cooperboating.com; or just shop around in this part of Granville Island.

Jericho Sailing Centre, Jericho Beach, T604-224 4177, www.jsca.bc.ca. Arranges trips, lessons, and rentals.

Simplicity Sailing Charters, north end of Denman St, T604-765 0074, www.simplicity sailingcharters.com. Offers sailing tours from $400 for 3 hrs.

Scuba-diving

Whytecliffe Park at the western tip of the North Shore, Cates Park in Deep Cove and Porteau Cove on Highway 99, are all renowned underwater reserves. **BC Dive and Kayak Adventures**, 1695 W 4th Av, T604-732 1344, www.bc dive.com, and **Rowand's Reef Dive Team**, 1512 Duranleau St, Granville Island, T604-669 3483, www.rowands reef.com, are recommended for courses, trips and rentals.

Diving Locker, 2745 W 4th Av, T604-736 2681, www.divinglocker.ca. PADI diving instructors for 30 years. Offer all-inclusive beginners' courses starting at $380. A wide range of advanced courses available, as well as 2- and 3-day dive trips. Sunday Safari day trips start at $75, all gear included.

Skiing

There is perfectly good skiing for all levels at **Grouse Mountain** (see page 34), **Cypress Mountain** (see page 35), and **Mount Seymour** (see page 34). The former in particular is a lively destination with lots of winter and summer activities for the whole family. Those with more time and/or experience, however, should note that Whistler-Blackcomb – just a few hours to the north (see page 69) – is infinitely superior.

Swimming

The 2 best swimming spots in town are the large open-air pool at Kits Beach (see page 29) and the heated saltwater pool in the **Vancouver Aquatic Centre**, 1050 Beach Av, T604-665 3424. The latter also contains a fitness centre.

Walking tours

Architecture Institute of BC, 100-440 Cambie St, T604-683 8588 ext 333, www.aibc.ca. 6 different guided architectural tours, Jul-Aug, Tue-Sat: Gastown, Chinatown, Downtown, West End, False Creek North/Yaletown. Tours start 1300, $10 per person.

⊖ Transport

Metro Vancouver *p16,*
maps p20, p24 and p30

Air

For airport details, see page 17; for flight information see Essentials, page 6.

Sample one-way fares from Vancouver in the summer are: $79 to **Kelowna** with West-Jet; $134 to **Castlegar** (for Nelson) with **Air Canada**; $129 to **Calgary** with West Jet; $195 to **Whitehorse** with **Air North**; $79 to **Victoria** with **Air Canada**, **West Coast Air** and **Pacific Coastal**; $62 to **Powell River** (Sunshine Coast) with **Pacific Coastal**.

Airline offices **Air Canada**, 1030 W Georgia, T1888-247 2262; **American**, T1800- 433 7300; **British Airways**, T1800-247 9297; **Continental**, T1800-2310856; **KLM**, T1800- 225 2525; **Lufthansa**, T1800-563 5954; **Qantas**, T1800-227 4500; **WestJet**, T1800-538 5696.

It is sometimes cheaper to book flights with a travel agent. **Flight Centre**, with many branches including 505 Burrard St, T1866-209 3282, and 1232 Davie St, T1866-246 2913, www.flightcentre.ca, is cheap and useful, as is **Travel Cuts**, 3065 W Broadway, T604-659 2870, www.flightcuts.com.

Floatplanes Fly to Victoria's Inner Harbour from Downtown (by Canada Place) or from the airport. The cost is about $140, saving at least an hour of bus time. **West Coast Air**, T604-606 6800, www.westcoastair.com, and **Harbour Air**, T604-274 1277, www.harbour-air.com.

Bus

Local Vancouver's relatively narrow streets make bus travel slow, and the system is not geared towards visitors,with few bus stops or vehicles carrying information. Think about buying a transit map, check online, or ask the usually friendly and helpful drivers. When boarding, drop the exact fare into a machine, which does not give change. If you have bought a ticket in the last 90 mins (time of expiry is on the ticket), feed it into the machine, which will give it back. Most routes run until 2400/0100.

There is also a transit service for the disabled called **HandyDART**. It mainly runs Mon-Fri 0630-1900, but for more information and booking call T604-430 2692. Additional information on all services, including maps and timetables for individual routes is available at the visitor centre, public libraries and SkyTrain ticket booths.

Long distance Buses and trains all leave from the VIA Rail Pacific Central Station, 1150 Station St, in a grim but handy part of town near the Main St/Terminal Av intersection and the Science World SkyTrain Station.

Greyhound, T604-482 8747, www.grey hound.ca, has connections to most Canadian towns and to Seattle. The following prices are one-way for adult/child and times are approx. Discounts are up to 50% if bought 21 days ahead, 25% 14 days ahead, and 10% 7 days ahead. Tickets are also cheaper when bought online. Look out for other discounts, such as 'City Pair Specials' between popular destinations. There are 5 daily buses to **Banff** (13½ hrs, $124); 4 to **Calgary** (15 hrs, $90); 2 to **Jasper** (11 hrs, $124); 5 to **Kamloops** (5 hrs, $58); 6 to **Kelowna** (6 hrs, $65); 1 to **Nelson** (12 hrs, $118); 3 to **Prince George** (12½ hrs, $86); 3 to **Toronto** (69 hrs, $214); and 7 to **Whistler** (2½ hrs, $25).

Pacific Coach Lines, T604-662 8074, www.pacificcoach.com, runs to **Victoria** from the bus station, $42 one-way, or airport, $49, including ferry (almost hourly); and to **Whistler** and **Squamish**, from various downtown hotels (eg Hotel Vancouver) $55 one-way, $67 from the airport.

TransLink

TransLink, T604-953 3333, www.trans link.ca, operates a reasonable network of city buses, a fast and generally efficient elevated rail system called the **SkyTrain**, and a passenger ferry between Waterfront SkyTrain Station and North Vancouver's Lonsdale Quay called the **SeaBus**. Tickets bought on these are valid for any number of journeys in any direction on all three within a 90-minute period. The system is divided into three fare zones, with Zone 1 covering almost everything of interest.

Fares are $2.50 for one zone, $3.75 for two and $5 for three. Concession fares (under 14 and over 65) are $1.75, $2.50 and $3.50. After 1830 and at weekends and holidays, tickets for all zones are $2.50/1.75. A day pass is $9/7. A FareSaver book of 10 tickets is $21/$17. Transit maps are posted on most bus shelters or are available at the visitor centre ($2), which also offers a free guide to reaching major attractions.

Perimeter Whistler Express, T604-266 5386, www.perimeterbus.com, runs 5 services daily during the ski season to Whistler and Squamish from the major hotels, $50 one-way, and the airport, $63. **Malaspina Coach Line**, T1877-227 8287, www.malaspinacoach.com, runs 2 buses daily to **Powell River** on the Sunshine Coast (6 hrs, $63, $75 from the airport).

Moose Travel Network, T604-7779905, www.moosenetwork.com, is the simplest way to get around BC and the Rockies. At least 16 different routes, mostly starting and ending in Vancouver, cover most itineraries. You can hop on and off and there are few time limits. Travel is in 11- to 24-seat mini-coaches, with lots of activities on the way.

To/from USA Greyhound, T1800-231 2222, runs 5 daily buses between **Seattle** and Vancouver (4 hrs, $29 one-way). The **Quickshuttle**, T1800-665 2122, www.quickcoach.com, also connects Vancouver with Downtown **Seattle**, 5 services daily from Downtown, stopping at the airport (4 hrs, $43/$20 one-way).

Car

For advice on travelling by car, including the cost of rental, see Essentials, page 8. All the major car hire agencies have offices downtown and at the airport. **Avis**, T604-606 2869; **Budget**, T604-668 7000; **Hertz**, T604-

606 4711; and **Thrifty**, T604-606 1666, offer a one-way service. **Rent-a-wreck**, T604-688 0001, rents minivans which you can sleep in. **RV Rentals** One-way RV rentals, often just to Calgary: **Candan**, T604-530 3645, www.candan.com; **Cruise Canada**, T604-946 5775, www.cruisecanada.com; and **Go West**, T604-528 3900, www.go-west.com.

Ferry

Local SeaBus ferries leave every 15 mins and take 12 mins to make the journey across Burrard Inlet from Waterfront Station to Lonsdale Market. They are wheelchair accessible and can carry bikes. 2 private ferry companies run services on False Creek. **Aquabus** T604-689 5858, www.theaqua bus.com, runs from the south end of Hornby St to Science World, stopping at the Arts Club on Granville Island, the end of Davie St in Yaletown and behind Monk McQueens at Stamp's Landing, $3.25 to $6.50 one-way. The little blue **False Creek Ferries**, T604-684 7781, www.granvilleislandferries. bc.ca, run from the Maritime Museum in Vanier Park to Science World, stopping at the Aquatic Centre on Beach Av, Granville Island Public Market, Stamp's Landing and BC Place, also charging from $3.25 to $6.50; $2.50-5 one-way.

Long distance BC Ferries, www.bc ferries.ca, run from Tsawwassen, about 30 km south of Vancouver, to **Victoria** (0700-2100, 95 mins), **the Southern Gulf Islands** and **Nanaimo** (0630-2100, 95 mins). To get to the ferry terminal from Downtown, take the Skytrain to Bridgeport Station, then bus No 620 ($5). Horseshoe Bay, some 15 km northwest of the city on Highway 99, is a far nicer terminal and much more convenient for Nanaimo, as well as **Bowen Island** and the **Sunshine Coast**. It is connected to Downtown by buses No 250 and No 257 ($3.75).

SkyTrain
A much better and faster service than the bus, but only a few stops are really useful for tourists: Waterfront in the old Canadian Pacific Station next to Canada Pl; Burrard at Burrard/Dunsmuir; Granville, beneath the Bay on Granville St; Science World-Main St; and Broadway at the Broadway/Commercial junction. The new Canada Line, built for the 2010 Olympics, now connects Downtown, via Yaletown, with the airport and gets you half way to Tsawwassen ferry terminal; a wonderful addition.

Taxi
Taxis are well regulated and compare favourably with public transport prices. After midnight they are about the only way to get around. The main companies are **Black Top/Checker Cabs**, T604-731 1111, and **Yellow Cab Co**, T604-681 1111.

Train
Canada's run-down train service is slower and more expensive than the bus. Trains leave from the **VIA Rail Pacific Central Station**, 1150 Station St. VIA Rail's **The Canadian**, T1888-842 7245, www.viarail.ca, connects Vancouver with **Toronto** (82 hrs) via **Kamloops** (9½ hrs, $96) and **Jasper** (18½ hrs, $200), leaving Fri, Sun and Tue. **Amtrak**, T1800-872 7245, www.amtrak.com, runs 5 daily trains to Seattle (3½ hrs, $40).

Directory

Metro Vancouver *p16,*
maps p20, p24 and p30
Banks
Finding an ATM in Vancouver is never a problem. The main Canadian banks are clustered in a few blocks around Burrard St and Georgia St. **Currency exchange Thomas Cook**, 777 Dunsmuir St in the Pacific Centre Mall; **Custom House** 999 West Hastings St or 355 Burrard St.

Emergencies
24-hr Crisis Centre, T604-872 3311; **BC Women's Hospital and Health Centre**, T604-875 2424; **Fire and Rescue**, T604-665 6000; **Police**, 2120 Cambie St, T911, T604-717 3321 (non-emergency); **Rape Crisis Centre**, T604-255 6344; **Women's Shelter**, T604- 872 8212.

Medical services
A & B2 Dental Clinic, 2561 Commercial Dr, T604-877 0664; **Care-Point Medical Centres**, 1123 Davie, T604-915 9517; 1175 Denman St, T604-681 5338; 711 W Pender, T604-687 4858; 1623 Commercial St, T604-254 5554; www.carepoint.ca, 0900-2000 but hours vary. **St Paul's Hospital**, 1081 Burrard St, T604-682 2344; **Travel Clinic**, L5 601 W Broadway, T604-736 9244; **Vancouver General Hospital**, 855 W 12th St, T604-875 4111.
Pharmacies London Drugs, 710 Granville St, 1187 Robson St, 665 Broadway and 1650 Davie St (24-hr); **Shoppers Drug Mart**, Pacific Centre at 700 Georgia St, 1006 Homer St, 1020 Denman St, 1125 Davie St, 2302 W 4th.

Post office
Canada Post The main post office with General Delivery (Poste Restante) is at 395 W Georgia. Others are at 595 Burrard St, 418 Main St, 732 Davie St. Letters can be posted at major pharmacies.

Contents

British Colombia

TransCanada and Crowsnest highways

Heading east from Vancouver, Highway 1 splits in three at Hope. Highway 5 (the Coquihalla Highway) is a high-speed, less attractive route to Kamloops (or Kelowna via Highway 97C). Highway 1 (the TransCanada) is the most direct route to the Rockies; there are few reasons to stop but it's a beautiful drive through some wonderfully varied landscapes: the steep walls and thrashing water of the Fraser Canyon; the arid vistas of the Thompson Valley; weirdly shaped expanses of water in the Shuswap; and increasingly sublime mountain scenery in the Columbia Mountains. Highway 3 – the Crowsnest – is mostly scenic with some boring stretches. It skirts the US border, offering direct access to Nelson (West Kootenays) and Osoyoos (Okanagan), with a few highlights of its own, such as Manning Provincial Park and the ski villages of Rossland and Fernie.

Ins and outs

Getting there and around

There are airports offering internal flights in Kamloops, **Kamloops Airport** ① *6 km northwest of town, T250-376 3613, www.kamloopsairport.com*, Castlegar and Cranbrook. **Greyhound** runs four buses daily between Vancouver and Calgary, serving most of the destinations in this section, as well as Banff; and two daily buses from Vancouver to the Alberta border, serving most of the Crowsnest Highway destinations in this chapter. The route is Vancouver to Hope (Highway 1) to Merritt (Highway 5) to Kelowna (Highway 97C) to Rock Creek (Highway 33) to the Alberta Border (Highway 3) via Nelson. **Via Rail** ① *T1800-561 8630, www.viarail.ca*, runs trains from Vancouver to Jasper via Kamloops three times a week. ▸▸ *See Transport, page 79.*

Tourist information

All but the smallest towns on these routes have visitor information centres. The most useful are in Hope, Kamloops, Revelstoke, Salmon Arm and Castlegar, and at the Highway 5/Highway 5A junction at Merritt.

TransCanada Highway → *For listings, see pages 68-80.*

Vancouver to Hope

The string of sprawling suburbs that line the TransCanada as it follows the Fraser River east from Vancouver barely lets up until you clear Chilliwack, some 120 km from Downtown. This suburban corridor is the main artery of the Lower Mainland, which contains most of BC's population. The first real diversion, north to **Harrison Hot Springs**, is only really worthwhile during the annual Festival of the Arts in July. A quicker, easier diversion is to the spectacular **Bridal Veil Falls**, a 15-minute leg-stretch reached via exit 135.

Most people drive right past **Hope** on their way somewhere else, but there's some good hiking and biking around, including the **Othello Quintette Tunnels**, a 90-m-deep solid granite wall that was blasted through in 1911 as part of the Kettle Valley Railway (see page). Ask for details at the **Hope Museum and Visitor Centre** ① *919 Water Av, T604-869 2021, www.travelthecanyon.com.*

Fraser Canyon

Between Hope and Lytton, the tumultuous Fraser River's massive volume of water is forced through a narrow channel between the sheer rock faces of the Cascade and Coast mountains, gouging out a steep, awe-inspiring canyon. Since the Fraser was the only river in southern BC to penetrate the mountain barrier, road and railway builders were obliged to follow this unlikely route. By either means, the journey is breathtaking.

The prettiest part of this spectacular drive is around tiny **Yale**, which is surrounded by sheer cliffs. It's hard to believe but, during the Fraser Valley Gold Rush, this sleepy village of less than 200 was a steamship navigation capital and one of North America's largest cities, with a population of over 20,000. You can find out all about it at the small **Yale Museum** ① *31187 Douglas St, T250-863 2324, www.historicyale.ca, May-Sep daily 1000-1700, by donation,* on the highway. Also here is the summer-only visitor information booth.

Fraser River reaches its awesome crescendo at **Hell's Gate**, where it is forced through a gorge 38 m wide and 180 m deep. The thrashing water reaches a depth of 60 m and thunders through with incredible power. The **Hell's Gate Airtram** ① *T250-867 9277, www.hellsgateairtram.com, Apr-Oct daily 1000-1600 to 1700 May-Sep, $20, under 18s $14, under 5s free, family $54,* carries up to 2500 people a day across the canyon for up-close views. Free canyon views can be had 8 km south at **Alexander Bridge Provincial Park**.

Heading north, the scenery remains spectacular, slowly taking on the dry, Wild West characteristics of the Thompson Valley, which the highway follows from Lytton. There's little to recommend the remaining towns, except as bases for some of the province's best rafting. There are excellent adrenalin-charged rapids just north of **Boston Bar** and further north between Spences Bridge and Lytton, with rapids such as the Jaws of Death.

At **Cache Creek**, Highway 1 veers eastwards. This funny little town, which has retained a distinctive 1950s feel, is surrounded by exceptional scenery, an arid, rocky moonscape of vast wrinkled mounds in shades of yellow and red, practically vegetation-free. The 'Painted Bluffs' between Savona and Ashcroft offer the best example of these colourful rock formations.

Kamloops

The sublime Thompson Valley landscape between Cache Creek and Kamloops provides a magnificent setting for this bland city. The endless hills of semi-desert, with their subtle hues and weird shapes, are an unlikely location for the second largest city in BC's interior, but a chance meeting of valleys has made this an important transport hub ever since the days when the canoe was the vehicle of choice. The Shuswap name, Cumloops, means 'meeting of the waters'. Today the Canadian Pacific and Canadian National railways, as well as two major highways connecting Vancouver, the Rockies and points east, south and north all converge here. It's a tough place to avoid, but there's little reason to stop except in August when one of the best powwows in the country takes place (see Festivals, page 75).

Five minutes north on Highway 5, **Secwepemc Museum and Heritage Park** ⓘ *T250-828 9749, www.secwepemc.org/museum, Jun-Sep daily 0800-1600, Oct-Apr Mon-Fri 0800-1600, $6, under 18s $3, under 5s free*, is an interesting place to learn more about the Secwepemc, or Shuswap, whose culture thrived here for thousands of years. As well as displays on hunting, fishing, clothing, games, food gathering and cooking, there are the archaeological remains of a 2000-year old Secwepemc winter village, four reconstructed winter pit houses, a summer village and a 5-ha park containing Ethnobotanical Gardens.

If you want to explore the surrounding area, a two-hour walk, starting 4 km west on Tranquille Road, leads to the **Hoodoos**, tall sandstone sculptures carved by wind and water. Alternatively, go hunting for semi-precious stones and fossils with a guided geological tour, or visit **BC Wildlife Park** ⓘ *20 km east on Hwy 1 at 9077 Dallas Dr, T250-573 3242, www.bczoo.org, May-Sep daily 0930-1700, otherwise 0930-1400, closed weekends Nov-Feb, $13, under 16s $12, under 12s $10, under 3s free*. This 50-ha park contains over 60 species including cougars, grizzly bears, wolves, moose and mountain goats.

Nearby **Sun Peaks Ski Resort** ⓘ *follow Hwy 5 north for 19 km to Heffley Creek, then right for 31 km at the Sun Peaks sign, www.sunpeaksresort.com, late Nov to mid-Apr, 0830-1530, lift passes are $58, youth $36, child $36 per day, cross-country $15/12/10*, is one of the interior's best. With 122 runs up to 8 km long on 1500 ha of skiable terrain, which includes two vast alpine bowls and a 881-m vertical drop, **Sun Peaks** is BC's second largest ski area, serviced by 11 lifts capable of handling 12,000 skiers per hour. The breakdown favours experienced skiers and snowboarders, with 58% of runs intermediate and 32% expert. There's also a kids' terrain garden, 40 km of cross-country trails and the bonus of 2000 hours of sun per year (hence the name). The village has everything you could need, including cafés, restaurants, bars, clubs, lessons, rentals and plenty of places to stay. There's also lift-assisted mountain biking and hiking in the summer.

The Shuswap

East of Kamloops, the arid vistas of the Thompson Valley give way to duller scenery and an abundance of water. The strangely shaped **Shuswap Lake** provides 1130 km of shoreline, beaches and waterways to explore. Of the many provincial parks in the Shuswap, the most popular and dramatic is **Cinnemousun Narrows**. The classic way to see the lake is in a houseboat from Sicamous (see Activities and tours, page 77) and the alternative is to rent a canoe and take a tent.

In summer, the Shuswap can get incredibly busy and booked up. The further you get from the highway, the smaller the hordes, but it is debatable whether the rewards justify the effort. One undeniable draw is **Roderick Haig-Brown Provincial Park** ⓘ *5 km north of* an excellent hostel in Squilax, on the north shore, which is the province's best place to witness the autumn return of migrating salmon, especially every fourth year when some 1.5 million fish turn the Adams River a brilliant red (the next is 2014).

The Shuswap's rapidly expanding main resort town, **Salmon Arm**, is a disappointment, but there's a pleasant 9-km boardwalk trail along the lake in Waterfront Park, starting at the **visitor centre** ① *101-20 Hudson Av NE, T250-832 2230, www.shuswap.bc.ca*. Pick up the very informative *Trail Guide* here. Between May and September you're likely to see one of the 250 pairs of endangered western grebe performing their extraordinary mating dance. Rock-climbing is big at nearby **Haines Creek** and there's a stunning historical suspension bridge at **Malakwa**, 17 km east of Sicamous.

Revelstoke

As the TransCanada enters the lofty Columbia Mountains, the scenery takes a dramatic upswing with increasingly frequent glimpses of the majestic Rockies. Situated amid giant trees halfway between Sicamous and Revelstoke, the **Enchanted Forest** ① *T250-837 9477, www.enchantedforestbc.com, Jun-Aug 0900-2000, May, Jun and Sep 1000-1800, $9, under 16s $8*, is a must for kids, featuring hundreds of fairy-tale settings and characters, some crazy giant tree houses, a long stretch of boardwalk and an 800-year-old cedar grove. **Revelstoke**, besides its splendid location, is a friendly, attractive town with top-notch outdoor pursuits and lots of heritage buildings sporting turrets and wrap-around balconies. A self-guided tour brochure is available from the two **visitor centres** ① *204 Campbell Av, T250-837 5345, www.seerevelstoke.com, open year round; and corner of Hwys 1 and 23 N, T250-837 3522, open summer only*. The town's only real sight is **Revelstoke Railway Museum** ① *Victoria Rd, opposite the bears, T250-837 6060, www.railwaymuseum.com, daily Jul-Aug 0900-2000, Sep-Oct and Apr-Jun 0900-1700, $10, under 16s $5, under 7s $2*, whose highlights include an entire passenger car, a locomotive and an interactive diesel simulator. Otherwise, Revelstoke is a major hub for outdoor activities. **Mount Revelstoke National Park** has some popular walking trails and fabulous wild flowers in July and August.

Following its major expansion and development, **Revelstoke Mountain Ski Resort** ① *4 km south of town, T250-814 0087, www.revelstokemountainresort.com, lift passes $74, under 18s $57, under 12s $26*, reopened in 2010, fulfilling its long-recognised potential to be one of the province's finest hills. It has 52 runs, the longest measuring 15.2 km, five alpine bowls, and 13 areas of gladed terrain, all accessed by four lifts, including an eight-passenger high-speed gondola which transports sightseers 900 vertical metres in seven minutes ($15). The 1214 ha of terrain breaks down as 7% beginner, 45.5% intermediate and 47.5% advanced. There are rentals and lessons, catskiing and heli-skiing, a hotel and restaurant. A shuttle leaves Revelstoke four times daily throughout the ski season ($2).

Glacier National Park

① *For daily updated information about snow conditions call Backcountry Report, T250-837 6867.*

With the Rockies so close, not many people stop to admire this chunk of the **Selkirk Mountains**, yet the peaks here are just as impressive and even more snow-laden. As its name suggests, Glacier National Park's defining feature is the 422 fields of permanent ice that cloak an incredible 14% of its area year round. Whereas most of the world's glaciers are rapidly retreating, the largest one here, **Illecillewaet Neve**, is still growing and some 70 new glaciers have been identified. The weather that fuels this ice-factory is wet and frequently abysmal.

Rogers Pass is recognized as one of the best backcountry skiing areas in the world, with some 1349 sq km of terrain featuring descents of up to 1500 m. For all but the most experienced, a professional guide is essential as avalanches are very common. Hikes in the park tend to be short and striking. Unfortunately, you're never very far from the highway. *Footloose in the Columbias* is a useful hiking guide to Glacier and Revelstoke National Parks. The very helpful **visitor centre** ① *1 km west of Rogers Pass, T250-837 6274, www.pc.gc.ca/eng/pn-np/bc/glacier/visit.aspx, Jun-Sep 0800-1800, May and Sep-Nov 0900-1700, Dec-Apr 0700-1700*, is due to reopen after renovations in 2011. As well as trail maps and information it has a number of impressive and entertaining hi-tech displays, and guided walks are offered in the summer. There's a very helpful map of the park in *The Mountain Guide*, available throughout the Rockies at visitor centres.

Hikes in Glacier National Park
Glacier Crest ① *10.4 km return; 1005-m elevation gain. Trailhead: turn into Illecillewaet Campground and proceed just over 1 km to car park.* This glorious trail takes you up the ridge between the park's two major glacier-bearing valleys, Illecillewaet and Asulkan, with ample views of both. You start in an old-growth forest, follow a burbling stream, ascend a steep canyon wall into a land of icy peaks and top out at a viewpoint offering dramatic 360° views. The last stretch is dangerous when wet, so do not attempt after recent rain.

Perley Rock ① *11.4 km return; 1162-m elevation gain. Trailhead: as above.* This steep and challenging trail would be a torment without the well-built switchbacks. The Illecillewaet Glacier is again on full display, along with the polished bedrock beneath its receding tongue. The higher you go, the better the views get and on the way back they're even better.

Hermit Basin ① *5.6 km return; 770-m elevation gain. Trailhead: 1.4 km northeast of Rogers Pass Information Centre.* Even steeper than the above but well maintained, this trail leads to a tiny alpine shelf with great views of the peaks and glaciers on the park's south side. There are four tent pads for overnight stays.

Bald Mountain ① *35.2 km return; 1354-m elevation gain. Trailhead: 11 km northeast of Rogers Pass; or 11.5 km south of northeast park entrance, turn onto Beaver Valley/ Copperstain Rd. Go left after 1.2 km and proceed 200 m.* This long and little-used trail slogs through old-growth forest for most of the first day but then rewards you with an 8-km-long ridge covered in wild flower meadows (prime grizzly bear habitat). The scenery is gobsmacking, with the glacier-supporting massif in full view across the valley.

Golden
Golden's location could hardly be more fortuitous: halfway between Glacier and Yoho National Parks, at the junction of the Columbia and Kicking Horse rivers, with the Selkirk and Purcell ranges to the west and the Rockies just to the east. Naturally enough, this is yet another magnet for adventure enthusiasts and, with the arrival of **Kicking Horse Ski Resort** ① *13 km from Golden, T250-439 5424, www.kicking*

horseresort.com, mid-Dec to mid-Apr 0900-1530, $73, under 18s $61, under 12s $35, the area is booming. The resort is the most recent large ski hill to be built in British Columbia, offering 1100 ha of award-winning 'champagne' powder, a pair of alpine bowls, over 85 inbound chutes, and a massive vertical rise of 1260 m. The eight-person Golden Eagle Express Gondola whisks skiers up 3413 m in 12 minutes to the highest peak, from where 106 runs (20% beginner, 20% intermediate, 45% advanced and 15% expert) fan out into the open spaces. All the usual rentals, lessons and facilities are available. There is a **snow shuttle** ① *daily, 0600, 0705, 0815, 1010, $3*, which runs during the season and leaves from various points in town. There are also shuttle from Calgary Aiport, Banff, and Lake Louise. In summer, the two main lifts stay open, providing access to a network of alpine hiking trails, stunning vistas from the fine dining restaurant up top, and a **Mountain Bike Park** ① *1030-1730, $41/36.*

Inevitably, the town fails to live up to its setting, though the ugly stretch of services on the highway bears no relation to the small, fairly pleasant centre. The **Golden Visitor Information Centre** ① *500 10th Av, T250-344 7125, www.tourismgolden.com*, is open year round and is one of the pick-up points for the snow shuttle. Ask about the endless activities available, particularly white water rafting on the Kicking Horse, hiking, mountain biking, and paragliding. There's also a **BC Visitor Centre** ① *111 Donald Upper Rd*. From Golden, it is about 60 km to Field in Yoho National Park (see page 144) and 11 km more to Lake Louise (see page 111), crossing the Alberta border (and putting clocks forward one hour) on the way.

Bugaboo Provincial Park
South of Golden, Highway 95 runs through the relatively disappointing Columbia Valley and a string of mediocre towns to join Highway 3 at dismal Cranbrook. Reached by a good 45-km gravel road from Spillimacheen, 65 km south of Golden, Bugaboo Provincial Park is famous in rock-climbing circles for its spectacular granite spires. Though the long access is off-putting, a couple of good trails allow hikers to enjoy the park's rugged beauty and extensive glaciers. Climbers should get the *Nat Topo Map 82K/10* and/or *82K/15* and might enjoy *Bugaboo Rock: A Climber's Guide* by R Green and J Benson.

Hikes in Bugaboo National Park
Bugaboo Spires ① *10 km return; 660-m elevation gain. Trailhead: parking lot at Km 43.3.* Leads to the base of the spires and Conrad Kain Hut, which sleeps 40 people and is equipped with propane stoves. Exploring beyond is recommended.

Cobalt Lake ① *17.4 km return; 930-m elevation gain. Trailhead: as above.* Involves a lot of hard work before mind-expanding views take over. A shorter trail (10 km return) leads from Bugaboo Lodge, which is operated by Canadian Mountain Holidays.

Crowsnest Highway → For listings, see pages 68-80.

Manning Provincial Park
From Hope, Highway 3 climbs quite steeply into the Cascade Mountains, through a vast area of wilderness with no communities to speak of until Princeton, which is 126 km away. This area is liable to have snow most of the year and, in winter, is excellent

for cross-country skiing, with some 130 km of ungroomed backcountry trails, a small ski hill and 30 km of groomed trails. Most of the hiking trails begin around the park's only accommodation, the **Manning Park Resort** (see Sleeping, page 71), also a good source of information. Some other good trails are accessed from Lightning Lake, including the hike to the east peak of **Frosty Mountain** (7½ hours return), the park's highest point; it's a steep climb, rewarded by a ridge walk with fantastic views. **Princeton**, the first town east of the pass, is renowned in angling circles, boasting 48 trout-fishing lakes within 60 km, 15 of them clustered together about 37 km north on Highway 5A.

Hedley

As the landscapes tend increasingly toward the arid, rolling hills of the Okanagan, the stretch east to Osoyoos is one of the most scenic sections of this highway. The tiny village of Hedley was once one of the most important gold-mining towns in BC. The **Hedley Mining Museum**, which doubles as a **visitor centre** ① *712 Daly St, signposted from the highway, T250-292 8787, www.hedleybc.com, mid-May to mid-Sep daily 0900-1700, mid-Sep to mid-May Thu-Mon, by donation*, has photos, artefacts and information about the interesting remains and historic buildings around town. Borrow their binoculars for a sneak preview of the Mine from the porch. The **Upper Similkameen Native Band** now operates a **Snaza'ist Discovery Centre** ① *161 Snaza'ist Dr, T250-292 8733*, showcasing their cultural heritage, and runs three-hour tours of **Mascot Gold Mine** ① *www.mascotmine.com, $37, child $29, Jul-early Sep daily 1200*, located 1 km up the adjacent cliff face, amongst dramatic swirls of rock. The 200 m underground tunnel, usually the highlight, will hopefully reopen for the 2011 season following safety maintenance. They also run an **Archeology Program** ① *daily May-Oct at 1330, 1½ hrs, $10/5*, which includes hunting for artefacts, and learning about the pictographs that abound in this area.

East to Christina Lake

East of picturesque Keremeos (see page) and the incredible arid vistas around Osoyoos (see page), the highway runs through some fascinating rocky landscapes, the scenery slowly shifting from the barrenness of the Okanagan to the densely forested mountains of the Kootenays. The best reasons to stop are the **Kettle River Museum** ① *T250-449 2614, www.midwaybc.ca/museum, May-Sep 1000-1630 Wed-Sun, daily Jul-Aug, $2*, in Midway, which celebrates the Kettle Valley Railway; and the quaint town of **Greenwood**, whose Wild West appearance is more natural than contrived.

The town of **Christina Lake** has few facilities and poor lake access. Fortunately over half of the beautiful, very warm lake is contained within **Gladstone Provincial Park** and easily accessed via the **Texas-Alpine turning** ① *5 km north on the highway; turn onto Alpine Rd and continue to the end for the campground*. A very satisfying hiking and biking trail begins here, hugging the lake to its northern tip. A right fork then continues deep into the park, the left leading to more private wilderness campsites, one close by on Christina Lake, another on Xenia Lake further west. You could also hire a canoe and cross the main lake to one of the remote wilderness campgrounds on the west shore. ▸▸ *See Sleeping, page 71.*

East to Rossland

At the junction with Highway 3B, **Nancy Greene Provincial Park** contains a lovely lake you can ski round, with a beach for summer swimming and fishing. Highway 3 carries on to Castlegar, but it's well worth making a diversion down Highway 3B to **Rossland**, one of the great unsung skiing Meccas and 'mountain bike capital of Canada'. Most people who live here are obsessed with one or both of these activities, so the atmosphere is saturated with an outdoor mentality. In winter the population doubles as the town fills up with ski-bums. Besides being young, lively and friendly, with a perpetual party atmosphere in winter, this is also an exceptionally picturesque little town with wide, impossibly steep streets, mountains all around and views above the clouds.

In the 1890s, Rossland was a booming gold-mining town, with 7000 people, 42 saloons and four local newspapers. The **Rossland Museum** ① *junction Hwys 22 and 3B, T1888-448 7444, www.rosslandmuseum.ca, mid-May to mid-Sep 0900-1700, $5, youth $3, child $1.50, tours leave every 30 mins Jul-Aug 0930-1530, 5 times daily May-Jun, with museum entry $9, youth $4, child $2,* documents this history and offers interesting 45-minute tours through the spooky (and chilly) turn-of-the-20th-century Le Roi Gold Mine, last operated in 1929 and filled with old equipment (closed 2010, hopefully reopening). The same building also houses the **Visitor Information Centre** ① *T250-362 7722, www.tourismrossland.com; there's also a smaller one open Dec-Mar at 2197 Columbia Av, T250-362 5666.*

Red Mountain Ski Hill ① *3 km W on Hwy 3B, T250-362 7384, www.redresort.com, Nov-Apr, day pass $79, youth $63, child $39,* boasts 682 ha of terrain, two mountains, two basins and an additional 1012 ha of easily accessible backcountry. The vertical gain is an impressive 890 m, but a relatively low elevation makes the snow-pack less reliable here than at most hills. When conditions are good, however, experienced skiers rate this hill as one of the province's best, thanks to the challenging terrain, and some of the best tree-skiing in the world. It really is geared to experts, with 45% of runs rated black diamond. The Paradise Basin is good for beginners and very pretty, with lots of views and sunshine. There's a terrain park for snowboarders, lessons, rentals, cross country skiing, cat-skiing, heli-skiing, and plenty of places to sleep and eat. Extensive development is planned, including 1400 sleeping units and 21,300 sq m of commercial space plus new lifts.

Fort Steele Heritage Town

① *9851 Hwy 93/95, 16 km northeast of Cranbrook, T250-417 6000, www.fortsteele.ca, daily May-Jun and Sep 0930-1800, Jul-Aug daily 0930-1900, Oct-Mar 1000-1600, $5, under 5s free. Steam train $10, under 12s $5, live 1890s variety shows in the Wild Horse Theatre, 1530, $15, under 18s $10, under 12s $5, horse-drawn wagon rides $5, under 5s free. All-inclusive 'Steele of a Deal' pass for 2 days $25, under 18s $15.*

At dreary Castlegar, you're advised to take Highway 3A to Nelson, then see Kaslo and New Denver, and head north through Nakusp to Highway 1. Highway 3 east via the Salmo-Creston pass is mostly a dull drive, as is Highway 93 north from dismal Cranbrook. If headed this way, however, it's worth stopping at the reconstructed late-19th-century town of **Fort Steele**, one of the best 'living museums' in BC. There are over 50 buildings, some original, some replicas and some brought in from elsewhere. The overall effect is a convincing step back in time. All the requisite shops and services are represented, with costumed staff acting out their roles while also filling in historical details and anecdotes. The blacksmith shoes horses, the sweet shop and bakery sell wares made on the spot, and the restaurant serves meals cooked in the wood-fired brick oven. There's a working printer, a tinsmith shop, general store, farm animals, street dramas and live shows in an old-time music hall. You can even be taken round in a steam train or horse-drawn wagon.

Fernie

Towards Fernie, the Crowsnest finally rewards its faithful with titillating previews of the Rockies. Surrounded by the soaring, jagged mountains of the **Lizard Range**, Fernie doesn't exactly do the setting justice but it comes closer than most. Recent expansion of its excellent ski hill has resulted in a fair amount of development, as hotels have sprung up along the highway, but the pretty little Downtown has been almost entirely spared. Most buildings here were constructed in brick or stone after a fire in 1908 wiped out the whole town in 90 minutes. A historical walking tour highlights these heritage buildings, many of which are clustered around Sixth Street and Fourth Avenue. A map is available at the **Visitor Information Centre** ① *102 Commerce Rd, T250-423 6868, www.ferniechamber.com.*

Until quite recently the copious challenging runs and plentiful powder of **Fernie Alpine Resort** ① *T250-423 4655, www.skifernie.com, 5 km from town, ski pass $76, under 18s $54, under 12s $25, night skiing 1730-2100 on limited days, $11, child $8,* were a fairly well-kept secret, along the lines of Red Mountain in Rossland. Like Rossland, Fernie is equally fine for skiing and mountain biking, resulting in a dynamic energy that helps save it from the backwater red-neck ambience of most of the East Kootenays. It remains a great choice for those who know their skiing and would rather stay in a real town, with good restaurants and bars and excellent cheap accommodation, rather than a purpose-built resort. The hill features 107 trails and five alpine bowls on 1013 ha of terrain that breaks down as 30% beginner, 40% intermediate, 30% advanced, and is serviced by 10 lifts capable of carrying up to 13,700 skiers per hour. There are also 14 kms of groomed and track-set cross-country trails. The hill has restaurants, rentals, lessons and lots of accommodation, and the **Smokie Mountain Ski Shuttle** ① *T250-423 8605,* runs frequently from Fernie.

TransCanada and Crowsnest highways listings

For Sleeping and Eating price codes and other relevant information, see pages 9-11.

🛏 Sleeping

Fraser Canyon *p61*

$$ Bear's Claw Lodge, 192 Hwy 97 N, Cache Creek, T250-457 9705. Far and away the nicest place to stay and eat on this stretch. The striking log-built lodge has comfortable rooms, a spacious guest lounge and a decent restaurant.

$$ Chrysalis Retreat B&B, 31286 Douglas St, Yale, T604-863 0055. Offers 3 rooms in a beautiful cottage with lovely gardens, hot tub and sauna. Also offers massage and hydro-therapy. Breakfast included.

$$ Teague House B&B,1 km west of Yale on Hwy 1, T250-363 7238, www.teaguehouse.com. Built in 1864, this quaint little blue house has 3 bedrooms, a full kitchen and a comfortable sitting room, all furnished with historical artefacts. There's a covered deck from which to enjoy the views over a full breakfast.

Camping

Kumsheen Rafting Resort, 1345 Hwy 1, 5 km east of Lytton, T250-455 2296, www.kumsheen.com. Has 2 de luxe cabin tents (**$**), a campground, trails, various sporting facilities, a restaurant, fabulous bar, swimming pool and spa. All-inclusive rafting packages available.

Skihist Provincial Park, 6 km east of Lytton, T250-455 2708. 58 decent sites, some dramatic views of the Thompson Valley, lots of Saskatoon berries and hiking trails on part of the Cariboo Wagon Rd.

Yale Campground, 28800 Hwy 1, T604-863 2407. Large sites, hot showers, laundry, playground and trails.

Kamloops p62

More upmarket accommodation is to be found near the junction of Rogers Way, on the highway above town. Columbia St, the road into town, has mid-range options.

$$$ Sun Peaks Lodge, T250-578 7878, www.sunpeakslodge.com. One of several lodges at the Ski Hill, offering rooms with balconies, and a spa, sauna and hot tub.

$$ A Desert Inn, 775 Columbia St, T250-372 8235, www.adesertinn.kamloops.com. Good rooms with large beds, balconies and fairly new furnishings. There's an indoor pool and an on site restaurant. The views of the valley are the best feature.

$$ Joyce's B&B, 49 Nicola St W, T250-374 1417, www.bbcanada.com/268.html. The 3 pleasant rooms in this spacious 1911 Banker's House in a nice part of Downtown are a great deal.

$$ Plaza Heritage Hotel, 405 Victoria St, T250-377 8075, www.plazaheritage hotel.com. The most appealing downtown choice. Rooms in this 1926 building are small, newly renovated and full of character.

$ Sun Peaks Hostel, T250-578 0057, www.sunpeakshostel.com. The budget option at the Ski Hill. All the usual facilities, including a kitchen, common room with TV, internet, canoes, lockers and skiing. Phone ahead for transport from Kamloops.

Camping

Paul Lake Provincial Park, 17 km east off Hwy 5 N, T250-828 9533. There is no decent camping in town but you might find this secluded spot on a lovely lake worth the drive. There's good fishing and a steep hike to the top of Gibraltar for views.

The Shuswap p62

$$$ Holiday Inn Express, 1090 22nd St NE, T250-832 7711, www.hiexsalmonarm.com. The friendliest, most agreeable of many chain hotels in town, with and indoor pool, exercise room, parking and breakfast.

$$ Alpiner Motel, 734 Hwy 1, Sicamous, T250-836 2290, www.alpinermotel.com. Fun little triangular cabins with large beds and kitchenette. Some very cheap tent sites. Great value.

$$ Artist's House Heritage B&B, 20 Bruhn Rd, 1 km west of Sicamous, T250-836 3537, www.artistshouse.ca. A friendly, antique-filled B&B, with 3 rooms, 1 with en suite shower. Library, living room, den, sun porch and a lovely big patio with views over the lake. Even has its own fallout shelter.

$$ The Trickle Inn, Tappen, T250-835 8835, www.trickleinn.com. 5 unique, sumptuously decorated rooms in a Victorian heritage home, overlooking the lake and surrounded by landscaped gardens. Superb restaurant, by prior reservation only.

$ Caboose Hostel, Squilax, T250-675 2977, www.hihostels.ca. Possibly the most interesting hostel in BC. The main building is a historic general store on the lake andthe dorm beds are in 3 converted cabooses (railway cars), each with its own kitchen and bathroom. Common room, TV room, native-style sauna, library, campfire and laundry. Friendly staff rent out canoes and a self-guided hiking kit, and can set you up with all manner of local activities. The **Greyhound** stops here and there's a nearby beaver lodge to check out. Phone ahead to arrange pick up.

Camping

There are remote campgrounds at **White Lake Provincial Park** and **Herald Provincial Park**, both T250-546 3790, which has a sandy beach and an easy trail to Margaret Falls.

Bush Creek Provincial Park, Adams Lake, 5.5 km up a rough logging road, T250-995 0861. One of the nicest, most peaceful and scenic places to camp in the area.

Shuswap Lake Provincial Park, 1210 McGill Rd, east of Squilax at Scotch Creek, T250-995 0861. 272 nicely wooded, private and well-equipped sites, as well as a large beach.

Sicamous KOA, junction of Hwys 1 and 97B, T250-836 2507, ww.salmonarmkoa.com. A well-equipped campground with laundry, showers, hot tub, heated pool, cabins, TV and a games room.

Silver Beach Provincial Park, Seymour Arm. A remote but spectacular forested location at the northernmost extremity of the lake. Great for swimming, fishing, and ideal for peace and quiet.

Revelstoke p63

$$$ Mulvehill Creek Wilderness Inn, 4200 Hwy 23, 19 km south towards Shelter Bay ferry, T250-837 8649, www.mulvehillcreek.com. A fabulous option for those with transport. This beautiful wood lodge stands on 40 ha of peaceful private land on the shore of Upper Arrow Lake. It has 8 rooms with en suite bath, a hot tub, games room and canoes. Friendly and interesting hosts, full breakfast included.

$$$ Regent Inn, 112 1st St E, T250-837 2107, www.regentinn.com. Large rooms with big beds and baths. Centrally located with an outdoor hot tub, sauna and gym access. Nice restaurant, lounge and pub downstairs.

$$ Minto Manor B&B, 815 Mackenzie Av, T250-837 9337, www.mintomanor.com. 3 plush en suite rooms decked out with period furniture. The 1905 Edwardian mansion has a veranda, large gardens, a sitting room, music room and TV room.

$$ Monashee Lodge, 1601 3rd St W, T250-837 6778, www.monasheelodge.com. A quiet, good-value motel, with hot tub and a light breakfast included.

$ Samesun Backpacker Lodges, 400 2nd St W, T250-837 4050, www.samesun.com. One of the great hostels. 76 beds in clean, bright, wood-finished dorms of up to 4, or doubles at no extra charge. Huge kitchens, a common room with TV, free internet, laundry and parking. Ask about their amazing skiing and cat-skiing packages.

Camping

Blanket Creek Provincial Park, 25 km south on Hwy 23, T250-837 5734. 63 sites on Arrow Lakes by Sutherland Falls.

Williamson Lake Campground, 1818 Williamson Lake Rd, 5 km south on 4th St/Airport Way, T250-837 5512, www.williamsonlakecampground.com. Well located on a warm lake away from the highway, with plenty of trees and greenery. Playground, canoe and rowboat rentals, showers, and laundry facilities.

Glacier National Park p63

$$ Glacier Park Lodge, right on Rogers Pass, T250-837 2126, www.glacier parklodge.ca. The only beds in the park and a great location. Heated outdoor pool, sauna, restaurant, 24-hr café and service station. There are also a number of lodges on the way to Golden.

Camping

Illecillewaet, Loop Brook and **Mt Sir Donald** campgrounds, 3, 5 and 6 km west of Rogers Pass respectively. Run by Parks Canada, non-reservable and rustic (especially the latter), these 3 sites give access to interpretive trails that pass through snow-sheds, bridges and other remains of the 1885 CPR railway line. The park also has backcountry campsites and cabins, or you can camp southeast of the park boundary where no fees or restrictions are in place.

Golden p64

Golden's mountain setting has led to a proliferation of log-built lodges, mainly west of the TransCanada, many of them accessed by helicopter only.

$$$ Kicking Horse River Lodge, 801 9th St N, T250-439 1112, www.khrl.com. This spectacularly restored historic fir-log building has a wrap-around balcony and views of the **Kicking Horse Ski Resort**. There are private rooms, loft rooms that sleep up to 9 (**$$$**), and dorm beds (**$**). Facilities include a 2-storey den with reading nooks and a stone fireplace, an entertainment area with TV, full kitchen, café and laundry.

$$ Goldenwood Lodge, 2493 Holmes Deakin Rd,15 km west, then 6 km east on Blaeberry School Rd, T250-344 7685, www.goldenwoodlodge.com. This rustic but handsome wood lodge offers tranquillity, glorious surroundings and a variety of sleeping options, such as rooms, family lodges, cottages with or without kitchenette and tepees. Vegetarian meals and bikes available, canoeing and horse riding trips arranged.

$$ Mary's Motel, 603 8th Av, T250-344 7111, www.marysmotel.com. With so little accommodation in Golden, apart from the undesirable strip on the highway, this makes a good standby, with an indoor pool, sauna, hot tub and 81 rooms.

$ Kicking Horse Hostel, 518 Station Av, take Hwy 95 exit off Hwy 1 then 1st left before the overpass, T250-344 5071, www.kickinghorse hostel.com. Dorms and camping. Kitchen, common room and sauna.

Camping
Waitabit Creek, 23 km to the west. Turn north onto Donald Rd for 500 m then left down Big Bend Rd for 2 km. A distance away, but the best camping that's right on the river.

Whispering Spruce Campground, 1430 Golden View Rd, off Highway 1 E, T250-344 6680, www.whisperingsprucecampground. 135 sites overlooking the Kicking Horse canyon, with good facilities including hot showers, laundry and games room.

Manning Provincial Park *p65*
$$$ Manning Park Resort, on the highway, T250-840 8822, www.manningpark.com. An impressive log building in a great location, decorated inside and out with artfully crafted chainsaw carvings and with a good range of rooms and cabins. Has a 50-ft indoor pool, hot tub, sauna, steam room, fitness room, games room with billiards, a café, restaurant and

lounge to warm up in. Bike, ski, canoe and kayak rental, an outdoor skating rink, volleyball, tennis, plenty of hiking and cross-country skiing trails.

Camping
Lightning Lake, 5 km from resort, T1800-689 9025. The most convenient of the park's 4 campgrounds, with 88 sites, canoeing and access to trails.

Hedley *p66*
$$ Colonial Inn B&B, 608 Colonial Rd, T250-292 8131, www.colonialinnbb.ca. Bursting with character from the outside, this historic house is spectacular from the inside too. Antique furnishings, chandeliers and hardwood floors. 5 equally impressive rooms, 3 en suite, are a steal at this price.

$$ The Gold House B&B, 644 Colonial Rd, T250-292 8418, www.thegoldhouse.com. A fabulous historic house occupying the mine's former office and storage room, which were built in 1904. The 4 lovely rooms, some sharing a bath, have access to the wrap-around balcony, with views of the mine and mountains. To the back are the scenic remains of a crushing plant, known as the Stamp Mill.

Camping
Stemwinder Provincial Park, just west of town. 27 nicely wooded and fairly private campsites on the river.

East to Christina Lake *p66*
$$ Hummingbird Haven B&B, 255 1st Av, T250-447 9293. Offers 3 very nice rooms in a spacious house. Peaceful location next to the golf course.

$$ Park Lane Resort & Motel, 31 Kingsley Rd, T250-447 9385, www.parklane-resort.com. Bright, pleasant and away from the highway. Some rooms come with kitchen, patio and BBQ. Also have tent and RV camping available.

$$ Sunflower Inn B&B, 159 Alpine Rd, T250-447 6201, www.sunflowerinnbb.com. Well situated next to the lake and park, with a private beach, canoes, deck with lake views and 3 pleasant rooms with shared bath.

Camping
Gladstone Provincial Park, accessed via the Texas-Alpine turning, 5 km north on the highway, T250-548 0076. A large and extremely busy campground by the lake, with access to several beaches and hiking trails. Reserve early or else keep your fingers crossed.

East to Rossland *p66*
If you want to stay at the Red Mountain Ski Hill, a package is the best bet through Central Reservations, T1877-969 7669, www.redreservations.com.

$$$ Prestige Mountain Resort, 1919 Columbia Av, T250-362 7375, www.prestigehotelsand resorts.com. A convenient downtown choice with a range of decent rooms and suites. Jacuzzi, fitness centre, restaurant, lounge and a noisy bar that's the best venue in town for live bands.

$$$ Red Mountain Village, 3 km north on Hwy 3B at the base of the hill, T250-362 9000, www.redmountainvillage.com. A wide range of options, from luxury chalets to large cabins and motel rooms. Prices drop by 50% mid-May to mid-Sep.

$$ Angela's B&B, 1520 Spokane St, T250-362 7790, www.visitred.com. A classically renovated 1920s house, with 2 suites that are geared to bigger groups but may suit a couple. Hot tub, fireplace, garden and a creek running through the property.

$$ Rams Head Inn, Red Mountain Rd, 400 m before ski hill, T250-362 9577, www.rams head.bc.ca. By far the best option around. Beautiful, comfortable and homely rooms. Common room with a stone fireplace, sauna, outdoor hot tub with views, a games room, full breakfast and use of snowshoes. Prices drop considerably mid-May to mid-Sep.

$ Mountain Shadow Backpackers Hostel, 2125 Columbia Av, T250-362 7160, www.mshostel.com. Dorms and private rooms, common room, kitchen and internet.

Camping
Rossland Lions Park, Red Mountain Rd, 1 km north on Highway 3B. 18 sites, some with hook-ups. Mid-May to mid-Sep only.

Fort Steele Heritage Town *p67*
Camping
Fort Steele Campground, 2 km south on Kelly Rd, T250-426 5117, www.fortsteele campground.com. This is a nicer, quieter spot with 60 wooded sites, heated pool, showers, RV hook-ups and lots of trails for biking and hiking.

Fort Steele Resort and RV Park, T250-489 4268, www.fortsteele.com. 176 sites right by the Village. Heated outdoor pool, hot showers, laundry, games room, playground and hook-ups.

Fernie *p68*
Fernie has lots of accommodation. Check www.fernie.com/lodging, for listings. You can also book what you need through **Fernie Central Reservations**, T1800-622 5007, www.ferniecentralreservations.com. Note that these prices are for the peak ski season, with rates up to 50% less during the summer months.

$$$ Park Place Lodge, 742 Hwy 3, T250-423 6871, www.parkplacelodge.com. Spacious and stylish rooms, some with balconies or kitchenettes. Indoor pool, hot tub, sauna, pub and bistro.

$$ Griz Inn, 5369 Ski Hill Rd, at the hill, T250-423 9221, www.grizinn.com. One of several decent lodges at the ski hill, offering rooms, studios and suites. Indoor pool, 2 outdoor hot tubs and sauna.

$$ Powder Mountain Lodge, 892 Hwy 3, T250-423 4492, www.powdermountain lodge.com. One of the finest hostels you will ever see. A beautiful, spacious building with dorms and private rooms with en suite baths. All facilities including a games room, hot tub, sauna, pool table, reading area, laundry, storage, shuttle to the hill or bus station and even a piano.

$$ Snow Valley Motel, 1041 7th Av/Hwy 3, T250-423 4421, www.snowvalleymotel.com. One of many motels on the highway downtown, with suites and kitchenette rooms.

$ Barbara Lynn's Country Inn, 691 7th Av, T250-423 6027, www.blci.ca. 10 small, slightly faded rooms just off the highway and close to town. Most with shared bath.

$ Raging Elk Adventure Lodge, 892 6th Av, T250-423 6811, www.ragingelk.com. An excellent hostel, with dorms, semi-private and private rooms. Huge common room, full kitchen, games room, movie room, sauna, garden and 2 patios. Breakfast included.

Camping
Mount Fernie Provincial Park, 3 km southwest on Hwy 3, T250-422 3003. Has 40 sites by the Elk River, wooded and private.

🍴 Eating

Kamloops *p62*
🍴 Brownstone, 118 Victoria St, T250-851 9939. A heritage building with an intimate interior and a lovely courtyard patio. Offers an ambitious, broad, international fine dining menu with a West Coast emphasis on freshness.

🍴-🍴 Chapters Viewpoint, 610 W Columbia St, **Panorama Inn**, T250-374 3224. A long-term favourite, offering fantastic views, outdoor seating and a menu that ranges from steak and seafood to salads, pasta and Mexican. Has an equally wide price range.

🍴 Bistro 326, 326 Victoria St, T250-374 2913. A hip little eatery with steak, seafood, great salads and some refreshingly original menu items like sweet and sour halibut cheeks or lobster ravioli.

🍴 The Commodore Grand Café and Lounge, 369 Victoria, T250-851 3100. A great place for a drink but also good for food. A menu of interesting fusion dishes and tapas, as well as regular pub fare.

🍴 Hot House Bistro, 438 Victoria St, T250-374 4604. Vegetarian cuisine with a laid-back South American atmosphere and international food from Mexico to India.

🍴 Sanbiki, 120 5th Av, T250-377 8857. Great sushi and offers some good choices for vegetarians.

The Shuswap *p62*
🍴 Minos Greek House, 720 22nd St, Salmon Arm, T250-832 1038. Good, reliable Greek fare.

🍴 Moose Mulligans, 1122 Riverside Av, Sicamous. Decent enough pub food and draft beer, but the real draw here is the views of the marina.

🍴 Table 24, 20 Hudson Av, T250-832 2410. Set in a former courthouse built in 1929, the best bet for a sophisticated dining experience, good for dinner, lunch, or weekend brunch.

Revelstoke *p63*
🍴 112 Restaurant, Regent Inn, 112 1st St E, T250-837 2107. The best choice for fine dining in romantic surroundings.

🍴 Bad Paul's Roadhouse Grill, 114 Mackenzie Av, T250-837 9575. One for the carnivores, specializes in prime rib.

🍴 Woolsey Creek, 600-2nd St, T250-837 5500. International, imaginative and well-executed cuisine, served in a colourful and comfortable interior, with couches, good art on the walls, and a patio.

🍴 Conversations, 205 Mackenzie Av, T250-837 4772. The nicest spot for a coffee, but the coffee itself is disappointing.

🍴 The Ol' Frontier, 112 Hwy 23 N and Hwy 1, T250-837 5119. With its Wild West saloon theme this is a fun place to have a big breakfast.

Golden *p64*
🍴 Cedar House, about 4.5 km south at 735 Hefti Rd, T250-344 4679. Expertly crafted Pacific Rim-style fine dining in the beautiful surroundings of this standout cedar building,

set in 4 ha of forest and organic gardens, with a lovely patio.

⫴ Eagle's Eye View, at Kicking Horse Resort, T250-439 5413. At the very top of the ski hill, accessible via the gondola (free with reservation), this is the highest restaurant in Canada. The fine dining menu is admittedly overpriced, but the timber-frame lodge has been thoughtfully built with vast windows to make the most of the priceless views.

⫴ Apostoles Greek Restaurant, 901 10th Av S, T250-344 4906. Authentic Greek cuisine at very reasonable prices.

⫴ Eleven 22 Grill and Liquids, 1122 10th Av S, T250-344 2443. Hands down Golden's hippest spot. Warm, intimate and stylish, with a menu strong on interesting international appetizers. Good drinks list.

⫴ Kicking Horse Grill, 1105 9th St S, T250-344 2330. International fusion cuisine in an authentic old log building on the banks of the river.

⫶ Bad Habit Bistro, 528 9th Av N, T250-439 1995. Wholesome lunches and breakfast served all day.

⫶ Bean Bag Coffee Roasters, 521 9th Av N, 250-344 6363. The best coffee in town.

Hedley *p66*
⫶ Gold Dust Pub, 5625 Hwy 3, east of town, T250-292 8552. The best bet in town for food and drink.

East to Christina Lake *p66*
⫶ Jimmy Beans, 9 Johnson Rd, T250-447 6610. Great coffee and light food, internet access and a pleasant garden and deck. A good place to stop for a break if you're driving through the area.

East to Rossland *p66*
⫴ Flying Steamshovel Inn, Washington/ 2nd Av, T250-362 7373. Superior pub food.
⫴ Gypsy at Red, 4430 Red Mountain Rd, at the ski hill, T250-362 3347. World cuisine with

an emphasis on Asian and Mediterranean flavours given a West Coast twist. Warm and intimate setting.

⫴ Idgies, 1999 2nd Av/Washington, T250-362 0078. A long-standing favourite with a mixed menu that covers seafood, curries, lamb, steaks and pasta dishes.

⫶ Alpine Grind, 2207 Columbia Av, T250-362 2280. Excellent home-made breakfast and lunches prepared by a top chef. The best coffee in town, and great views from the deck.

⫶ Clansey's Capuccino, 2042 Columbia Av, T250-362 5273. A great atmosphere, good for breakfast.

⫶ Sunshine Café, 2116 Columbia Av, T250-362 7630, daily 0730-1500. Good for breakfast and paninis. The play area makes it a great choice for families.

Fernie *p68*
⫴ The Old Elevator, 291 1st Av, T250-423 7115. Down-to-earth but excitingly original environment, housed in a 1908 grain elevator. The menu focuses on steak and game, cooked to perfection and artfully presented. There's also tapas in the lounge.

⫴⫴-⫴ Picnic, 701 2nd Av, T250-423 7666. A beautiful room, casual but classy, serving fresh and innovative cuisine. Also a choice spot for drinks, open Thu-Sat till 0200.

⫴ Blue Toque Diner, 601 1st Av, T250-423 4637. Situated in an old train station, this attractive and intimate spot is understandably popular, especially for breakfast/brunch. The food is great and plentiful, plus there's a wonderful outdoor patio, and a decent drinks menu.

⫴ The Curry Bowl, 931 7th Av, T250-423 2695. A cosy little place with a friendly atmosphere. The broad menu is pan-Asian, the food fresh and tasty and there are 50 import beers to wash it down with. Try the panang curry.

⫶ Mug Shots Bistro, 592 3rd Av, T250-423 8018. Good breakfast and coffee, fresh juices, second-hand books and internet access.

Kamloops *p62*
The Commodore Grand Café and Lounge, 369 Victoria, T250-851 3100. With brick walls, booths and relaxed music, this is a perfect spot for a glass of wine or 2.

The Shuswap *p62*
Hideaway Pub, 995 Lakeshore Dr, Salmon Arm, T250-832 9442. A nice spot where connoisseurs can sample excellent locally brewed Crannog organic beers on tap.

Revelstoke *p63*
The 112 Lounge and **River City Pub & Patio**, in the **Regent Inn**, 112 1st St, T250-837 2107, are both good at what they do.
Big Eddy Inn, 2108 Big Eddy Rd, T250-837 9072. The best regular boozer in town.

East to Rossland *p66*
Flying Steamshovel Inn, Washington/2nd Av, T250-362 7373. An atmospheric pub with a lingering flavour of the Wild West saloon. Small, intimate and very light, with a pool table, a good selection of beer on tap, drink specials and excellent pub food.
Rock Cut Neighborhood Pub, 3052 Hwy 3B, T250-362 5814. Situated across from the ski hill, there are great views from the patio of this popular pub. Decent après-ski munchies too.

Fernie *p68*
The Brickhouse Bar & Grill, 401 2nd Av, T250-423 0009. Housed in a former Imperial Bank, spacious and atmospheric, with brick walls, soft lighting and an open kitchen, this new favourite of locals and visitors is equally recommended for food or drink. **The Underground** downstairs has a fire red ceiling, local art on the walls, live or DJ-driven music, and stays open till 0200 Tue-Sat.
Grizzly Bar, above the **Daylodge** at the ski hill, T250-423 4655, is the après-ski bar of choice. **The Pub Bar and Grill**, in the Park Place Lodge, 742 Hwy 3, T250-423 6871, is a great neighbourhood pub, and a long-time favourite for locals and ski-bums alike. As pub-grub goes, the food is also very good.

Kamloops *p62*
For information and tickets, call **Kamloops Live!** on T250-374 5483 and to find out about all live music, visit www.kamloopsmusic.com.
The Blue Grotto, 319 Victoria St, T250-372 9901, www.thebluegrotto.ca. Live, predominantly rock, music on Thu-Sun.
Kamloops Art Gallery, 465 Victoria St, by the library, T250-377 2400, www.kag.bc.ca, Mon-Sat 1000-1700, Thu 1000-2100, $5, child $3. One of the town's finest features, with a collection of quality works by inspiring artists.
Paramount Twin Theatres, 503 Victoria St, T250-372 3911. The handiest cinema.
Sagebrush Theatre, 1300 9th St, T250-372 0966. Home of the Western Canada Theatre company and the Kamloops Symphony Orchestra. A major venue for visiting shows.

Revelstoke *p63*
The Roxy Theatre, 115 Mackenzie Av, T250-837 5540. Cinema.

Fernie *p68*
Vogue Theatre, 321 2nd Av, T250-423 3132. Cinema.

Kamloops *p62*
Mar Kamloops Cowboy Festival, T1888-763 2223, www.bcchs.com/festival. A celebration of all things cowboy. One of the biggest and best of its kind in Canada.
Jul Merritt Mountain Music Festival, www.mountainfest.com. Held over 4 days in Merritt, 72 km south of Kamloops, one of Canada's most celebrated country music festivals.
Aug Kamloopa Powwow, T250-828 9700, www.tkemlups.ca. One of the best powwows

in the country. Everyone is welcome, and it's the most enjoyable way to get an authentic taste of contemporary aboriginal culture. Brightly clad dancers from over 30 bands across Canada and the northern US perform to the rhythms of drumming and singing.

The Shuswap *p62*

Jul Shuswap Lake Festival of the Arts, T250-955 6401, www.artsfestivalshuswap.ca. A week-long judged exhibition of various art media held in Sorrento Memorial Hall, with demonstrations, workshops and an art walk. Switzmalph Cultural Day & Powwow, T250-803 0395. Held in Salmon Arm, this is the biggest of 3 local powwows, with numerous First Nations events and shows. **Aug** Roots and Blues Festival, T250-833 4096, www.rootsandblues.ca. For 3 days in mid-Aug, this superb festival brings Salmon Arm to life with acts performing on 6 stages, $135 in advance, $158 at gate, $60-70 per day. There is camping available. **Nov** Shuswap International Film Festival, T250-832 2294, www.shuswapfilm.net. A 3-day event held at the unique Salmar Classic Theatre.

Revelstoke *p63*

Jun Revelstoke Music Festival, T250-837 5500, www.revfest.ca. Held for 3 days on the 3rd weekend, with various musical shows on 2 open-air stages.

Fernie *p68*

Mar Griz Days Winter Festival, T250-423 6868. A 4-day event in early March, featuring a parade, the Mardi Gras Cabaret, and the Raging Elk Dummy Downhill. **Apr** Powder Pedal Paddle, marks the closure of the ski hill, and is an excuse for a big party disguised as a fun variation on the gruelling triathlon. **Sep** Taste of Fernie, T250-423 4842. The chance to sample the fare of local restaurants, with live entertainment throughout the day.

▲ Activities and tours

Fraser Canyon *p61*
Rafting
Fraser River Raft Expeditions, on the riverside at the south end of Yale, T1800-363 7238, www.fraserraft.com. A small, friendly company offering 1- to 7-day rafting tours on powerful rivers like the Fraser and Thompson, or smaller but equally exciting rivers like the Nahalatch and Coquihalla, starting at $130 a day. **Kumsheen Raft Adventures**, T250-455 2296, www.kumsheen.com. The most professional operation around, offering 1- to 5-day rafting trips on all the local rivers, gear rental, kayaking, bike tours, fishing, rock climbing, and accommodation.

Kamloops *p62*
Fishing
This area is famous for its trout fishing, with over 200 nearby lakes. Among the closest and best are Paul Lake, 23 km northeast and Lac Le Jeune, 35 km south.

Fossil hunting
Earthfoot, T250-554 2401, www.earthfoot.org. A local expert leads geologiy and fossil tours in the mountains around Kamloops, searching for 36- to 60-million-year-old fossils, minerals and crystals. Suitable for all levels of rock-hound. Tools are supplied but your own vehicle is required. $100 per day, or $60 per person, child $25. 30-day advanced booking recommended.

Golf
There are 11 golf courses in the area, visit www.golfkamloops.com for more information. **Rivershore**, T250-573 4622, www.rivershoregolflinks.com; **The Dunes**, T250-579 3300, www.golfthedunes.com.

Mountain biking
There are a lot of good trails around Kamloops and it's a great way to explore

the weird landscapes. The best places are Sun Peaks and Lac Dubois.

Full Boar Bike Store, 310 Victoria, T250-314 1888, www.fullboarbikes.com. Rents out bikes and can provide information.

Skiing

See Sun Peaks Ski Resort, page 62.

The Shuswap *p62*
Houseboats

All the rental companies are clustered together on the marina in Sicamous, so you can shop around and see what you're getting. Unfortunately, they're prohibitively expensive unless you're with a group and they can only be rented by the week.

Bluewater Houseboat Rentals, T250-836 2255, www.bluewaterhouseboats.ca. There are many houseboat rental companies, but this outfit is as good as any. Best value is the 4-day sport cruiser mid-week rate of $1095 for up to 8 people.

Watersports

Adams River Rafting, 3993 Squilax-Anglemont Rd, Scotch Creek, T250-955 2447, www.adamsriverrafting.com. $65 pp for a 1-hr trip on the Adams River.

Get Wet Rentals Ltd, 1130 Riverside Av, Sicamous, T250-836 3517, www.getwet rentals.com. All kinds of water toys for hire, including fishing boats for $60 per day and canoes for $40 per day.

Sicamous Water Tours and Charters, T250-836 4318. Guided lake tours with narrative and petroglyph-viewing. Water taxi service.

Revelstoke *p63*
Hiking

A 10-km trail up Mt Revelstoke starts behind the Railway Museum. It can also be snow-shoed in winter. Keystone and Standard Basins is a 1st-class 14.6- or 22-km hike with grand views of the Columbia Range, but the trailhead is 63 km away. Ask at the information centre if interested.

Mountain biking

Revelstoke has some great trails. Get a map from the information centre.

High Country Cycle and Sports, 188 Mac-Kenzie Av, T250-814 0090. Rentals, tours and advice. Also cross-country and back-country ski gear rentals.

Skiing

For years, Revelstoke has been revered for its ample powder and fabulous backcountry skiing, and skiers have dreamed about the day when the local hill's potential would be realized. Well, it's finally happenied with Revelstoke Mountain Ski Resort (see page184).

Most locals go backcountry skiing across the river on the Five Fingers of Mt McPherson. This is the best, most convenient spot, with northern exposure insuring good snow conditions. The Resort organizes cat-skiing in the Selkirk Mountains for $400 per day.

Free Spirit Sports, 203 1st St W, T250-837 9453. Backcountry, cross-country, snowshoe and snowboard equipment and rentals.

Revelstoke Nordic Ski Club, Snow Phone T250-837 7303, www.revelstokenordic.org. Maintains 24 km of groomed cross-country ski trails on Mt Macpherson, whose trailhead is 7 km south of Revelstoke on Hwy 23. Day fee $7.50, under 18s $4.

Selkirk Tangiers, T250-837 5378, www.selkirk-tangiers.com. Heli-skiing in 200,000 ha of terrain, from 1-day tasters ($725) to 7-day all-inclusive packages.

Golden *p64*
Flightseeing

Alpenglow Aviation Inc, T250-344 7117, www.purewest.com. Flightseeing tours over Rocky Mountain Icefields, departing from Golden airport, from $145 for 45 mins.

Hang-gliding

Mt Seven is considered Canada's premier site, hosting the annual Western Canadian Hang-gliding Championships and the Canadian

National Paragliding Champion- ships in Aug. Check www.flygolden.ca for more information.

Horse riding

Bear Corner Bed & Bale, 2054 Blaeberry Rd, 20 km W of Golden, T250-344 4785, www.bearcornerb-b.com. Horse riding trips from 1 hr ($40) to multi-day tours, or packages that include accommodation and meals. They have a cabin, or you can camp.

Ice-skating

There is an outdoor ice-rink in the Kicking Horse Ski Resort, with on-site skate rentals.

Mountain biking

Mountain biking is huge around Golden, with top trail networks at Mount 7, Moonraker and Dawn Mountain. Full details can be found at www.goldencyclingclub.com.
Selkirk Source for Sports, 504 9th Av, T250-344 2966. Mountain bike rentals, service and information on local trails.

Rafting

Between May and Sep the aquamarine untamed Kicking Horse River provides Grade III and IV rapids for exciting rafting and kayaking. Gentler trips explore the unique wetlands of the Columbia River.
Kootenay River Runners, T250-347 6595, www.raftingtherockies.com. Rafting the Kicking Horse from $87 for 3½ hrs, and more gentle all-day trips on the Kootenay River for $97. Also floating down the Columbia, and voyageur canoe trips.
Wet'n'wild, 1509 Lafontaine Rd, T250-344 6546, www.wetnwild.bc.ca. Offers a range of different trips on the Kicking Horse, including the possibility of combining rafting with horse riding or a jet boat tour.

Skiing

Dawn Mountain Nordic Ski Trails, at the base of the Kicking Horse Ski Resort, www.golden nordicclub.ca, has 25 km of groomed and track-set cross-country skiing trails. There are more trails at the golf course. There is also a 4 km trail net- work for snowshoeing off Palliser Trail Rd. For rentals and trail maps, contact **Canyon Creek Outfitters** in the Glacier Lodge in the Kicking Horse Resort Village.
Purcell Helicopter Skiing, T250-344 5410, www.purcellhelicopterskiing.com. Heli-skiing from $730 for 3 runs.

East to Christina Lake *p66*

Wild Ways Adventure Sports, 1925 Hwy 3, T250-447 6561, www.wildways.com. Bikes and general outdoor gear to buy or rent and mountain biking tours. Kayak rentals, tours, instruction and information.

East to Rossland *p66*

Mountain biking and hiking

Rossland is the self-styled 'Mountain bike capital of Canada', surrounded by a mountain network comprising over 100 km of progressive, well marked and maintained trails, many of them on old railway grades and logging skid roads. Visit the Kootenay Columbia Trails Society's site at www.kcts.ca, or www.bikerossland.ca for up-to-date information and maps. There are also several good hiking and skiing trails from town, including Old Glory, a classic 8-hr return hike to 360° views of the mountain ranges. The trailhead is 11 km north of town on Highway 3B.
Revolution Cycles and Service, 2044 Columbia Av, T250-362 5688, www.revolutioncycles.ca. Rentals, sales, shuttles and your best source of information.

Skiing

Black Jack Trails 500 m north of Red Mountain Resort, T250-364 5445, www.ski blackjack.ca, 35 km of groomed, track-set cross-country trails, including 1 km of night-lit trail, plus snowshoeing and dogsledding. There are rentals available at the hill or at **Powder Hound**, 2040 Columbia Av, T250-362 5311, where bikes can also be rented.
Rossland Mountain Adventures, T250-

368 7375. Ski touring, hiking, alpine hut tours, backpacking and backcountry equipment rentals.

Swimming
Trail Aquatic and Leisure Centre, 1875 Columbia Av, Trail, T250-368 6484. The best facilities in the Kootenays, including a large, unchlorinated pool, sauna, hot tub and fitness room.

Fernie *p68*
Mountain biking
Fernie is famed for its biking and hiking, much of it in Mt Fernie Provincial Park and at the ski hill. For full trail information, visit www.crankfernie.com, or www.bikefernie.ca. **Board Stiff**, 542 2nd Av, T250-423 3473, www.boardstifftouring.com. Bike rentals, sales and parts; kayak rentals; ski and snowboard gear and rentals.
Ski Base, 432 2nd Av, T250-423 6464, www.skibase.com. Bike rentals and trail information. Ski and snowboard sales, gear, rentals and repairs.

Rafting
Mountain High, T1877-423 4555, www.raft fernie.com. Gentle floats or whitewater rafting and kayak trips on the Elk or Bull Rivers, from $60 for 3 hrs to $120 per day.

Skiing
Fernie Wilderness Adventures, T250-423 6704, www.fernieadventures.com. Cat-skiing, wildlife viewing, ice fishing and fly fishing.
Mountain Pursuits, T250-423 6739, www.mountainpursuits.com. Year-round guided hiking and backcountry skiing, day-trips or overnighters.

⊖ Transport

TransCanada Highway *p61*
Bus
In summer, there are 7 daily **Greyhound** buses between **Vancouver** and **Kamloops** (4.5-5 hrs, $58), travelling up the Coquihalla Hwy via **Hope** (2½ hrs, $25). The 0030, 0630, 1345, 1845 services continue east on the TransCanada, stopping at **Salmon Arm** (7½ hrs, $72), **Revelstoke** (9 hrs, $90) and **Golden** (11½ hrs, $118), continuing to **Banff** (13½ hrs, $124) and **Calgary** (15-17 hrs, $90).

Fraser Canyon *p61*
Greyhound, www.greyhound.ca, runs 3 daily buses from **Vancouver** to **Cache Creek** (5½ hrs, $58), stopping at all towns along the way.

Kamloops *p62*
Air
Air Canada, www.aircanada.com, flies daily to **Vancouver** ($109-149) and **Calgary** ($109-129). **Central Mountain Air**, T1888-865 8585, www.flycma.com, flies daily to **Vancouver** ($163) and **Prince George** ($331).
  BC Transit, T250-376 1216, runs a regular public bus service downtown. The **Airporter Shuttle**, T250-314 4803, charges about $12 for the same trip. **Sun-Star Shuttle**, T250-544 8005, www.sunstarshuttle.com, runs 8-10 times daily to and from Sun Peaks Ski Resort, $42.50, under 12s $24 one-way.

Bus
Local BC Transit bus No 1 (Tranquille) goes to the North Shore, airport and city park; bus No 6 (Cityloop) runs round town to the youth hostel and Greyhound station.
Long distance The Greyhound station is at 725 Notredame Dr, T250-374 1212, with 7 daily buses to **Vancouver** (4½-5 hrs, $58), 4 to **Calgary** (9 hrs,$82), 4 to **Prince George** (7 hrs, $83) and 4 to **Kelowna** (2 fast, 2 slow, $31).
  Kamloops Ski & Ride Bus, T250-314 9923, www.canadawestcoach.com, runs a week-end shuttle bus to the hill leaving Kamloops 0740, $15 one-way, $25 same-day return.

Taxi
Kami Cabs, T250-554 1377; **Yellow Cabs**, T250-374 3333.

Train

Via Rail, T1800-561 8630, www.viarail.ca, runs west to **Vancouver** on Mon, Thu, Sat (9 hrs, from $64); and east to **Jasper** on Mon, Wed, Sat (8½ hrs, from $85).

The Shuswap *p62*
Bus

Salmon Arm receives 4 buses daily to and from **Kamloops** or **Kelowna** (2 hrs) and several to and from **Vancouver** (7-9 hrs).

Revelstoke *p63*
Bus

The **Greyhound** station, T250-837 5874, is on Fraser Dr, just off Hwy 1. There are 4 buses daily to **Vancouver** (8½ hrs) and 4 to **Calgary** (6 hrs) via **Banff** (4 hrs).

Golden *p64*
Bus

The **Greyhound** station, 1050 Hwy 1, T250-344 2917, with 4 buses daily (1 via Vernon) to **Vancouver** (11½ hrs), 4 to **Calgary** (4 hrs) and 1 to **Invermere**.

Crowsnest Highway *p65*
Bus

Greyhound runs 2 daily buses (0030, 0645) to Manning Park (3-4 hrs, $42) 1 of which continues east on Hwy 3 to **Midway** (89 hrs, $74), **Greenwood** (9 hrs, $90), **Grand Forks** (9½ hrs, $95), **Christina Lake** (10 hrs, $95), **Castlegar** (11 hrs, $107), **Nelson** (12 hrs, $118), **Creston** (14 hrs, $127), **Cranbrook** (16 hrs, $140), and **Fernie** (18 hrs, $148).

East to Rossland *p66*
Bus

The **Greyhound** station is in Trail at 1355 Bay Av, T250-368 8400. Local buses between Rossland and **Trail** leave every 1½ hrs from Cedar/Spokane in Trail and from Jubilee/St Paul in Rossland. The buses tend to be at inconvenient times, so you might need a taxi (T250-364 3344, $15).

Fernie *p68*
Bus

The **Greyhound** station is at Parks Place Lodge, 742 Hwy 3, T250-423 6871, with 2 buses daily in each direction. A shuttle to the ski hill leaves from several spots in town including the hostels. **Rocky Mountain Sky Shuttle**, www.rockymountainsky shuttle.com, runs a shuttle to Fernie from **Calgary** and **Cranbrook** airports.

Directory

Kamloops *p62*
Internet Library (free); PC Doctors Digital Café, 350 Seymour St, T250-372 5722. **Laundry** McCleaners Drycleaning & Laundromats, 301 Tranquille Rd, T250-554 2131. **Library** 465 Victoria St, T250-374 7042. **Medical services** Royal Inland Hospital, 311 Columbia St, T250-374 5111. **Post office** Canada Post, 217 Seymour St, T250-374 2444.

Revelstoke *p63*
Internet Samesun Hostel, free for guests. **Laundry** Family Laundry, 409 W 1st St, T250-837 3938. **Medical services** Queen Victoria Hospital, 1200 Newlands Rd, T250-837 2131. **Post office** Canada Post, 301 W 3rd St, T250-837 3228.

East to Rossland *p66*
Internet Page One Used Books, 1703 2nd Av, Trail, T250-368 8004. **Medical services** Trail Regional Hospital, 1200 Hospital Bench, Trail, T250-368 3311. **Post office** Canada Post, 2096 Columbia Av, T250-362 7644.

Fernie *p68*
Internet Mug Shots Bistro, 592 3rd Av, T250-423 8018. **Library** 492 3rd Av, T250- 423 4458. **Medical services** Sparling East Medical Centre, 402 2nd Av T250-423 4442. **Post office** Canada Post, 491 3rd Av, T250-423 7555.

Contents

Footprint features

Canadian Rockies

Ins and outs

Getting there and around

Calgary has the closest major airport to the Rockies, a mere 128 km east of Banff, receiving international and domestic flights. Several shuttle services run directly from Calgary Airport to Banff, Canmore and Lake Louise. **Greyhound** runs daily buses to Banff from Vancouver and Calgary and to Jasper from Prince George. **VIA Rail** operates three weekly trains to Jasper from Vancouver and Kamloops and three more from Prince Rupert and Prince George.

The best way to get around the Rockies is with your own vehicle or bike (starting at Jasper is easier for cyclists). Be aware that some people are prone to slam on their brakes in the middle of the road if they spot a sheep or deer so drive defensively. Greyhound buses connect Banff with Lake Louise, Field and Jasper. ▸▸ *For details of flights from Calgary Airport, see Essentials, page 6 and Transport, page 101.*

Visitor information

There are first-class **Visitor Centres/Park Offices** in Banff, Lake Louise Village, Field (Yoho) and Jasper. Staff here are excellent sources of information about hikes and all other park activities and usually keep a small library of key hiking guides. They hand out very useful maps with trail descriptions and backcountry guides, and issue compulsory wilderness passes for backcountry camping. They also organize guided hikes and other activities, and operate a voluntary safety registration programme for those engaging in potentially hazardous activities.

Friends of the Parks ⓘ *www.friendsofbanff.com, www.friendsofjasper.com, www.friendsofyoho.ca, www.friendsrevglacier.com*, sell an assortment of guidebooks and maps. The *DEMR 1:50,000* topographic maps are expensive and tend to cover a limited area; the *Gem Trek*, www.gemtrek.com, maps cover more terrain and so can be more useful. Most hikes are clearly marked, well maintained and much trodden, so finding your way is rarely an issue. **Parks Canada** ⓘ *T1888-773 8888, www.pc.gc.ca*, produces two 1:200,000 maps – one for Banff, Yoho and Kootenay; one for Jasper – which are recommended as an overview.

Visitor centres keep track of local accommodation vacancies. If turning up without a reservation, their assistance can save a lot of time and hassle. They even have a courtesy phone. For a useful overview of all the parks, including maps that show the major trails, campgrounds and hostels, be sure to pick up the invaluable *Mountain Guide* from any visitor centre. Weather information is available at T403-762 2088 for Banff, Yoho and Kootenay national parks and T780-852 3185 for Jasper. For some inspiring images, visit www.experiencemountainparks.ca.

Best time to visit

Summer is best for most people, specifically July and August, when the days are warm and long and the trails most likely to be dry. Naturally, this is also when the trails and towns are at their busiest, which can be horrifying if you've come to get away from it all. Spring and autumn are much calmer and certain trails can be hiked as early as mid-May and as late as October. The majority, however, are snow-bound until July and in autumn the weather can be dangerously unpredictable. September is a favourite month for many people, as all the larches turn a glorious gold. Even at the height of summer, the Rockies receive a lot of rain, especially on the west of the divide. You could have clear blue skies every day for a week, or just as easily endure three weeks of solid downpours. At high altitude anything can happen any time and snow is never out of the question. The winter ski season generally runs from mid-December to the end of May, but conditions are best in March when days are warmer and longer and the powder is most plentiful.

Park fees

Banff and Jasper have booths on the main access roads collecting park fees. **Day passes** ① *$9.80, senior $8.30, under 16s $4.90, under 6s free, family $19.60*, are valid for all the parks up to 1600 the following day. Day passes can also be bought at visitor centres and campgrounds. No fee is charged for through traffic. An annual **Discovery Pass** ① *$67.70, senior $57.90, youth $33.30, family $136.40*, is valid for entry to 27 National Parks and 77 National Historic Sites in Canada. If staying for a week or more, it is well worth getting one of these, as they also entitle you to discounts at a number of sights and on certain tours. They can be bought by phone, T403-760 1343, or online at www.pg.gc.ca.

Mandatory **Wilderness Passes** ① *$9.80 per person per night*, are for backcountry camping. An **annual pass** ① *$68.70*, is good for unlimited wilderness camping in all Western Canada national parks. If you buy one, you still have to register. You can trade seven day-pass receipts for one of these. The fee for backcountry reservation (which is not mandatory, but necessary for Yoho) is $11.70. Front country campgrounds range from $38.20 for RV sites with water, sewer and electrical, to $10.80 for primitive overflow sites. A campsite day use permit is $8.80. A fire permit is $8.80 per day, including firewood. **Reservations** ① *T1877-737 3783, T1905-426 4648 (for outside North America), www.pccamping.ca*, can now be made, with a $11.70 fee. Fishing permits are $9.80 per day or $34.30 annually.

Flora and fauna in the Rockies

Flora From mid-July to mid-August, the Rockies' many meadows come alive with an exciting display of multicoloured wild flowers, including Indian paintbrush of all shades, alpine forget-me-nots, lousewort, western anemone, buttercups, daisies, alpine fleabane, false azalea, arnica, columbine, spring beauty, pearly everlasting and many more. Several types of orchid bloom about a month earlier. Red and white heather, mosses and multicoloured lichens are present throughout the temperate months. In autumn, larches and deciduous trees brighten the predominantly evergreen forests with their spectacular golden hues. Other vegetation includes a host of berry bushes, rhododendrons, red elder, cinquefoil and several species of saxifrage.

Fauna You are almost guaranteed a sighting of elk, deer and bighorn sheep, often on the roads or at campgrounds, causing a degree of excitement that after a while seems excessive. There's also a chance of seeing moose, black or grizzly bears, mountain goats and coyotes, as well as a host of smaller animals like otters, beavers, pikas and porcupines. Hoary marmots inhabit rocky slopes and make a distinctive whistling sound to warn each other of your presence. On rare occasions you'll catch a glimpse of a wolf, badger, wolverine, marten, cougar, caribou or lynx. Some first-class birdwatching spots attract of waterfowl and there's a good chance of seeing jays, ptarmigans, finches, chickadees, ospreys, various eagles and many other species.

Suggested day hikes in the Rockies

There are only a couple of hundred grizzly bears left in the Rockies and the same number of black bears. As well as being much bigger, grizzlies have a dished face, a big, muscular shoulder hump and long, curved front claws. You are more likely to see one by the side of the road than in the bush, but to minimize the chances of a scary encounter, take a few simple precautions. Any animal can be unpredictable and dangerous if scared, so keep a respectful distance. More people are attacked by elk than by bears. Female elk are most aggressive during the May to June calving season; males are especially dangerous during the September to October rutting season. According to a po-faced notice spotted at Lake Louise ski hill, the greatest number of injuries in Banff National Park result from people getting too close to squirrels.

Small creatures are indeed the ones most likely to prove a nuisance. At lower elevations, especially on dry overcast days, mosquitoes are sure to bug you. From early to mid-June ticks are prevalent, especially on sunny, grassy slopes. Check vigilantly for them at the end of the day and ideally remove them using fine-pointed tweezers: grab hold of the mouth without squeezing the body and gently pull back until the tick lets go. Pull out any remaining parts like a splinter. Then there are black flies, deer and horse flies, and no-see-ums, so named because they're too small to see.

Calgary

One of North America's youngest and most modern cities, Calgary possesses a youthful brand of energy and optimism. The Downtown area is a grid of sleek glass, chrome and granite skyscrapers, the result of an oil boom that began in the 1970s. Despite a lingering redneck turned oil baron attitude, three decades of affluence have made the town increasingly cosmopolitan and sophisticated, resulting in a wealth of interesting restaurants, bars, clubs and art galleries. Still nicknamed Cow-Town, however, Calgary is overtly proud of its cattle-ranching heritage and everyone from bank managers to ski guides dons their 10-gallon hats, leather boots and chaps to embrace their inner cowboy during the famous Stampede. Symbolically, two of the best Westerns of modern times, Brokeback Mountain and The Assassination of Jesse James, were shot here. The obvious starting point for those whose primary focus is the Rockies, Calgary merits a day of discovery. Most of what's worth seeing, including the excellent Glenbow Museum, is handily concentrated around the lively, pedestrianized Stephen Avenue Walk. With a day to spare, the fascinating Badlands and Dinosaur Museum of Drumheller, 148 km to the northeast, make a recommended day trip.

Ins and outs

Getting there

Calgary International Airport (YCC) ① *T403-735 1200, www.calgaryairport.com*, is 10 km northeast of Downtown. **Calgary Transit** bus No 57 runs to Whitehorn C-train station for connections into town. **Allied Airport Shuttle** ① *T403-299 9555, www.airportshuttle calgary.ca, 0530-2130, $15, under 12s $10, one-way, daily every 30 mins 0800-2400*, runs to numerous downtown locations.

Sun Dog Tours ① *T1888-786 3461, www.sundogtours.com, 1130-2000*, operate seven shuttles daily from 1130-2000 to Kananaskis, Canmore, Banff (all $50/25 one-way), Lake Louise ($70/35) and Jasper ($129/65) (reservations recommended). The **Greyhound** station is at 877 Greyhound Way SW. A free shuttle runs to the Seventh Avenue and Tenth Street C-train from Gate 4. ▸▸ *See Transport, page 101.*

Getting around

Greater Calgary is a vast ever-expanding metropolis that is difficult to negotiate, but the Downtown area is small enough to tackle on foot. The **Plus 15 Walking System** is a 16 km maze of walkways connecting offices, shopping centres, restaurants and boutiques, designed to avoid the cold outside in winter. It's the world's longest such system, and lots of fun to explore. **Calgary Transit** ① *www.calgarytransit.com*, runs a cheap and efficient system of buses and the electric C-train. The grid of streets is divided into quadrants, with Centre Street dividing east from west and the river dividing south from north. In a three-digit street number, the first digit refers to the block, so 130 Ninth Avenue SE means that the building is No 30 on Ninth Avenue in the block between Central and First streets southeast.

Driving in Calgary is difficult and parking is always a problem. Drivers should be aware that the **TransCanada Highway** runs north of Downtown as 16th Avenue Northeast. Highway 2, the major north-south artery, splits the town in two. **Macleod Trail** is Highway 2 heading south, **Deerfoot Trail** is Highway 2 heading north. Signs often refer to the highway's name and not its number.

Best time to visit

With an average low of -15.7°C in January, Calgary is too cold to visit in the winter. The best month is July, which has the Stampede, a microbrewery festival, the folk festival and Shakespeare in the Park. September, which is also a great time to visit the nearby Rockies, has Art Week and the International Film Festival and enjoys a climate that is midway between the too-cold winter and too-hot summer.

Tourist information

Calgary's main **Visitor Centre** ① *101 9th Av SW, T403-750 2362, www.tourism calgary.com*, is at the base of the Calgary Tower. There are also desks on the Arrivals level of the airport, T403-735 1234, and at Southcentre Mall between The Bay and Centre Court, T403-271 7670. Be sure to pick up their excellent *Visitor Guide* and also *Where Calgary*, www.where.ca/calgary, which is a useful bi-monthly magazine usually found at the visitor centres or high-end hotels. It's also worth checking www.downtowncalgary.com, and www.calgaryattractions.com.

Downtown Calgary → *For listings, see pages 94-101.*

Calgary Tower

ⓘ *101 9th Av/Centre St, T403-266 7171, www.calgarytower.com, daily 0900-2100, to 2200 Jul-Aug, $14, under 17s $10, under 12s $6, family $40.*

Since it contains the Visitor Centre, **Calgary Tower** is a good place to begin your explorations. This has been the city's most distinctive landmark since it was built in 1968, when its 190-m height was unchallenged by the surrounding structures. Even today, great views of the city, with the Rockies as a backdrop, can be enjoyed from the Observation Terrace where the glass walls are complemented by glass floors and give the novel sensation of being suspended in space. Next door is one of Calgary's oldest, most impressive buildings, the **Fairmont Palliser Hotel**, whose opulent interior, featuring marble columns and floors, handmade rugs and public art, is worth a quick look.

Glenbow Museum

ⓘ *130 9th Av SE, T403-268 4100, www.glenbow.org, daily 0900-1700, Thu 0900- 2100, $14, youth $9.*

Spread over three floors, the large and varied collection of the Glenbow Museum represents Calgary's most compelling attraction. The second floor contains the permanent exhibitions **Many Faces, Many Paths: Art of Asia**, an impressive collection of Asian religious sculptures, and **Historical Art**, a collection of pieces from the 18th to 20th centuries arranged thematically, plus the semi-permanent **Modernist Art** collection, which focuses on 20th-century Canadian artists, especially those from the West. Also here is the **ARC Discovery Room**, where children are encouraged to explore some of the museum's current topics through interactive multimedia learning stations, and reveal their artistic side. The third floor presents an intense introduction to Native Canadian culture. **Niitsitapiisinni: Our Way of Life** uses interactive displays, artefacts and a circular narrative path to explore the history and culture of the Blackfoot. **Native Cultures from the Four Directions** features artworks by various First Nations of the northwest. There are some fine examples of carving, beadwork, textiles and even music, such as the eerie throat music of the Inuit. **Mavericks: An Incorrigible History of Alberta** recounts the history of Southern Alberta through the stories of 48 spirited and adventurous individuals, using interactive technology to present this instructive material in a fresh, dynamic way. On the fourth floor are **Treasures of the Mineral World**, **Where Symbols Meet: A Celebration of West African Achievement**, and **Warriors: A Global Journey through Five Centuries**, which traces the history of warfare across different cultures. There are also always a few temporary and visiting exhibitions of a high calibre. The ground floor contains a good gift shop and a café.

Around Stephen Avenue Walk

After the museum, the obvious thing to do is wander down the pedestrianized section of Eighth Avenue between Macleod Trail and Barclay Mall. Known as **Stephen Avenue Walk** this is the most intact turn-of-the-century downtown street in Western Canada, with many of Calgary's finest and oldest buildings rubbing shoulders with the brand new. Those hungry for more culture could check out the nearby **Art Gallery of Calgary** ⓘ *117 8th Av SW, T403-770 1350, www.artgallerycalgary.org, Tue-Sat 1000-1700, $5, under*

Calgary

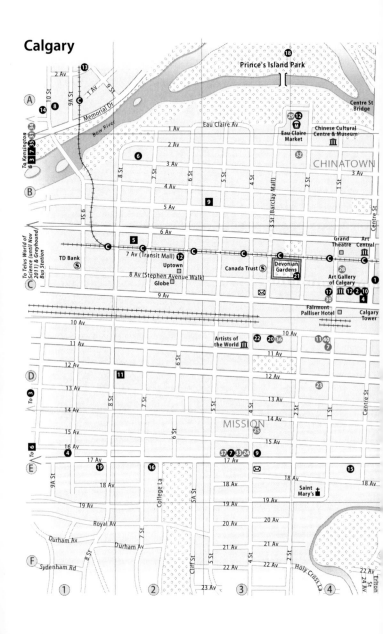

200 metres
200 yards

Sleeping 🛏

5 Calgary Downtown
  Suites **9** *B3*
Auberge Chez Nous
  Hostel **8** *B5*
Calgary City View **10** *D6*
Calgary International
  Hostel **1** *C6*
Foxwood B&B **6** *E1*
Good Knight B&B **3** *A1*
Inglewood B&B **2** *C6*
Le Germain **4** *C4*
Nuvo Hotel & Suites **11** *D2*
River Wynde Executive
  B&B **7** *B1*
Sandman **5** *C2*

Eating 🍴

Belvedere **2** *C4*
Bistro Piq Niq **17** *C4*
Brava Bistro **16** *E2*
Buchanan's **6** *B2*
Caffe Beano **4** *E1*
Catch Restaurant
  & Oyster Bar **1** *C4*
Cilantro **9** *E3*
Divino Wine & Cheese
  Bistro **10** *C4*
Galaxie Diner **3** *D1*
Good Earth Café **12**
  A4/C2/C4
Heartland Café **13** *A1*

Jing Jang Bakery **5** *B5*
La Chaumière **15** *E4*
Living Room **7** *E3*
Marathon **8** *A1*
Mother Tucker's **20** *D3*
Muse Restaurant &
  Lounge **35** *A1*
River Café **18** *A3*
Roasterie Too **14** *A1*
Silver Dragon **27** *B5*
Sultan's Tent **19** *E1*
Teatro **21** *C4*
Thai Sa-On **22** *D3*

Bars & clubs 🍸

Auburn Saloon **28** *C4*
Barley Mill **29** *A4*
Beat Niq Jazz
  & Social Club **30** *C4*
Café Meditteranean **7** *D4*
Don Quijote **32** *B4*
Hifi Club **11** *D4*
Hop in Brew Pub **23** *D4*
Local 510 **24** *E3*
Milk Tiger Lounge **25** *E3*
Ming **33** *E3*
Molly Malone's **34** *B1*
Muse **31** *A1*
Ship & Anchor **37** *E3*
Vicious Circle **40** *D4*
Whiskey **36** *D3*

18s $2.50, under 12s free, lunch-hour programmes Tue-Fri 1200-1300, $2, which hosts 15 to 20 exhibitions each year, showcasing the works of 35 to 40 Calgary and Canadian artists. Across the road is **Art Central** ① *100 7th Av SW/Centre St, T403-543 9600, www.artcentral.ca, Mon-Sat 1100-1800, free*, which contains 57 individual spaces dedicated to artist studios, galleries, cafés, arty boutiques and a restaurant. Also nearby are the **EPCOR Centre for the Performing Arts** and the **Cathedral Church of the Redeemer** ① *9th Av and 1st St SE*, one of Calgary's most attractive buildings.

While Stephen Avenue Walk's ground level is lined with pubs, restaurants, street vendors, buskers and some funky shops, just above (connected by the Plus 15 walking system) is a world of cinemas, offices and nine department stores, such as the massive **Toronto Dominion Square** between Second and Third streets. This block is now dominated by a set of odd 20- to 25-m white steel sculptures called *The Trees*. Each 'tree' holds a large light that projects dozens of colour combinations at timed intervals, providing a weird atmosphere. Equally strange, spanning three floors of TD Square are some real full-sized trees, as well as 20,000 varieties of plant, fountains, waterfalls, ponds, bridges, pathways and art exhibitions. Known as the **Devonian Gardens** ① *317 7th Av, T403-268 2489, Sat-Wed 0930-1800, Thu-Fri 0930- 2000, free*, this is a perfect place to escape the Calgary weather. Currently under renovations, it should reopen spring 2011, better than ever, with a new playground.

Seventeenth Avenue and Fourth Street
Seventeenth Avenue Southwest ① *just south of Downtown between 2nd and 10th sts*, and **Fourth Street** are hands-down Calgary's most interesting night-time areas, with lots of good restaurants and pubs, and the highest concentration of clubs. While here, check out the nearby **St Mary's Cathedral** ① *1st St and 18th Av*, one of the latest Gothic-revival churches in Western Canada, with an incredibly striking symmetrical brick tower which is best appreciated at night. **Mission District** ① *4th St, southwest from 12th Av going south*, was originally settled by French Canadian priests and now has some classy restaurants and art galleries.

Along the Bow River → *For listings, see pages 94-101.*

Apart from the sights concentrated in the Downtown core, most places of interest are to the north, scattered along the banks of the Bow River. It makes most sense to wander down the pedestrianized **Barclay Mall** ① *3rd St SW*, to Eau Claire Market, then venture east or west to whatever appeals.

Eau Claire Market and Prince's Island Park
Pleasantly situated on the Bow River between 2nd and 3rd streets **Eau Claire Market** brings together fruit and vegetable stalls, a food hall of fast-food joints, a few cinemas and some tacky craft shops. Though this doesn't compare with Vancouver's Granville Market, it is worth a wander. Outside is an open area surrounded by pubs, which offers a welcome respite from Downtown Calgary's teeming streets, as well as acting as a meeting place and venue for cultural events. Across a pedestrian bridge is **Prince's Island Park**, a nice place for a stroll, with a wonderful café.

Kensington

Situated on the north bank, reached via a footbridge from Prince's Island Park or more directly from the **Louise Bridge** ① *4th Av SW*, the colourful and culturally stimulating neighbourhood of Kensington is as close as Calgary gets to a bohemian, alternative scene, with lots of pubs, tasteful restaurants and interesting shops. Those who dislike cities but are obliged to spend a day in Calgary should head straight here.

Telus World of Science

① 701 11th St SW, T403-268 8300, www.calgaryscience.ca, daily 1000-1600, to 2200 Fri, $19.75, under 17s $16.75, under 12s $12.25. C-train to 10th St station.

Predictably enough, this place is aimed predominantly at kids. Through hands-on mini experiments and intriguing snippets of information, they're taught about the human brain, the five senses, engineering, design, farming, ecology, the universe and much more. The **Discovery Dome** shows 40-minute IMAX-style films, while the **Creative Kids Museum** gives younger children the chance to let rip, dramatize, make art and music, and get messy. There's a playground made to resemble the caves, rocks and hoodoos of Alberta's landscapes, surrounded by murals, and another fun exhibit based on sensory illusions. The **Shaw Millennium Park** next door is a giant purpose-built skateboard park which also has some volleyball courts. Decent as it may sound, the Centre falls way short of most similar venues elsewhere. However, in autumn 2011 it is due to reopen in a location north of the Calgary Zoo, and promises to be infinitely better. Check out their website for the latest news.

Chinatown

A few blocks east of the market, Calgary's Chinatown is small but clean and packed with cheap bakeries and restaurants offering dim sum. The **Chinese Cultural Centre and Museum** ① *197 1st St SW, T403-262 5071, www.culturalcentre.ca, daily 1100-1700, $4, youth/child $2 for museum, dome interior daily 0900-2100, bus No 31*, is its main attraction, featuring a magnificent dome copied from the 15th-century Temple of Heaven in Beijing. Its interior features 561 individually crafted gold dragons and 40 phoenixes. There are temporary art galleries on the second and third floors (free entry) and a very worthwhile museum downstairs with a number of fascinating exhibits, such as a big picture of tigers made entirely of feathers, a 'transparent' bronze mirror and a bronze bowl which spurts water when it's rubbed.

Fort Calgary and Inglewood

Fort Calgary ① *750 9th Av SE, T403-290 1875, www.fortcalgary.com, daily 0900- 1700, $11, under 17s $7, under 6s $5, under 2s free, bus No 1, 75 or 41 from Downtown*, is a reconstruction of the 1875 North West Mounted Police fort built to control the trouble caused by rogue whisky traders. It's staffed by costumed guides, whose stories about Calgary's roots supplement the exhibits. Just to the east, on Ninth Avenue Southeast between 10th and 12th streets, is Inglewood which is Calgary's oldest district. This is where some of the city's grandest houses and cottages can be found, as well as a concentration of antiques shops. Still further east is **Inglewood Bird Sanctuary** ① *2425 9th Av SE, T403-221 4500, May-Sep daily 1000-1700, Oct-Apr Tue-Sun 1000-1600, paths open year round till dusk, by donation, bus No 411 from Downtown, No 1 back*, with 32 ha of paths, 250 bird species, 300 plant species and an interpretive centre.

Calgary Zoo

ⓘ *1300 Zoo Rd NE, via Memorial Dr, T403-232 9300, www.calgaryzoo.com, daily 0900-1700, $19, under 12s $11, under 2s free, train tours for children, $3, take the C-train.*

Across from the fort, situated on St George's Island between two branches of the Bow River, are the **Botanical Gardens**, **Prehistoric Park** and **Calgary Zoo**. With over 1000 animals from all over the world, including the usual favourites, this is a good place to spend the day, with lots of facts about the animals dotted around to make it an educational experience. The Prehistoric Park, entered via a suspension bridge across the river, has plastic life-sized dinosaurs in rather unconvincing settings. The botanical gardens are 2 ha of colour. The conservatory, containing tropical, arid and butterfly gardens, is well worth a visit. There's also a great playground and tours on a little train for children under 12.

Drumheller and the Badlands → *For listings, see pages 94-101.*

Apart from the Rockies, the most worthwhile destination in Alberta is centred on the small, unexceptional town of Drumheller, an easy day excursion from Calgary. The Badlands scenery here is truly exceptional, easily enjoyed thanks to a circular driving route that connects some great vantage points, and takes in one of the world's finest palaeontology museums.

On the way to Drumheller, you'll pass **Horseshoe Canyon**, one of the most dramatic viewpoints for admiring the Badlands. Just before you reach town, **Reptile World** ⓘ *95 3rd Av E, T403-823 8623, www.reptileworld.net, May to Aug 0900-2200, Sep-Oct, Mar-Apr 1000-1700, Nov-Feb 1200-1700 Thu-Mon, $7.50, under 8s $5, under 5s free,* cashes in on the dominant theme, with a collection of 200 reptiles and amphibians, including cobras, anacondas, snakes and toads that can be handled, and Fred the 270-kg (600-lb) alligator. **Drumheller** itself remains hidden in the canyon until the last moment, which is no bad thing as it's a fairly drab place. The nicest part of town is on its north side just over the bridge. As well as a wading pool, which offers some relief from the intense summer heat and the **World's Biggest Dinosaur** ⓘ *26 m high, $3 to climb up and stand in its mouth,* this is where you'll find the **Visitor Information Centre** ⓘ *60 1st Av West, T403-823 8100, www.travel drumheller.com, Jul-Aug daily 0900-2100, Sep-Jun 1000-1730.* This is the place for maps and self-guided tour information. If here in July, ask about the celebrated **Passion Play** ⓘ *17th St SW/Dinosaur Trail, T403-823 2001, www.canadianpassion play.com,* staged for six days in a dramatic natural amphitheatre.

Royal Tyrrell Museum of Palaeontology

ⓘ *6 km northwest of Drumheller on Hwy 838 (North Dinosaur Trail), T403-823 7707, www.tyrrellmuseum.com, mid-May to mid-Sep daily 0900-2100, Sep-May Tue-Sun 1000-1700, $10, under 18s $6, under 6s free. There are 2 walking trails: a 1-hr and a 2½-hr loop, that lead from the museum through the Badlands in Midland Provincial Park. It's difficult to reach the museum without your own transport, so it makes good sense and is good value to go with a tour company.*

Half a million visitors a year flock to the Royal Tyrrell Museum to see the world's largest collection of complete dinosaur skeletons, almost 40 in all, including the ever-popular Tyrannosaurus rex. With this many people, you can expect it to be very crowded in summer, so think about arriving early or late. State-of-the-art technology is used to talk visitors through the Earth's history, from the primordial soup to the present. Displays explain matters such as evolution, plate tectonics and geology, how fossils are created and how they are found and prepared. One engrossing exhibit deals with the findings at **Burgess Shale** in Yoho National Park, using a stunning display set in a dark tunnel to represent an ocean bed from 500 million years ago, with the bizarre prehistoric creatures blown up to 12 times their original size and floating around in a surreal, illuminated landscape. In the Cretaceous Alberta gallery, you can wander through a recreated 70-million-year-old riverbed amidst a pack of Albertosaurus. The Lords of the Land gallery showcases some of the Museum's rarest, most fragile and scientifically significant pieces.

The whole experience builds you up to the almost overwhelming climax of the **Dinosaur Hall**, where a mind-blowing collection of skeletons is exhibited in front of artistic backdrops evoking the deltas, swamps and lush vegetation that would have constituted this valley's scenery 75 million years ago. The story is completed with a series of displays that deal with the extinction of the dinosaurs, the dawn of the Age of Mammals and the occurrence of ice ages. As well as a museum, this is one of the world's premier palaeontological research facilities and runs many educational programmes. In the summer, you can assist the experts (for a fee) on one of their Day Digs.

Dinosaur Trail and Hoodoo Trail

A perfect complement to the museum is the well-signed 48-km road circuit known as the **Dinosaur Trail**, an excellent way to see the stunning Badlands. Highway 838 is the North Dinosaur Trail, Highway 837 the South Trail. They join at the Bleriot Ferry. Which way you drive the loop depends on whether you want to visit the museum at the beginning or end, it's the first stop if you follow Highway 838. The next key attraction is **Horsethief Canyon**, which has superb views. Thereafter the road drops down to cross the river, with a lovely campground on the south bank. Views from this side have a different quality, so be sure to stop at the **Orkney Hill Viewpoint** on the way back to town.

The less essential **Hoodoo Trail** runs 25 km southeast along Highway 10 to a minor collection of hoodoos, mushroom-shaped sandstone pillars that would have appealed to Dr Seuss. On the way, you pass yellow canola fields dotted with nodding donkeys, a suspension bridge and the **Atlas Coal Mine National Historic Site** ① *T403-822 2220, www.atlascoalmine.ab.ca, daily Jul-Aug 0930-2030, May-Jun 0930-1730, Sep-Oct 1000-1700, $7*, one of many remnants of the once-booming local mining industry. Various guided tours are available: a 1¼-hour tunnel tour underground ($12); a 45-minute tour of Canada's last-standing wooden tipple mine, eight stories high amongst giant machinery and miles of conveyor belts ($9); a 45-minute mine train tour on a coal car; and a one-hour Ghost Walk tour that explores the shady side of mining towns. All tour prices include admission; take two tours for $14, or 3 for $16. A detour to the ghost town of **Wayne** is a pretty drive, with 11 bridges along the way, and highly recommended in September when the Wayne Music Festival takes place.

Cowboy Trail

① *For more information pick up a brochure, call T1866-627 3051 or visit www.thecowboytrail.com.*
Southern Alberta's tourist board has put together a number of self-guided tours for visitors. The most tempting is the **Cowboy Trail**, most of which follows Highway 22, which can be

picked up just west of Calgary. It runs south from Rocky Mountain House National Historic Site, some 385 km north, to Cardston near Waterton Lakes (see page 156), via a number of ranches and heritage sites, including Longview's Bar U Ranch, Head-Smashed-In-Buffalo-Jump (see page 159) and the Kootenai Brown Heritage Village in Pincher Creek.

Calgary listings

For Sleeping and Eating price codes and other relevant information, see pages 9-11.

Sleeping

Downtown Calgary *p87, map p88*
There are disappointingly few mid-range options in Downtown Calgary. The major routes into town are lined with cheap chain motels, especially Banff Trail NW, which is known as Motel Village. Note that rates go up by at least 50% during the stampede (see Festivals), when reservations are essential.
$$$$ Hotel Le Germain, 899 Centre St, T403-264 8990, www.germaincalgary.com. Gorgeous rooms and suites, bright, modern and very comfortable, in a super stylish downtown boutique hotel.
$$$ 5 Calgary Downtown Suites, 618 5th Av SW, T403-451 5551, www.5calgary.com. A pretty good deal considering the handy downtown location. A range of reasonable suites with outdoor swimming pool, hot tub, fitness room, sauna and internet access.
$$$ Nuvo Hotel and Suites, 827 12th Av, SW, T403-452 6789, www.nuvohotelsuites. com. Nicely situated between Downtown and 17th Av, this very chic and contemporary hotel has stylish suites that are good value.
$$$ Sandman, 888 7th Av SW, T403-237 8626, www.sandmanhotels.com. The best centrally located mid-range hotel, offering comfortable rooms, an indoor pool, hot tub and fitness room. Also has a lounge and restaurant.
$$ Calgary City View, 2300 6th St SE, T403-237 0454, www.calgarycityview.com. 3 pleasant rooms and a studio in an interesting wood buikding close to the Stampede Grounds, with big balconies offering great views. Good value.

$ Auberge Chez Nous Hostel, 149 5th Av SE, T403-232 5475, www.auberge-cheznous. com. Very central, bright and clean, with French-style decor. Dorm rooms each have 5-6 beds (not bunks) separated by lockers to afford some privacy. Communal living room and small kitchen. Friendly staff and a relaxed atmosphere.
$ Calgary International Hostel, 520 7th Av SE, T403-283 6503, www.hihostels.ca. Conveniently close to Downtown, with newly decorated dorms and private rooms. Great facilities, including common room, a fully equipped kitchen, lockers, laundry facilities and free internet.

Seventeenth Avenue and Fourth Street *p90, map p88*
$$$ The Foxwood B&B, 1725 12th St SW, T403-244 6693, www.thefoxwood.com. A beautiful Edwardian house furnished with antiques, close to the lively 17th Av district. 2 plush rooms and a suite with private bath and its own balcony. A living room, cosy den, hot tub, big veranda at the front and garden with a deck at the back.

Along the Bow River *p90, map p88*
$$$ Inglewood B&B, 1006 8th Av SE, Inglewood, T403-262 6570, www.inglewoodbed andbreakfast.com. 3 pleasant rooms in a Victorian-style house near the river.
$$ A Good Knight B&B, 1728 7th Av NW, T403-270 7628, www.agoodknight.com. 2 nice rooms with private bath and an apartment in a Victorian-style house close to Kensington.
$$ River Wynde Executive B&B, 220 10A St NW, Kensington, T403-270 8448, www.riverwynde.com. Lovely heritage

home, with 4 rooms, with features such as hardwood floors, private balconies and wood-burning fireplace. There's also a sunny patio, a garden, library and use of bikes.

Drumheller and the Badlands p92
$$$ Jurassic Inn by Canalta Hotels, 1103 Hwy 9 S, T403-823 7700. Probably the most comfortable hotel in town, with an indoor pool, hot tub and exercise room, but overpriced.

$$ Badlands Motel, 801 North Dinosaur Trail, on way to museum, T403-823 5155. About the cheapest of the standard motels in town.

$$ McDougall Lane B&B, 71 McDougall Lane, T403-823 5379, www.bbcanada.com/1787. A large house with 2 plush rooms and 1 suite, a very nice living room, hot tub and a fabulous sunken flower garden featuring fountains, ponds and decks. Full breakfast included.

$$ Newcastle Country Inn, 1130 Newcastle Trail, T403-823 8356, www.newcastlecountry inn.net. 11 pleasant rooms in a rather plain house. Clean and quiet, with friendly, helpful hosts, who provide a good continental breakfast. Highly rated by former guests.

$$ Taste the Past, 281 2nd St, T403-823 5889, www.bbcanada.com/taste. A nicely restored turn-of-the-century home, with 3 reasonable rooms. Antique decor, a billiards table, fireplace, piano, library, and a garden veranda. Full breakfast included.

Camping
Bleriot Ferry Provincial Rec Area, 23 km west on the south side of the ferry crossing, on the South Dinosaur Trail, T403-823 1749. A pleasant little site right on the river, good for swimming. Great views of the landscape.

Dinosaur Trail RV Resort, 11 km west on North Dinosaur Trail (Dinosaur Trail North), T403-823 9333. A nice spot with a swimming pool and canoe rentals. Reservations necessary in summer.

Little Fish Lake Provincial Park, T403-823 1749, 25 km east of the Hoodoos off Hwy 10 on Hwy 573. A great campground down a dirt road, next to a lake that's usually dry.

River Grove Campground and Cabins, 25 Poplar St, off Hwy on north side of bridge, T403-823 6655, www.camprivergrove.com. The best of a few campsites around town, with semi-private pitches on the river. They also have 7 rustic log cabins and some tepees (**$$**).

Eating

Downtown Calgary p87, map p88
¶¶¶ Belvedere, 107 8th Av SW, T403-265 9595, Mon-Sat. One of Calgary's most long-running and respected restaurants, this New York-style dining room has a romantic atmosphere, a seasonal, international menu, and a top wine list.

¶¶¶ Buchanan's, 738 3rd Av SW, T403-261 4646. Dominated by a huge, well-stocked bar, this old-fashioned San Francisco-style chop house is renowned for its steaks and burgers. Also has a broad range of wines by the glass and 146 malt whiskies.

¶¶¶ Catch Restaurant & Oyster Bar, 100 8th Av SE, T403-206 0000. With its hardwood floors, chandeliers and classic furnishings, this long, elegant room is a beautiful place to enjoy international dishes prepared with French flair. There's also a handsome dark-wood oyster bar, serving San Francisco-style seafood and draught beer at more affordable prices.

¶¶¶ Divino Wine and Cheese Bistro, 113 8th Av SW, T403-234 0403. With its red-brick walls, wood floor and open kitchen, this is a gorgeous, intimate little space. Broad menu of international, California-style cuisine, including gourmet apple wood-fired pizzas and plenty of wines and cheeses.

¶¶¶ River Café, Prince's Island Park, T403-261 7670. The best location in town, with views of the river and the Downtown skyline. A wonderful interior reminiscent of an upmarket mountain fishing lodge, with an open fireplace. The menu is broad and very sophisticated, with plenty of fish and a West Coast-style emphasis on freshness and locality of ingredients.

Teatro, 200 8th Av, T403-290 1012. A long-standing favourite, set in an elegant vintage bank building with sumptuous decor, attentive service, and a lively but romantic ambience. The menu focuses on high-end Italian-style cuisine with international influences, using only the freshest ingredients, and the wine list is huge.

Bistro Piq Niq, 811 1st St SW, T403-263 1650. Gourmet French-style cuisine in an intimate setting that's genuinely reminiscent of a French bistro. Great service and value. Downstairs is a small venue for live jazz, Thu-Sat.

MotherTucker's, 345 10th Av SW, T403-262 5541. Popular with big eaters, this rustic, Western-style eatery specializes in prime rib but is most renowned for its buffet lunches, Sun brunch and 60-item salad bar.

Silver Dragon, 106 3rd Av SE, T403-264 5326. The place to go for the full dim sum experience or for very authentic Cantonese dishes. A locals' favourite for 40 years. Try the pan-fried prawns.

Thai Sa-On, 351 10th Av SW, T403-264 3526. Rated the best Thai food in town for 15 years. Also has a surprisingly good wine list.

Galaxie Diner, 1413 11th St SW, T403-228 0001. Great breakfasts in an old-style diner, complete with booths and bar stools.

Good Earth Café, Eau Claire Market; 119 8th Av SW; 707 7th Av SW; 602 1st St SW; 333 5th Av SW; and 1502 11th St SW. Casual atmosphere, speciality coffees, baked goods and vegetarian snacks.

Jing Jang Bakery, downstairs at 100 3rd Av SE, T250-265 9588. Delicious Chinese buns, like the BBQ pork, curried beef or honey.

Seventeenth Avenue and Fourth Street *p90, map p88*

Cilantro, 338 17th Av, T403-229 1177. A long-standing favourite, serving California-fusion eclectic cuisine in a setting dominated by dark wood and wrought iron. Has an open kitchen and an inviting outdoor patio.

La Chaumière, 139 17th Av SW, T403-228 5690. French-style haute cuisine with an emphasis on game and seafood, served in almost excessively opulent surroundings.

Brava Bistro, 723 17th Av SW, T403-228 1854. A warm, intimate, stylish setting for French/Canadian cuisine focusing on organic and vegetarian dishes. Excellent wine list and a nice patio.

The Living Room, 514 17th Av SW, T403-228 9830. The decor here is modern, sophisticated, minimalist and sleek. The food puts a contemporary twist on French and Italian cuisine, with fondues, shared meals and encouraged wine pairings. There's also one of the best outdoor patios in town.

Caffe Beano, 1613 9th St, T403-229 1232. A quaint, cosy café that's favoured by artists and intellectuals.

Kensington *p91, map p88*

Muse Restaurant and Lounge, 107 10A St NW, T403-670 6873. A fabulous dining experience. The interior is intimate and sophisticated, the West Coast-style dishes are adventurous, exciting, and perfectly executed. The ambience, service and wine list are also spot on.

Marathon, 130 10th St NW, T403-283 6796. Delicious Ethiopian curries. Popular and intimate. Lunch buffet.

Sultan's Tent, 4 14th St NW, T403-244 2333. Delicious authentic Moroccan dishes such as tajines and couscous. Decor made to resemble a Berber tent, with floor seating.

Heartland Café, 940 2nd Av NW, T403-270 4541. Pleasant local hang-out with a wholefood attitude.

The Roasterie Too, 227 10th St NW, T403-270 3304. Fresh roasted coffee, in a comfy spot with outdoor seating.

Drumheller and the Badlands *p92*

Eating choices in Drumheller are mostly family-dining joints catering to tour buses.

Bernie and the Boys Bistro, 305 4th St W, T403-823 3318. A classic diner serving superior burgers, shakes and ostrich egg omelettes.

Molly Brown's, 233 Centre St, T403-823 7481. Cosy café serving homemade lunches and good desserts.

Sizzling House, 160 Centre St, T403-823 8098. Excellent, cheap Szechuan and Thai food without the MSG or the sugar. Great value and a good veggie selection.

Whif's Flapjack House, 801 North Dinosaur Trail, in the **Badlands Motel**, T403-823 7595. Mostly breakfast but also serves lunch specials.

Bars and clubs

Downtown Calgary *p87, map p88*

Auburn Saloon, 115 9th Av SE, T403-266 6628. An arty downtown spot with a theatrical, loungey vibe and martinis and cocktails on cosy couches.

Barley Mill, 201 Barclay Parade, T403-290 1500. The most tempting choice of the many pubs around the courtyard outside **Eau Claire Market**, whose inviting summer patios offer a reprieve from the Downtown traffic. A range of beers on tap.

Café Mediterranean, 1009 1st St, T403-286 8452. Classic Middle Eastern decor, with dim lighting, low tables and chairs, gentle music, tapestries, and backgammon. The food and drinks are great, but this is recommended as the best place to smoke a hookah, a current Calgary trend.

Don Quijote, 309 2nd Av SW, T403-205 4144. A Spanish restaurant and tapas bar that turns into a Latin dance club with dancing till 0200 Fri and Sat. Not recommended for the food, though.

The Hifi Club, 219 10th Av SW, T403-263 5222. A tiny, friendly dance club often playing old school music.

Hop In Brew Pub, 213 12th Av SW, T403-266 2595. An old house converted into a cute little pub, with various rooms, a relaxed atmosphere, and an impressive selection of beers.

Vicious Circle, 1011 1st St SW, T403-269 3951. A cosy café/lounge with sofas, candlelight, good art, varied music, an appealing menu of small dishes and 140 different martinis. Attracts a mixed but sophisticated crowd.

The Whiskey, 341 10th Av SW, T403-770 2323. About the best surviving mainstream nightclub, with various spaces, including a massive illuminated glass dance floor, and a lounge.

Seventeenth Avenue and Fourth Street *p90, map p88*

Local 510, 510 17th Av, T403-229 4036. The sleek interior here strangely mixes urban sophistication with a rustic Wild West feel. The exterior wraparound patio is possibly the best in town. The food menu is simple but excellent, and the drinks are also fine, especially cocktails. The DJ music is modern but unobtrusive. A great place for a night on the town.

Milk Tiger Lounge, 1410 4th St SW, T403-261 5009. A very hip, understated, New York-style lounge, intimate and sophisticated. Excellent drinks, especially cocktails, good music, and friendly staff. Food is mostly gluten-free.

Ming, 520 17th Av SW, T403-229 1986. A very enticing, trendy martini lounge with dim lighting and an atmosphere of casual sophistication without a hint of pretence. Good food.

Ship and Anchor, 534 17th Av SW. Very popular with the locals and arguably the best pub in town. Outside seating that's perfect for people watching and an unbeatable selection of draught beers, including the whole range by excellent local brewers Big Rock.

Kensington *p91, map p88*

There are far too many British-style pubs here, all with very slight variations, so just walk (or crawl) around. You can't knock their vast selections of quality draught beers. Happy hour is 1600-1900.

Molly Malone's, 1153 Kensington Cres, T403-296 3220. A little Irish-style pub with seating on the roof and live music.

Muse Restaurant and Lounge, 107 10A St NW, T403-670 6873. A chic lounge, casual but sophisticated.

⊕ Entertainment

Downtown Calgary *p87, map p88*
Check the listings in Calgary's free listings magazine, *FFWD*, www.ffwdweekly.com, free from cafés and elsewhere.

Art galleries
Calgary has many galleries besides the **Art Gallery of Calgary** and **Art Central**. **TRUCK Contemporary Art**, 815 1st St SW, T403-261 7702, www.truck.ca. Contemporary art with a focus on hybrid and emerging work.

Cinema
Globe, 617 8th Av SW, T403-262 3308; **IMAX**, at 200 Barclay Pde SW, T403-974 4629; **Plaza**, 1133 Kensington Rd NW, T403-283 2222; and **The Uptown Stage and Screen**, 612 8th Av SW, T403-265 0120, www.theuptown.com. Mainly 1st-run indie, foreign and art-house films.

Live music
Beat Niq Jazz and Social Club, downstairs from **Bistro Piq Niq**, 811 1st St SW, T403-263 1650. Live music Thu-Sat 2130, generally small, vocal-led acts, with a cover charge.
Bookers BBQ Grill, 316 3rd St SE, T403-264 6419. This is a great place to eat, with a rustic warehouse interior and cajun dishes like jambalaya or catfish po'boy. There's live blues and jazz on Fri and Sat nights.
Broken City Social Club, 613 11th Av SW, T403-262 9976, www.brokencity.ca. A great little gritty venue for local bands, with live music – usually indie – most

nights, decent pub-style food, cheap drinks and a rooftop patio.
EPCOR Centre for the Performing Arts, 205 8th Av SE, T403-294 7455, www.epcorcentre.org. Calgary's most important performance venue, it includes a 1800-seat concert hall renowned for its beauty and fine acoustics, which hosts all genres of music from classical to rock, as well as live theatre and dance. There are also 4 theatres, some galleries, workshops and a café.
Jubilee Auditorium, 1415 14th Av, T403-297 8000, www.jubileeauditorium.com. Home of the Calgary Opera and a major venue for all kinds of touring acts.
Ranchman's, 9615 Macleod Trail S, T403-253 1100, www.ranchmans.com. An authentic cowboy saloon with live country bands Mon-Sat and a big dance floor for all that two-stepping.
Rose and Crown Pub, 1503 4th St SW, T403-244 7757. A lively pub that's a great venue for live music on Fri and Sat nights.

Spectator sports
Baseball The Calgary Cannons play at **Burns Stadium**, across Crowchild Trail from the NW Banff Trail C-train.
Canadian football McMahon Stadium, across from the NW Banff Trail C-train, T403-289 0258. Where the Calgary Stampeders, www.stampeders.com, play.
Horse racing Takes place at **Stampede Park**, 17th Av/2nd St SE, T403-261 0214.
Ice hockey Pengrowth Saddledome, 555 Saddledome Rise SE, T403-777 2177. Where **Calgary Flames**, www.flames.nhl.com, play.
Show-jumping Takes place at **Spruce Meadows**, 3 km west of Macleod Trail on Hwy 22X, T403-974 4200.

Theatre
EPCOR Centre for the Performing Arts, see above, is home to **Theatre Calgary** and other major companies.

Pumphouse Theatre, 2140 Pumphouse Av, T403-263 0079, www.pumphousetheatre.ca. Numerous small theatre groups produce plays throughout the year.

Theatre Junction at The Grand, 608 1st St SW, T403-205 2922, www.theatrejunction. com. Recently renovated, **The Grand** is Western Canada's oldest theatre, now hosting small contemporary plays, as well as music and dance.

Vertigo Theatre, 115 9th Av SE, T403-221 3707, www.vertigotheatre.com. Mystery plays.

❂ Festivals and events

Downtown Calgary *p87, map p88*
Calgary is famous far and wide for its sensational **Stampede** (see page), but there are plenty of other events scattered throughout the year.

Feb Calgary Winterfest, T403-543 5480. A month-long celebration of the cold, featuring snowboarding competitions, ice sculptures, and dogsled races.

Mar $100 Film Festival, www.100dollar filmfestival.org/fest/. A 3-day festival that showcases work from local, national and international filmmakers working with Super 8 and 16 mm film.

May FunnyFest Comedy Festival, www.funnyfest.com. 11 days and nights of live comedy performances. **International Children's Festival**, T403-294 7414, www.calgarychildfest.org. Celebrating its 25th anniversary in 2011 with 5 days of kid-friendly shows and events around town.

Jul Calgary Stampede in early Jul. **Calgary Folk Music Festival**, T403-233 0904, www.calgary folkfest.com. Held later in the month at Prince's Island Park, lasts for 4 days. Attracts some big names.

Jul-Aug Shakespeare in the Park, T403-440 6374. Performances of the Bard's plays, 3 per year, with entry by donation, on scheduled days throughout Jul and Aug in the lovely environment of Prince's Island Park.

Big Valley Country Music Jamboree in Camrose, 231 km NE, T403-672 0224 www.bigvalley jamboree.com. A major 4-day event that attracts big crowds and some major artists.

Aug Calgary Fringe Festival, T403-265 3378, www.calgaryfringe.ca. Held at the start of the month, 10 days of small shows at various venues. **Calgary International Blues Festival**, www.calgaryblues fest.com. A 7-day open-air blues bonanza. **Shady Grove Bluegrass Music Festival** in High River, 52 Km SE, T403- 652 5550, www.foothills bluegrass.com/shadygrove.php.

Sep International Film Festival, www.calgaryfilm.com. 15 days in late Sep.

O Shopping

Downtown Calgary *p87, map p88*
Antiques
There are several antiques shops in Inglewood, 9th Av SE between 11th and 13th St.

Arts and crafts
Fosbrooke Fine Arts, 2nd floor, Penny Lane, 513 8th Av SW, T403-294 1362. Displays a rotating selection showcasing 15-20 artists. **Galleria**, 907 9th Av SE, T403-270 3612. Handmade works in a variety of media from over 500 Canadian artists and potters. **Masters Gallery**, 2115 4th St SW, T403-244 2502. More classic, high-brow pieces.

Books and music
HMV, TD Sq, 8th Av SW, T403-233 0121; **McNally Robinson**, 120 8th Av SW, T403-538 1797, set in an attractive historic building, with 3 floors of books, including a good range of Prairie authors; **Pages Books on Kensington**, 1135 Kensington Rd, T403-283 6655.

Clothes and accessories
Boutik, in Hotel Arts, 119 12th Av SW, T403-698 4987. Trendy fashions and accessories from several cutting-edge designers. **Eye on Design**, 1219 9th Av, T403-266 4750.

A funky little store in Inglewood, carrying unique items by smaller designers, including lots of jewellery.

Lammle's Western Wear, 11 shops including 209 8th Av SW, T403-266 5226. The place for all your cowboy needs. What could be a better souvenir of Calgary than an authentic 10-gallon hat or cowboy boots?

The Pendulum, 1222 9th Av SE, T403-266 6369. Carries a selection of brand-name consignment clothing.

Riley and McCormack, 220 8th Av SW, T403-228 4024, also at Calgary Airport. Another fine purveyor of all things cowboy, as well as native crafts, gifts and souvenirs.

Shisomiso, 105 7th Av SW, T403-266 4211. Showcasing the clothes of 2 local designer-owners and that of other local designers.

Sporting and outdoor equipment

Coast Mountain Sports, 817 10th Av SW, T403-264 2444. A wide selection of high-end sports and mountain clothing and footwear.

Mountain Equipment Co-op, 830 10th Av SW, T403-269 2420. A massive store with all the sport and camping equipment you could need.

Patagonia, 135 8th Av, T403-266 6463. Outdoor clothing and accessories.

Ski West, 300 14th St NW, Kensington, T403-270 3800. Skis, snowboards and accessories from many leading brands.

▲ Activities and tours

Downtown Calgary p87, map p88
Tour operators

Chinook River Sports, T403-263 7238, www.chinookraft.com. Whitewater rafting on the Kicking Horse and Kananaskis rivers, and through the Horseshoe Canyon section of the Bow River.

Creative Journeys, T403-272 5653, www.creativejourneys.com. A variety of 1-day tours, including 2- to 3-hr walking tours of Calgary ($30), 3- to 4-hr bus tours of town ($40) and longer trips to Banff ($80), Jasper

($100), Waterton ($100) and the Prairies and Badlands. Also offer day trips to Drumheller ($70), Footlands and Ranchlands, including Head-Smashed-In-Buffalo-Jump ($70).

Hammerhead Scenic Tours, T403-590 6930, www.hammerheadtours.com. 1-day tours to the Badlands, Banff, Waterton and Head-Smashed-In-Buffalo-Jump. Tours tend to be a bit more expensive than **Creative Journeys**, but also a couple of hours longer.

Home On The Range, T403-229 9090, www.homeontherange.ca. Cowboy tours geared to individual needs, including authentic western experiences like cattle drives, ranch stays, historic sites, powwows, rodeos and horseback tours of the Rockies.

Inside Out Experience, T403-949 3305, www.insideoutexperience.com. A broad range of adventure tours, including white-water rafting, hiking, mountain biking, snowshoeing, cross-country skiing, horse riding and hiking.

Legendary Tours, T403-285 8376, www.legendarytravels.net. Full-day sightseeing tours to Banff and Lake Louise, Drumheller, Blackfoot Crossing, Head-Smashed-In-Buffalo-Jump, and a mixed Western Adventures trip (all $115), and to the Columbia Icefields ($249).

University of Calgary Outdoor Centre, T403-220 5038, www.calgaryoutdoorcentre.ca. Whether you want instruction, tours or gear rental, they have it all. Climbing, canoe trips, biking, kayaking, caving, hanggliding, skiing, you name it they do it.

Drumheller and the Badlands p92
Dinosaur Trail Golf Club, across from the museum, T403-823 5622, www.dinosaur trailgolf.com. One of the most interesting settings imaginable.

Wild West Badlands Tours, T1888-823 3118, www.wildwestbadlandstours.com. A variety of tours of the Badlands in an 8-passenger van, $40 for 2½-3 hrs.

⊖ Transport

Calgary *p87, map p88*
Air

For airport details, see page 86. Calgary has flights to and from all major cities within Canada with **Air Canada**, T1888-247 2262, www.aircanada.com, and **West Jet**, T1800-538 5696, www.westjet.com. Example one-way fares are $159 to **Vancouver** and $119 to **Kelowna**.

Travel agents Travel Cuts, 815 10th Av SW, T403-686 7633, 109 10th St NW, Kensington, T403-270 3640, www.travel cuts.com. Offering student discounts.

Bus

Local Calgary Transit has its own information centre at 224 7th Av SW, T403-262 1000, www.calgarytransit.com, Mon-Fri 0600-2100, Sat-Sun 0800-1800. They can provide very helpful maps. Tickets costing $2.75, youth $1.75, under 6s free, can be bought here, from machines on C-train platforms, or from shops with the **Calgary Transit** sticker. Bus drivers require the exact fare. Day passes cost $8.25, child $5.25. If you need to take more than 1 bus or C-train to complete a journey, ask the driver for a transfer (valid for 90 mins). The C-train is free downtown on 7th Av between Macleod Trail and 8 St SW.

Long distance Greyhound, T1800-661 8747, www.greyhound.ca, runs 5 daily buses to **Banff** (1½-2 hrs, $29); at least 6 to **Vancouver** (15-17 hrs, $95); and 3 direct to **Kamloops** (9 hrs, $87). **Sun Dog Tours**, T1888-786 3641, www.sundogtours.com, operate 3 shuttles daily from Downtown (1020, 1450 and 1725) and 7 from Calgary Airport (1130-2000) to **Kananaskis**, **Canmore**, **Banff** (all $50/25 one-way), **Lake Louise** ($70/35) and **Jasper** ($129/65). **Brewster**, T1800-760 6934, www.brewster.ca, operates a near-identical service.

Taxis
Associated Taxi, T403-299 1111; **Calgary Cab Co**, T403-777 2222.

Vehicle rental
Car hire All Season Rentals, 1510 10th Av SW, T403-204 1771, www.allseason motorsports.ca, offers motorbike hire; **Budget**, 140 6th Av SE, T403-226 1550, www.budget.ca; **Thrifty**, 123 5th Av SE, T403-262 4400, www.thrifty.com.
RVs Canadream Campers, 2510 27th Av NE, T403-291 1000, www.canadream.com; **Cruise Canada**, 2980 26th St NE, T403-291 4963, www.cruisecanada.com.

Drumheller and the Badlands *p92*
Roughly 150 km northeast from Calgary, Drumheller is reached on Hwy 9 north from the TransCanada Hwy. **Greyhound** buses leave Calgary daily at 0845, 1745 and 1945 (2 hrs, $35 one-way), returning at 0355, 0920 and 1725 ($64 return, $35 21 days in advance) making this just about possible as a daytrip, though tours (see above) are a better idea.

Taxi
JB Taxi Services, T403-823 7433.

❶ Directory

Calgary *p87, map p88*
Banks National Bank of Canada, 2700-530 8th Av SW, T403-294 4946; **Bank of Montreal**, 222 5th Av SW, T403-234 1810. **Currency exchange Citizens Bank of Canada**, 150-505 3rd St SW, T403-266 7321; **Olympia Trust Foreign Exchange**, 100-237 8th Av, T403-770 6350. **Medical services Foothills Medical Centre**, 1403 29th St NW, T403-944 1110; **Health Resource Centre**, 1402 8th Av NW, T403-220 0410; **Rockyview General Hospital**, 7007 14th St SW, T403-943 3000. **Post office Canada Post** 135-315 8th Av SW, T403-233 2400; 224-205 5th Av SW, T403-266 4304; 1702 4th St SW, T403-228 3788.

Banff National Park

Banff National Park, the oldest and most famous in the Canadian Rockies and Canada's number one tourist attraction, receives some 4.7 million visitors per year. This is partly due to its 6641 sq km of jaw-dropping scenery, including 25 peaks over 3000 m and 1500 km of trails, many of which are accessed from the highway and gentle enough for almost anyone. Of equal significance is its location on the country's main highway, a mere 128 km from Calgary. The park's popularity is its only drawback.

Banff Townsite is the park's main hub, a pleasant but absurdly busy place with services catering to every budget. A short hop north is Lake Louise, the single most famous location in the Rockies. From here, a nice loop leads through Yoho and Kootenay national parks, while the incredible Icefields Parkway runs north to Jasper, lined with the most drool-inducing scenery of all, peaking around the extraordinary Columbia Icefields.

Ins and outs

Getting there and around

Two companies run regular shuttles from Calgary Downtown and Airport to Banff (see page 101) and onward to Lake Louise and Jasper. **Greyhound** ① *100 Gopher St*, also run numerous daily buses to Calgary and Lake Louise. The TransCanada Highway connects Banff with Vancouver and all points east.

Banff Townsite can be easily explored on foot, as almost everything is on or near Banff Avenue. **Banff Transit** ① *T403-762 1215*, operates two Roam shuttles that cover the whole town ($2). ►► *See Transport, page 126.*

Tourist information

The **Banff Information Centre** ① *224 Banff Av, Jun-Sep daily 0800-2000, Sep-May daily 0900-1700, May-Jun daily 0900-1900*, comprises the **Parks Canada Office** ① *T403-762 1550, www.pc.gc.ca/banff*, and the **Banff Lake Louise Tourism Bureau** ① *T403-762 8421, www.banfflakelouise.com*. The former is an excellent source of information about hikes and all other park activities. It issues very useful maps for day-hikes and cycling, and one showing longer trails and backcountry campgrounds. To stay at one of the latter you must register here and buy a **Wilderness Pass** ① *$9.80 per person per night*. The Tourism Bureau can help out with sleeping arrangements. It keeps track of which hotels, B&Bs and campsites still have spaces and provides a courtesy phone. It can also provide brochures for the *Banff Historical Walking Tour*. The **Friends of Banff National Park** ① *T403-762 8918, www.friendsofbanff.com*, sells maps and all kinds of books on hiking and other activities as well as natural and cultural history. It also runs free guided walks throughout the summer. For park radio, tune in to 101.1 FM.

Banff Townsite → *For listings, see pages 116-127.*

Banff enjoys a stunning location and was once a pretty little village. Today, however, the 50,000 visitors it receives daily throughout the summer have taken their toll. The streets are perpetually heaving, the roads choked with tour buses. The relentless commercialism soon becomes tiresome and there is little to do but shop, eat and party. Those craving creature comforts will find them here in abundance, but if you are camping or staying in hostels there are nicer places to be. The main reason to visit the Townsite is for its excellent information centre to help plan your excursion, then for a little R&R when you get back. The nicest part of Banff lies at its west end, where a picturesque bridge over the Bow River gives an idea of how the village might have looked before its popularity got out of hand.

Whyte Museum of the Canadian Rockies

① *111 Bear St, T403-762 2291, www.whyte.org, daily 1000-1700, $8, under 18s $5, under 6s free, 90-min Historic Banff walking tour leaves once a day, $8.*

Created by artists Peter and Catherine Whyte, Banff's most worthwhile sight includes thousands of volumes of archives and Alpine Club records of early expeditions. Of greater significance to visitors is the fine collection of mountain-related art, much of it by the founders and a half dozen temporary exhibitions by local and international contemporary artists, usually of a documentary or educational nature. Most fascinating of all is an excellent collection of photos that vividly documents the early days of the park and the changing attitudes that have prevailed regarding its wildlife. Countless black and white pictures depict fancily dressed Edwardian tourists standing next to their vintage cars, grinning stupidly as they feed a bear by hand; or a self-satisfied ranger standing smugly over some poor dead beast. The museum presents lectures and various tours.

Banff Park Museum and around

ⓘ *91 Banff Av, T403-762 1558, mid-May to mid-Sep daily 1000-1800, daily tours 1500, mid-Sep to mid-May daily 1300-1700, weekend tour 1430, $4, youth/child $2.*

The Banff Park Museum is housed in a splendid wood cabin built in 1903, its age explaining all the skylights, which compensated for the lack of electric light. Like the building itself, the interior is more a relic from the past than a place where the past is documented. Indeed, it is described as a "museum of a museum". A large collection of dusty, old stuffed animals, dating back as far as the 1860s, pay their politically incorrect tribute to a time when people's idea of wildlife watching was taking high tea in a room lined with animal heads, and even the official park approach to wildlife preservation was to shoot all predators like cougars, lynx and eagles so that innocents such as elk, deer and sheep could multiply unhampered.

Across the river, the **Buffalo Nations Luxton Museum** ⓘ *1 Birch Av, T403-762 2388, May-Sep daily 1000-1800, Oct-Apr daily 1300-1700, $8, child $2.50*, has a small collection of First Nations artefacts such as beadwork, costumes, headdresses, a decorated tepee and a number of poorly executed dioramas. The gift shop is its best feature.

Cave and Basin Hot Springs

ⓘ *311 Cave Av, T403-762 1566, closed for renovations till Nov 2011, regular hours: mid-May to mid-Sep daily 0900-1800, mid-Sep to mid-May Mon-Fri 1100-1600, Sat-Sun 0930-1700, tours mid-May to mid-Sep daily 1100, 1400, 1600, mid-Sep to mid-May Sat-Sun 1100, $4, youth/child $2.*

A couple of kilometres southwest of Banff centre is the site of the thermal waters whose discovery prompted the park's formation. Upon seeing them for the first time, Canadian Pacific Railway builder William Van Horne exclaimed, "These springs are worth a million dollars", and how right he was. The story is told through a collection of exhibits on the second floor, and the film *Steam, Schemes and National Dreams*, shown in the replica 1887 bathhouse. The cavernous, atmospheric setting of that first pool is the highlight, making you wish it was still open for bathing. The outdoor 'basin' pool is only slightly less enticing. Look out for Banff springs snails.

The grounds are also attractive and contain a couple of short and popular walks. The interpretive **Marsh Loop Trail** ⓘ *2.7 km*, leads on boardwalks around a wetland area whose warm microclimate has made it unusually lush and flower-filled and a rewarding spot for birdwatchers. The easy and popular **Sundance Canyon Trail** ⓘ *7.4 km round trip*, follows a paved path to the canyon mouth.

Banff Springs Hotel

ⓘ *It's a boring walk up Spray Av from the centre, so take the No 1 local transit.*

After the discovery of the springs, the Canadian Pacific Railway quickly saw tourism as a

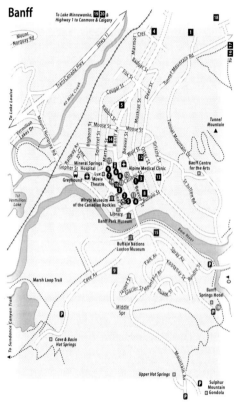

Banff

N

500 metres
500 yards

Sleeping
Banff Boutique Inn 9
Banff Y Mountain Lodge
& Sundance Bistro 15
Blue Mountain Lodge 3
Bumpers Inn 4

Driftwood Inn 14
HI Banff Alpine Centre,
  Storm Centre &
  Sundance Bistro 1
Mountain Home B&B 8
Rocky Mountain B&B 12
SameSun Banff Lodge 5
Tan-Y-Bryn 13
Tunnel Mountain I 17
Tunnel Mountain II 18
Tunnel Mountain
  Trailer Court 16
Two Jack Lakeside 19

Two Jack Main 20

Eating
Aardvark Pizza 1
Coyotes 3
Elk & Oarsman Pub
  & Grill 5
Evelyn's Coffee Bar 9
Grizzly House 8
Le Beaujolais 4
Maple Leaf Grille &
  Hoodoo Lounge 2
Nourish Vegetarian Bistro 6

Saltlik Steakhouse 7
Sushi House 10

Bars & clubs
Aurora Night Club 11
Lik Lounge 14
Rose & Crown 12
St James's Gate
  Olde Irish Pub 13
Waldhaus Pub 16
Wild Bill's Legendary
  Saloon 15

means to pay for its expensive line and went about building a series of luxurious hotels. First of these was the **Banff Springs Hotel**, the largest in the world when finished in 1888. Unfortunately, the Gothic giant was constructed back to front, with wonderful views from the kitchens and none at all from the guest rooms. Since then it has been rebuilt and developed, its 250 rooms expanded to 770, all of which are full in summer, mostly with Japanese tour groups. Known as the 'Castle in the Rockies', it is now more village than hotel, a vast, confusing labyrinth of restaurants, lounges, shops and other facilities. Utterly over-the- top, its sheer excessiveness makes it the only unmissable sight in Banff. Be sure to pick up a map from reception before exploring.

Upper Hot Springs
ⓘ *End of Mountain Av, T403-762 1515, www.hotsprings.ca, mid-May to mid-Oct daily 0900-2300, mid-Oct to mid-May daily 1000-2200, to 2300 Fri-Sat, $7.30, child $6.30.*
If the Cave Springs have put you in the mood, head here, an outdoor thermal swimming pool with great views where the very sulphurous water is cooled to 37-40°C. The **Hot Springs Spa** offers massage, aromatherapy and a steam room.

Banff Gondola
ⓘ *End of Mountain Av, T403-762 2523, www.banffgondola.com, May-Aug daily 0830-2100, Sep 0830-1830, Oct-Nov 0830-1630, Nov-Jan 1000-1600, Feb-Apr 1000-1700, $29, under 15s $14, under 5s free, bus No 1 to Fairmont then walk.*
Just down the road is the **Banff Gondola**. This eight-minute ride takes you up 700 m at a 51° angle to the top of Sulphur Mountain, where there is a restaurant, observation decks for taking in the exceptional panoramic views and a couple of short trails leading to even more vistas. From Sanson's Peak, the South East Ridge trail runs along the mountain's ridge to its true summit.

Vermilion Lakes and Lake Minnewanka
The **Vermilion Lakes**, just west of town off Mount Norquay Road, are easily explored by bike or car. The marshes around them are home to a wide range of birds, such as ospreys and bald eagles, as well as like muskrat, beaver, elk and coyote. **Lake Minnewanka**, north of the eastern highway junction, is a focus for hiking, biking, fishing and boating.

Hikes around Banff Townsite → See map, page 110.
Fenland Trail ⓘ *1.5 km. Trailhead: Mt Norquay Rd.* A loop through the wetlands near the first Vermilion Lake, a haven for birds and other wildlife.

Marsh Loop ⓘ *2 km. Trailhead: the Cave and Basin hot springs.* This trail explores a similarly rich area for flora and fauna.

Tunnel Mountain ⓘ *3.6 km return; 200-m elevation gain. Trailhead: St Julien Rd.* This short, steep but easily attainable hike leads to fine views of Banff Village.

C-level Cirque ⓘ *8 km return; 455-m elevation gain. Trailhead: 3.5 km north on Lake Minnewanka Rd.* This is a short, easy hike leading to some heart-warming mountain scenery. You'll also see mining remains and wild flowers.

Lake Minnewanka ① *6-60 km return with little elevation gain.* This trail is suitable for anyone and is open even in April and November when most others are closed. You can also go as far as you like. The **Ghost Lakes** are at Km 24, with frequent campgrounds along the way. At Km 7.8, you can turn left for the steep climb to **Mount Aylmer Lookout/Pass**, 23.6 km or 27 km, 615-m or 845-m elevation gain. This route also enjoys a longer season than most. From the lookout are great views of the lake and mountains towering above the opposite shore. From the pass the views are bigger but mostly limited to vast expanses of desolate grey rock.

Cory and Edith passes ① *13-km circuit; 960-m elevation gain. Trailhead: 0.5 km on Bow Valley Parkway after it leaves Hwy 1, turn right and continue 1 km.* Cory Pass can usually be hiked by late June. An extremely tough trail involving steep sections and some scree slope scrambling, this is only for the fit and reasonably experienced but if you can manage it, the rewards are an adrenalin-pumping quest and some exhilarating views. Edith is less exciting but makes for an easier descent and a neat loop.

Around Banff → *For listings, see pages 116-127.*

Canmore

Though the highway around Canmore is now entirely engulfed by satellite suburbs of hotels and condos, its Downtown core, centred on Main (Eighth) Street, just about manages to retain the comfortable feel of an authentic small town, making this an attractive and cheaper alternative to the insanely busy and commercially-oriented Banff, just 21 km to the west. There are some decent, down-to-earth pubs, fine restaurants and as many sports equipment shops as anyone could desire. Moreover, many fine hikes into Banff and Mount Assiniboine Parks are most easily accessed from Canmore, a number of tour operators are based here, and all kinds of outdoor activities are seriously pursued in the region, particularly climbing, Nordic skiing and mountain biking. ➤ *See Activities and tours, page 123.*

Across the bridge from town, past the Nordic Centre, a steep, rough road leads to the **Spray Lakes**, a nice quiet spot to camp. On the way, this road passes Canmore's most worthwhile attraction, **Grassi Lakes**. The unreal aquamarine/lime green colour of these lakes is extraordinary, even by local standards, and the whole area is a lovely, relaxing place. North of the lakes is a very popular spot for rock climbing; there's always plenty of action to watch for those who do not partake. Those who do will find lava cliff faces riddled with holes and all levels of climb with routes already anchored by locals.

For maps and trail information, call in at **Tourism Canmore** ① *907 7th Av, T403-678 1295, www.tourismcanmore.com.* They can provide a brochure for the self-guided *Historic Walking Tour* of the town. More useful for general enquiries is **Travel Alberta** ① *at the south side of Hwy 1 on west end of Canmore service road, T403-678 5277, www.travel alberta.com, May-Oct daily 0800-2000, Nov-Apr daily 0900-1800.* The national HQ of the **Alpine Club of Canada** ① *201 Indian Flats Rd, T403-678 3200, www.alpineclubofcanada.ca,* is a short drive from town. They're very helpful and knowledgeable about climbs and hikes, and sell a good selection of maps and guidebooks. They also have a hostel, and numerous backcountry huts dotted throughout the parks. For locations follow links from their website.

Mount Assiniboine Provincial Park

Canmore is the main jumping-off point for hikes into the south of Banff National Park. These are reached on the Smith-Dorrien Highway (No 742) beyond Spray Lakes. Just past the south end of Spray Lakes reservoir, turn right onto Watridge logging road and drive 5.3 km for Mount Shark trailhead, one of the starting points for hikes into Mount Assiniboine Provincial Park in BC. Mount Assiniboine is one of the most recognizable and visually gratifying peaks in the Rockies, a pyramid-shaped icon that has been compared to the Matterhorn in the Swiss Alps. The rest of the park is equally sensational and certainly one of the top backpacking destinations in the range.

From Mount Shark, the easiest route is via **Bryant Creek** ① *27.5 km one-way, with a 480-m elevation gain*, and the Assiniboine Pass. A strong hiker can do it in a day. Otherwise there is a campground at Km 9.7 and a warden hut, campground and shelter at Km 13.6. To stay at either, make arrangements with the Banff Visitor Centre. The easiest route back to Mount Shark, making a nice loop, is over **Wonder Pass** ① *27.5 km, 230-m elevation gain and then a lot of downhill*, and by Marvel Lake. A second access route and probably the best, is over **Citadel Pass** ① *29 km, 450-m elevation gain*, from Sunshine Village. This is a delightful, slightly easier hike. The ultimate trip would be to enter this way and exit via Wonder Pass, but arranging a shuttle would be tricky. None of this should be done without a map and a more detailed trail description.

The core area of this triangular park is its southeast corner, which contains Mount Assiniboine, eight other peaks over 3000 m and several beautiful lakes. The main focus and campground is at **Lake Magog**. There is also a park headquarters/warden's cabin. Some excellent one-day hikes from here give the chance to see some of the park and recover from the trek in. **Nub Peak** ① *a moderate 11.6-km round-trip, from Magog*, offers excellent views of the surroundings. **Windy Ridge** ① *a moderate 17.4-km round-trip*, is one of the highest trail-accessible points in the Rockies, with even better views and wild flower meadows on the way. An easier excursion is the 8-km loop to **Sunburst, Cerulean** and **Elizabeth Lakes**, which can be extended to 18.6 km to take in the views from **Ferro Pass**. Whatever the skies are doing and the forecasts say, always come prepared for the worst the weather can throw at you.

Sunshine Village Ski Area

① *T403-705 4000, snow phone T403-277 7669, www.skibanff.com, Sat-Thu 0800-1730, Fri 0800-2230, lift pass $78, under 18s $55, under 12s $26, there are 3 daily shuttles from Downtown Banff and major hotels, free with pre-bought ski passes, or $15, child $10 return.*
Bow Valley Parkway is the scenic route east from Banff to Lake Louise and beyond. Highway 1 is still a beautiful drive, but much faster with less chances to stop and hike. After 8 km, a road heads from the latter to **Sunshine Village Ski Area**. Twelve lifts, including a high-speed gondola, provide access to 107 uncrowded runs on 1330 ha of skiable terrain on three mountains (20% beginner, 55% intermediate, 25% expert). Situated right on the Great Divide, these receive a much higher calibre of snow than nearby Mount Norquay, with 9 m per year of first-class powder, Canada's biggest snow-pack. There are also three Freeride zones for experts only, and a Terrain Park. The hill also has one of the longest seasons, running from mid-November until late May. The highest elevation is 2730 m, with a vertical drop of 1070 m. All the usual rentals and lessons are available, as well as numerous restaurants, bars and places to stay. Note that it's very cold up here.

Mount Norquay Ski Area

ⓘ *T403-762 4421, www.banffnorquay.com, lift pass $55, under 17s $43, under 12s $17, 0900-1600, night skiing Wed and Fri 1700-2200, $20, there are 3 shuttles from major Banff hotels, $15 return, $10 to pass holders, T403-762 4421 for more information.*

Just 6 km to the north of Banff, Mount Norquay Ski Area receives 3 m of snow per year and employs a snow-maker. Five lifts access terrain that is 20% beginner, 36% intermediate, 28% advanced and 16% expert. This has long been considered the domain of experienced skiers, with plenty of steep, deep runs and the only night skiing in the Rockies. The highest elevation is 2133 m, with a vertical drop of 503 m. There's also a Terrain Park, and snow tubing, $24 per day, under 17s $20, under 12s $17. The lodge has a restaurant, café, rentals and lessons. The season runs from early December to mid-April.

Hikes from Sunshine Village

The beauty of ski hills is the speed with which you can be whisked to elevations that would take hours of hard walking to reach otherwise. Then you can maximise your time and effort, because the views are already fantastic, especially up in the Sunshine Meadows. During the summer (June-September), **White Mountain Adventures** ⓘ *T403-762 7889, www.sunshinemeadowsbanff.com, hourly 0900-1545, $26, under 12s $15 return, or from Banff Townsite 0815 only, $55/30* run a shuttle bus 5.5 km from the base parking lot to Sunshine Village, or from Banff. They also run guided five-hour hikes, daily at 0900, $35 per person, and some longer treks.

Sunshine Meadows At the top of the gondola the meadows stretch for 15 km along the Great Divide, receiving copious amounts of rain and snow that feed one of the most glorious midsummer wild flower displays you'll ever see. Naturally, such an easily accessible Eden draws crowds of visitors. Most go only as far as **Rock Isle Lake**, an easy 1.6-km trail to a beautiful viewpoint. To avoid the crowds set a brisker pace towards **Citadel Pass** ⓘ *18.6 km return, 343-m elevation gain*. On a clear day many of BC's mighty and rugged peaks are visible, including Mount Assiniboine. Continue a little further towards Fatique Pass, 2.5 km away, for even better views. This is a popular way to begin a multi-day backpacking trip into Mount Assiniboine Provincial Park in BC.

Healy Pass ⓘ *18.4 km return; 360 m or 655-m elevation gain. Trailhead: there are 2 ways to reach Healy Pass, from Sunshine Village via the shuttle and Simpson Pass or from the Sunshine parking lot via Healy Creek.* The distance is the same but starting from the Sunshine parking lot involves a lot more climbing, though at a gentle pace. If you are fit and don't want to pay the shuttle fare, go via Healy Creek. Either way, the flowers are wonderful. The pass itself is unexceptional but offers good views of Egypt and Scarab Lakes and the Pharaoh Peaks. You could also explore the Monarch Ramparts south of the pass. **Egypt Lake** campground and a basic, cheerless hut is 3 km further on. To stay here book at the **Banff Visitor Centre** ⓘ *T403-762 1550, $17 per person (including Wilderness pass).* There are some worthwhile side-trips if you do. **Whistling Pass** is a fine 6.6-km round-trip, which could be extended to **Shadow Lake** beneath the lofty Mount Ball (26 km return from Egypt Lake).

Bow Valley Parkway

The Bow Valley Parkway leaves Highway 1 just west of Banff. Its speed limit is

Banff National Park

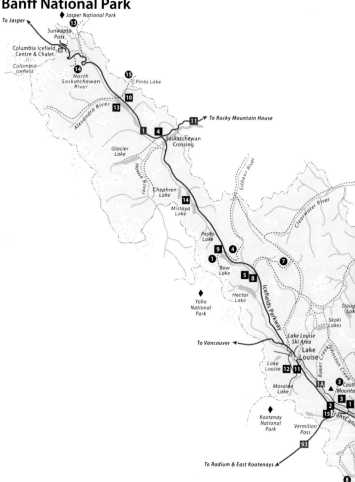

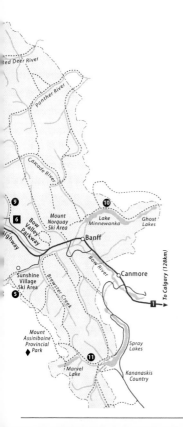

a sometimes-frustrating 60 kph but when drivers are liable to hit the breaks at any moment if a sheep appears, this is a good thing. Along the road are three campgrounds, a hostel, a few lodges and numerous hikes and viewpoints. At Km 16 is **Johnston Canyon** and its eponymous trail of the same name ① *11.6 km return, 215-m elevation gain*, which is the most worthwhile hike along the parkway. The chasms and waterfalls of this canyon are famous and perpetually flooded with tourists, but it's a lovely walk. The canyon is at its most beautiful in winter, when the waterfalls are frozen (see Activities and tours, page 123). You can continue beyond the falls to the multicoloured cold-water springs of the **Inkpots** and views of Johnston Creek Valley.

Castle Mountain, 30 km from Banff, marks the junction with Highway 93, which heads south through Kootenay National Park to Radium Hot Springs. The mountain itself is a magnificent and aptly named sight, worth pulling over to admire. The nearby **Rockbound Lake Trail** is more trouble than it's worth but **Silverton Falls** from the same trailhead is a nice 1.6-km jaunt. About 5 km to the west is the **Castle Crags Trail** ① *7 km return, 520-m elevation gain*. This short but steep hike leads to an old fire lookout and an outstanding panorama of the Bow Valley from Banff to Lake Louise. It is also free of snow earlier and later than most trails. On the way up you'll pass wild flower gardens and a dilapidated old cabin.

Lake Louise

→ *For listings, see pages 116-127.*

Magnificent Lake Louise is the single most famous icon in the Rockies and consequently receives far more visitors than any place of natural beauty should ever have to endure. This is the only focus in the park other than Banff Townsite, with

---

a better assortment of trails and things to see, but far fewer facilities. There are actually four components to Lake Louise: the Village, the Lake, Moraine Lake and the Ski Hill.

The Village

You'll come to the village first, close to the important junction where Highway 1 veers west through Yoho towards Golden and Revelstoke. Highway 93 then becomes the sole route north, henceforth known as the **Icefields Parkway**. This 'village' is little more than the ugly, overpriced Samson Mall, though it does contain most of the limited local accommodation, including one of the best hostels in the country, and the excellent **Lake Louise Visitor Centre** ① *T403-522 3833, daily Jun-Aug 0800-2000, Sep 0900-1700, Oct-Jun 0900-1600 or 1700*. The parks office and information centre helps out with hikes and accommodation, handing out brochures and maps and issuing backcountry permits. A number of interesting natural history exhibits explain some of the local geographical features, including displays on the Burgess Shale in Field (see page 144).

The Lake

① *4.5 km from the Village up a steep hill, 2.7 km on foot.*

There are many lakes in the Rockies with water that has an opaque, milky quality due to the presence of glacial silt known as 'rock flour', mineral deposits that glaciers have scraped from the mountain rock. These particles absorb all colours of the light spectrum except green and blue. Far and away the most famous is **Lake Louise**, where the water is of the most exquisite aquamarine colour, or colours as the hue changes dramatically according to the time of year and angle of the sun. Add to this the lake's sheer size and dramatic location at the foot of an incredibly powerful, towering rock rampart, and it is not difficult to understand why this is the definitive picture-postcard image of the Rockies, and the single most popular sight in the range.

Around 10,000 people come here every day in peak season, so if you want to see its shores crowd-free, arrive at sunrise. It comes as little surprise that this was the spot chosen by the CPR for the second of their giant hotels, the Château, originally built in 1890. Many visitors are shocked by this behemoth and consider its monstrous presence on the shores of the heavenly water an outrage that would never be allowed today. The best thing is to ignore it and go for a walk, or hire a canoe and go for a paddle. **Lake Agnes Tea House** and **Plain of the Six Glaciers Tea House** are each situated on popular trails about one or two hours' hike above the lake.

Moraine Lake

① *Expensive canoes can be rented at the lodge for a paddle, T403-522 3733. Note that parking is often a problem here.*

Halfway to Lake Louise, a left fork leads 12.5 km to Moraine Lake, another striking emerald product of rock flour. Half the size of its sister, it's equally beautiful and almost as popular, and the location might even be more dramatic. Stretching away from its shores is the **Valley of the Ten Peaks**, a wonderfully scenic cluster of mighty mountains, also known as the **Wenkchemna**, the Stoney word for 10. Some excellent trails lead into the valley and up to viewpoints.

Lake Louise Ski Area

ⓘ *T403-522 3555, snow phone T403-244 6665, www.skilouise.com; day pass is $76, under 18s $55, under 12s $25, under 6s free; the turning is just before the Bow Valley Parkway crosses Hwy 1 on its way to Lake Louise.*

This is the biggest ski hill in Canada, with 1700 ha of skiable terrain featuring world-class, vast, alpine bowls. With excellent dry powder and stupendous views, it ranks for almost all ski aficionados as one of the best hills in North America. A high-speed gondola and eight lifts service 139 runs that break down as 25% beginner, 45% intermediate and 30% expert. The top elevation is 2637 m, with a vertical drop of 911 m. The only drawbacks are the low snowfall of 360 m and the fact that it is bitterly cold, not helped by the fact that most runs are above the tree line. The lodges at the bottom are open year round, with restaurants, pubs, lounges, a cappuccino bar, equipment rentals, and lessons. A free shuttle bus to the hill leaves the Château Lake Louise and Lake Louise Inn every 30 minutes mid-December to mid-April.

In summer, the **Lake Louise Sightseeing Gondola** ⓘ *T403-522 3555, www.lakelouise gondola.com, May-Sep daily 0900-1830, $26, under 15s $15, $3 extra for breakfast buffet, $6 extra for lunch buffet,* runs people to the top of the hill to enjoy the views, a 14-minute journey; at the top, the **Wildlife Interpretive Centre** gives a number of different educational presentations at 1000, 1200 and 1400, and runs 45-minute **guided nature walks** at 1100, 1300 and 1500, $5. They also run longer hikes that change seasonally.

Hikes from the Lake

Saddleback/Fairview Mountain ⓘ *7.4-10.6 km return; 600- to 1014-m elevation gain. Trailhead: by the canoe rental at northeast end of lake.* The hike to Saddleback, despite its steepness, is very popular, especially in September when the larches turn to gold. This is a great viewpoint; even better is Saddle Mountain, 90 m straight up above it. Best of all is Fairview Mountain, a further steep 1.6-km climb. The panorama from here is to die for, with gargantuan peaks all around Lake Louise 1000 m below.

Plain of the Six Glaciers ⓘ *13.8 km; 380-m elevation gain.* This popular trail takes you up to the Teahouse and is perpetually crowded. Go anyway, because the views are astounding, embracing the giant peaks of mounts Lefroy and Victoria and their extensive glaciers and icefalls. Try starting after 1600 to minimize the company.

Hikes from Moraine Lake Road

Paradise Valley/Lake Annette ⓘ *18.2-km circuit/11.4 km return; 400-m/250-m elevation gain. Trailhead: 2.5 km from junction with Lake Louise Dr, 10 km before Moraine Lake.* Though this is a valley hike, the views it offers are as good or better than most ridge walks, with plenty of peaks and sheer rock faces. A return hike to Lake Annette is phenomenal in itself, but the longer circuit is recommended and best done in a clockwise direction. Horseshoe Meadow has a backcountry campground for those who want to take their time and extend it into a two-day trip. A possible worthwhile detour is to Giant Steps, where a river cascades slowly over some truly enormous slabs of quartzite. The paths there are confusing.

Hikes from Moraine Lake

Valley of the Ten Peaks/Sentinel Pass ⓘ *11.6 km return; 725-m elevation gain. Trailhead: past the lodge.* This wonderful, exhilarating trail leads through Larch Valley, a particularly popular spot in the autumn when the trees turn to gold. It is a fairly gentle hike most of the way until the final switchback ascent to the pass, which is not as hard as it looks. The view from the top is spectacular, taking in most of the 10 peaks and looking down on the other side into Paradise Valley. This hike can be combined with the Paradise Valley one to make a 17-km one-way trip ending 10 km down Moraine Lake Road. The best bet is to leave a vehicle here and hitch or take the shuttle up to Moraine Lake. This is a very popular trail but only takes four or five hours so think about starting early or late.

Consolation Lakes ① *6 km return; 60-m elevation gain.* Though no substitute for the above, this is a short and easy walk and the cliffs that tower over the lakes are undeniably impressive. The rough trail beyond the first lake means that the second is always less busy.

Hikes from the Ski Area
Skoki Valley ① *31.6 km, 785-m elevation gain. Trailhead: follow Whitehorn Rd towards the Ski Area, turn right at Km 2 onto Fish Creek Rd and follow for 1.1 km.* The high point of this hike are the alpine meadows and numerous lakes surrounded by rugged mountains with a romantically desolate air. The downside is that many hikers come this way, meaning trails are muddy if it's been raining. At least the first 4 km are on a boring fire-road. Think of doing it as a day trip and cycle that section. If camping, Merlin Meadows and Baker Lake are the best options, or you could stay at the **Skoki Lodge**, see page 118. A fine day-hike from here is the 6.2-km round-trip to the beautiful Merlin Lake. A 1.6-km scramble up Skoki Mountain leads to 360° views. This is also a very popular area for cross-country skiing.

Icefields Parkway → *For listings, see pages 116-127.*

The 230-km road between Lake Louise and Jasper runs through some of the Rockies' most spectacular scenery, bridging the two major parks, and must qualify as one of the most exciting drives in the world. In fact, the endless parade of lofty snow-capped peaks and vast glaciers is likely to push you towards sensory overload. The climax comes just beyond the Sunwapta Pass that separates Banff and Jasper National Parks. This is the Columbia Icefield, the single largest and most accessible area of ice and snow in the Rockies.

Distances given below are from Lake Louise. Dotted along the road at fairly regular intervals are youth hostels, campgrounds and a host of long and short trails. Pick up the Icefields Parkway map and guide from the Visitor Centre in Banff, Lake Louise or Jasper.

Lake Louise to the Columbia Icefield
Bow Lake ① *Km 37,* is a beautiful lake whose turquoise hue seems almost preternaturally vivid. **Bow Summit** ① *2069 m, 3 km further north,* is the highest pass in the Rockies and the highest highway crossing in Canada. Just beyond, a short side road leads to the exceptional but very busy viewpoint above **Peyto Lake**, another of those Rocky Mountain icons whose undeniable beauty can get lost among the throngs and clamour. It's named after Bill Peyto, a legendary Rocky pioneer who was as famous for his exploits around town as for his wilderness exploration.

Saskatchewan Crossing ① *Km 78,* is a grim crossroads with Highway 11 but a useful service centre offering a rare chance to get gas and essential supplies. At 114 km the road enters a dramatic giant switchback known as the 'Big Bend'. At the top are the impressive

Panther Falls and a couple of viewpoints where you can stop and enjoy the sweep of mountains back to the south. Look out also for the **Weeping Wall**, where water plunges down from a series of cracks in the apparently solid rock face.

Just beyond **Sunwapta Pass** ⓘ *2023 m*, which marks the border between the national parks, comes the highlight of the drive. For further information on the Columbia Icefield and the surrounding area, visit the **Icefield Centre**, see page 131.

Hikes around Columbia Icefield

Fish Lakes/Pipestone Pass/Devon Lakes Trail ⓘ *29.6-62.8 km; 762 m- to 1116-m elevation gain. Trailhead: park at Mosquito Creek, at Km 28, then walk across the road and over the bridge.* This trail leads through mostly open terrain with scenery that is consistently wonderful. There are a few possible itineraries. North Molar Pass makes a good 23-km day-hike. On this route, a scramble east of the pass gives views of the Fish Lakes and Pipestone River valley. Upper Fish Lake is reached at Km 14.8, a day trip for fast hikers. The campground, right on the lake beneath a towering rock wall, is a fine spot. To make it a four-day trip, continue to Pipestone Pass, with extensive views that include 19 km of the Siffleur River Valley, through the Clearwater Pass and on to the quiet and remote Devon Lakes at Km 31.4.

Cirque Peak/Helen Lake Trail ⓘ *15 km return; 1043-m elevation gain. Trailhead: Crowfoot Glacier viewpoint, at Km 34.* One of the best hikes in the Rockies, leading quickly to open sub-alpine meadows covered with heather and wild flowers, offering views of the impressive mountains. The marmots at Helen Lake are daring and entertaining. It's a long, slow scramble up a scree slope from here to Cirque Peak, but easier than you'd think and amply rewarded by 360° views of the Dolomite Valley, Bow and Peyto Lakes and Crowfoot and Bow Glaciers.

Bow Glacier Falls ⓘ *9 km return; 148-m elevation gain. Trailhead: Bow Lake at Km 37.* Stroll along the shore of this striking lake and witness the birthplace of the Bow River.

Bow Hut Trail ⓘ *14.8 km return; 500-m elevation gain.* This follows the same trail as Bow Glacier, above, almost to the falls, then heads uphill through a canyon to a mountaineering hut close to the edge of the vast Wapta Icefield. The rock and ice views are wonderful but those scared of heights might baulk at the final ascent.

Bow Lookout Trail ⓘ *6 km return; 260-m elevation gain. Trailhead: Peyto Lake at Km 40.* Leads up to a former fire lookout and gets you away from the crowds below. Commanding views take in the many lofty peaks and offer another perspective on the fabulous Bow Lake.

Sunset Pass Trail ⓘ *16.4 km return; 725-m elevation gain. Trailhead: just north of Rampart Creek at Km 89.* This long expanse of meadows is usually snow-free by late June but can be very wet and is prime grizzly habitat. The landscape climaxes at the north end with views of the deep-blue Lake Pinto.

Nigel Pass Trail ⓘ *14.4 km return; 365-m elevation gain. Trailhead: Km 113.* A gentle hike offering constant expansive views. At the pass, look beyond to the more starkly beautiful, formidable peaks of the upper Brazeau Valley. This is the opening section of a multi-day trek to Jonas Pass and Poboktan Pass (80 km return, 1913-m elevation gain). Among the best long hikes in the range, this network of trails presents many options and factors that require thought and research. The highlight of the trip is Jonas Pass, an 11-km-high meadow valley with pristine mountain scenery. Poboktan Pass is also a delight to explore but both the loop via Brazeau Lake and the one-way exit along Poboktan Creek have major drawbacks. Better is to camp at Jonas Cutoff, day-hike to Poboktan Pass, pass another night at the Cutoff, then hike out the same way. The lack of camping throughout Jonas Pass means either hiking 33 km to the Cutoff camp- ground, then 33 km out on the third day, or breaking the journey by camping at Four Point (14 km), making it a five-day trip.

Parker Ridge Trail ① *4.8 km return; 270-m elevation gain. Trailhead: Km 117.* A hike whose rewards far outweigh the effort expended. Breathtaking views take in the awesome expanse of the 9-km-long Saskatchewan Glacier, the longest tongue of the Columbia Icefield.

Wilcox Pass Trail ① *8 km return; 335-m elevation gain. Trailhead: just south of Wilcox Creek campground.* A short and easy hike that everybody should do, quickly leading to views that many longer hikes fail to equal. After a brief ascent through mature forest, the Columbia Icefield is suddenly visible in all its glory. Wild flower meadows and resident bighorn sheep complete the idyllic picture. With so much to be gained from so little effort, don't expect to be alone.

Banff National Park listings

For Sleeping and Eating price codes and other relevant information, see pages 9-11.

🛏 Sleeping

Banff Townsite *p103, map p105*
Accommodation in Banff is overpriced and heavily booked. On midsummer weekends, every single bed and vehicle-accessible campsite in the park will often be full, so reservations are strongly recommended. You can book through **Banff Accommodation**, T403-762 0260, T1877-226 3348, www.banffinfo.com. If you turn up without a reservation, head straight for the visitor centre; they know exactly what is left. To plan ahead, check www.banfflakelouise.com, which has full details and links for just about everywhere in town.
$$$ Banff Boutique Inn, 121 Cave Av, T403-762 4636, www.banffboutiqueinn. com. A very beautiful house with hardwood floors. Most of the 10 rooms have an en suite bath, half have mountain views and some have fireplaces, prices vary accordingly. Guests enjoy a common room and a front terrace with a fireplace. Breakfast included.
$$$ Blue Mountain Lodge, 137 Muskrat St, T403-762 5134, www.bluemtnlodge.com. 10 small but attractive en suite rooms in a centrally located turn-of-the-20th-century building with period decor and a shared lounge and kitchen.
$$$ HI Banff Alpine Centre, 801 Coyote Dr, Tunnel Mountain Rd, T403-762 4122, www.hihostels.ca. 3 km from town but the Transit Bus passes by. The best budget option, with excellent facilities and plenty of choice. Lovely cabin suites with a lounge area that sleep up to 5 (**$$$**), private rooms with (**$$$**) or without (**$$**) shared bath, and dorm rooms (**$$**), some with en suite bath.

There are 2 kitchens, a common room, deck, laundry, internet access, lockers, a pub, game house with a pool table, and a cheap restaurant serving good food and big portions. They also have a 10-m ice-climbing wall, and can organize activities. Be sure to book ahead.

$$$ Mountain Home B&B, 129 Muskrat St, T403-762 3889, www.mountainhomebb. com. 3 nice en suite rooms and a common room in a renovated 1940s home with antique furnishings.

$$$ The Driftwood Inn, 337 Banff Av, T403-762 4496, www.bestofbanff.com. Reasonable, fairly spacious rooms with pine furnishings. Guests are allowed to use the spa and fitness room of the **Ptarmigan Inn**.

$$ Bumpers Inn, 603 Banff Av/Marmot Cres, T403-762 3386, www.bumpersinn.com. Fairly nice, spacious rooms. Situated on the edge of town and quiet as a result, with forest at the back, which can be enjoyed from the courtyard deck or 2nd-floor balconies.

$$ Banff Y Mountain Lodge, 102 Spray Av, T403-762 3560, www.ymountainlodge. com. A cheap, reliable option by the river at the pretty end of town. They have dorms and private rooms, a pleasant common room, kitchen, laundry, internet access and a bistro with an outdoor patio.

$$ Rocky Mountain B&B, 223 Otter St, T403- 762 4811, www.rockymtnbb.com. 9 decent rooms and a large suite in a 1918 house. Shared common room has a historic feel.

$$ SameSun Banff Lodge, 449 Banff Av, T403-762 5521, www.samesun.com. Situated downtown, with more of a party atmosphere than the HI. All beds are in pleasant dorm rooms and there's a kitchen, TV room, games room, internet, courtyard with BBQ, hot tub, lockers, and activities can be arranged.

$$ Tan-Y-Bryn, 118 Otter St, T403-762 3696, www.tanybryninbanff.com. 8 no-frills rooms, most with shared bath, at a great price.

Camping

There are 5 campgrounds around Banff Townsite and sites can be reserved, T1877-737 3783, www.pccamping.ca, with a $10.80 reservation fee.

Tunnel Mountain I and **Tunnel Mountain II**, Tunnel Mt Rd. Big and ugly with 618 and 188 crowded sites respectively. The latter is the only one open year round.

Tunnel Mountain Trailer Court, Tunnel Mt Rd. A big parking lot with full hook-ups for RVs.

Two Jack Lakeside, 12 km northeast of Banff, Lake Minnewaka Rd. The nicest by far, with 74 sites including some tent-only spots on the lake and showers.

Two Jack Main, across the road from **Two Jack Lakeside**. Has 380 fairly nice sites.

Canmore p107

Canmore has a dearth of decent hotels but there are dozens of nice, reasonably priced B&Bs. Many are close to Downtown on 1st and 2nd St. Call the **B&B Hotline**, T403-609 7224, www.bbcanmore.com, or try www.tourismcanmore.com.

$$$ Bear and Bison Inn, 705 Benchlands Trail, T403-678 2058, www.bearandbisoninn.com. 10 incredibly opulent, honeymoon-style rooms. Gourmet breakfast included.

$$$ The Georgetown Inn, 1101 Bow Valley Trail, T403-678 3439, www.georgetowninn. net. 20 lovely rooms in a wonderful Tudor-style inn with patios and gardens. Guest lounge and an English-style restaurant/pub.

$$ Bow Valley Motel, 610 Main St, T403-678 5085, www.bowvalleymotel.com. A very central location and reasonable rooms, some with balconies.

$$ Drake Inn, 909 Railway Av, T403-678 5131, www.drakeinn.com. The best Downtown option by far. Rooms are above average, with large windows. Those overlooking the creek have private balconies. Downstairs is a popular pub.

$$ Riverview & Main, 918 8th St, T403-678 9777, www.riverviewandmain.ca. 3 bright and pleasant rooms with decks and mountain views. Very nice private sitting room.

$ HI-Canmore Hostel, in the **Alpine Club** on Indian Flats Rd, a short drive east, no public transport, T403-678 3200, www.hihostels.ca. Made up of 2 buildings, each one has its own fully equipped kitchen, living room, fireplace, deck and BBQ. Sauna, library and laundry available in the main building.

Camping

Spray Lakes Campground, T403-591 7226. 16 km south on a rough and sometimes steep dirt road, with no public transport. A wonderful campground that hugs the lakeside for 6 km, making for private sites right on the crystal-clear lake and surrounded by mountains.

Mount Assiniboine Provincial Park *p108*

$ Naiset Huts, Lake Magog, T403-678 2883. Bunk beds in this basic cabin can be booked and you're advised to do so. Despite the long walk, don't expect to have the place to yourself.

Camping

Lake Magog Campground. The park's main campground. There's a quieter one 6 km north at Og Lake. $5 per night, cash only.

Bow Valley Parkway *p109, map p110*

$$$ Castle Mountain Chalets, T403-762 2281, www.castlemountain.com. A range of sleeping options, including attractive pine or cedar chalets that could sleep 4-6, with kitchens, bathroom, and wood-burning fireplaces. There's also an exercise room, hot tub, and laundry, and they rent bikes and snowshoes.

$$$ Johnston Canyon Resort, T403-762 2971, www.johnstoncanyon.com. A good alternative to staying in Banff. Attractive,

semi-rustic cabins and bungalows with showers and fireplaces, but they're far too close together. Large 2-bedroom cabins (**$$$$**) are a good deal for 2 couples sharing, they're modern and fully equipped with kitchen, clawfoot tub, TV, porch and fireplace. On site dining room, coffee shop, BBQ area and tennis court.

$$$ Storm Mountain Lodge, 10 mins SW from Castle Mtn on Hwy 93, T403-762 4155, www.stormmountainlodge.com. Gorgeous log cabins, immaculately furnished with wood fires and soaker tubs, in a remote, forested 2-ha site. No kitchens, but gourmet meals are available. Their restaurant is one of the finest in Banff.

$ HI Castle Mountain Wilderness Hostel, T403-670 7580, www.hihostels.ca. A fairly basic but picturesque little hostel with 28 dorm beds, laundry, kitchen and a cosy common room with a wood-burning fireplace and bay windows.

Camping

Castle Mountain Campground. With just 43 sites, this is one of the smaller, nicer sites in the park. No showers.

Johnston Canyon Campground, has showers and 140 not very private sites, but it's a great location.

Lake Louise *p111, map p110*

$$$$ Skoki Lodge, T1800-258 7669, www.skoki.com. The only way to the lodge is by skiing or hiking an 11-km trail that starts behind the ski resort. The lodge has rooms and cabins but no electricity or running water. The price (starting at $113 per person in winter, $144 per person in summer) includes a buffet-style breakfast and dinner. Sitting at 2000 m, surrounded by mountains, this is an excellent base for getting into the backcountry and has been used as such since the 1930s when it put Lake Louise on the Nordic ski map.

$$$ Deer Lodge, 109 Lake Louise Dr, The Lake, T403-522 3991, www.crmr.com. Built in 'vintage national-park Gothic' style with antique furnishings, this hotel has plenty of character but its rooms are very small and rather ordinary. There's a rooftop hot tub and a decent but expensive restaurant with a patio.

$$$ Mountaineer Lodge, 101 Village Rd, The Village, T403-522 3844, www.mountaineerlodge.com. The most reasonable of a hideously overpriced collection of hotels in the village. Spacious but fairly standard rooms, many with views. Also has hot tub and steam room.

$$ HI Lake Louise Alpine Centre, Village Rd, The Village T403-670 7580, www.hihostels.ca. A spacious, attractive, well-equipped hostel, with dorms and private double rooms, some with en suite bath. Facilities include 2 kitchens, laundry, library, lots of common places to relax, a sunny outdoor patio, fireplaces, internet, access to maps, storage and an excellent cheap restaurant. Some guided tours. Open year round. Reservations well in advance are essential.

Camping
Lake Louise Tent, The Village, T403-522 3833, May-Sep. 220 not especially nice sites and showers.
Lake Louise Trailer, The Village, T403-522 3833, open year round. 189 less pleasant sites designed for RVs, with hook-ups.

Icefields Parkway p114, map p110
$$$$ Simpson's Num-Ti-Jah Lodge, T403-522 2167, www.num-ti-jah.com. In a prime location on the shore of Bow Lake, this octagonal construction was built in 1920 by Jimmy Simpson, a legendary pioneering guide. Age has lent a lot of charm to the rooms, which include some cheaper options with shared bath. There is a fine restaurant, a library with fireplace, and a lounge with pool table. Its popularity is a little off-putting and makes advance booking a necessity.

$$$ The Crossing, Saskatchewan Crossing, T403-761 7000, www.thecrossingresort.com. An overpriced but heavily booked motel with an exercise room, hot tub, laundry and internet access. There's also a fast-food cafeteria, restaurant, grocery store and a tacky gift shop. Closed for the winter.

$ Mosquito Creek Hostel, Km 28, T403-670 7580, www.hihostels.ca. 20 dorm beds and a few private rooms in 4 log cabins nicely situated by the creek. Rustic, with no electricity or running water but with a kitchen, a cosy common room and sauna.

$ Rampart Creek Hostel, Km 89, T403-670 6580, www.hihostels.ca. 24 beds in 2 cabins. Rustic, with no running water or electricity but a small kitchen, common room and sauna. Popular in winter, with over 150 ice climbs within 30 mins' drive.

Camping
Mosquito Creek Campground, at Km 28. A small, basic year-round campground with 32 sites, of which 20 are walk-in only.
Rampart Creek Campground, at Km 89. Basic but pleasant, with 50 sites by the river.
Waterfowl Lake Campground, at Km 57. 116 nice sites close to the lake.

🍴 Eating

Banff Townsite p103, map p105
Banff's expensive restaurants often have 'tasting menus' which are 4- to 8-course meals for around $90 per person.

♥♥♥ Grizzly House, 207 Banff Av, T403-762 4055. A good choice for something fun and highly unusual, including the bizarre retro decor. An absurd selection of meats is offered, mostly game, with even more exotic choices like rattlesnake, alligator or shark, cooked at your table in fondues or on hot rocks. Great service, but small portions and very expensive.

♥♥♥ Le Beaujolais, 212 Buffalo St, T403-762 2712. Very upmarket, with a dress code and an extensive wine list. The small French-inspired menu features game and seafood with delicious sauces, as well as favourites like stroganoff or steak-frites, and a 3-course 'prix fixe' menu. Great service and atmosphere, but not for those with a large appetite or tight budget.

¶¶¶ Saltlik Steakhouse, 221 Bear Av, T403-762 2467. A relaxed but classy spot, specializing in top-notch Alberta steaks, cooked to perfection. It's also a great place for a glass of wine, martini or cocktail.

¶¶ Coyotes, 206 Caribou St, T403-762 3963. Sophisticated southwest-style food such as orange chipotle prawns, nicely spicy and very tasty. Subtle decor, with an open kitchen: you can sit at the bar and watch the chefs at work. A great breakfast option, too.

¶¶ Elk & Oarsman Pub & Grill, 119 Banff Av, T403-762 4616. A nice pub atmosphere with superior food. Recommended for game such as elk or bison, served BBQ, as a burger, ribs or sandwich. They're all excellent. Good portions and prices. Popular with locals, too.

¶¶ Maple Leaf Grille,137 Banff Av, T403-760 7680. The inviting lodge-style interior concentrates on Canadiana, with lots of wood and leather, and a genuine birch-bark canoe. The menu features lots of seafood, game, steak, pasta and other favourites, while the comfy lounge is a good spot for a quiet drink. Great views from the dining room, and a neat little coffee corner.

¶¶ Nourish Vegetarian Bistro, 2nd floor of Sundance Mall, 215 Banff Av, T403-760 3933. You don't have to be vegetarian to enjoy this delicious food, and if you're vegan or need gluten-free food, this is your lucky day. Tapas-style entrées come in big portions, made to share.

¶ Aardvark Pizza, 304 Caribou St, T403-762 5500. Open till 0400. Take-out menu, and very good pizzas.

¶ Evelyn's Coffee Bar, 201 Banff Av, T403-762 0352. Good coffee and great light food, from sandwiches to rhubarb pie.

¶ Sundance Bistro, at the Banff Y Mountain Lodge. A charming bistro with an outdoor patio, serving wraps and salads and the best-value breakfast in town.

¶ Sushi House, 304 Caribou St, T403-762 4353. Cheap and delicious sushi, made before your eyes, then placed on a model train that circles around the customers.

Canmore *p107*

¶¶¶ Murrieta's Bar & Grill, 737 Main St, T403-609 9500. With its hardwood floors, big windows and elegant long bar, the atmosphere is sophisticated and the menu features seafood, pasta and European-style fine dining choices. A locals' favourite for years, it's also a great place for a drink with a good selection of wines and cocktails.

¶¶¶ Trough Dining Co, 725B 9th St, T403-678 2820. A small house with an elegant, intimate interior and a contemporary West Coast menu that is innovative, ambitious and cosmopolitan. 1st-class food, and a good wine list.

¶¶ Chef's Studio Japan, 709 Main St, T403-609 8383. A casual and inviting spot for innovative sushi.

¶¶ Chez François, 1602 Bow Valley Trail, T403-678 6111. Consistently excellent French cuisine with an emphasis on fresh ingredients, served in elegant surroundings with an inviting mahogany wine bar. Try the duck.

¶¶ Crazy Weed Kitchen, 1600 Railway Av, T403-609 2530. The menu here is international and surprisingly eclectic, from curries to tenderloin or scallops, all done to perfection. Almost everybody loves it, some even rate it the best in town.

¶¶ Grizzly Paw Brewing Co, 622 Main St, T403-678 9983. Fine ales brewed on the premises, superior versions of casual pub food like fish and chips, and burgers. A fantastic, busy patio in summer.

¶¶ Quarry Dining Lounge, 718 Main St, T403-678 6088. Bright, airy, sophisticated and modern, with open beams and a long bar. The menu focuses on French and Italian bistro cuisine, with an emphasis on the freshness of ingredients. Try the pork tenderloin.

♥♥ Sage Bistro, 1712 Bow Vallet Trail, T403-678 4878. Wine bar with great views, but most highly recommended for breakfast.

♥♥ Tapas Restaurant, 633 10th St, T403-609 0583. With much more than just tapas on the menu, this is the real deal. Impressively broad menu of very authentic Spanish and Portuguese dishes, exquisitely prepared and presented. Live flamenco Thu and Fri nights.

♥♥ Zona's Late Night Bistro, 710 9th St, T403-609 2000. A cosy house decorated with eccentric pieces of art, and a garden courtyard that's perfect for those warm summer evenings. The food is international, creative and perfectly executed. Try the Moroccan lamb and molasses curry. After the kitchen closes, drinks and tapas are available till late.

♥ The Coffee Mine, 802 Main St, T403-678 2241. Coffee, snacks and outdoor seating.

♥ The Summit Café, 1001 Cougar Creek Dr, T403-609 2120. Great Canadian and Mexican breakfasts. Organic coffee.

Bow Valley Parkway p109, map p110
♥♥♥ Baker Creek Bistro, at the Baker Creek Chalets, T403-522 2182. Very good food, with a pleasant patio and a licensed lounge.

Lake Louise p111
♥♥♥ Deer Lodge, Upper Lake Louise, T403-522 3747. 'Rocky Mountain Cuisine' such as elk and wild mushrooms. Great patio.
♥♥♥-♥♥ Lake Louise Station, 200 Sentinel Rd in the Village, T403-522 2600. The interior is very nice, with lots of wood, high ceilings and big windows, and there's a lovely garden patio with BBQ in the summer. The menu is fairly small but varied, ranging from gourmet burger to the duck confit. It's also a fine spot for a drink.

♥ Bill Peyto's Café, at the HI Alpine Centre. Cafeteria-style, good-value large portions, with great breakfasts, pasta and salads.

♥ Laggan's Bakery, in Samson Mall, T403-522 2017. Good bakery items and sandwiches to go, and an increasingly popular choice for tasty breakfasts and lunches. Try the beef pot-pie.

♥ Village Grill and Bar, in Samson Mall, T403-522 3879. Family-style joint with all-day breakfast, sandwiches, burgers, BBQ, Chinese food and some more expensive options.

Icefields Parkway p114, map p110
♥♥♥♥ Num-Ti-Jah Lodge (see Sleeping). The famous lodge has a good fine dining restaurant and a lounge.

♥♥ The Crossing, at Saskatchewan Crossing (see page 114). Contains a fast-food cafeteria and a 2nd-rate restaurant.

♥♥ Icefield Centre (see page 131). An over-priced Chinese restaurant and a hamburger/hotdog cafeteria.

🎵 Bars and clubs

Banff Townsite p103, map p105
Aurora Night Club, 110 Banff Av, T403-760 5300. Combines heaving DJ-led dance floor action with an elegant martini bar. The best place for dancing.

Hoodoo Lounge, 137 Banff Av, T403-760 8636. An ener- getic, somewhat youthful spot for DJs, live music or drink specials every night.

The Lik Lounge, 221 Bear St, T403-762 2467. An upbeat martini lounge, with live bands on Thu, and DJs on Sun.

Rose & Crown, upstairs at 202 Banff Av, T403-762 2121. Varied live bands every night, a good atmosphere, decent pub food.

St James's Gate Olde Irish Pub, 207 Wolf St, T403-762 9355. Banff's most appealing pub, with 33 beers on tap, 30 malt whiskeys and upscale pub food. Really does feel like an Irish pub.

Waldhaus Pub, downstairs behind the Banff Springs Hotel, T403-762 6860.

An authentic German-style boozer with low ceilings and Becks on tap. A good pub menu that features fondues from the more highbrow restaurant upstairs.

Wild Bill's Legendary Saloon, 2nd floor, 201 Banff Av, www.wbsaloon.com. An attractive saloon-style setting, with different live music almost every night, that doesn't necessarily entail line dancing. Large portions of Western and Tex-Mex and an inviting a patio.

Canmore *p107*
Bandoleer's, 120 1st Av, Deadman's Flats, 5 mins east of Canmore, T403-609 3006. A Tex-Mex restaurant with live jazz and blues on Fri and Sat nights.

The Drake Inn, 909 Railway Av, T403-678 5131. Canmore's most popular night spot, with live bands on weekends and generous portions of pub fare.

Grizzly Paw Brewing Co, 622 Main St, T403-678 9983. The obvious pub of choice, with beers brewed on the premises and a summer patio.

Rose and Crown, 749 Railway Av, T403-678 5168. 14 beers on tap and a patio. Popular with locals, offers decent pub grub.

☻ Entertainment

Banff Townsite *p103, map p105*
Banff Centre for the Arts, 107 Tunnel Mountain Dr, T403-762 6281, www.banff centre.ca. One of the most highly respected art schools in North America, organizing all sorts of cultural events, including art exhibitions, theatre, dance, cabaret and regular music of all genres, including some big names. Their **Walter Phillips Gallery**, specializing in contemporary visual arts, is open Wed-Sun 1230-1700, to 2100 Thu, free.

Canada House Gallery, 201 Bear St, T403-762 3757, www.canadahouse.com. Sun-Wed 0930-1800, Thu-Sat 0930-2000. One of Alberta's most important private galleries, representing dozens of Canadian artists

and sculptors for over 30 years. Well worth checking out.

Lux Cinema Theatre, 229 Bear St, T403-762 8595.

☻ Festivals and events

Banff Townsite *p103, map p105*
Jan Winter Festival, 10 days of winter-related competitions and events in late Jan, including the Mountain Madness Relay race.

May Rocky Mountain Wine and Food Festival, www.rockymountainwine.com/banff. For 1 day at the end of May, hosted by the Banff Springs Hotel.

May-Jun Art Banff Jazz Festival, attracts some big names, with Dave Douglas a regular contributor.

May-Aug Banff Summer Arts Festival, organized and partly hosted by the Banff Centre, www.banffcentre.ca. Includes the **Jazz Festival**, cabarets, dance, opera, literary events, lots of music, art walks, exhibitions and lectures. Much of it is free and many events take place at the Central Park Gazebo, downtown.

Jun Banff Bike Fest, T403-762 0284. 7 challenging road races held over 4 days.

Aug Dragon Boat Festival. Over 500 participants race across Lake Minnewanka.

Oct-Nov Banff Mountain Film and Book Festival, at the Banff Centre. More than 30 events held over 9 days, including screenings of the best 50-60 films worldwide in mountain subjects, including alpinism, culture, environment and sport. The top 20 will then tour the rest of Canada and abroad.

Canmore *p107*
Jun ArtsPeak Arts Festival, www.artspeak canmore.com. 4 days in mid-Jun, featuring an Art Walk, street performers, films, art sales, competitions and musical events

Aug Canmore Folk Music Festival, T403-678 2524, www.canmorefolkfestival.com. Held on the 1st weekend of the month, this is the town's main annual event, with lots of acts outside in Centennial Park.

◆ Shopping

Banff Townsite *p103, map p105*
All along Banff Av are the often tacky gift
shops offering souvenirs such as smoked
salmon (which keeps well), maple syrup
and copies of Aboriginal art.
Banff Book and Art Den, 94 Banff Av,
T403-762 3919, in the Banff Springs. Big
selection of outdoor recreation guides.
Friends of Banff, 214 Banff Av, T403-
762 8918. Educational books and maps.
All profits go to Banff Park.
The Glacier Shop, 317 Banff Av, T403-
760 5130. Outdoor clothing, sports gear
and ski equipment.
Mountain Magic Equipment, 224 Bear
St, T403-762 2829. Massive selection of
outdoor gear. Rentals for camping, climbing
and biking.
Standish Home Hardware, 223 Bear St,
T403-762 2080. Good for camping gear.
Weeds and Seeds Health Co, 211 Bear St,
T403-760 5060. A health food shop offering
bulk organic goodies.

Canmore *p107*
The Second Story Used Books, 713 Main
St, T403-609 2368. Stock up here because
second-hand bookshops in the Rockies are
a rarity.
Sobeys, 950 Railway Av, in front of the **IGA**
supermarket, T403-609 6636. The perfect
place to stock up on healthy camping food.
Sports Consignment, 718 10th St, T403-
678 1992. Good deals on used sports or
camping equipment.
Valhalla Pure, 726 Main St, T403-678 5610.
Camping gear and sports equipment.

Lake Louise *p111*
Village Grocery, Samson Mall. Overpriced,
but essential for stocking up on food for
your trip.
Wilson Mountain Sports Ltd, Samson Mall,
T403-522 3636, www.wmsll.com. Rents skis,

snowboards, snowshoes, and a range of
bikes. Also climbing, camping and fishing
gear to buy or rent.

▲ Activities and tours

Banff Townsite *p103, map p105*
Boat tours
Lake Minnewanka Boat Tours, T403-
762 3473, www.explorerockies.com/
minnewanka/. 1-hr sightseeing boat tours,
$44, under 15s $19, under 5s free. May-Oct
3-9 tours daily; Jun-Sep hourly 1000-1800.
Also boat rentals ($45 per hr, $100 per half
day, $120 per day) and fishing charters
($500 per day for 1 or 2).

Canoeing and kayaking
Blue Canoe, at Bow River Canoe Docks,
end of Wolf St, T403-760 5465, www.banff
canoeing.com. Canoe and kayak rentals,
including all equipment, basic instruction,
safety tips and a route map, $34 1st hr, then
$20 per hr. Paddling is also possible on Two
Jack Lake, Vermilion Lakes, Echo Creek and
40 Mile Creek. They also arrange trips in a
14-person voyageur canoe, $39/15 for 1 hr,
and rent cruiser bikes.

Climbing and ice climbing
Yamnuska Mountain Adventures, T403-
678 4164, www.yamnuska.com. A broad
range of guided mountain trips with
experienced experts: climbing,
mountaineering, ice climbing, hiking
and backcountry skiing.

Dog sled tours
Howling Dog Tours, T403-678 9588,
www.howlingdogtours.com.
Snowy Owl Sled Dog Tours, T403-678
4369, www.snowyowltours.com.

Fishing
Banff Fishing Unlimited, T403-762 4936,
www.banff-fishing.com. The largest guiding
and outfitting company in the region. Lake

Minnewanka and the Upper Bow River are obvious local sites. They also do ice fishing. Gear and licences can be obtained from **Lake Minnewanka Boat Tours** (see above).

Helicopter tours
Icefield Helicopter Tours, T403-721 2100, www.icefieldheli.com. Sightseeing tours of the icefields and glaciers, from $189 per person for 20 mins.

Hiking and ice canyon tours
Great Divide Nature Interpretation, T403-522 2735, www.greatdivide.ca. Daily interpretive hikes and walks led by naturalists. Also snowshoeing.

White Mountain Adventures, T403-678 4099, www.whitemountainadventures.com. Highly recommended tours through the frozen waterfalls of Johnston or Grotto Canyons, ($330 for up to 6 people), snowshoeing at Sunshine Meadows, ($84 per person), and half- or full-day guided hikes.

Willow Root Nature Tours, T403-762 4335. Walks, hikes and wildlife watching with full interpretation from a professional naturalist.

Horse riding
Trail Rider Store, 132 Banff Av, T403-762 4551, www.horseback.com. Arrange horse riding from their 2 local stables, 1- to 3-hr trips or multi-day rides using their lodges as bases, or sleeping in tents. Also covered wagon rides or horse-drawn sleigh rides in winter.

Ice-skating
Outdoor skating is possible on **Bow River**, end of Wolf St; **Banff High School**, Banff Av and Wolf St; and **Banff Springs Hotel**.
   There's an indoor rink at **Banff Recreation Centre**, Mt Norquay Rd, T403-762 1235.

Mountain biking
Mountain biking is possible on many of the local trails, though **Lake Louise** is better and **Canmore** is better still. Highest calibre is

the **Brewster Creek Trail** which extends the **Sundance/Healy Creek trails** from Cave and Basin Hot Springs to a possible 37-km one-way ride to Allenby Pass. An exciting 5.2-km downhill run is the **Lower Stoney Squaw** at Mt Norquay Ski Area. The **Rundle Riverside** is a 14-km rollercoaster ride to Canmore Nordic Centre and more trails. Good gentle cycling can be had at Lake Minnewanka, Vermilion Lakes or Sundance Canyon. **Bactrax**, 225 Bear St, T403-762 8177, www.snowtips-bactrax.com. Offers bike rentals and tours ($20 per hr per person). They also provide shuttles to and from trailheads. **The Ski Stop**, 203A Bear St, T403-760 1650, www.theskistop.com. Run a number of bike tours, easy or hard, including a backcountry shuttle and ride package. Also rent bikes.

Rafting
Hydra River Guides, T403-762 4554, www.raftbanff.com. Whitewater rafting trips on the Kicking Horse River; gentle (75 mins, $74/49), medium (2-2½ hrs, $105) and intense (5½ hrs, $149). Also packages combining rafting with horse rides, ATV, zipline, or accommodation.

Rentals and sales
Whatever you need – skis, snowboards, ice skates, snowshoes, sleds, hiking boots, tents, sleeping bags, mopeds, rafts, climbing or fishing gear – you're likely to find it at **Bactrax**, see Mountain biking, above. **Mountain Magic Equipment**, 224 Bear St, T403-762 2591, www.mountainmagic.com. **Monod Sports**, 129 Banff Av, T403-762 4571, www.monodsports.com. Sell a wide range outdoor clothing, footwear, books and maps, and equipment for hiking, camping, rock and ice climbing. Skiing and snowshoeing.

Skiing
Banff is very much a year-round resort, with 2 ski hills right on its doorstep. As well as the excellent Sunshine Village Ski Area, 18 km

southwest of Banff off Hwy 1 (see page 108), there's Mt Norquay Ski Area, just 6 km to the north (see page 109).

Many local trails are groomed in winter for cross-country skiing. Pick up the *Nordic Trails* pamphlet from the visitor centre.

Tour operators
Banff Adventures Unlimited, 211 Bear St, T403-762 4554, www.banffadventures.com and **Discover Banff Tours Ltd**, T403-760 1299, www.banfftours.com. These 2 giants can set you up with any of the activities available within the park, including ATV tours, boat cruises, cave tours on Grotto Mountain, helicopter tours, hiking, horse riding, kayaking, rock climbing, sightseeing, wildlife viewing, skiing, dog-sledding, heli-skiing, ice-climbing, sleighing, snowmobiling, snowshoeing and the list goes on.
Brewster, 100 Gopher St, T403-760 6934, www.sightseeingtourscanada.com. Sight-seeing coach tours to just about every destination in the Rockies.
Moose Travel Network, www.moosenetwork.com As well as arranging budget hop-on hop-off trips from Vancouver, some of which take in the Rockies, they run 2- ($139) and 4-day ($250) trips from Banff to Jasper along the Icefields Parkway that enable car-less travellers to make multiple stops along the way.

Canmore *p107*
Climbing
This is Canmore's local speciality. There are climbs at Grassi Lakes, Yamanuska, on Hwy 1A E and Cougar Canyon for a more challenging climb.
Alpine Club, T403-678 3200, www.alpineclubofcanada.ca. The best place for advice and to find out about mountain huts.
Yamnuska Mountain Adventures, T403-678 4164, www.yamnuska.com. Ice and rock climbing, backcountry skiing, mountaineering lessons and tours.

Cross-country skiing
Canmore Nordic Centre, off Spray Lakes Rd, well signposted from town, T403-678 2400, has over 65 km of groomed and track-set trails that are the best in the Rockies. The day lodge has a café, fireplace and showers. Day passes are $10, under 17s $7.50, under 11s $6, under 6s free. There is now a 6.5-km illuminated loop for night skiing $5/3.75/2.50.
Trail Sports, beside the Day Lodge, T403-678 6764, www.trailsports.ab.ca, provides rentals, lessons, tours and trail information.

Hiking
Access to excellent long-distance hikes, mostly in the south of Banff Park, is via Spray Lakes Rd and its extension, the Smith-Dorrien Hwy, a distance of some 40 km. Follow signs to the Nordic Centre and keep going up the steep, rough road, ignoring the right turn to Spray Lakes campground. Local hikes include the Three Sisters area and Ha Ling Peak, across from the Goat Creek parking lot, both on Spray Lakes Rd; Grotto Mountain is accessed from the Alpine Club.

Horse riding
Cross Zee Ranch, T403-678 4171, www.canadianrockies.net/crosszeeranch. Day horse-riding trips.

Mountain biking
There are excellent networks of trails at Mt Shark and Mud Lake, both on the Smith-Dorrien Hwy. Considerably closer, Canmore Nordic Centre (see above) has over 100 km of mountain bike trails.
Trail Sports, at the Centre, T403-678 6764, www.trailsports.ab.ca, rents bikes.

Rafting
Canadian Rockies Rafting Co, T403- 678 6535; www.rafting.ca. Whitewater rafting for all ages and abilities on the Bow, Kananaskis, and Kicking Horse rivers.

Inside Out Experience, T403-949 3305, www.insideoutexperience.com. Whitewater rafting on the Kananaskis River (2 hrs for $75), the Bow River's Horshoe Canyon (2 hrs for $82), and gentler float trips (1½ hrs for $49).

Rentals
Gear Up, 1302 Bow Valley Trail, T403-678 1636, www.gearupsport.com. Your best bet for all rentals, including bikes, kayaks, climbing and camping gear, skis, snowboards, skates, and snowshoes.

Lake Louise p111
Horse riding
Timberline Tours, T403-522 3743, www.timberlinetours.ca. Horse-riding trips starting from the corral behind Deer Lodge. 10 mins for $15, 3 hrs for $105, 1 day for $179, then anything up to 10 days. They will drop off or pick up at **Skoki Lodge** ($179 per person).

Lake sports
Canoes can be rented from the lodges at both lakes. When the lake gets cold enough it provides an idyllic location for skating.
Brewsters, T403-522 3522, www.brewster.ca. Organizes sleigh rides along the shoreline of Lake Louise, $28 per person for 45 mins. Leaves most hours 1300-2000 Dec-Apr.
Monod Sports, in Château Lake Louise, T403-522 3628, www.monodsports.com, daily 0800-2100. Rents skates, skis, snowshoes, snowboards, and sells outerwear and footwear.

Mountain biking
Some local trails are ideal for riding. The 14.6-km return Ross Lake Trail starts behind the **Château** and leads through forest to a small lake beneath a steep rockwall. The more demanding 10-km Moraine Lake Highline leads from the Paradise Valley trailhead to the scenic lake; sometimes closed due to

grizzly activity. The 13.4-km Pipestone Trail starts off Slate Rd just west of the Village and follows the Pipestone River to the valley. The 7-km Bow River Loop is a gentle trail on both sides of the river. The 10.5-km one-way Great Divide Path is a paved but traffic-free route starting at Km 3.6 on Lake Louise Dr and ending at Hwy 1 in Yoho.

Rentals
Wilson Mountain Sports, in the Village, T403-522 3636, www.wmsll.com. Rents bikes, fishing rods, climbing, mountaineering and camping gear, skis, snowboards, skates and snowshoes.

Skiing
As well as top notch downhill skiing at Lake Louise Ski Area, there is fine cross-country skiing in the Skoki Valley, around the picturesque log **Skoki Lodge**.

⊖ Transport

Banff Townsite p103, map p105
Bus
Banff Transit, T403-762 1200, runs 2 bus routes. One connects the Banff Springs Hotel with the Tunnel Mountain Trailer Court; another connects the Luxton Museum with the campgrounds on Tunnel Mountain Rd. Both run along Banff Av, $2, child $1.

Greyhound, T1800-661 8747, www.greyhound.ca, runs 5 daily buses to **Calgary** (1½ hrs, $26), 4 to **Canmore** (15-30 mins, $10), 4 to **Lake Louise** (45 mins, $15), 3 to **Jasper** (12½-16 hrs, $118), 4 to **Field** (65 mins, $20), 2 direct to **Kamloops** (7½ hrs, $79) and 4 direct to **Vancouver** (12½-15½ hrs, $124).

Sun Dog Tours, T1888-786 3461, www.sundogtours.com, run 7 shuttles daily to **Lake Louise** ($20), and 7 to **Canmore** and **Calgary** ($50). They also run a daily service to **Jasper** from Banff (1345, $65) and **Lake Louise** (1445, $55).

Rail

Rocky Mountain Rail Tours, T1877-460 3200, www.rockymountaineer.com. Prohibitively expensive, though admittedly spectacular, rail trips from **Vancouver** to **Banff** or **Jasper**, with an option to continue on to **Calgary**. Prices start at $789 one-way for 2 days and 1 night.

Taxi

Banff Taxi, 103 Owl St, T403-762 4444.

Vehicle rental

Budget Car & Truck Rental, 202 Bear St, T403-762 4565, www.budget.com.

Canmore *p107*
Bus

The **Greyhound** station is at 701 Bow Valley Trail, T403-678 0832, www.greyhound.ca, with 4 daily buses to **Calgary** and **Banff**. Both shuttle services stop here on the way from Banff to Calgary. **Sun Dog Tours** (see Banff transport) run regular shuttles from Calgary Airport to Canmore, continuing to **Lake Louise** and **Jasper**.

Taxi

VIP Taxi, T403-678 5811.

Lake Louise *p111*
Taxi

Lake Louise taxi and Tours, in the Samson Mall, T403-522 2020.

⊙ Directory

Banff Townsite *p103, map p105*
Banks Bank of Montreal, 107 Banff Av, T403-762 2275. **Emergencies** Banff Warden Office, T403-762 4506; Police, T403- 762 2226; Medical and Fire, T403-762 2000.
Internet Cyberweb Internet Café, 215 Banff Av, T403-762 9226; the **Library** is cheaper.
Laundry Cascade Coin Laundry, 317 Banff Av, T403-762 3444. **Library** 101 Bear St, T403-762 2661. **Medical services** Alpine Medical Clinic, 211 Bear St, T403-762 3155; Mineral Springs Hospital, 305 Lynx St, T403-762 2222. **Post office** Canada Post, 204 Buffalo St, T403-762 2586.

Canmore *p107*
Bank Bank of Montreal, 701 8th St, T403-678 5568; **Royal Bank**, 1000 Railway Av, T403-678 3180. **Internet** Free at the library. Two Moose Internet Cafe, 717 10th St, T403-609 2678. **Library** 950 8th Av, T403-678 2468. **Medical services** Canmore General Hospital, 1100 Hospital Pl, T403-678 5536. **Post office** Canada Post, 801 Main St, T403-678 4377.

Lake Louise *p111*
Internet Samson Mall has internet and ATMs. **Medical services** Lake Louise Medical Clinic, 200 Hector St, T403-522 2184.

Jasper National Park and around

Jasper National Park feels much closer to wilderness than Banff. Neither as famous nor as convenient to reach, it receives far fewer visitors and has 10,878 sq km over which to spread them, an area bigger than Banff, Yoho and Kootenay National Parks combined. Vast tracts of this land are extremely remote and practically inaccessible, the overall emphasis being less on instant gratification, more on the long backcountry hikes that account for much of Jasper's 1000 km of trails. Apart from those on the Icefields Parkway, most of these are close to the pleasant town of Jasper, or around the attractive Maligne Lake, 48 km away.

Ins and outs

Getting there and around

The airport closest to Jasper is in **Edmonton International Airport (EIA)** ① *www.flyeia. com*, 370 km to the west, about four hours' drive. The **Sky Shuttle** ① *T780-465 8515, www.edmontonskyshuttle.com, $18, under 12s $10*, runs from the airport to the **Greyhound station** ① *10324 103rd St NW, T780-428 1908*, from where there are four buses daily to Jasper (five hours, $63). Trains run from the **Via Rail station** ① *12360 121st St*, to Jasper three times a week (five hours, $90); to get there take a taxi.

Note that **Calgary Airport** (see page 86) is not much further, just 412 km south of Jasper and the journey is infinitely more exciting. **Sun Dog Tours** ① *T1888-786 3461, www.sundogtours.com*, run shuttles from the airport, also picking up at Banff and Lake Louise, December to April only. The 281-km journey from Banff to Jasper is spectacular and for the best views, sit on the left-hand side. There are few services along what remains a region of extreme wilderness. Road closures are common from October to April after heavy snow. If cycling, note that Jasper is 500 m higher than Banff, so the journey is better made from north to south. Bikes can be rented in Jasper for one-way trips.

Jasper's train and bus stations are in the same attractive building, downtown at 607 Connaught Street. **Greyhound** ① *T780-852 3926, www.greyhound.ca*, runs regular daily buses from Edmonton, Vancouver via Kamloops and Prince George. **VIA Rail** operates three trains per week from Edmonton and Vancouver and Prince Rupert via Prince George. **The Rocky Mountaineer train** ① *T604-606 7245*, takes two days from Vancouver with a night in Kamloops, a beautiful journey. ▸▸ *See Transport, page 142.*

Tourist information

The Jasper National Park Information Centre ① *T780-852 6176, T780-852 6177 for trail information, www.jasper.travel, open daily Apr-Jun and Oct 0900-1700, Jun-Aug 0900-2100, Sep 0900-1800, Nov-Mar 0900-1600*, is situated in an attractive 1914 stone building in the city park at 500 Connaught Drive. They have information on accommodation and trails, issue Park and Wilderness passes and hand out a number of useful maps such as the *Backcountry Visitors' Guide*, the *Day-hiker's Guide* and a *Cycling Guide*. They also operate a voluntary safety registration system. **Friends of Jasper National Park** ① *T780-852 4767, www.friendsofjasper.com*, run free 1½-hour guided walks around the townsite nightly from June to September at 1930, and sell books and maps. There is also a Parks Canada counter in the Icefield Centre (see page 131).

Columbia Icefield → *For listings, see pages 136-142.*

The northern hemisphere's most extensive glacial area south of the Arctic Circle, the Columbia Icefield provides a dramatic introduction to Jasper National Park. As well as feeding three giant watersheds, its melt waters are the source of some of the continent's mightiest rivers, including the Columbia, Saskatchewan and Athabasca and drain into three oceans, the Atlantic, Pacific and Arctic. The only other icefield of equal scope and importance in the world is in Siberia. Most of the icefield's staggering 325-sq-km terrain is high in the mountains out of view, but three of the six major glaciers are clearly visible from the road, including the huge **Athabasca Glacier** ⓘ *6 km long, 1 km wide and 100 m thick*, which you can walk or even be driven on.

The ultimate way to see this spectacle is from the **Wilcox Pass Trail** ⓘ *8 km return, 335-m elevation gain*, which starts just south of Wilcox Creek Campground. This is one hike that everybody should do. Short and easy, it quickly whisks you to views that many longer hikes fail to equal. After a brief ascent through mature forest, the Columbia Icefield

Jasper National Park

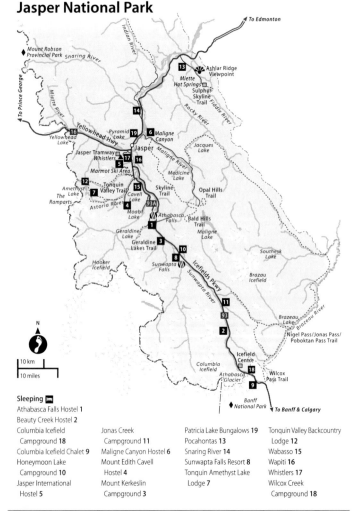

is suddenly visible in all its glory and from an angle far more gratifying than you'll get taking the Ice Explorer. Wild flower meadows and resident bighorn sheep complete the idyllic picture. With so much to be gained from so little effort, don't expect to be alone.

A joint venture by Brewster and Parks Canada, the **Icefield Centre** ① *T780-852 6288, http://www.explorerockies.com/columbia-icefield/, Apr-Oct daily 0900-2100*, resembles an airport and totally takes the edge off the wondrous surroundings, although it is a fine vantage point from which to ogle the Athabasca Glacier. The Glacier Gallery contains well-mounted informative displays, explaining glaciation, the icefield and the stories behind it. The **Parks Canada counter** ① *T780-852 6288, daily May and Sep to mid-Oct 0900-1700, Jun-Aug 0900-1800*, is helpful and can provide maps and leaflets for whichever park you are entering. **Brewster's Ice Age Adventure** tours take you onto the glacier in a specially built Ice Explorer bus (see page 141). Don't be tempted to walk on the glacier alone: people are killed and injured every year. Either they fall into one of its many crevasses, or injure themselves on the sharp sediment embedded in the ice.

North to Jasper

Distances below are from the Columbia Icefield, where many people choose to turn round anyway: understandable, as it is the high point of the drive. After so much rich fare, the easy **Beauty Creek Trail** ① *3.6-km*, which starts 15.5 km to the north, provides a nice change. This tiny chasm and its chain of pretty scaled-down waterfalls can be an uplifting sight. The mountains along this stretch of highway are striated at a 45° angle and resemble cresting waves.

At 53 km, a side road leads to **Sunwapta Falls**, which are mostly interesting for the canyon they have carved through the valley. **Athabasca Falls**, some 25 km further, are less worth a stop. At this point Highway 93A, the old Parkway, branches off from Highway 93 and runs parallel for 30 km, providing access to a campground, a hostel, Marmot Basin ski hill and a number of hikes.

Marmot Basin Ski Hill

① *T780-852 3816, www.skimarmot.com, mid-Nov to early-May, lift tickets are $74, under 17s $59, under 12s $27, cheaper in Jan, a shuttle runs daily from Jasper hotels at 0800, 0930 and 1145.*

Marmot has a reputation for being one of the most spacious, friendly and uncrowded ski hills in the country. It receives 4 m of powder per year, with no need for snow-makers. Eight lifts service 84 trails on 678 ha of skiable terrain, which breaks up into 30% beginner, 30% intermediate, 20% advanced and 20% expert. The top elevation is 2612 m, with a vertical drop of 914 m and a longest run of 5.6 km. There are three lodges, one at the base and two mid-mountain, with lounges, dining rooms, rentals and lessons.

Hikes from Highway 93A

Tonquin Valley ① *43-km loop; 920-m elevation gain*. The Tonquin Valley is one of Jasper's most popular backpack trips, leading to the beautiful Amethyst Lakes and an incredible 1000-m rock wall known as The Ramparts that shoots straight up from their shores. Before considering this hike, be aware that it could easily turn into a nightmare. There are two possible routes to the valley and both of them are used by operators whose horses churn up the trails. If it rains, or has done so in the last few days, the hike in is likely to be a long, frustrating trudge through ankle-deep mud. To do the trip by horse, see Activities and tours, page 140. If it's not raining, the mosquitoes and other biting insects are ferocious.

Astoria River Trail ① *7.2 km south on Parkway, turn west onto Highway 93A, continue 5.3 km south, then right onto Mt Edith Cavell Rd and 12.2 km to parking area just past the hostel, known as the Tonquin Expressway.* This is an easier, flatter route into the valley.

Portal Creek Trail ① *2.5 km south on Highway 93A, right onto Marmot Basin Rd, 6.5 km to car park over Maccarib Pass (which is steeper but consequently offers better views and is a more staisfying route).* Ideally, hike in on one and out the other, arranging a shuttle or hitching between trailheads. There are plenty of campsites to choose from, Surprise Point being a good choice. Reserve sites well in advance. Nearby is the Wates-Gibson Hut, reserved through the **Alpine Club of Canada** ① *T403-678 3200, www.alpineclubofcanada.ca*.

Eremite Valley The best day-hike side-trip, leading to more glacier-bearing peaks. In winter, you can ski 23 km into the valley and stay at the Tonquin Valley Backcountry Lodge or Tonquin Amethyst Lake Lodge.

Geraldine Lakes ① *10.5 km return to second lake, 13 km return to fourth lake; 407- to 497-m elevation gain. Trailhead: 1 km north of Athabasca Falls on Highway 93A, then 5.5 km up Geraldine Fire Rd.* The first lake is an easy hike to an unremarkable destination, but after that, things get more difficult and more rewarding. It's a fairly tough climb to the second and biggest lake with ridge top views and a waterfall as compensation. Beyond there is no trail and much bushwhacking to reach pristine pools set in wild, alpine meadows.

Cavell Meadows ① *8-km loop, 370-m elevation gain, trailhead: 13 km south on Highway 93A, 14 km on Cavell Rd.* This easy hike leads to spectacular views of the giant Angel Glacier. In mid-summer, these are also some of the finest wild flower meadows in the Rockies. The pay-off is marching along with crowds of people.

Jasper Townsite → For listings, see pages 136-142.

Jasper is a far more relaxed base than Banff, having managed to hold on to its small-town charm despite a turnover of some three million visitors per year. There is little in the way of out-of-control commercialism, and not much to do. Almost everything is on Connaught Drive, the road in and out of town, or Patricia Drive, which runs parallel to it. The only possible 'sight' in town is the **Yellowhead Museum and Archives** ① *400 Pyramid Lake Rd, T780-852 3013, www.jaspermuseum.org, mid-May to mid-Sep daily 1000-1700, mid-Sep to mid-May Thu-Sun, $5, child $4*, with a number of predictable displays exploring the town's First Nations, fur trade and railway, and a temporary exhibition in the Showcase Gallery.

Around Jasper Townsite

There are many loop day-hikes around the Pyramid Bench area, some leading to Pyramid Lake. Start at the **Activity Centre** ① *401 Pyramid Lake Rd*, and climb up to the bench. The Old Fort Point is a 3.5-km return trail leading to marvellous views of Athabasca River and

Jasper. Take Highway 93A from town to the Old Fort Point access road. Turn left and cross the iron bridge. You can continue from here on signposted No 7 trail to **Maligne Canyon** ① *9.5 km one-way*, and return along the river for an easy 20.7-km loop.

Just 5 km east of town on Lodge Road are **Annette Lake** and **Edith Lake**, whose shallow waters are the warmest around in summer, making their beaches very popular for swimming and sunbathing. There is a wheelchair-accessible path around the former. The winding Pyramid Lake Road leads 8 km northwest of town to **Pyramid Lake** and **Patricia Lake**. Apart from good views of Pyramid Mountain, this duo offers a couple of alternatives to sleeping in Jasper, and fishing, boating and horse riding.

The longest and highest of its kind in Canada, **Jasper Tramway** ① *3 km south on Hwy 93, then 4 km west on Whistler Mountain Rd, T780-852 3093, www.jasper tramway.com, daily Apr-May and Sep-Oct 1000-1700, May-Jun 0930-1830, Jul-Aug 0900-2000, $29, under 14s $15, under 5s free*, takes seven minutes to climb almost 1000 m in 2.5 km to an elevation of 2277 m. At the top is an interpretive centre, some boardwalks, excellent views, and a restaurant offering four-course meals June-August 1730-1930, $35, and breakfast June-August 0900-1030, free with your ticket. Expect queues in summer. A steep trail gains another 600 m to reach **Whistlers Summit** ① *2470 m*, and even more awe-inspiring vistas as far as Mount Robson, 80 km away.

Jasper

200 metres
200 yards

Sleeping 🛏
Amethyst Lodge 2
Bear Hill Lodge 4
Castle Guest House 12
Jasper International Hostel 9
Juniper House 13
Patricia Lake Bungalows 5
Pine Bungalows 10
Raven House B&B 6
Tekarra Lodge 3
Whistlers Inn & Pub 11

Eating 🍴
Andy's Bistro 1
Coco's 2
Earl's 3
Evil Dave's Grill 6
Fiddle River 5
Kimchi House 8
La Fiesta 7
Patricia Street Deli 16
Pines 4
Soft Rock Café 10
Villa Caruso 11

Bars & clubs 🍸
Atha B Nightclub 9
De'd Dog Bar & Grill 12
Downstream Bar 13
Jasper Brewing Co 14
Pete's Nightclub 15

Maligne Lake

The busy Maligne (pronounced 'maleen') Lake Road branches off Highway 16 east of town, leading 48 km to the most popular attraction in the park, with a few major sights on the way. In summer it is perpetually crowded with a stream of vehicles. The Maligne Lake Shuttle makes the journey several times daily. **Maligne Canyon**, 11.5 km from Jasper, is a spectacular gorge, 55 m deep and almost narrow enough to jump across. A number of short walking trails and footbridges lead to viewpoints. Unfortunately, the area is far too busy and taking on the unpleasant feel of a tourist trap. The canyon is at its best in winter, when the water freezes into an ice palace with 30-m icefalls and incredible, blue-ice caves. In winter a few operators run three-hour tours, with crampons, head lamps and other equipment provided. There is a hostel here and the northern terminus of the famous Skyline Trail.

A further 21 km is **Medicine Lake**, whose water level fluctuates dramatically with the seasons because it fills and empties through sink-holes into an elaborate network of underground limestone caves. In summer the water is high, but in winter it sometimes disappears altogether. While such temporal variations fascinated Native Americans, the one-time visitor will see nothing but another lake.

At 22 km long, beautiful **Maligne Lake** is the largest lake in the Rockies and the second largest glacier-fed lake in the world. Surrounded by white-peaked mountains, it is a sight to behold, though not as overwhelming as Lake Louise. The best views open up from the middle of the lake, accessible on cruises and boat tours. Lots of hikes begin here, including the excellent Skyline Trail. For something shorter, the 3.2-km Schäffer Viewpoint loop leads along the east shore from Car Park 2. There is no accommodation at the lake apart from two backcountry campgrounds on the lakeshore that can only be reached by canoe (a four-hour trip) and must be booked at Jasper Information Centre. ▶▶ *See Activities and tours, page 140.*

Hikes from Maligne Lake

Skyline ⓘ *44.5 km; 820-m elevation gain.* This is one of the all-time great backpack trips, offering everything you come to the Rockies for: drool-inducing views of lofty peaks, including some of the range's highest and sweeping meadows full of wild flowers. Fast hikers can do it in two days, but three is more realistic. It is a one-way hike best started at Maligne Lake. If driving, leave your vehicle at the Maligne Canyon terminus and hitch or take a bus to the lake. Book sites in the backcountry campgrounds well ahead, because this is one hike that is almost impossible to get onto at short notice. Plan your trip for after late-July, when the steepest section of the trail, known as 'the Notch', should be snow-free. This is the only steep section of a hike that is surprisingly level, considering that almost all of it is above the treeline. This last fact means you're particularly at the mercy of the weather, so go prepared for anything.

Bald Hills ⓘ *12.6 km return; 610-m elevation gain.* The Bald Hills are actually a 7-km-long ridge. The lack of trees that gave them their name makes for excellent views of the surroundings, including Maligne Lake and the Queen Elizabeth Ranges, with razorback ridges, gleaming glaciers, rugged rock faces, green forests, alpine meadows and extraordinary rock formations. After about 45 minutes, take the cut-off trail through the trees and look out for wild flowers. Most people stop at the old fire lookout but you can continue for greater panoramas and less company.

Opal Hills ⓘ *8.2 km; 460-m elevation gain*. This trail is short but very steep. The rewards are gorgeous views of mountains and the lake and a host of tiny wild flowers.

Miette Hot Springs

ⓘ *T780-866 3939, daily Jul-Aug 0830-2230, mid-May-Jun and Sep to mid-Oct 1030-2100, $6, under 16s $5.15, road closed in winter.*

A favourite excursion from Jasper is to **Miette Hot Springs**, 61 km east on Highway 16, then 17 km south on Miette Road. Near the junction of these roads is an interpretive trail to the abandoned mining town of Pocahontas, a pleasant wander through a forest that has grown around the ruins. **Ashlar Ridge Viewpoint** ⓘ *8.5 km Miette Rd*, offers great views of this impressive rock wall, which can also be appreciated from the newly renovated springs themselves, which are the hottest in the Rockies. Cooled from 54°C to 40°C, the water is chlorinated and runs into two large outdoor pools. Interpretive displays explain the local geology and an interpretive trail leads to the source of the springs.

If you've driven this far, hike the short but steep **Sulphur Skyline** ⓘ *8 km return, 700-m elevation gain*, offering views out of all proportion to the energy expended. It's also a good early-season hike.

Mount Robson Provincial Park → *For listings, see pages 136-142.*

ⓘ *The only public transport into the park is the Greyhound. Ask to be dropped at the Mt Robson viewpoint, also site of the Visitor Centre, T250-566 4038, May-Sep daily 0800-1700, mid-Jun to Aug 0800-1900. The nearby café/garage is about the only place to get food. The reservation fee for hiking Berg Lake, $6 per night up to $18 for 3 or more nights, is paid at the time of booking T1800-689 9025, a credit card is essential. The camping fee, $5 per person per night, is paid at the time of registration at the visitor centre, which also retains a few first-come, first-served sites: be there before it opens to get one.*

The Yellowhead Highway (Highway 16) accompanies the railway west from Jasper to the **Yellowhead Pass** ⓘ *1131 m*, which has been used as a route across the Continental (or Great) Divide by fur-traders and gold-seekers for over 150 years. This is the border between Alberta and British Columbia, Mountain and Pacific time zones (BC is one hour behind) and Jasper and Mount Robson parks. There are few facilities in the latter, so if planning to do the overnight hike discussed below, stock up in Jasper. The next closest town is **Tête Jaune Cache** ⓘ *16 km beyond the park's western boundary*, though Valemount to the south is more substantial.

More than any other of the Rocky Mountain parks, this one is utterly dominated by its crowning feature. At 3954 m, **Mount Robson** is the highest peak in the Canadian Rockies and possibly the most spectacular. It was one of the last mountains in the Rockies to be climbed and even today represents a difficult challenge. Whether you're approaching on Highway 16 or from Kamloops on Highway 5, the first sight of this colossal rock pyramid is likely to take your breath away: the perfection of its shape, highlighted by the pointed triangle of ice at its apex and the distinct layering of rock which inspired the native name Yuh-hai-has-hun, 'Mountain of the Spiral Road'. The only way to fully appreciate the peak's awesome beauty is by doing the hike, which reveals the incredible vast glaciers that cover its north side.

Hikes in Mount Robson Provincial Park

Mount Robson/Berg Lake ⓘ *39.2 km return; 786-m elevation gain. Trailhead: 2 km north of the visitor centre on a side road.* This is the most popular and one of the very best backpacking trips in the range and can be attempted as early as mid-June. Most people reach Berg Lake in a day, spend a day exploring, then hike out on the third. The trail is extraordinary and varied, leading through lush, flower-dotted rainforest, past open gravel flats, over suspension bridges in a rugged river gorge, through the Valley of a Thousand Faces and past three powerful waterfalls, including the 60-m Emperor Falls. At Berg Lake, Mount Robson rises 2316 m directly from the shore, its cliffs wrapped in the vast ice-cloaks of Mist and Berg Glaciers. Huge chunks of ice regularly crash from the latter into the lake. There is a campground right here, a more private one 600 m further, another 1.4 km further still, and four more elsewhere in the park. A recommended 9-km day-hike is to Snowbird Pass. The path leads to the toe of Robson Glacier and for the next 3 km the views of the glacier are stupendous.

Yellowhead Mountain ⓘ *9 km return; 715-m elevation gain. Trailhead: 8.5 km west of the pass on Hwy 16, 1 km on a gravel road across Yellowhead Lake on an isthmus. Park below the railway where road splits.* Passing through meadows and aspen forest, this trail is particularly attractive in autumn. The best day-hike in the park, it offers wonderful views of Yellowhead Pass.

Jasper National Park and around listings

For Sleeping and Eating price codes and other relevant information, see pages 9-11.

😴 Sleeping

Columbia Icefield *p129, map p130*
$$$ Columbia Icefield Chalet, in the Icefield Centre, T1877-442 2623, www.columbiaicefield.com/hotel.asp. Spacious, comfy rooms with high ceilings, some with glacier views and some with lofts. Book ahead. Prices halve mid-Sep to mid-Jun.
$$$ Tonquin Amethyst Lake Lodge, T180-852 1188, www.tonquinadventures.com. Private, heated cabins with log beds and warm blankets, and shared guest chalets with dining area and log fire. Price includes meals. Access is only possible on foot or on horseback along an 18.6-km trail.
$$$ Tonquin Valley Backcountry Lodge, Eremite Valley, T780-852 3909, www.tonquinvalley.com. Rustic but comfortable chalets, which sleep 1 to 6 people in bunk beds. Price includes meals, boat use, and dayrides. Access is only possible on foot or on horseback.

Camping
Wilcox Creek and **Columbia Icefield** campgrounds, right next to each other on the Jasper side and 5 mins' walk from the Icefields Centre, enjoy one of the prime locations in the Rockies and are both predictably very crowded. The latter is for tents only and has very nice walk-in sites.

North to Jasper *p131, map p130*
$$$ Sunwapta Falls Resort, T1888-828 5777, www.sunwapta.com. Small but very nice, cosy, newly renovated en suite rooms, some with sun decks and some with fireplaces. There's a reasonable restaurant and bikes for rent.
$ Athabasca Falls Hostel, T1877-852 0781, www.hihostels.ca. 20 beds in 3 rustic cabins with no running water, showers or flush toilets. The location is fantastic.
$ Beauty Creek Hostel, 14 km north of the Icefield Centre, T1877-852 0781, www.hihostels.ca. A very basic, summer-only hostel with 24 beds in 2 cabins, no flush toilets or running water but sun showers and a small

propane-fuelled kitchen. Situated right next to the creek, which through 8 sets of waterfalls along a limestone gorge.

$ Jasper International Hostel, 7 km southwest, near gondola on Whistlers Mountain Rd, T1877-852 0781, www.hihostels.ca. A chalet-style hostel with 84 beds, full kitchen, showers, laundry and bike rentals. Shuttles from Downtown.

$ Mount Edith Cavell Hostel, 5.3 km south on Hwy 93A, then 12 km on Mt Edith Cavell Rd, T1877-852 0781, www.hihostels.ca. 32 beds in 2 cabins with views of the Angel Glacier and the 3363-m peak. Popular, as it's the perfect base to start backcountry hikes into the Tonquin Valley. Book ahead.

Camping

Jonas Creek Campground, 9 km beyond Beauty Creek. 25 sites by the creek, some walk-in only.

Honeymoon Lake Campground, just past Sunwapta Falls. One of the nicer places to camp with 35 spacious sites, some right on the lake.

Mount Kerkeslin Campground, 10 km further. 42 attractive sites.

Jasper Townsite *p132, maps 130 and p133*
Jasper's hotels are not much better value than Banff's and are just as likely to be full in summer. There are, however, plenty of private homes close to town with reasonably priced rooms (**$$**). Ask at the information centre, or visit www.stayinjasper.com, for a detailed list of over 120. This site also provides availability reports for the following 7 days. Make hostel reservations online at www.hihostels.ca, or call T1877-852 0781.

$$$ Amethyst Lodge, 200 Connaught Dr, T780-852 3394, www.mpljasper.com. Central location with big rooms, balconies, 2 outdoor hot tubs, restaurant and lounge.

$$$ Bear Hill Lodge, 100 Bonhomme St, T780- 852 3209, www.bearhilllodge.com. A wide range of cabins, lodge rooms

and duplexes with full bath, some with kitchenettes or gas fireplace. Situated on a forested 1-ha lot on the edge of town, with hot tub, sauna, internet and laundry facilities.

$$$ Patricia Lake Bungalows, 6 km north towards Pyramid Lake at Patricia Lake, T780-852 3560, www.patricialakebungalows.com. Lots of options in a quiet spot by the lake, including luxury suites (**$$$**), attractive, spacious cottages or cabins with kitchens and/or fireplaces, (**$$$**) and good value motel style suites (**$$$**). Facilities include hot tub, laundry and canoe rentals.

$$$ Pine Bungalows, 2 km east at 2 Cottonwood Creek Rd, T780-852 3491, www.pinebungalows.com. Situated in a forest setting on the banks of the Athabasca River, with 72 very nice, cosy, modern cabins, bungalows and motel rooms, all with tubs, most with kitchenettes and many with stone fireplaces. The 2-bedroom cabins for 4 people (**$$$**) are quite a bit nicer.

$$$ Raven House B&B, 801 Miette Av, T780- 852 4011, www.ravenbb.com. 2 pleasant rooms in a private house in town.

$$$ Tekarra Lodge, 1 km south off Hwy 93A, T780-852 3058, www.tekarralodge.com. In a quiet spot in the trees by the confluence of the Athabasca and Miette rivers. Tasteful cabins with hardwood floors, stone fireplaces, balconies and kitchens, or plain B&B lodge rooms. Common area with fireplace, good restaurant, continental breakfast, bike rentals and hiking trails nearby.

$$$ Whistlers Inn,105 Miette Av, T780-852 3361, www.whistlersinn.com. Economy (**$$$**) and standard (**$$$**) rooms and much nicer suites (**$$$$**) in a very central property with an outdoor rooftop hot tub, a steam room, 2 restaurants and a nice pub.

$$ Castle Guest House, 814 Miette Av, T780-852 3994, www.bbcanada.com/ 12351. 2 comfortable rooms in a splendid modern wood house with a garden patio.

$$ Juniper House, 713 Maligne Av,

T780-852 3664, www.visit-jasper.com/juniperhouse. 2 very tasteful suites in a newly renovated heritage home, which is also very central. Good value.

$ Maligne Canyon Hostel, 11 km east on Maligne Lake Rd, T780-852 3215, T1877-852 0781, www.hihostels.ca. 24 beds in 2 cabins near the canyon. Open year round (closed Wed in winter). Rustic, with no running water or flush toilets but a small propane kitchen.

Camping

Campgrounds close to town fill up very fast in summer, with queues starting about 1100, but **Pocahontas**, **Whistlers**, **Wapiti** and **Wabasso** can all be reserved ahead by calling T1877-737 3783, or online at www.pccamping.ca. When all the campgrounds are full, overflow sites are put into effect (cheaper, but not very nice). Jasper has over 100 backcountry sites. Wilderness Passes cost $9 per person per night, refundable till 1000 on proposed date of departure. Reservation (with $12 fee) at information centre or T780-852 6177, up to 3 months before departure. Campsite day-use permit $7.

Pocahontas, 45 km east then 1 km on Miette Hot Springs Rd. 140 reasonable sites.
Snaring River, 15 km north off Hwy 16 on the road towards Celestine Lake. This is the nicest campground, with 66 sites. When all others are full, there is overflow camping here with space for 500.
Wabasso, 15 km south on Hwy 93A. 228 sites. The inconvenient location tends to mean it's the last one to fill up.
Wapiti, 4 km south on Hwy 93. Has 362 sites, some with hook-ups. Showers available. The only campsite open year-round, although less sites are available in winter and cannot be reserved. OK, for being so close to town.
Whistlers, 3 km south off Hwy 93. There are 781 sites, including some with full hook-ups. Campers should try to get a walk-in site.

Mount Robson Provincial Park *p135*
$$$ Mount Robson Mountain River Lodge, 4 km west of the **Visitor Centre** on Hwy 16, T250-566 9899, www.mtrobson.com. Situated close to the trail (phone for directions), offering a couple of lovely log cabins with kitchens (**$$$**), and 4 rooms in the splendid wood lodge (**$$**). Breakfast available ($12) but not included. Spectacular location and views, with a lovely deck to enjoy them from.

$$ Mount Robson Heritage Cabins, 2 km from the Hwy on Hargreaves Rd, T250-566 4654, www.mountrobsonranch.com. 7 lovely rustic cabins, some with kitchenettes, in a very quiet, private spot near the Berg Lake Trail. Also has a campground for tents and RVs, and a restaurant offering all meals.

Camping

Emperor Ridge Campground, within walking distance of the **Visitor Centre** on Kinney Lake Rd, T250-566 8438. Offers 37 decent sites and hot showers.
Robson Meadows and the much smaller **Robson River Provincial Park** campgrounds, are both close to the **Visitor Centre** on the park's west side. 144 sites between them, showers and lovely riverside locations.
Robson Shadows Campground, 5 km west of the park boundary on Hwy 16, T1888-566 4821. Nice sites on the Fraser River, with showers available. Panoramic views of Mt Robson.

🍴 Eating

Jasper Townsite *p132, maps 130 and p133*
🍴🍴🍴 **The Pines** at Coast Pyramid Lake Resort, Pyramid Lake Rd, 6 km from town, T780-852 4900. Sumptuous dishes like smoked trout chowder and seafood pasta flavoured with black sambuca, served in a comfortable interior or on a patio overlooking the lake. Also good breakfasts.
🍴🍴 **Andy's Bistro**, 606 Patricia St, T780-852

4559. European-influenced cuisine in an intimate setting, with a frequently changing menu that focuses on meat dishes and fondue. Chef Andy is undoubtedly one of the best in town.

†† Earl's, 600 Patricia St, T780-852 2393. The standard broad menu covering many popular bases, but they do it well and there are good views from the 2nd-floor balcony. One of the nicest locations in town.

†† Evil Dave's Grill, 622 Patricia St, T780-852 3323. A laid-back, bright and sophisticated newcomer, with a diverse international menu that's daring and exciting but overpriced. Also has a good wine, cocktail and martini list.

†† Fiddle River, 1st floor, 620 Connaught Dr, T780-852 3032. A cosy, pine-finished loft that's casual but stylish. The place to go for seafood, immaculately cooked in a variety of imaginative or tried and tested ways. Also has a big wine list.

†† Kimchi House, 407 Patricia St, T780-852 5022. A real cultural experience, serving authentic Korean BBQ dishes that are big enough for 2. Choose between the cosy interior or outdoor patio.

†† La Fiesta, 504 Patricia St, T780-852 0404. One of the nicest interiors in town, with exposed wooden beams and hardwood floors, simple, elegant and romantic. The Spanish menu has lots of choice, but paella and tapas (3 for $25) are their speciality. Generous portions, a changing menu, and good sangria.

†† Villa Caruso, 640 Connaught Dr, T780-852 3920. A classic steak-and-seafood-style menu, in a downtown location dominated by lots of wood. Good atmosphere with 2 fireplaces and 3 outdoor patios. The bar is also a nice place for a drink.

† Coco's, 608 Patricia St, T708-852 4550. A good place to hang out, with a bright and breezy atmosphere, good coffee, music, breakfast, scones, magazines, and decent breakfast and lunch items that are vegan and coeliac friendly.

† Patricia Street Deli, 606 Patricia St, T780-852 4815. Take out only, but delicious sandwiches made with fresh ingredients and house-baked bread.

† Soft Rock Café, 632 Connaught Dr, T708-852 5850. Tasty breakfast and grilled sandwiches; internet access.

🔾 Bars and clubs

Jasper Townsite *p132, maps 130 and p133*
Most of Jasper's hotels have lounges for a quiet drink, but with big-screen TVs.

Atha-B Nightclub, 510 Patricia St, T708-852 3386. recently renovated nightclub with DJs and live music.

De'd Dog Bar and Grill, Astoria Hotel, 404 Connaught Dr, T708-852 3351. A casual place to hang out, popular with locals, boasting a good selectioy of ales on tap, darts and a pool table.

The Downstream Bar, 620 Connaught Dr, T708-852 9449. A cosy spot for a glass of wine. with a rustic oak and brick interior, a more mature clientele, and very good food.

Jasper Brewing Co, 624 Connaught Dr, T708-852 4111. A decent pub that brews its own beers and serves high-quality, contemporary pub food.

Pete's Night Club, 2nd Floor, 614 Patricia St, T708-852 6262. A party bar, with dancing, drink specials and occasional live music.

Whistler's Inn Pub, 105 Miette Av, T780-852 3361. A cosy neighbourhood favourite, with a huge oak bar, fireplace and pool table.

⊛ Festivals and events

Jasper Townsite *p132, maps 130 and p133*
Aug Heritage Folk Festival, T780-852 3615. A major folk music event held biennially in Centennial Park (next in 2011).
Jasper Heritage Pro Rodeo, www.jasper heritagerodeo.com. For 4 days in mid-Aug the rodeo attracts top cowboys and stock from around the world, with events like bull riding, bareback and saddle bronco riding, steer wrestling, calf roping, barrel racing and more. Dances on Fri and Sat nights featuring top Country entertainers.

O Shopping

Jasper Townsite *p132, maps 130 and p133*
Everest Outdoor Stores, 414 Connaught Dr,
T708-852 5902. Maps, outdoor clothing, and
sports equipment to buy or rent.
Friends of Jasper National Park, opposite
the **Visitor Centre** on Connaught Rd, T780-
852 4767, www.friendsofjasper.com. Profits
go to the park.
Gravity Gear, 618 Patricia St, T708-852 3155.
The place for climbing gear.
Jasper Source for Sports, 406 Patricia St,
T708-852 3654. Fishing equipment, boat
rentals, bike and camping gear rentals.
Nutters Bulk Food, 622 Patricia St, T708-
852 5844. Health food and hiking snacks,
good salamis and cheeses.

▲ Activities and tours

Jasper Townsite *p132, maps 130 and p133*
Biking
Pick up the *Jasper Cycling Guide* at the visitor
centre. There are several good trails starting
from town. Experienced bikers will enjoy the
Saturday Night Lake Loop, 27 km, starting at
the Cabin Lake Rd parking lot, west end of
town, with views of Miette and Athabasca
Valley. There is some good riding across the
river at Old Fort Point, which is also the start
of the 23-km Trail No 7, a good all-level ride
passing through Maligne Canyon.
Freewheel Cycle, 618 Patricia St, T780-852
3898, www.freewheeljasper.com. Trail maps,
rentals and information. Also rent skis and
snowboards.

Climbing
Gravity Gear, 618 Patricia St, T780-852 3155,
www.gravitygearjasper.com. Ask them about
climbing at Maligne Canyon, Rock Gardens
and Boulder Gardens. Hidden Valley, 30 km
east, is good for the experienced.
Jasper Activity Centre, 303 Pyramid Av,
T708-852 3381. Has an indoor climbing wall.

Dog sledding
Cold Fire Creek, T780-968 6808, www.dog
sleddinginjasper.com. Dog-sledding trips,
1 hr ($125), 3 hrs ($190) and longer. Also
3-hr moonlight tours ($250).

Fishing
Currie's Guiding & Tackle, T780-852 5650,
www.curriesguidingjasper.com. Full and ½-
day fishing trips, mostly on Maligne Lake,
in a 21-ft cedar strip freighter canoe.
They can obtain your permit for you.

Hiking, walking and ice canyon tours
Overlander Trekking and Tours, T780-
852 0167, www.overlandertrekking.com.
Backcountry hikes in and around the park.
Guided cross-country skiing and snowshoe
tours. The 3-hr Maligne Canyon Icewalk
departs 3 times daily, $55, $27.50 child,
and is highly recommended.
Walks and Talks Jasper, 626 Connaught
Dr, T780-852 4994, www.walksntalks.com.
Interpretive guided hikes, walks, and ice walks,
which focus on wildlife and the environment.
Also offer guided ski and snowshoe tours.

Horse riding
Pyramid Riding Stables, T780-852 7106,
www.mpljasper.com/jasper/pyramid_
riding.html. 1-hr to 1-day horse rides above
town on Pyramid Bench with views of the
Athabasca Valley. Also offer carriage and
wagon rides.
Skyline Trail Rides, T780-852 4215,
www.skylinetrail.com. 3-day horseback trips
to their Shovel Pass Lodge, $825 including
food, lodging, horses and guides. Also daily
trail rides from Jasper Park Lodge, from
1¼ hrs ($43) to 4½ hrs ($125), and children's
pony rides, $20 for 30 mins.
Tonquin Valley Pack Trips, T780-852 1188,
www.tonquinadventures.com. 3- ($795), 4-
($1050) or 5-day ($1295) horse-riding trips up
Tonquin Valley to their Amethyst Lake Lodge,
with meals and accommodation included.

Icefield tours

Brewster, T403-762 6700, www.sightseeing
tourscanada.ca. The Icefield Glacier
Experience tour takes you onto the Athabasca
Glacier in an Ice Explorer, a specially built
bus that moves at a snail's pace, doing the
5-km round trip in 80 mins. Tours leave
every 15-30 mins Apr and Oct 1000-1600,
May and Sep 0900-1700, Jun-Aug 0900-1800,
and cost $49, under 15s $24.

Ice-skating

Jasper Activity Centre, 303 Pyramid Av,
T780-852 3381, has an indoor rink; **Lac
Beauvert**, by Jasper Park Lodge; **Pyramid
Lake**, Pyramid Lake Rd.

Rafting

All of the rafting companies offer similar trips
and prices: 2-hr ($59) and 3-hr ($79) trips on
the Athabasca River, with mellow Grade II
runs, and 4-hr trips on the Sunwapta River
($89) for more dramatic Grade III trips.
Maligne Rafting Adventures, T780-852
3370, www.mra.ab.ca, also run 5-hr trips
on the Fraser ($99) and multi-day trips on
the Kakwa River; **Raven Rafting**, T780-852
4292, www.ravenadventure.com; **Rocky
Mountain River Guides**, T780-852 3777,
www.rmriverguides.com; **Whitewater
Rafting**, T780-852 7238, www.whitewater
raftingjasper.com.

Rentals

Edge Control Ski & Outdoor Store, 626
Connaught Dr, T708-852 494, specializes
in ski and snowboard equipment rentals;
Jasper Source for Sports, 406 Patricia St,
T780-852 3654; **On-Line Sport**, 600 Patricia
St, T780-852 3630. Canoes at a couple of
lakes, including Maligne, and fishing gear.

Skiing

For downhill skiing, see Marmot Basin Ski Hill,
page 131. For cross-country skiing there are
20 km of groomed trails at Maligne Lake. The
Bald Hills up above offer plenty of space for
telemarking and touring, but the 480-m
elevation gain over 5.5 km makes it hard work
getting there. The 5 km Beaver/Summit Lake
Trail, Km 27 on Maligne Lake Rd, gives easy
access to the backcountry. There are 1- to
30-km trails at Pyramid Bench and around
Patricia Lake. Jasper Park Lodge, on Lodge
Rd just east of Jasper, also has a network of
groomed loops from 5 km to 10 km. The
4.5-km Whistlers Campground loop is flat,
easy and lit up at night. Moab Lake is a nice,
easy 18-km trail with great views, 20 km
south on Hwy 93A.

Tour operators

Air Jasper, T708-865 3616, www.airjasper. com.
Flightseeing tours of the Icefield and Maligne
Lake or Mt Robson and Amethyst Lakes in a
Cessna (75 mins, $185 per person). The tours
can be combined (105 mins, $270 per person).
Price includes the shuttle to Hinton Airport.
Jasper Adventure Centre, 604 Connaught
Dr (mid-May to mid-Sep); 618 Connaught
Dr (mid-Sep to mid-May), T780-852 5595,
www.jasperadventurecentre.com.
Representing many of the other companies
in this listing, these guys can set you up with
any activity around Jasper. They also run 2-hr
'voyageur' canoe trips, walking and hiking
trips, and a number of van tours for those
without transportation to places like Jasper
Tramway, Maligne Lake or Canyon, and
Miette Hotsprings.
Sun Dog Tours, T780-852 4056, www.sun
dogtours.com. As well as providing shuttles,
they can also book any tours you need.

Mount Robson Provincial Park *p135*
Headwaters Outfitting, T250-566 4718,
www.davehenry.com. Backcountry skiing,
hiking or trail riding based out of the remote
Dave Henry Lodge or Swift Creek Cabins,
both close to Mt Robson Park. A 4-day
guided hiking trip is $604 per person
including lodging but not meals.

Mount Robson Whitewater Rafting, T250-566 4879, www.mountrobsonwhitewater.com. Float trips (2½ hrs, $49), whitewater trips (3 hrs, $89), or the 2 combined ($129) on the Fraser River.

Snow Farmers, T250-566 9161, www.snowfarmers.com. Guided horse riding, from 1 hr, $40 to 1 day, $150.

⊖ Transport

Jasper Townsite *p132, maps 130 and p133*
Bus
Local Most of Jasper's important trails are far from the town. For those without their own transport the choices are to hitchhike or use one of the rather expensive shuttle services: **Jasper Adventure Centre**, T780-852 5595; **Walks and Talks Jasper**, T780-852 4945. From May-Oct the **Jasper Shuttle**, 616 Patricia St, T780-852 3370, www.jaspershuttle.com, connects the Townsite with Maligne Lake, late Jun to late Sep 0830, 1130, 1415, 1630, leaving the lake at 1000, 1300, 1515, 1800; otherwise 0845, 1230 and 1530, returning 1000, 1400 and 1700. One-way $20, $15 to **Maligne Canyon**. Will also drop you at trailheads.

Long distance Greyhound, T1800-661 8747, runs 4 daily buses to **Edmonton** (5 hrs, $62), 2 to **Vancouver** (11-12 hrs, $124) via **Kamloops** (5½ hrs, $65) and 1 to **Prince George** (5½ hrs, $65). **Sun Dog Tours**, T1888-786 3641, www.sundogtours.com, runs a shuttle to **Banff** ($65) and **Calgary** ($129).

Train
VIA Rail, T1888-842 7245, www.viarail.ca, operates 3 trains per week to **Edmonton** (5 hrs) and **Vancouver** (17½ hrs) or to **Prince Rupert** (31 hrs) with a night in **Prince George** (6½ hrs). **The Rocky Mountaineer** train, T604-606 7245, www.rockymountaineer.com. A beautiful 2-day journey to **Vancouver** with 1 night's accommodation in Kamloops, starting at $789.

Mt Robson Provincial Park *p135*
Greyhound, T1800-661 8747, buses will drop you off at the visitor centre. 3 daily to **Jasper** (1½ hrs, $27), 1 daily to **Prince George** (3½ hrs, $51) and 2 from **Kamloops** (4½ hrs, $58).

ⓘ Directory

Jasper Townsite *p132, maps 130 and p133*
Banks TD Bank, 606 Patricia Av, T708-852 6270. **Internet** Library; Soft Rock Internet Café, 632 Connaught Dr, T708- 852 5850. **Laundry** Coin Clean Laundry, 607 Patricia Av, T708-852 3852, also has coin-operated showers. **Library** Jasper Municipal Library, 500 Robson St/Elm Av, T708-852 3652. **Medical services** Cottage Medical Clinic, 507 Turret St, T780-852 4885; Seton General Hospital, 518 Robson St, T780-852 3344. **Post office** Canada Post, 502 Patricia St, T708-852 3041.

Yoho National Park

Yoho is a Cree exclamation of awe and wonder, something like 'Wow!' The scenery in this park is indeed astounding, with many waterfalls and 28 peaks over 3000 m. Banff may be the most famous of the parks and Jasper the biggest, but get any Rocky Mountain aficionado talking and they'll soon start waxing passionate about Yoho. Comparatively small, it contains the greatest concentration of quality hikes in the range, mostly clustered in two major areas and one minor. Lake O'Hara has proved so popular that a complete traffic ban has been imposed, and visitor numbers are now strictly limited. A good second choice, if that's too much hassle, Yoho Valley has the park's only hostel and a fabulous campground. Emerald Lake is a pretty destination and offers one very good hike. The pleasant little village of Field makes a good base for those not camping.

Ins and outs

Getting there and around
Field is on the TransCanada Highway and therefore receives three **Greyhound** ① *www.greyhound.ca*, buses from Vancouver, Calgary and all points in between, including Banff and Lake Louise. ▸▸ *See Transport, page 149.*

There is no public road to Lake O'Hara and bikes are not allowed. A shuttle bus runs from mid-June to early October from the Lake O'Hara Fire Road parking lot, off Highway 1, 15 km east of Field, 11 km west of Lake Louise. Buses leave at 0830, 1030, 1530 and 1730, departing from Lake O'Hara Lodge at 0930, 1130, 1430, 1630 and 1830; early October 1000 and 1500 in, 1100 and 1600 out. To get a place on the bus it is essential to reserve at T250-343 6433 up to three months in advance. You will need to know your plans, as bus, campground and reservation fees are all to be paid by credit card when booking. Six seats on the bus and three to five places in the campground are left open per day for bookings by phone the day before. The office opens at 0800 (Mountain time) and the fare is $14.70 return, under 16s $7.30, with a $12 reservation fee. Once up there a place on the return bus is first-come, first-served, but practically guaranteed at 1630 or 1830. For more info, visit www.pc.gc.ca.

Tourist information
Unless you know specifically what you want to do, a sensible first port of call is to the village of Field which is close to all of Yoho's sights and contains the excellent **Visitor Centre/Parks Office** ① *T250-343 6783, www.field.ca, mid-Jun to early-Sep daily 0900-1900, mid-Sep to mid-May daily 0900-1600/1700, backcountry camping reservations T250-343 6433, $12.* They can help organize accommodation and camping arrangements, give sound advice on what hikes to choose and issue the very useful backcountry guide, as well as maps. They also take backcountry camping reservations up to three months ahead, a must for Lake O'Hara.

Field → *For listings, see pages 148-149.*

Field is a remarkably attractive one-horse town of 250 people built on the side of a mountain and dotted with beautiful flower gardens, and makes a delightful base for day hikes around the park. There are no sights as such, but Field Mountain, visible across the valley, is the site of the **Burgess Shale**, an ancient seabed that has yielded a host of 515 million-year-old fossils. Remains of more than 120 species of soft-bodied marine animals have been found, some so well preserved that scientists can tell what they ate just before they died. This is one of only three places in the world where such fossils are found. An excellent exhibit recreating the sea and explaining its inhabitants is one of the highlights of the Royal Tyrell Museum in Drumheller, Alberta (see page 92). There are also displays at the Field and Lake Louise visitor centres. Long and strenuous guided hikes to the fossil beds are run between July and mid-September by the **Yoho Burgess Shale Foundation** ① *T1800-343 3006.* Numbers are limited to 15 per hike.

There is also a **viewpoint** ① *8 km east of Field and 2 km up the Yoho Valley Rd,* for contemplating the Spiral Tunnels, two enormous figure-of-eight galleries blasted out of the mountains in 1909 in order to reduce the original 4.5% railway grade to a much safer 2.2%. For railway buffs, the sight of a long goods train tying itself in knots through these tunnels is an extraordinary phenomenon not to be missed.

Yoho National Park

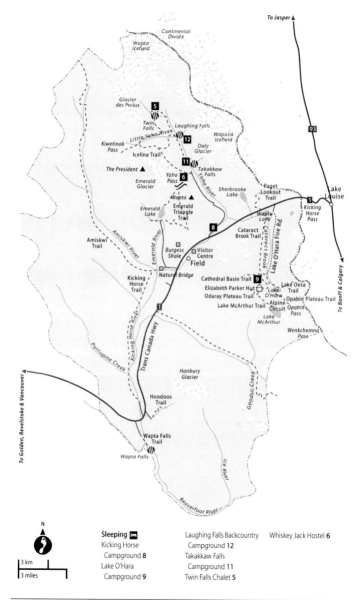

Continental Divide
Wapta Icefield
To Jasper
Glacier des Poilus
5
Twin Falls
Laughing Falls
Little Yoho River
12
Kiwetinok Pass
Iceline Trail
Waputik Icefield
Daly Glacier
The President ▲
11
Takakkaw Falls
Emerald Glacier
Yoho Pass
6
Sherbrooke Lake
Paget Lookout Trail
Emerald Lake
Wapta ▲
Emerald Triangle Trail
Wapta Lake
93
Lake Louise
Kicking Horse Pass
8
Cataract Brook Trail
Amiskwi Trail
Burgess Shale
Visitor Centre
Field
Canada Brook
Lake O'Hara Fire Rd
1
To Banff & Calgary
Emerald River
Kicking Horse Trail
Natural Bridge
Cathedral Basin Trail
9
Lake Oesa Trail
Elizabeth Parker Hut
Odaray Plateau Trail
Lake O'Hara
Opabin Plateau Trail
Lake McArthur Trail
Alpine Circuit
Opabin Pass
Lake McArthur
Wenkchemna Pass
Amiskwi River
Kicking Horse River
Porcupine Creek
Trans Canada Hwy
1
Hanbury Glacier
Goodsir Creek
To Golden, Revelstoke & Vancouver
Hoodoos Trail
Wapta Falls Trail
Wapta Falls
Ice River
Beaverfoot River

N
3 km
3 miles

Sleeping 🛏
Kicking Horse
  Campground **8**
Lake O'Hara
  Campground **9**

Laughing Falls Backcountry
  Campground **12**
Takakkaw Falls
  Campground **11**
Twin Falls Chalet **5**

Whiskey Jack Hostel **6**

Lake O'Hara → *For listings, see pages 148-149.*

The camping fee here is $10 per person per night. Anybody can hike the 11-km trail to the lake, but it's still essential to have reserved a campsite. These days places in the Alpine Club of Canada's **Elizabeth Parker Hut** are allotted by a lottery, which only members can enter.
➤ *See Ins and outs, page 144.*

The Lake

Exquisitely framed by the two lofty mountains, Victoria and Lefroy, which tower over Lake Louise on the other side of the Continental Divide, Lake O'Hara is a rare jewel even in the overflowing treasure chest of the Rockies. When it was first discovered by Canada's hiking community, news of its extraordinary natural beauty and network of quality day hikes spread like wildfire and soon the area was too popular for its own good. Parks Canada have taken measures to protect it, so visiting can be difficult unless you book ahead. No traffic is allowed into the region, not even bikes.

Hikes from Lake O'Hara

Hiking in the Lake O'Hara region is among the most popular and rewarding in the Rockies. On the Continental Divide between here and Lake Louise are a number of the highest and most awe-inspiring peaks in the range. Within a relatively small area are 25 named lakes and an extensive, well-maintained network of trails that radiate out from Lake O'Hara like the spokes of a wheel. There are five main sub-regions that can be combined in any number of ways.

Lake Oesa ⓘ *5.8-km loop; 240-m elevation gain.* This is a short and easy hike to a stunning turquoise lake set in a rugged cirque. Towering above are the Continental Divide summits of Mounts Lefroy and Victoria, the other side of the stunning massif that towers so dramatically over Lake Louise.

Opabin Plateau ⓘ *7.2-km loop; 250-m elevation gain.* Set in a beautiful hanging valley, this easy hike offers many temptations for casual exploration among small flower-filled tundra meadows. The loop follows the east and west sides of the same valley. A 600-m side-trail leads from the west side to outstanding views from Opabin Prospect. From the east side, a detour leads along Yukness Ledge, a possible highline traverse to Lake Oesa.

Lake McArthur ⓘ *7 km return; 315-m elevation gain.* This half-day hike is one of the area's finest. The 1.5-km-long lake is the biggest in the area and an exquisite, deep blue colour due to its 65-m depth. Sheer cliffs rising straight up, more than 600 m above the water, make for a dramatic location.

Odaray Plateau ⓘ *7-10-km loops; 290- to 655-m elevation gain.* This is one of the most spectacular routes in the park, but is often closed, or visitor numbers are limited due to grizzly bears. The trail climbs quickly and steeply. Odaray Prospect offers a 180° panorama centred on Lake O'Hara, backed by the wall of high peaks that comprise the Great Divide. Further along, the trail branches off to Odaray Grandview, the only spot in the park from which all of its major lakes can be seen simultaneously. To achieve this prize you have to face a difficult 1.1-km scramble that requires endurance and some experience. At Km 4.5 a junction at McArthur Pass leads back to the start making a 6.5-km loop, or on to Lake McArthur as part of a 9.5-km loop.

Cathedral Basin ⓘ *13-15 km return; 300-m elevation gain.* This is one of the longest and least crowded day-hikes in the area, but is also one of the lowest and least dramatic. However, after skirting the pretty Linda and Cathedral Lakes, the trail starts to climb towards the mouth of the Cathedral Basin. The wonderful views all along this stretch peak at Cathedral Prospect, which offers one of the most complete overviews of the whole Lake O'Hara region. The climb to the Prospect is fairly steep on a poor, rocky surface.

Alpine Circuit ⓘ *9.8-12.4 km; 495-m elevation gain.* The classic way to combine some of the area's sights, this is one of the highlights of the Lake O'Hara region, but it's a fairly tough circuit, more route than trail, following cairns and paint-marks across scree slopes and along exposed ledges. Those scared of heights, worried about getting lost, or not in tip-top condition should probably choose another hike. Use a good trail description and carry a good map. Starting the circuit with the toughest section, the ascent to Wiwaxy Gap, is a good idea. Views from the gap are exceptional. The loop can be extended or shortened in a couple of places. The short detour to Opabin Prospect is worth the effort, while the ascent to All Souls' Prospect is an excellent conclusion to the hike.

Yoho Valley → *For listings, see pages 148-149.*

Logistically easier than Lake O'Hara and almost equally wonderful, is the Yoho Valley, which is lined with waterfalls, including the dramatic **Twin Falls** and the 380-m **Takakkaw Falls**, one of Canada's highest, whose name comes from a Stoney Indian word meaning 'magnificent'. This is also one of the most exceptional areas for glaciers: the enormous Wapta and Waputik Icefields are both easily visible, as is the beautiful Emerald Glacier. The valley is ringed with monster peaks. To get there, drive 3.7 km northeast of Field, or 12.5 km southwest of the Continental Divide, turn north on Yoho Valley Road and drive about 13 km up a very steep, winding road, not suitable for RVs or trailers.

Hikes in the Yoho Valley
Iceline ⓘ *12.8-21.3 km; 690-m elevation gain. Trailhead: Whiskey Jack Hostel.* The steep ascent of this popular hike takes you up to the Emerald Glacier, on a level with truly extraordinary scenery that includes the Daly Glacier and Takakkaw Falls opposite and the vast Wapta Icefield to the north. Once at the top, the hiking is high, easy and scenically uplifting. A return journey to the highpoint is 12.8 km. Circuits can be made by continuing to the Yoho Valley and possibly the Little Yoho Valley as well, though neither option adds anything that compares to the views from the top. A two-day backpack trip would entail a night at Little Yoho campground or the nearby Stanley Mitchell hut (book with the **Alpine Club**, T403-678 3200, www.alpineclubofcanada.ca), a possible diversion to Kiwetinok Pass and a return via the stupendous vantage point of the Whaleback.

Yoho Valley ⓘ *16.4 km; 290-m elevation gain.* This flat trail through the trees leads to a few waterfalls, ending at the dramatic Twin Falls. It is a nice stroll and good for a rainy day, but there seems no point if you're able to do the spectacular Iceline trail, which offers much more.

Emerald Lake → *For listings, see pages 148-149.*

This is a lovely spot and the name is accurate, if lacking in imagination. To get here, drive 2.6 km southwest of Field, then 8 km on Emerald Lake Road, passing on the way the Natural Bridge, a giant rock that has been carved by the powerful Kicking Horse River. In addition to those listed below, a number of longer trails are better suited to mountain biking. The **Amiskwi Trail** ① *35 km one-way*, follows a river, starting at Emerald Lake Road. The **Kicking Horse Trail** ① *19.5 km*, starts at the same point or at the Chancellor Peak campground.

Emerald Triangle ① *19.7 km; 880-m elevation gain.* The clear-cut choice for a day hike. A satisfying loop, the climb is gentle (more so in a clockwise direction), but the descent at the end is rapid. As well as the lake, views are of the glaciated ramparts of The President, the sheer cliffs of Wapta Mountain, the Kicking Horse Valley and the fossil-fields of the Burgess Shale.

Hikes (and biking) from the TransCanada Highway
Paget Lookout ① *7.4-km return, 520-m elevation gain. Trailhead: Wapta Lake Picnic Area, 5.5 km southwest of BC/Alberta border.* This short but steep climb leads to astounding views that include the mountains encircling Lake O'Hara and the Kicking Horse Valley. Scramblers can ascend a further 430 m to Paget Peak for even better views.

Hoodoos ① *3.2 km, 455-m elevation gain. Trailhead: 22.7 km southwest of Field, before campground entrance, 1.5 km to parking area.* A short but very steep hike leads to these fascinating, elongated-mushroom-shaped rock formations. Follow the trail above them for the best views. This can be enjoyed whatever the weather and combines nicely with **Wapta Falls** ① *4.8 km, 45-m elevation gain. Trailhead: 25 km southwest of Field, 1.8 km down Wapta Falls access road*, a powerful waterfall in a raw setting. The short, level hike is good for spring or autumn, a rainy day, or just a leg-stretch to see the cascade.

Yoho National Park listings

For Sleeping and Eating price codes and other relevant information, see pages 9-11.

🛏 Sleeping

Field *p144*
Almost every residence in Field functions as an informal guesthouse, offering self-catering suites with kitchen for about $150-175. Contact the visitor centre, which has a full, up-to-date list, or check www.field.ca.
$$$ Alpine Guesthouse, 2nd Av, T250-343 6878, www.alpineguesthouse.ca. Spacious 2-bedroom suite with private entrance and kitchen. Incredible views.
$$$ Canadian Rockies Inn, T250-343 6046, www.bbcanada.com/7896. Has 4 suites,

all with private bathroom and living room, 1 with kitchen, and 2 bedrooms.
$$$ Kicking Horse Lodge, end of Kicking Horse Av/Stephen Av, T250-343 6303, www.trufflepigs.com. The only hotel in town, housed in a grand structure, offering big, recently renovated rooms, with kitchenettes for an extra $20. It also has a renowned restaurant.
$$$ Mount Burgess Guesthouse, T250-343 6480, www.mtburgessguesthouse.ca. 2 suites with kitchens, private bath and TV. Good value.
$$ Alpenglow B&B, 306 Kicking Horse Av, T250-343 6356. Good rooms with shared bath.
$$ Mount Stephen Guesthouse, T250-343 6441, www.mountstephen.com. 2 en suite rooms with kitchen.

Camping
Kicking Horse Campground, 3.7 km north-east at the Yoho Valley turn-off. 86 very nice private sites and good showers.

Lake O'Hara *p146, map p145*
Camping
Lake O'Hara Campground. Doesn't cater to RVs. For further details, see page 144.

Yoho Valley *p147, map p145*
$$$$ Twin Falls Chalet, at the far end of the valley, a 10-km hike, T403-228 7079, Jul-Sep only. A real backcountry experience, with no electricity or running hot water but wonderful meals included in the price.
$ Whiskey Jack Hostel, on the way to the campground, T1800-762 4122, www.hi hostels.ca, late Jun-Sep. The park's only hostel and one of the best in the Rockies. Friendly and cosy, with 27 beds in 3 dorms. Kitchen, showers and great views from the front deck. Reservations recommended.

Camping
Laughing Falls Backcountry Campground, halfway to Twin Falls. Basic but private, with just 8 sites.
Takakkaw Falls Campground. Beyond the hostel, a group of car parks signals the end of the road. The campground is a 500-m walk from here and for tents only. It has wagons on which you can cart in as much food and equipment as you wish. The sites are fairly private and very ocated close to the falls, with a view of the Wapta Icefield. Some excellent hikes begin here.

❷ Eating

Field *p144*
🍴 **Truffle Pigs Bistro**, in the **Kicking Horse Lodge** (see Sleeping). A freshly renovated bright, uncluttered space serving gourmet West Coast-style comfort food with some nice wines on offer. Open breakfast to dinner in summer, though dinner reservations (essential) may be limited to hotel guests.

Emerald Lake *p148*
🍴 **Cilantro On the Lake Restaurant**, next door to the **Emerald Lake Lodge**, T1800-343 3006. Set in an impressive post and beam structure on the water, this is a perfect spot for a splurge or at least a drink. The menu, inspired by Californian, West Coast and First Nations cuisine, incorporates lots of wild game and fish from the area. The atmosphere is that of a casual but upmarket bistro.

⛰ Activities and tours

Field *p144*
There are plenty of trails for cross-country skiing from Field. The 12 km Tally Ho Trail winds its way round Mt Burgess to Emerald Lake. The information centre has maps.

There are some world-class ice-climbing routes in the Field and Yoho Valleys, but you will have to look elsewhere (Jasper or Banff) for tour operators. A few old fire trails and longer hikes make for good mountain biking, but the closest rentals are in Lake Louise.
Alpine Rafting, T1888-599 5299, www.alpinerafting.com. Whitewater rafting on the Kicking Horse River. All levels.

Emerald Lake *p148*
The Emerald Lake Loop is a popular 5-km hiking trail. Fishing is good here and a portion of the lake is cleared in winter for ice-skating.
Emerald Sports and Gifts, beside the lodge, T250-343 6000. Rents canoes, rowboats, fishing tackle and permits, cross-country skis, snowshoes and all gear.

⊖ Transport

Field *p144*
3 **Greyhound** buses daily from the visitor centre running: east to **Lake Louise** (20-35 mins, $15), **Banff** (80 mins, $20) and **Calgary** (3 hrs, $38); west to **Golden** (1 hr, $14), **Revelstoke** (3-3½ hrs, $38), **Kamloops** (6-8 hrs, $67) and **Vancouver** (12-14 hrs, $117).

Kootenay National Park

Situated on the other side of the Continental Divide from Banff and bounded to the north by Yoho, it would be wrong to expect anything but spectacular scenery from Kootenay National Park, yet this is far and away the least visited of the big four. Besides the relative tranquillity, this park has two major assets: the Rockwall, which is one of the top five backpacking trips in the range; and a large number of short walks right from the highway, ideal for the less athletic, leading to diverse destinations including a forest fire burn and the Paint Pots, a series of multicoloured mineral pools. A much more comprehensive overview of the Rockies can be gained by taking our suggested loop from Lake Louise through Yoho to Golden, down Highway 93, then through Kootenay Park arriving back near Banff. Entering from this direction, you'll be greeted by the dramatic red walls of Sinclair Canyon.

Ins and outs

There is no public transport to or within the park. The only **Visitor Centre** ① *Jul-Aug daily 0900-1800, mid-May to Jun, Sep to early Oct daily 1000-1700*, in the park is in Kootenay Park Lodge at Vermilion Crossing. They hand out the *Backcountry Guide*, whose map and trail descriptions are all you need and issue backcountry passes ($9 per person per night). There is another, more helpful but less convenient **Parks Canada Visitor Centre** ① *7556 Main St E, T250-347 9505, T250-347 9331 for Chamber of Commerce, www.radium hotsprings.com, mid-May to Jun daily 0900-1700, Jul-Aug daily 0900-1900, Sep-early Oct daily 0900-1600*, in the town of Radium Hot Springs.

Sights → *For listings, see pages 154-155.*

Radium Hot Springs

Kootenay National Park's boundaries neatly parallel the winding course of the Banff-Windermere Parkway (Highway 93) as it makes its way from Castle Junction on Highway 1 to Radium Hot Springs in the East Kootenays. This rather brash and unpleasant town is little more than a string of cheesy motels, which tend to be full throughout the summer. The only thing to see is the **Thousand Faces Sculpture Gallery** ① *Hwy 93/ Madsen Rd, T250-347 9208, www.radiumwoodcarver.com, $1*. This large collection of carvings and masks, many of them done with a chainsaw, has a lot of legends and stories built into it. The eccentric artist, Rolf, is a curiosity himself. He has two pet goats – Goofy and Spoofy – which live on his roof.

Those entering from the south are treated to a fine introduction to the park, as the road snakes its way through the steep and narrow Sinclair Canyon, its cliffs a rich red due to the high iron content. Just to the north are **Radium Hot Springs Pools** ① *T250-347 2100, May-Oct daily 0900-2300, Oct-May Sun-Thu 1200-2100, Fri-Sat 1200-2200, $6.30, child $5.40*, with a large hot pool (39°C) and a cool pool (27°C) surrounded by rugged rocky scenery. These are packed in summer with up to 4000 people a day. You do not have to pay the National Park entry fee to enter the pools, but you do if you go any further. Note that the park is on Mountain Time, an hour ahead of most of BC. The park's other attractions are all reached via hikes, described below.

Hikes in Kootenay National Park → *For listings, see pages 154-155.*

Short hikes from north to south

Fireweed Trail ① *1 km, Trailhead: just south of park boundary*. In 1968 a forest fire started by a single lightning bolt laid waste to a 24-sq-km area just south of Vermilion Pass (1651 m). In 2003, the park's most active fire season in living memory, 12.6% of the park burned. This short trail talks you through the regeneration process and reveals how such fires are an integral part of the forest's natural cycle, to the point that lodgepole pine cones actually require the heat of a forest fire in order to open and spread their seeds. Already, a new forest has begun to appear within the blackened remains.

Marble Canyon ① *800 m or more. Trailhead: 7 km south of park boundary*. An easy trail takes you to this lovely 600-m-long, 37-m-deep canyon which Tokumm Creek has carved

Kootenay National Park

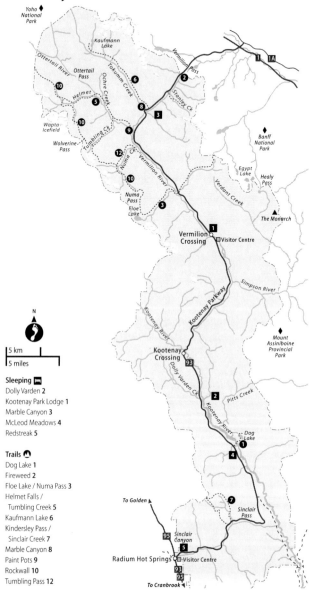

Yoho ◆
National
Park

Kaufmann
Lake

Ottertail River

Ottertail
Pass

Tokumm Creek

Vermilion Pass

1 **1A**

2

Ochre Creek

6

Stanley Ck

Helmet

5

8

3

Banff
National
Park

◆

Wapta
Icefield

10

10

Tumbling Ck

9

Egypt
Lake

Wolverine
Pass

12

Numa Ck

Vermilion River

Verdant Creek

Healy
Pass

10

Numa
Pass

3

Floe
Lake

The Monarch

▲

Vermilion
Crossing

1

☐ Visitor Centre

Simpson River

Kootenay River

Kootenay Parkway

Mount
Assiniboine
Provincial
Park

◆

N

⬆

| 5 km |
| 5 miles |

Kootenay
Crossing

93

Dolly Varden Ck

2

Pitts Creek

1

Dog
Lake

4

Sleeping 🛏

Dolly Varden **2**
Kootenay Park Lodge **1**
Marble Canyon **3**
McLeod Meadows **4**
Redstreak **5**

7

Sinclair
Pass

Trails ⛰

Dog Lake **1**
Fireweed **2**
Floe Lake / Numa Pass **3**
Helmet Falls /
  Tumbling Creek **5**
Kaufmann Lake **6**
Kindersley Pass /
  Sinclair Creek **7**
Marble Canyon **8**
Paint Pots **9**
Rockwall **10**
Tumbling Pass **12**

To Golden ◀

95

Sinclair
Canyon

5

Radium Hot Springs ☐ Visitor Centre

93

95

To Cranbrook ◀

out of the white dolomite limestone that was once mistaken for marble. The highlight is a striking view of a powerful waterfall where the creek forces its way through a narrow opening. In winter, the whole canyon turns into a magical palace of blue and green ice. This trail is currently closed.

The Paint Pots ① *3 km return. Trailhead: 9.5 km south of park boundary.* This trail leads to a series of fascinating pools where iron-laden mineral springs push through clay sediments to create shades of red, orange and yellow. Native Americans came from far and wide to collect these coloured clays, which were then baked, ground into powder and added to fat or oil to make paint, which was then used in a number of creative and ceremonial ways.

Dog Lake ① *5.2 km return. Trailhead: 500 m south of Mcleod Meadows campground.* About the best of the short hikes in the southern half of the park. This shallow, marsh-edged lake sits in one of the Rockies' most temperate valleys, making it a good spot for wildlife. Orchids also abound in early summer.

Longer hikes
The Rockwall ① *54.8 km; 1490-m elevation gain. Trailhead: 22.5 km south of park boundary.* The Rockwall is the name of the Vermillion Mountains' eastern escarpment, a solid sheet of grey limestone whose sheer cliffs run for 35 km along the Great Divide. Instead of running along a ridge like some highline trails, this one goes up and down like a rollercoaster, crossing three alpine passes then plunging down into valleys, passing on the way a number of hanging glaciers, flower-strewn meadows, gorgeous lakes and stunning waterfalls. It is one of the most demanding but rewarding hikes in the Rockies and is comfortably done in four days. Four trails lead to the Rockwall, along Floe, Numa, Tumbling and Helmet Creeks. The optimum approach is to hike up Floe Creek, spending night one at Floe Lake campground (10.5 km), night two at Tumbling Falls (27.9 km) and night three at Helmet Falls (39.7 km). A few shorter hikes take in sections of the Rockwall, although the greatest reward is hiking the whole thing.

Floe Lake/Numa Pass ① *21-26.4 km; 715- to 1030-m elevation gain. Trailhead: 22.5 km south of park boundary.* This is the best of the Rockwall day-hikes. Floe Lake is one of the most majestic sights in the Rockies: sheer cliffs rise 1000 m straight up from the azure blue waters, their ice floes mirrored on its crystal surface. The ascent is long, quite steep and mostly through forest, making this more suited to an overnighter than a day hike. Views from Numa Pass, 2.7 km (one hour) further, are even more striking, another reason to spend an extra day. It's the best place to take in the lake and the rockwall that towers above it. From here, it is possible to descend to the highway via Numa Creek, making a total loop of 27.3 km, though it means hitching 8 km back to the trailhead.

Tumbling Pass ① *24.4-km loop; 800-m elevation gain, 840-m loss. Trailhead: 9.5 km south of park boundary.* As a day hike, this is extremely long and tough. It starts pleasantly enough by passing by the Paint Pots, but soon sets into a steady ascent with little reward until you reach Tumbling Falls at 9.4 km, where there is a nice campground. The pass is a tough 3.6 km further, but worth it for the awesome sight of the Rockwall and Tumbling Glacier. A 6-km detour to Wolverine Pass is also worth the effort, but as a day-hike there's no time. From the pass, return to the trailhead along Numa Creek, a steep but pleasant descent.

Helmet Falls/Tumbling Creek ⓘ *37-km loop. Trailhead: 9.5 km south of park boundary.* As a two-day trip, it is worth hiking up Ochre/Helmet Creeks to Helmet Falls at the north end of the Rockwall. This impressive cascade is one of the highest in Canada. It is possible to stay at the campground here then ascend through Rockwall Pass and exit to the trailhead along Tumbling Creek, though this is a tough second day.

Kindersley Pass/Sinclair Creek ⓘ *16.5- to 20.5-km loop, 1055-m elevation gain. Trailhead: across the highway from the parking area 9.5 km from the west gate at Radium.* This is one of the park's most scenic and most strenuous hikes. The trail ascends steadily for 8.4 km with little reward. From Kindersley Pass, views start to appear northward of the countless peaks of the Brisco Range. For the next 1.4 km to Kindersley Summit vistas of this ocean of summits keep getting better. From here the indistinct trail along Sinclair Creek makes for a convenient loop back to the Highway, though it leaves you 1.2 km northeast of your vehicle.

Kootenay National Park listings

For Sleeping and Eating price codes and other relevant information, see pages 9-11.

💤 Sleeping

Kootenay National Park *p150, map p152*
$$$ Kootenay Park Lodge, Vermilion Crossing, T250-762 9196, www.kootenay parklodge. com. Very small, fairly basic log cabins with front patios. The only beds in the park itself.

Camping
There are 8 campgrounds in the park, mostly on the **Rockwall** and **Kaufmann Lake** trails.
Marble Canyon. The only campground in the more interesting northern part of the park, Jun-Sep. 61 sites.
McLeod Meadows, 25 km north of Radium. 98 basic sites on the river, Jun-Sep. Just to the north and only open in winter, is the tiny (free) **Dolly Varden**.
Redstreak, just north of Sinclair Canyon, T1877-737 3783, www.pccamping.ca, May-Sep. The park's biggest campground and the only one that can be reserved, with 242 sites, showers and full hook-ups.

Radium Hot Springs *p151*
$$$ Chalet Europe, 5063 Madsen Rd, T250-347 9305 www.chaleteurope.com. This Swiss-style chalet is situated on a hill adjacent to the park entrance, a healthy 180 m above the madding crowd. The 6 very attractive suites have kitchens, and private balconies with telescopes to make the most of the incredible views. Sauna and jacuzzi.
$$ Misty River Lodge and HI Hostel, Hwy 93, by the park entrance, T250-347 9912, www.radiumhostel.bc.ca. A small, friendly hostel with 11 dorm beds, 2 private rooms and 2 family rooms. Lounge, kitchen, deck with BBQ, and bike and canoe rental.
$$ Rocky Mountain Springs Lodge, 5067 Madsen Rd, T250-285 9743, www.milliondollarview.ca. Up on the hill above town by the park entrance. Plain but decent sized rooms with balconies and great views. Very reasonable price and breakfast is included. Also serves the best food.
$$ Village Country Inn, 7557 Canyon Av, T250-347 9392, www.villagecountryinn.bc.ca. The nicest of many places to stay in town. Comfortable rooms with big beds and TVs.

Eating

Kootenay National Park *p150, map p152*

Old Salzburg, 4943 Hwy 93, 2 km west of the park gates in Radium, T250-347 6553. Serves traditional Austrian food such as schnitzel and spaetzle, as well as seafood, steak, pasta and delicious desserts. Excellent food, service and atmosphere.

Radium Hot Springs *p151*

Citadella Restaurant, in Rocky Mountain Springs Lodge, see Sleeping, T250-285 9743, www.milliondollarview.ca. Generous portions of delicious meat-based fare, with Hungarian specialities. There's also the amazing view.

Horsethief Creek Pub and Eatery, 7538 Main St, T250-347 6400. Good pub grub. Try the beef dip.

Waterton Lakes National Park

Despite its modest size, a mere 525 sq km – the most southerly of Canada's Rocky Mountain parks delivers landscapes and hiking to rival almost anything further north, but without the crowds. The scenery has a unique flavour of its own, a strange juxtaposition of prairies and mountain. The park's remarkable diversity of geographic zones – prairie, wetlands, aspen parkland, montane forest – has also led to a far greater variety of flora and fauna than any of Western Canada's other parks, with about 1200 plant species, including 55% of Alberta's wild flowers. In 1932, the park combined with Glacier National Park in Montana to become the world's first International Peace Park and was recognized as a Biosphere Reserve in 1979 and UNESCO World Heritage Site in 1995.

Ins and outs

Getting there and around
The closest **Greyhound station** ① *1018 Waterton Av, Pincher Creek, 51 km to the north, T403-627 2716*, receives daily buses from Vancouver via Highway 3 and from Calgary. The nearest **US border crossing** ① *Jun-Aug daily 0700-2200, late May and Sep daily 0900-1800*, is at Chief Mountain on the park's eastern edge. At other times, the closest border crossing is east on Highway 2 at Carway, Alberta/Peigan, Montana, open year round (daily 0700-2300).

A **Hiker Shuttle Service** from Tamarack Outdoor Outfitters, at 214 Mount View Road, T403-859 2378, will take you to Cameron Lake, Red Rock Canyon and other trailheads. **Crypt Lake Water Shuttle Service** at the marina, T403-859 2362, delivers hikers to Crypt Lake Trailhead ($18 return) and points such as Rainbow Falls and Francis Lake.

Best time to visit
The park is open from the long weekend in May until Labour Day weekend in September, though many of the hikes are still under snow well into June. Prairie flowers bloom in the spring and early summer, while higher elevation wild flowers arrive in late summer/ autumn, which is also the best time to see animals such as bears and elk. Waterton receives Alberta's highest average annual precipitation levels and is one of the province's windiest places.

Tourist information
The **Parks Canada Visitor Information Centre** ① *Entrance Rd, T403-859 2445, www.watertonchamber.com, Jun-Aug daily 0800-1900, May-Jun and Sep-early Oct daily 0900-1630*, is on the way into town. The rest of the year information is available at the

Parks Administration Office ① *215 Mt View Rd, T403-859 2477, Mon-Fri daily 0800-1600.* Also useful is the Heritage Centre, operated by **Waterton Natural History Association** ① *117 Waterton Av, T403-859 2624, www.wnha.ca,* which has exhibits, an art gallery, a museum and sells park-related books and maps. Hikers can buy a 1:50,000 map here or at the visitor centre, though for most people the free map will suffice. A park permit costs $7.80 per day, under 16s $3.90.

Waterton Townsite → *For listings, see pages 160-162.*

As a tribute to the herds that once roamed freely on this land, a Bison Paddock is maintained just north of the park entrance off Highway 6. As you approach the core of the park, the first thing you'll see is the magnificently grandiose **Prince of Wales Hotel**, a fascinating building erected by the Great Northern Railway in 1927, with a steeply sloping gabled roof, myriad balconies and an extraordinary post and beam lobby. Its location could hardly be more photogenic: high on a bluff overlooking broad expanses of crystal aquamarine surrounded by towering snowy peaks. Be sure to go in and explore.

Waterton Townsite cannot hope to live up to this opening gambit, but it's a pleasant enough spot that gains much from the lake setting. More resort than genuine village, it still feels rather quaint, with mule deer and bighorn sheep wandering freely over the lawns and Cameron Falls just on the edge of town. Hiking is the main activity around here. Wonderful views are easily attained and a few of the many day hikes lead right from the townsite. Thanks to the strong local winds, windsurfing is very popular on **Cameron Bay**, as are fishing (with a licence), canoeing and scuba-diving.

Hikes in Waterton Lakes National Park → *See map, page 158.*

Hikes from town

Crypt Lake ① *17.2 km return; 685-m elevation gain. Trailhead: by boat.* This is one of the most popular and exciting trips in the park, with a bit of everything thrown in. You start with a boat trip across the lake, hike an undulating trail through Hell Roaring Valley, pass four waterfalls including the stunning Crypt Falls, stoop through a dark 20-m tunnel, then ascend a mountainside using a safety cable. The views are fine throughout and the emerald lake itself sits in a steep and dramatic cirque. You can expect to have plenty of company. There is a backcountry campground at Km 8.

Bear's Hump ① *1.4 km; 200-m elevation gain. Trailhead: above information centre.* Short but steep, leading to great views of mountains, lake and townsite. Snow-free from late May.

Bertha Lake ① *11 km return; 460-m elevation gain. Trailhead: car park opposite the town campground.* The popularity of this hike is due mainly to its being easy and conveniently located. The trail's highlight arrives at just Km 1.5, with views of the lake and distant prairie. A fork here leads right to Bertha Lake. The left fork descends to the Waterton Lakeshore Trail. This leads to the decent beach at Bertha Bay and beyond to Goat Haunt (15 km in total), where you can catch a boat back. This is only really recommended as a spring or autumn hike, as it's usually snow-free from April to October.

Hikes from the Akamina Parkway

Lineham Ridge/Rowe Lakes ⓘ *17-20 km return; 920- to 1060-m elevation gain. Trailhead: Km 10.5 on the parkway.* This trail follows a creek up gentle slopes with valley views and through mature forest before cutting up bare, rocky slopes to the ridge. The pretty Row Lakes are a worthwhile side-trip best saved for the return leg if time and energy allow, because the highlight is Lineham Ridge, which offers excellent views of many of the jagged peaks in Waterton and Glacier Parks.

Wall and Forum lakes/Akamina Ridge ⓘ *10- to 20-km return; 915-m elevation gain. Trailhead: at Km 14.6 on the parkway.* There are three possible hikes in Akamina-Kishinena

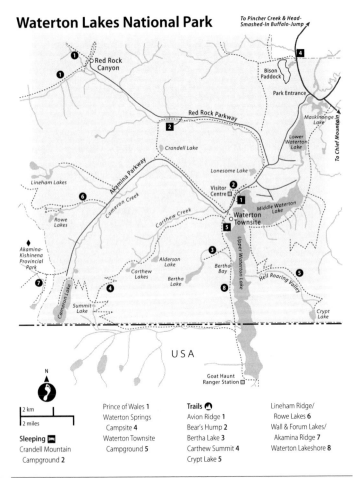

Waterton Lakes National Park

To Pincher Creek & Head-Smashed-In Buffalo-Jump

Red Rock Canyon

Bison Paddock

Park Entrance

Red Rock Parkway

Maskinonge Lake

To Chief Mountain

Crandell Lake

Lower Waterton Lake

Lonesome Lake

Lineham Lakes

Visitor Centre

Middle Waterton Lake

Cameron Creek

Rowe Lakes

Carthew Creek

Waterton Townsite

Akamina-Kishinena Provincial Park

Alderson Lake

Bertha Bay

Upper Waterton Lake

Hell Roaring Valley

Carthew Lakes

Bertha Lake

Cameron Lake

Summit Lake

Crypt Lake

USA

Goat Haunt Ranger Station

N

2 km
2 miles

Sleeping 🛏
Crandell Mountain
Campground **2**

Prince of Wales **1**
Waterton Springs
Campsite **4**
Waterton Townsite
Campground **5**

Trails ⛰
Avion Ridge **1**
Bear's Hump **2**
Bertha Lake **3**
Carthew Summit **4**
Crypt Lake **5**

Lineham Ridge/
Rowe Lakes **6**
Wall & Forum Lakes/
Akamina Ridge **7**
Waterton Lakeshore **8**

Provincial Park, adjacent to Waterton in British Columbia. Forum and Wall Lakes are distinct, easy hikes to pretty lakes at the base of sheer rock walls. Between the two is Akamina Ridge, the real prize for those not averse to a bit of scrambling, with great views into Waterton and Glacier Parks. The Forum–Ridge–Wall circuit is best done in this order. Be sure to get full details before attempting it and be ready for strong winds on the ridge.

Carthew Summit ① *20 km one-way; 700-m elevation gain. Trailhead: at Km 15.7, the end of the road.* This is a one-way hike from Cameron Lake to Cameron Falls on the edge of Waterton Townsite, so is best done using a shuttle to the trailhead. The highlight is the view from Carthew Summit itself, with the steep peaks of Glacier National Park to the south and the curious sight of endless Alberta prairies stretching off to the northeast horizon. From here it's all down hill, in every respect.

Hikes from Red Rock Parkway
Avion Ridge ① *22.9-km loop, 944-m elevation gain. Trailhead: canyon car park at road's end.* This long, high, narrow ridge has few truly inspiring viewpoints, but offers panoramas whose very size makes an impression. The loop is best done clockwise, past Snowshoe Campground, over the ridge and down past Goat Lake. Otherwise, take the worthwhile 7-km detour from Snowshoe to Twin Lakes, the campground is much nicer.

Head-Smashed-In-Buffalo-Jump → *For listings, see pages 160-162.*

Native Americans had thousands of years to refine their techniques for the large-scale slaughter of bison, their ultimate method being the ruthlessly efficient 'buffalo jump'. Situated 18 km west of Fort Macleod on Highway 785, Head-Smashed-In-Buffalo-Jump was named a UNESCO World Heritage Site because it is one of the oldest and best preserved of its kind. Over 11 m of bone deposits at the base of the cliff bear witness to at least 5500 years of continual use.

A masterpiece of invention that blends into the sandstone cliff over which the herds were driven, the four-storey **Interpretive Centre** ① *T403-553 2731, www.head-smashed-in.com, mid-May to mid-Sep daily 0900-1800, mid-Sep to mid-May daily 1000-1700; $9, under 17s $5, no public transport, taxis from Fort Macleod cost about $25*, uses archaeological evidence and the verbal records of the local First Nations to explain the functioning and history of the jump and its relation to the ecology, mythology, lifestyle and technology of the Blackfoot people.

The process of the buffalo hunt presented by the centre includes: pre-hunt ceremonies; the **Gathering Basin** – a 40-sq-km grazing area of plentiful grass and water to attract the herds; the network of **Drive Lanes**, consisting of stone cairns that helped hunters to funnel the bison towards the cliff; the **Kill Site**, which is just north of the centre, with another visible 1 km north; and the **Processing Area**, where the meat was sliced into thin strips and hung on racks to dry, much of it pounded with grease, marrow and berries to make pemmican. Displays also cover the lifestyle of prehistoric Plains people, their techniques of food gathering, social life and ceremonies; and the geography, climate, flora and fauna of the northwest plains.

Trails at the lower and upper level allow you to explore the site and have a good look at the Drive Lanes and cliff. Tours are conducted by Blackfoot guides and **drum and dance performances** ① *Wed in Jul and Aug, 1100 and 1330*, are given on the Centre's Plaza.

Cardston

The obvious route between Waterton and Fort Macleod is via Highways 6 and 3, passing through Pincher Creek. An alternative route (and about the same length) is on Highways 5 and 2, which meet at Cardston, a small town with a couple of worthwhile attractions. The **Remington-Alberta Carriage Centre** ① *623 Main St, T403-653 5139, www.remington carriagemuseum.com, Jul and Aug daily 0900-1700 Sep-Jun 1000-1700, $9, under 17s $5, free guided tours, carriage rides can be taken mid-May to mid-Jun, $4, youth $2.50, 15-20 mins,* has over 250 horse-drawn carriages from around the turn of the 20th century, which are displayed in a superbly equipped, purpose-built museum. Most of the carriages are original and in tip-top condition. Videos, panels, displays and live demonstrations deal with the carriage business from factory to blacksmith to fire station.

While in town, the amazing **Alberta Temple of the Latter Day Saints** ① *348 3rd St, T403-653 3552, mid-May to mid-Sep daily 0900-2000, free,* is well worth seeing. Built in 1912 from 3680 tons of premium white gold-bearing granite quarried around Kootenay Lake, this geometric structure successfully blends ancient and modern styles, with traces of the Temple of Solomon, Mayan-Aztec pyramids and the Prairie School of Frank Lloyd Wright. The inside sounds equally impressive, but non-Mormons cannot enter.

Waterton Lakes National Park listings

For Sleeping and Eating price codes and other relevant information, see pages 9-11.

☺ Sleeping

Waterton Lakes National Park *p156, map p158*
Camping
There are 9 designated wilderness camp-grounds in the park. Limited spaces have resulted in a quota system, with reservations possible 90 days in advance, T403-859 5140 Apr to mid-May, then T403-859 5133. The full fee, $7.80, under 17s $3.90 per person per night, plus a reservation fee of $7.80, child $3.90 per person, must be paid by credit card when booking. You'll need to know how many nights you intend to stay. Passes are issued at the visitor centre if there are places left.

Waterton Townsite *p157, map p158*
$$$ Aspen Village Inn, 111 Windflower Av, T403-859 2255, www.aspenvillageinn.com. Small, pleasant rooms with balconies, plus attractive and expensive 2-bedroom cottage suites, in an agreeable building. Use of hot tub.

$$$ Crandell Mountain Lodge, Mountain View Rd, T403-859 2288, www.crandell mountainlodge.com. A very attractive old-fashioned country cottage, offering a range of pleasant rooms, and some suites with kitchenette.

$$$ Northland Lodge, 408 Evergreen Av, T403-859 2353, www.northlandlodge canada.com. 9 colourful and distinctive rooms in a country-style home.

$$$ Prince of Wales Hotel, T403-236 3400, www.glacierparkinc.com. A must for those who can afford it, this beautiful timber-frame building is brimming with character and a sense of history. Ask for a lake view. There's also a restaurant, lounge, tea room, and gift shop.

$$$ Waterton Lakes Lodge Resort, 101 Clematis Av, T403-859 2150, www.watertonlakeslodge.com. Many different types of appealing chalet-style rooms and suites in 11 buildings, including the impressive lodge. There's a heated indoor pool, hot tub, fitness centre, games room with ping-pong tables, and restaurant.

$$ Bear Mountain Motel, 208 Mount View Rd, T403-859 2366, www.bearmountain motel.com. Plain rooms with 1 or 2 beds. Some have kitchen and/or living room.

$$ Waterton Alpine Hostel, 101 Clematis Av, T403-859 2150, www.hihostels.ca. 21 beds in dorms or private rooms in a choice wood lodge, with kitchen, sauna and café.

Camping

There are several walk-in sites and some private campgrounds north on Hwy 6 and east on Hwy 5.

Crandell Mountain Campground, 8 km west on Red Rock Canyon Rd. The nearest pleasant campground to town. 129 sites with fire pits and a kitchen. Also has 5 traditional tepees for rent (**$**), which need to be reserved at T403-859 5133.

Waterton Springs Campground, 3 km northeast of gate on Hwy 6, T403-859 2247. Has the best facilities of those on the highway, with 190 sites, showers, laundry, games room, and internet café.

Waterton Townsite Campground, T1877-737 3783, www.pccamping.ca. An ugly parking lot with 238 sites, but it's right in town, and is the only one that takes reservations.

Head-Smashed-In-Buffalo Jump *p159*
Buffalo Plains RV Park and Campground, 3 km east of the site, T403-553 2592, www.buffaloplains.com. 30 pleasant sites with views and laundry, but no showers.

Eating

Waterton Townsite *p157*
The better choices for food in Waterton are all hotel dining rooms.

Royal Stewart Dining Room, in the **Prince of Wales** (see Sleeping). European and Canadian dishes, open for breakfast, lunch and dinner, decent but nothing exceptional. The views are superb.

Vimy's Ridge Lounge & Grill, at **Waterton Lakes Resort**, 101 Clematis Av,

T403-859 6343. A fairly predictable menu, but one of the most attractive rooms in town.

Bel Lago Ristorante, 110 Waterton Av, T403-859 2213. For many people, the best food in town. Mostly pastas, but also game, lamb, daily specials and (our favourite) great calamari. Great service and wine list too.

Pearl's, 305 Windflower Av, T403-859 2284. The best place for breakfast or lunch, featuring wraps, bagels, pies, French toast and baked goods.

Pizza of Waterton, 303 Windflower Av, T403-859 2660. A great choice for quality, value, and attractive surroundings. The pizzas are very good, plus there are big salads, home-made soups, and desserts. Also has an outside deck, and gets very busy.

Trapper's Mountain Grill, 106 Waterton Av, T403-859 2240. A reliable place for a meat fix for breakfast, lunch or dinner. Good service and portions, and better value than most.

Wieners of Waterton, 301 Windflower Av, T403-339-1079. Raises the humble hot dog to an art form. Incredibly friendly owners, who have made this one of Waterton's social hubs.

Bars and clubs

Waterton Townsite *p157*
Thirsty Bear Saloon, 111 Waterton Av, T403-859 2211. The most boisterous place in town, with a games room, theme nights, karaoke, drink specials, DJs, dancing, and weekly bands.

Vimy's Ridge Lounge & Grill, at Waterton Lakes Resort, 101 Clematis Av, T403-859 6343. The most attractive and sophisticated choice for a quiet drink. Their **Wolf's Den Lounge** has more of a pub-style atmosphere, and a good choice of local beers.

Windsor Lounge, Prince of Wales Hotel. Probably the best value way to soak up the atmosphere of this fascinating building is by sipping a beer or glass of wine in this sophisticated lounge. There's also sometimes live entertainment.

✷ Festivals and events

Waterton Townsite *p157, map p158*
Jun Waterton Wild Flower Festival,
www.watertonwildflowers.com. 9 days
of events and guided excursions to see,
photograph, paint and behold the park's
plants and flowers.

◯ Shopping

Waterton Townsite *p157*
Gust Gallery Fine Arts, 112A Waterton
Av, T403-859 2535, www.gustgallery.com.
Showcases the work of numerous local artists.
Tamarack Outdoor Outfitters, 214 Mount
View Rd, T403-859 2378. The obvious place
for outdoor clothes, footwear, camping
and backpacking gear, and trail maps.

▲ Activities and tours

Waterton Lakes National Park *p156*
Hiking
There are over 200 km of trails in the park.
A hiker shuttle service to Cameron Lake,
Red Rock Canyon and other trailheads is
operated by **Waterton Outdoor Adventures**,
in Tamarack, 214 Mount View Rd, T403-859
2378, www.watertonvisitorservices.com.
**Waterton Inter-Nation Shoreline Cruise
Co**, T403-859 2362 (see also Tour operators,
below) operates the all-important **Crypt Lake
Water Shuttle Service** from the marina, daily
1000, Jul-Aug daily 0900, 1000 ($18 round trip,
under 12 $9), delivering hikers to the Crypt
Lake trailhead for one of the park's best, most
popular outings. After returning from a hike
in spring and early summer, check for ticks.

Waterton Townsite *p157*
Tour operators
Alpine Stables, T403-859 2462, www.alpine
stables.com. Horse riding and pack trips to
many places in the park. 1 hr for $35, 3 hrs
for $80, 8 hrs for $145. May-Aug.
Cameron Lake Boat Rentals, Cameron
Lake, 17 km west. Canoes and row boats.
Kimball River Sports, just south of
Cardston, T1800-936 6474,
www.raftalberta.ca. Rafting, canoeing,
kayaking and fishing tours.
Mountain Meadow Trail Rides, Mountain
View, halfway to Cardston, T403-653 2413,
www.mountainmeadowtrailrides.com.
Horseback adventures from 1½-hr rides
to overnight pack trips. Also packages
including canoeing or rafting.
Pat's Cycle Rental, 224 Mountview Rd,
T403-859 2266. Bike and scooter rentals,
and sales.
**Waterton Inter-Nation Shoreline Cruise
Co.**, T403-859 2362, www.watertoncruise.com.
2-hr interpretive tours of the lake, up to
4 times daily, $36, under 17s $18.
Waterton Lakes Golf Course, T403-859
2114, www.golfwaterton.com. Surely one
of the most scenic in the country.

◑ Directory

Waterton Townsite *p157*
Banks ATM in Tamarack Village Sq; **Rocky
Mountain Food**, Windflower Av. **Currency
exchange** Tamarack Village Sq.
Emergencies Ambulance T403-859
2636; **Police** T403-859 2244. **Laundry**
301 Windflower Av. **Medical services** Closest
hospitals are in Cardston, T403-
653 4931 and Pincher Creek, T403-627
3333. **Post office** Canada Post,
Corner Fountain Av/Windflower Av.

Contents

Footnotes

Index

Titles available in the Footprint *Focus* range

Latin America	UK RRP	US RRP
Bahia & Salvador	£7.99	$11.95
Buenos Aires & Pampas	£7.99	$11.95
Costa Rica	£8.99	$12.95
Cuzco, La Paz & Lake Titicaca	£8.99	$12.95
El Salvador	£5.99	$8.95
Guadalajara & Pacific Coast	£6.99	$9.95
Guatemala	£8.99	$12.95
Guyana, Guyane & Suriname	£5.99	$8.95
Havana	£6.99	$9.95
Honduras	£7.99	$11.95
Nicaragua	£7.99	$11.95
Paraguay	£5.99	$8.95
Quito & Galápagos Islands	£7.99	$11.95
Recife & Northeast Brazil	£7.99	$11.95
Rio de Janeiro	£8.99	$12.95
São Paulo	£5.99	$8.95
Uruguay	£6.99	$9.95
Venezuela	£8.99	$12.95
Yucatán Peninsula	£6.99	$9.95

Asia	UK RRP	US RRP
Angkor Wat	£5.99	$8.95
Bali & Lombok	£8.99	$12.95
Chennai & Tamil Nadu	£8.99	$12.95
Chiang Mai & Northern Thailand	£7.99	$11.95
Goa	£6.99	$9.95
Hanoi & Northern Vietnam	£8.99	$12.95
Ho Chi Minh City & Mekong Delta	£7.99	$11.95
Java	£7.99	$11.95
Kerala	£7.99	$11.95
Kolkata & West Bengal	£5.99	$8.95
Mumbai & Gujarat	£8.99	$12.95

Africa	UK RRP	US RRP
Beirut	£6.99	$9.95
Damascus	£5.99	$8.95
Durban & KwaZulu Natal	£8.99	$12.95
Fès & Northern Morocco	£8.99	$12.95
Jerusalem	£8.99	$12.95
Johannesburg & Kruger National Park	£7.99	$11.95
Kenya's beaches	£8.99	$12.95
Kilimanjaro & Northern Tanzania	£8.99	$12.95
Zanzibar & Pemba	£7.99	$11.95

Europe	UK RRP	US RRP
Bilbao & Basque Region	£6.99	$9.95
Granada & Sierra Nevada	£6.99	$9.95
Málaga	£5.99	$8.95
Orkney & Shetland Islands	£5.99	$8.95
Skye & Outer Hebrides	£6.99	$9.95

North America	UK RRP	US RRP
Vancouver & Rockies	£8.99	$12.95

Australasia	UK RRP	US RRP
Brisbane & Queensland	£8.99	$12.95
Perth	£7.99	$11.95

For the latest books, e-books and smart phone app releases, and a wealth of travel information, visit us at: www.footprinttravelguides.com.

footprinttravelguides.com

Join us on facebook for the latest travel news, product releases, offers and amazing competitions: www.facebook.com/footprintbooks.com.